KINGS of KINK

WHEN A QUEEN NEEDS A KING... OR THREE

N.O. ONE

Copyright © 2023 by N.O. One

Kings Of Kink

All rights reserved.

No portion of this book may be reproduced in any form without written permission from the publisher or author, except as permitted by U.S. copyright law.

This book is licensed for your personal enjoyment only.

This book may not be re-sold or given away to other people. If you would like to share this book with another person, please purchase an additional copy for each recipient. If you're reading this book and did not purchase it, or it wasn't purchased for your use only, then please return to your favourite book retailer and purchase your own copy. Thank you for respecting the hard work of this author.

All Rights Reserved ©

This is a work of fiction. Names, characters, places, brands, media and incidents are either the product of the author's imagination or are used fictitiously. The author acknowledges the trademark status and trademark owners of various products referred to in this work of fiction, which have been used without permission. The publication/use of these trademarks is not authorized, associated with, or sponsored by the trademark owners.

Cover Design – The Pretty Little Design Co

Editing – Encompass Press Ltd

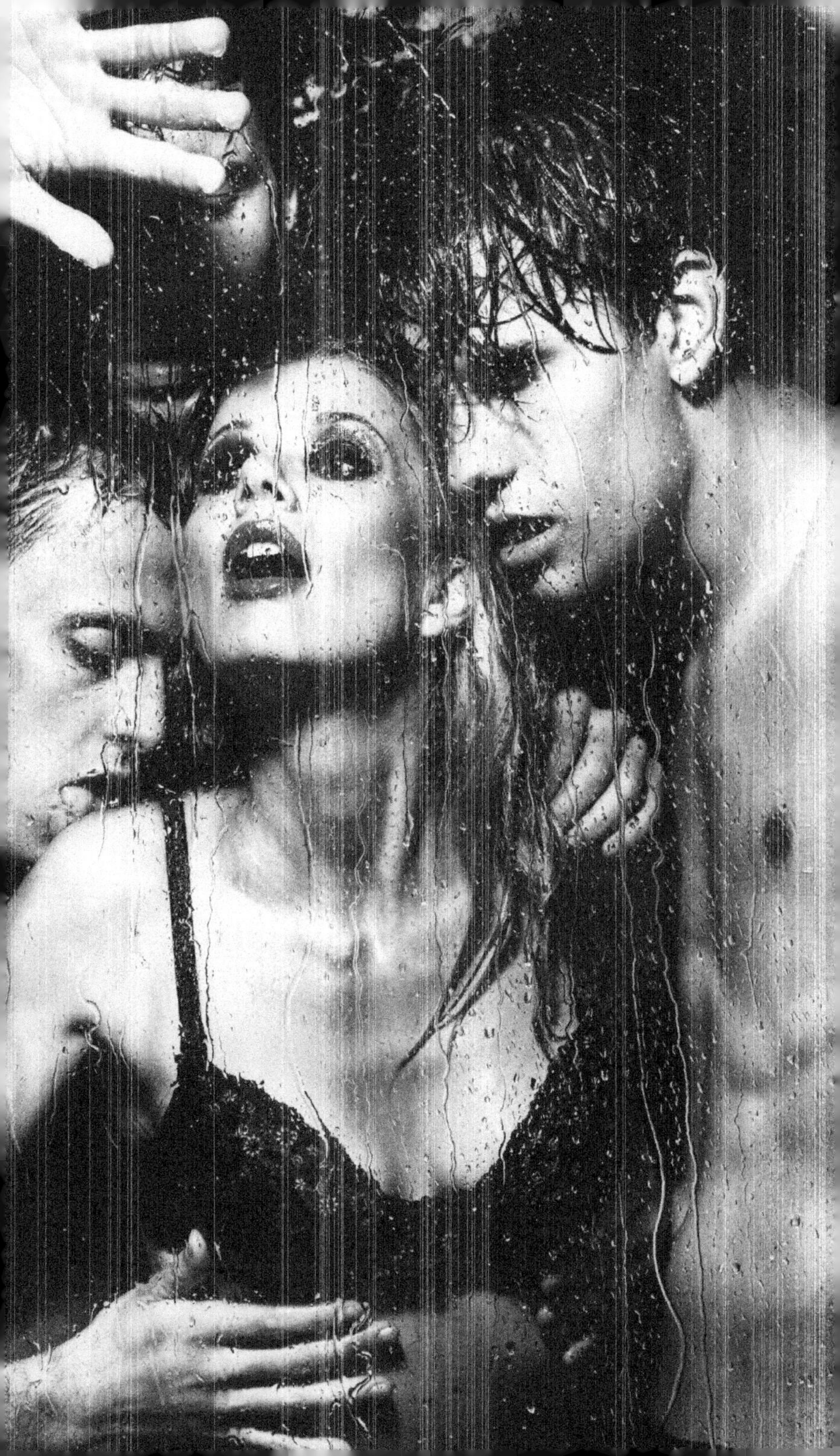

Warning / Foreword

KOK is an RH/Why Choose standalone (which does include some MM between main characters)... However, if you want to have a fuller background on some of the characters and story, we suggest you read The Escort series first—starting with The Rich One. The Escort is a complete MF 6-book series and follows River Fox. There are major spoilers in KOK as to who River ends up with and some of the outcomes of her story, so we'd recommend you read that series before this if you don't want all the spoilers for it.

Onto the rest, we do have a list of warnings on our website. We felt it was better to describe them there, because we don't want to give away spoilers to anyone who doesn't want them. But we do encourage anyone with any kind of triggers at all to please check our website or send us a message to ask.

www.author-no-one.com

This book does deal with the aftermath of SA. It isn't on page, and doesn't happen during this timeline, but it is something that occurred before this story begins.

Now, if you're the parents or children of Blondie or Brunette, please close the book and walk away...

Everyone else... strap in and strap on!

To all of you sexy bitches. Yes, you. Keep on surviving, keep on being awesome, keep on being kinky AF ;)

Chapter One

Lina

Sucking off Batman, while dressed as a slutty bunny, isn't how I pictured this night going. But here I am, on my pink, stocking-covered knees, with Batman's cock in my mouth. The bright-pink lipstick marks at his base make me smile, and the guttural groan he releases when I flick my tongue over his tip fills me with the kind of power I've been craving.

Having this kind of hold over a man is intoxicating, addictive, and I suck dick like a fucking champion. With a long, hard, satisfying suck, I pop him out of my mouth, the balls of his piercings grazing my lips as I grip him with my palm and stroke up and down. My eyes make brief contact with his deep-blue ones as I twist my neck for a good angle to suck his balls into my mouth. Batman smirks, a deep growl escaping his throat as he exhales, trying to contain himself, his hands behind his head as he leans back against the bathroom door.

It's obvious he wants to touch me, to twist his fingers into my hair and control my movements, but that wasn't part of the deal. As much as part of me really wants him to, I just know I won't cope with that.

With a mouthful of balls and a handful of cock, I wink at him, humming my own pleasure through his body. He's close, I can tell. Swapping my hand and mouth around, so I'm now cupping his balls, I suck him down once more. In and out, squeezing, rolling, flicking my tongue, until warm ropes of cum hit the back of my throat. His satisfaction and weakness in this moment make me feel powerful.

I did that. I made this man literally weak in the knees.

Swallowing him down, I wipe at my mouth and stand. My pink stilettos put my eyes level with his chin, and I look up at him through my lashes. The mask he's wearing is hot as fuck, accentuating his strong jawline that could cut glass, and with the black all around his eyes, they're almost mesmerizing.

He doesn't speak as he bends to pick up his cape—being careful not to touch me—after insisting I knelt on that rather than the rank floor to save my pretty stockings from the filth. The sentiment was kinda sweet, but I really couldn't give two shits.

Batman stands behind me as I wash my hands, our eyes connecting in the mirror. He still doesn't touch me, but his hands are fisted at his sides, telling me he's restraining himself. I wonder what it would be like if he didn't?

Could I handle that yet?

No, I don't think I can.

Having my power stripped from me in a horrifically brutal way, just four months ago, is going to stay with me for a long time. My vision begins to glass over at the memory and I quickly shake it away.

Fucking fuck this shit.

"See you around, Batman." With all the confidence I can muster, I smile, wink, and shake my ass as I walk away.

"Until next time, Treacle." His deep voice somehow soothes everything inside of me as I exit the bathroom, trailing through the crowd of people to find Freya.

I see her at the bar, a line of shots all ready for us, and I knock them back quickly.

"Whoops, I had them all. Guess we should order more." Laughing, I grab the bartender's attention and order another few rounds for us.

"The rest of the night is on you then, Bitch. That's your punishment." Freya laughs, even though I bristle at the word punishment, but the alcohol swirling through my system helps the brief panic quickly fade.

"Whatever. Most nights are on me anyway. Time to get fucked up!" I raise two glasses, because one isn't enough, and knock them back, slamming them onto the bar and picking up two more.

I'm not totally dumb, I'm aware that Freya is taking advantage of my wealth, but at the same time, I feel like she's the only person who doesn't look at me with pity in her eyes. The only expectation she has of me is to get fucked up with her, which is exactly what I need. It's the only way I can forget his hands on me...

Shuddering, I allow the alcohol to do its thing, blurring my mind and separating myself from reality as the music in the club rings through my ears. Freya is dressed as a slutty cop—which is ironic, considering the amount of cocaine she has stuffed in her cleavage—and almost every other person here is in some kind of fancy dress.

The large crowd doesn't bother me like intimate situations do, and I know Harris is lurking in a corner somewhere, watching out for anyone who might get handsy. Having a bodyguard is actually pretty normal for me, considering they've been around for the majority of my life. Being the daughter of a mafia don means getting used to it, there is no alternative option.

Although my father died last year, leaving my big brother, Marco, as New York's mafia don, I'm still on a constant watch. Our family has enemies, and I understand the need for security... one enemy in particular has a sick fascination with me. In fact, he's the one responsible for my need to forget.

So forget, I will.

The fumble in the bathroom with Batman was just one step on my journey to a new me. A me that doesn't give a shit about anyone or anything other than getting lost in my own mind as I get wasted. In a way, I was testing myself with him, and like with Freya, the look in his eyes wasn't one of pity. When he approached me earlier this evening, I almost turned him away, but he didn't try to touch me or force himself on me, he kept a safe distance and asked permission in his own way. I liked it.

After officially breaking up with Tyler and Enzo because of the pain that ripped through me every time I was with them, I'm still not ready for anything more than what I had with Batman.

Baby steps, I suppose.

While I wallow in my own misery, I've tried running, going back to work in my sister-in-law's club, and visiting the salon I own, but none of them have helped. They're too familiar. I need new. Fresh. And that's what Freya is. An escape from reality as we spend our days sleeping and our nights partying.

Sweat trickles down my back as we dance, the lights a blur of color and the music thump, thump, thumping with the writhing bodies around me. I close my eyes and the room spins uncontrollably, but I carry on regardless, because this is exactly what I want. My face is numb and I think Freya's offering me some of her coke, but I turn it down; I'm already flying, with images of the Batmobile whisking me away at high speeds.

The song changes, the crowd of dancers cheering like it's their favorite tune, so I cheer with them, throwing my hands in the air and joining the masses. Oh the lights are so pretty, the flashes of color mesmerizing, and I try to match my movements to the changes, imagining myself dancing on stage in an empty room.

Freya hands me another shot—I didn't even realize she'd disappeared—and I take it eagerly, needing to top off the alcoholic buzz I've got going on right now. I spin and down it, wobbling a little before regaining my unsteady balance.

A hand comes down on my shoulder and I flinch away, ready to throat punch whoever touched me. I throw my fist out, but it hits empty air. I could've sworn someone was there...?

"Miss Lina, are you ready to go home now?"

"Pfft." It's Harris. "I thought you were cool. Go away. I'm dancing." Talking only accentuates the numbness of my face and I giggle, finding the feeling funny as I twirl again, ignoring Harris.

"Sorry? Listen, your brother will scalp me if anything happens to you on my watch. I can barely understand you. It's time to go home." He reaches his arm out to grip mine and my immediate reaction is to knee him in the balls. He knows better than to touch me.

Only, as I lift my knee, I stumble, falling into him, slapping him away from me as he catches me.

"No. Touching. I'm fine. I'm going to tell on you if you stop being cool. And you'll be scalped anyway. Ha." I think I got all the words out okay. His eyes are wide with fear, so I must have gotten my point across.

I grab a drink from a nearby table, winking at the guy I stole it from before downing it. His brows furrow, but I ignore him, slamming the glass down and throwing my hands back in the air to the music. Freya is grinding against some dude, which is pretty normal for our nights out. Not my circus, let her have at it.

The music takes me again and I get lost in it, twisting, swaying, singing at the top of my lungs while the room continues to spin.

Glimpses of Batman keep filling my vision...

Music...

Lights...

Wait, are we in a taxi?

Whatever, I don't fucking care.

Chapter Two

Tyler

It's well past two in the morning and I'm still in my office. The Halloween party goers are fumbling around the streets of Manhattan as one after the other, the clubs close their doors. From up here, the top floor of the Walker building just two blocks east of the Empire State Building, everyone looks like an ant as they scramble along the sidewalks, hoping to find someone to warm their beds after drinking to excess.

Same shit, different holiday.

I imagine Lina out there somewhere—dressed in the most provocative thing she has in her closet and placing herself in dangerous situations—and it makes my blood pressure rise to alarming levels. I take in a deep breath and slide my hands in the pockets of my slacks while I stare out the wall of windows, hoping to catch a glimpse of her.

My logical brain knows damn well that I won't, but my heart, that stupid motherfucker, is still hoping, even after everything that's happened.

In just four months my entire life has taken a U-turn from utter bliss to complete, fiery Hell. Four fucking months. I can't even wrap my head around this shit. One day, I'm making love to Lina, contemplating taking our relationship to the next level. The next, she's sobbing in my arms, begging me to lend her my private jet so she can fly to Italy and save her brother and Enzo.

I dare any man in love to say no to that.

So, I made the call, got the jet ready, and flew across the Atlantic with her and River. Not once during those eight hours in flight did they tell me the gravity of the situation. I figured with the ten men we had in the plane we would go in, get our friends, and get the fuck out of Dodge, all within a few hours.

Except, as soon as I stepped out of that town car in the middle of no-fucking-where, white hot pain followed by complete darkness is all I remember. Next thing I knew, someone tore off the black bag covering my head, almost blinding me in the process. Lina was standing there, looking like the devil himself had ripped out her very soul.

It's only later—as she spent the entire first night before we flew back out, nestled in my arms—I learned just how true my words rang. Without giving me details, River filled me in on what that motherfucker did to her and from that moment on, Lina has been avoiding me. She texted me that she needed some time to process and from what I've heard, she's processing a lot of fucking alcohol and God knows what else.

"Fuck." Dark thoughts invade my mind as I wonder where she is, what she's doing. With whom.

Taking my phone out, I scroll down my list of contacts until I find Marco's number and press the green call button before I change my mind.

It rings twice before my best friend's groggy voice fills the silence.

"You better be on your fucking death bed, asshole." Did I mention he's my best friend?

"Am I interrupting something?" This is our usual banter. His control issues and my dominant gene always fight for the last word in any given situation.

Last year, I feared our friendship wouldn't survive the tsunami that was River Fox. I knew her as Rose, hired her to be my escort at functions and, in doing so, I was putting distance between me and my ex-wife while also giving Rose protection from Nathaniel Reed's ongoing threats. Truth be told, Marco and I thought protecting this girl he was obsessed with would be the best way to protect the third member of our small circle of trusted friends. He was talking like a madman, throwing out words like revenge and her getting what she deserved.

It's only when I started falling in love with her that Marco took control of the situation, eventually discovering her true identity. River Fox was the long-lost heir to the Volpe family and the young girl Marco was destined to marry when she was only seventeen years old.

It's a story as old as time itself. He saw her and lightning struck harder than a steel beam to the head.

And there I was, fucking her every opportunity I had. To say things got a little awkward is like saying the Antarctic gets a little chilly. A complete and utter understatement.

"Yes, it's the dead of night and I've had to walk away from my wife. This better be a fucking emergency." I can hear the rustling of sheets or clothing and the soft click of a door as Marco's voice grows louder. "What's up?" He's got a loud bark, but his bite is only deadly when you cross him.

"I'm worried about Lina." Silence grows between us as he heaves a pregnant sigh before admitting the same sentiment.

"Yeah, we all are. We're trying to navigate the situation without pushing her away. River asked me to put a tracker on her but Lina's smart, she'd find it without a second's thought." He's right. The number of times she lost her security detail so she could sneak over, back when we were keeping our relationship under wraps, makes me worry even more. "But, Tyler, we've got Harris parked with her twenty-four-seven. Poor guy sounds like he's afraid of me, tells me her every move. In fact, he called earlier to tell me they were at some club in Midtown and then they were going back to Freya's. FYI, I don't like that psycho."

I grunt as my only response. I have no doubts that Harris pisses his pants every time Marco barks at him, but I'm willing to bet the very jet plane that got us in this mess that Harris would rather face Marco's wrath than Lina's disappointment. Nothing feels worse than falling from grace when it comes to Madelina Mancini. Absolutely nothing.

"You have to assume she's got him wrapped around her little finger. I know you're not naïve enough to think she's letting him give you a play by play of her days and nights."

He'd be a fool to accept that and my best friend is many things, but an idiot is not one of them.

On the other end of the line, Marco sighs like he's carrying the entire weight of the world on his Godfatherly shoulders. "I do, but every time I double up her security, they get fired. She seems to like Harris." I frown at his words, my mind spinning with the possibility that she may very well be sleeping with him.

Before I even know what I'm doing, my body swings around and my arms sweep everything right off my desk. The neatly stacked files and ready-to-sign documents go flying across the room, floating like unwanted feathers from a soaring bird headed toward warmer weather. I watch the paper as it rocks from side to side before joining the rest on the carpeted floor.

"Feel better?" I'm still holding my phone, Marco's voice bouncing off the four walls of my office.

"Yes, actually. I do." Suddenly, I'm the one heaving a sigh big enough to shake my entire chest as I let myself fall onto my swiveling chair. "But I still don't know how to fix this. Fix... her."

"I'm guessing that's your problem, right there, Tyler. You can't fix her, none of us can. She has to heal. Not the same thing." Rolling my eyes, a small chuckle escapes my mouth.

"Since when are you the sane one here?" I know what his answer is going to be before he even utters the first syllable.

"Since River." And there it is. The force of nature that is his wife was strong enough to lift him even higher than he already was before they met.

"Figured." And I mean it.

"Now, get your head out of your ass and go get your girl, will you? Quit moping around like a lovesick Romeo. That guy was a complete jack off." I laugh at that, more out of duty than from actual humor.

"How do you figure I do that? She doesn't want to see me." Staring off into the empty office, a few scenarios cross my mind, each one creepier than the last.

"By all means, Brother. By any and all fucking means."

I nod, even though he can't see me, and think about the illegal shit he did to get his wife back and figure, what the hell? It worked for him.

When I don't answer and silence gets the better of him, I hear the rustling of clothes all over again.

"I'm going back to my wife now. Do not call me again until you've got my sister back." Without waiting for my response, the line goes dead and I know what I need to do.

The only good thing about insomnia is being able to up and go in the middle of the night without the worry of losing sleep. It's lost anyway so I may as well ride that silver lining and take a stab at getting my woman back.

It's the dead of night by the time I arrive at Freya's house, a Cape-Cod-style home with a steep roof and wide bay windows. It's what I'd imagine a young, middle-class couple would choose as their first home. I'm not surprised. It even has the sought-after white picket fence.

I kill the engine and lean my head back on the seat, asking myself for the millionth time if this is a good idea. Then I hear Marco's voice in my head as it patronizes me for being an idiot and it gives me the kick in the ass that I need to get out of the car and make my way to the imposing red door. The lights are out, there's no movement behind the violet curtains hanging from the windows, so I hesitate before I knock.

Harris opens for me mere seconds later, the outside light turning on at the same time.

"Thank God!" His words do not inspire the warm and fuzzies. In fact, I'm sure the feral sound I hear is coming from me.

"What the fuck does that mean, Harris?" The guy's relieved features quickly transform into worry with his furrowed brow and wide eyes.

"They've been partying, but Miss Mancini made me promise not to tell her brother what she does." I'm not a violent man, but right now I'm close to punching some sense into Harris and hoping he'll get to the point. Quickly.

Without asking for permission, I shoulder check him as I cross the threshold until I realize I have no fucking clue where I'm going. He must see my hesitation because he points upstairs to the half story with a mumbled, "Second door on the left."

I'm there in the time it takes my heart to pump three times. The knob in hand, I take a moment to breathe in and out, afraid of what I might find on the other side. I cannot be held responsible for my actions if she's in bed with some random guy.

The wood creaks as I push the door just enough to slink inside, my gaze searching for Lina. The bed is empty, the floor is littered with discarded clothes piled high next to the chair. With all the lights out, I can't see properly but when I swivel around and find the entrance to the en-suite bathroom, the air whooshes from my lungs and my heart freezes. It takes me a couple of seconds to register what I'm seeing and another for my conscious brain to kick my body into action.

"Lina!!" All I can see are her legs lying on the floor, her body straddling the entrance. She's got one shoe on and what looks like some kind of bunny costume if that fluffy button tail on her ass is any clue.

Sliding across the floorboards, my hand flies to her delicate neck, seeking out her pulse. It's faint but it's there, thank fuck.

"Lina! Lina, wake up, Baby. Come on." She's completely limp in my arms as I pull her up, her long-eared headband getting caught on my dress shirt. Definitely a bunny. Whiskers and all.

Her naturally tanned skin is pale, the healthy glow she worked hard maintaining has vanished, leaving her pasty and almost gaunt.

"Fuck, Lina, what are you doing to yourself?" I don't think she can hear me and I almost cry when I hear her groan, followed by a heave which is my only warning before her entire body sits up and her head flies back.

I act on pure instinct as I twist us around, grab her long hair in my fist, and aim her mouth at the toilet before she empties her stomach of bile. It's obvious she hasn't eaten or maybe she's already thrown up whatever food she *did* have earlier tonight. It doesn't matter. All I know is that I have to take her home where someone will take care of her. Someone needs to watch her to make sure she doesn't sleep in her own vomit. Or worse, drown in it.

I wish I could take away her pain, maybe even bleach her memory of that horrific night, and it pisses me off that I can't. Rage floods my bloodstream knowing this is a battle she has to fight alone.

And I'm responsible for it all.

Although I would love nothing more than to bring Madelina back to my place so she can rest without having pitying or judgmental eyes on her, I opt for the safest alternative.

The sun is peeking over the horizon and through the glass and steel buildings as the city begins its morning ritual when we walk through Marco's front door. I texted Stefano before I even left Freya's place so he could prepare her room with a bucket, a tall glass of water, and ibuprofen for the pain she'll no doubt feel once she wakes up.

As I lay her down on her bed, I nod to Stefano, mouthing a thank you, just as he bows and walks out of the room. The rich royal-blue curtains are drawn with just enough of a sliver open so I can see what I'm doing.

She stirs beneath my touch as I'm pulling off her shoes and stockings. Her whimpers stab me in the heart, the slow wail-like sounds so similar to something a child in pain would utter that it makes me want to gather her in my arms and fight her demons for her.

"Shh, it's okay, Gumdrop. I've got you." I don't take her clothes off, even though I should. The smell alone might bother her as she sleeps if the tightness of her bunny corset doesn't. But it's not my place to undress her, no matter who I am or what we've already done together. No matter that I've seen her naked and writhing beneath my touch over a hundred times, I refuse to expose her skin without her consent. Period.

Behind me, a soft knock at the door tears my attention away from my girl as River comes in and tiptoes to my side. Worry is etched across her face, her eyes glassy with a mixture of sleep and concern.

"What happened?" Her question is legitimate but, again, it's not my place to give her all the information. So, I give her a watered-down version of what I'm guessing were the night's events.

"She was out with Freya, got drunk, threw up, passed out." I willfully leave out the part about the drugs I saw on the bathroom counter. Not one, but multiple. A clear baggie with the unmistakable white powder and the bag with at least five to seven blue pills I'm guessing were ecstasy. Once Lina wakes up and we can have a sober conversation, we'll fix this.

I will fucking fix this.

"Hmm, it's becoming a habit, Tyler. We need to do something." River's words are filled with the love and care of a sister.

"I'll take care of it. Don't worry, okay?" I pin her with my gaze, hoping she gets my message. I need to do this.

"Okay, but I have to tell Marco. You get that, right?"

Yeah, I get it but I don't like it.

"Whatever you think is best."

River actually growls at me like I'm shitting on her rocky road ice-cream. It would be cute if it weren't unnecessary. "Do not try to manipulate me into keeping secrets from my husband, Tyler. Secrets are the reason Lina is suffering."

Fuck. She's right but I just cannot have Marco going all big brother on Lina. Just like Newton's Third Law tells us, she'll react in the opposite direction and with equal force.

"Honestly, River, I get it, but my only concern right now is Lina. And Marco has elephant feet that will inevitably destroy the china shop." It's late and my metaphor may not be the clearest but it has the merit of making River giggle softly.

"You're not wrong, but still. I'll talk to him." I nod at her words, knowing full well that River is never one to break her promises.

"Thank you." I bend over my girl as River walks back out, and kiss Lina on the forehead.

"Sleep, Gumdrop. I'll be right here."

I watch her sleep for the better part of the morning, keeping a close eye on her and making sure she has help if she gets sick. With my phone on silent, I ignore all my calls but answer, when possible, by email or text message.

It's only when her breathing gets more and more shallow that I tear myself away and gently make my way out of her room after kissing her on the forehead one last time.

"Come back to me, Gumdrop. I miss you."

Then I leave the house behind, hoping somewhere deep inside her she heard me.

Chapter Three

Lina

"Polo... Polo..."

The half-whispered words are getting more insistent with each passing second and it's causing the throbbing in my head to send shooting pains behind my eyes.

"Come on, boy."

Then there's a tiny furry paw on my cheek, followed by a snuffling sound in my ear and a teeny wet nose. I'd be mad as Hell at the intrusion... if it were anyone other than this little fluffball belonging to my sister-in-law, River.

Slowly opening one eye, I spy said sister-in-law sitting on the armchair from the corner of my room—which is now beside my bed. I groan, actually groan, knowing that she's here because of what happened last night. Not that I can remember much after dancing in that club.

There were many more drinks after I handed my credit card over to Freya because bar-waiting time meant less dancing time. Batman... oh God, that was the third time this week. I remember Tyler at one point. Why do I remember Tyler...? Shit, wasn't I at Freya's house? How am I home?

"Hey, Gorgeous. There's some Ibuprofen and some fresh cold water here." River's voice is soft, soothing, with a hint of worry in her tone. Normally she'd be laughing her Louboutin's off at my hangover misery. My head hurts too much to be even a little bit bothered by her pity for me.

Polo has curled himself up into my side, resting his tiny head on my thigh, and I gently stroke my palm over his soft fur. Well, I can't move now, can I? Not that my body would obey me right now anyway. My limbs are heavy, sluggish, and my eyes don't feel like they want to open all the way just yet, so I close them again.

"Daddy's got himself a little fun to have first... hold her legs down."

Screaming, that's all I can hear, all I can do, all that there is...

"Lina, honey, it's okay, you're safe. Come on, wake up. You're safe..."

Pain shoots through my skull as I open my eyes wide, sitting up sharply to wrap my arms around my legs. It was a nightmare. He's not here. I think I'm going to be si—

"Here you go, beautiful." A red plastic bowl is suddenly in front of me as I climb onto my knees and spew my guts up, at the same time my hair is pulled back from my face with River's other hand.

With a now-empty stomach, I remain where I am and slowly look up to River. Her eyes hold more than just concern for me, there's a hint of disappointment mixed in there too and I don't like it. Mostly because it makes me feel even worse.

I'm well aware I'm spiraling down a seemingly never-ending rabbit hole, but I just don't have it in me to stop yet.

Silently, River removes the bowl and heads into my bathroom where I hear the toilet flushing followed by running water before she comes back out.

"Tyler brought you home at about four this morning." My sister-in-law always has a way of knowing what I need to hear.

I slowly nod, annoyance rumbling through my chest, but not at River. With a tight smile, I close my eyes and take a deep breath, immediately wishing I hadn't because it feels like alcohol has replaced my blood stream.

"Don't be mad at him, he was worried about you. He stayed until a couple of hours ago when he had to go for some work meeting."

"Wait, what time is it now?" The curtains are drawn, making it impossible to see outside.

"Three in the afternoon. Listen, I love you, okay? I know you're struggling and I'm not going to diminish any of your hurt by assuming anything I can do will make you feel better, but please remember I'm here. For whatever you need. If you want to talk, I'll talk. If you want me to just listen, I will. If you need to scream, I'll scream with you. If you want to sit in silence, play board games or watch movies, literally, whatever you need, I'm here."

All I can do is slowly nod once more as tears prick at my eyes. Silence isn't usually my thing, but I can't find the words to express my gratitude for her. If only it were that simple. I'm not ready for any of those things. I thought I was, I even tried running for a while, hoping my mind would stay clear as my feet pounded the pavement, but I found myself searching him out.

Ugo Ambrosio.

Any time I'd see someone even remotely similar, I'd reach for my gun, only to remember I wasn't carrying it, then the panic attacks would start.

At first, it was just the standard loss of breath, like I couldn't inhale enough air to keep me breathing, but as the attacks continue, more frequent and longer-lasting, they feel as though fingers are creeping up the inside of my throat and squeezing every ounce of oxygen right out of me. Ripping away my breaths and robbing me of my life source. Like lying in a grave with my eyes wide open and my soul slipping away into the earth.

It's terrifying, sure, but at the same time, it tastes a little bit like freedom.

Luckily for me, Harris knew what was happening and managed to eventually bring me back. I made him swear not to tell Marco or River about them; it'd only make them worry more and they have enough of their own shit to deal with without adding mine to the mix.

A tear escapes my eye as I take in my sister-in-law's beautifully kind face. I can see she wants to say more, but she's hesitating, which is unlike River. She leans forward and wipes away my tear with the satin sleeve of her red shirt before standing and wrapping her arms around my shoulders. Kissing the top of my head, she squeezes me, and I revel in the warmth radiating off her. I hug her back, because it's impossible to do anything else around this formidable woman.

"All I have left to say is be safe, Gorgeous. Please, for the love of all the gods, be safe. I recognize the kind of hangover you have, not just from alcohol, and I won't preach because that's not who I am, but you're in dangerous territory, babe. If you won't talk to me, please talk to *someone*, okay?" She holds me by the shoulders and looks me in the eyes, love shining through them and an eyebrow raised as she waits for me to answer.

I nod, barely tipping the corners of my lips up, knowing full well I haven't been to see the therapist for too long. The last time was just after the first panic attack, the therapist felt really judgey and tried to prescribe me more pills that I didn't want. They were useless compared to the cocaine I've been taking with Freya.

"Words, Madelina." Marco's growl from the doorway startles me and I jump back from River, anger suddenly bubbling through my insides at his intrusion.

"Marco, really?" River rests her hands on her hips and turns to my brother, a little of the anger I'm feeling flashing on her face as her brows furrow.

"Yes, really, Tesoro. You might not preach, but I sure as hell will." He turns his glare to me, unmoving from his place just inside my open door. "One, I know you haven't been seeing your therapist; she called. Sounded like an uptight bitch so I've booked you in with someone in a few days. Two, you're not fucking stupid, so stop with the snow before it becomes a problem. And three, Enzo and Tyler have been like sad puppies—"

"One, big brother of mine, that's none of your fucking business. Two, that's also none of your fucking business. And three, woah, we're going for a hat trick, because that's also none. Of. Your. Fucking. Business. You know what? It's been a long time coming. I'm going to find my own place, away from your prying, nosy-as-fuck eyes." My tone is scathing, and I know he's coming from a good place with it, taking control is how he deals with shit, but it's not what I want from him. Hell, I don't even know what I do want, all I know is that it isn't this right now.

"Madel—"

"No, Marco! I don't want to hear it. I'm twenty-seven tomorrow; who even lives with their big brother at the age of twenty-seven? I don't need you all up in my business anymore. I'm a big girl and I need to do this for me." What started as a rant, has turned into a solid new plan. The anger has subsided a little, with determination seeping in at my new task. Something shiny and new to put all my focus into. "Now please, kindly, fuck off."

Marco's face is full of anger, his fists are tight by his sides, but he closes his eyes and takes a deep breath after glancing at River. "*Ti voglio bene, Sorellina.*"

Before leaving the room, he looks to River again, heat in his eyes as she sucks her middle finger and uses it to blow a kiss to him. As quickly as the anger rose within me, it's completely gone. Instead, I'm kind of happy in this moment and I want to bask in it. I still feel like shit and want to sleep for days, but knowing how my emotions have been so up and down, I want to take advantage of the natural up.

"You're really doing it, aren't you?" River turns her attention back to me, a little excitement flashing through her eyes.

"Yeah." I shrug, and find myself smiling at the idea of my own place now that I'm more settled in New York. Staying here was only ever supposed to be a stop-gap anyway.

"Well then, everything I said still stands, okay?"

"Okay. Thanks, River."

"Anytime, Gorgeous."

Harris drives me past Rapture, River's club where I dance from time to time, on the way to visit my salon. The urge to go and dance pulls at me, and I know River's held my position there as a dancer, but as with a lot of things, I haven't been ready.

Maybe soon.

For now, The Belle-Vu is my destination. It's been a while since my last visit. Since I hired people to basically run things for me here when I started dancing, I haven't needed to come. Although, pre-Italy, I did try to make a point to visit once every couple of weeks to catch up with the staff and make sure they're all getting on okay. After-Italy, I haven't been once.

Pulling up outside the salon a few blocks away from Rapture in Hell's Kitchen, I breathe a sigh of relief. This feels like a little slice of normal and, as with every time I come here, I look up at the gold lettering of my sign, allowing the achievement to settle in. This place is all mine. I did this. I built this salon from the ground up. Yes, I had a little financial help from my dad when he was alive, but

I made sure to pay back every penny he poured into my business.

Walking inside is like a serene dream, the warmth of the artificial pink and lilac roses covering the information desk, the gold accents surrounding each of the workstations and beauty areas; it's luxurious perfection. And busy as usual, which is always a nice sight.

"Lina! Oh my God, it's so good to see you." Sandy rushes toward me from behind the counter, wrapping her arms around me. "Ooh, girl, you've lost some weight. Have you been ill?"

"Yeah. But I'm fine, better now. Is Rex in today?" I'm starting to think I'm not ready to come here, but maybe if I just have a talk with Rex, who is managing the place for me, then I won't feel like this was a wasted journey. Usually, I'd stay for a good few hours, but I don't think I have it in me today.

After finding an apartment and putting in the paperwork yesterday—having money helps make a lot of things happen quickly in this city, my surname helps a lot too—I have been on a natural high. But the one comment about my weight has me feeling self-conscious and wanting to leave already.

Rubbing at my arm, my skin prickles in irritation, the scab that's formed from God-knows-where becoming raw. Luckily, I'm wearing long sleeves so it's not visible.

It's fine. I can stay. Today is a good day.

"He'll be here in the next hour if you want to wait. I can make you a coffee and set you up with Stacey to give you a blow-out."

As much as I'd love that, especially considering it's my birthday today so there's no reason not to get pampered, the annoying anger that keeps rearing its ugly head begins to make an appearance. My stomach is in knots just because Rex isn't available when I'm here. It's irrational of me, I'm aware, but it's difficult to control. Rolling my eyes, I flip my hair and turn to leave.

"No. Tell him to call me as soon as he gets in."

I don't spend any time with my employees, I don't say goodbye, I just leave. And now I'm pissed off at my own rude behavior as well as Rex not being in the salon.

Fuck this shit.

Pulling my cell from my small black clutch bag, I hesitate over who to call, my thumb hovering over Enzo, then Tyler... then him.

Nope. Not today. After basically being told how skinny I look, throwing all my happy down the drain, I know what I need to do.

Get fucked up and forget the world around me for another day.

Trying to be some semblance of normal is too difficult right now, and I tell myself I'll try again tomorrow.

I hit dial, holding my cell to my ear as I wait for an answer.

"Biiiiitch! Where were you last night? I had to go out all on my lonesome. You coming over? I've just had a delivery."

A stone sits in my stomach, knowing that I'm on a self-destructive path of up and down emotions, but also, I really can't find it inside myself to care. While Freya wouldn't be my first choice of who to spend my birthday with, she's the only one who won't judge what I want.

I mean, I know River wouldn't either, but she wouldn't let loose with me the way Freya does, and while I love how caring she is as a person, in my own way, I'm protecting her from myself. Plus, she comes with a giant tag-along known as Marco.

"Get your sparkliest outfit on. It's my birthday and we're going out."

Chapter Four

Enzo

"Get it fucking done!"

Marco slams his office phone down on the receiver like it's to blame for all his frustrations.

"No luck?" I know I sound bored but my bouncing knee and tapping index finger on the arm of his fancy office chair say the exact opposite.

"When did my men become incompetent? It's been months and that fucker is still out there… living." They're my boss's words but it's like he's taking them right out of my brain. Tension rolls off his shoulders as he overlooks The City, giving me his stone-faced profile, the ticking of his jaw beating to the rhythm of the pelting rain against the floor-to-ceiling windows.

"I told you, he's underground. I've got my ears to the beat, making friends with some shady fuckers, but I think it'll be worth it in the end." Marco's eyes find mine as he turns his head away from the view and I swear there's a crackle in the air, like electricity seeking out an overflowing pool.

"Same shady fuckers that are giving you a new black eye every week?" I snort, one shoulder rising and falling like it's no big deal and barely worth mentioning.

"So I let them get a punch in once in a while. It's good business." I'm making light of the situation because if he knew the whole truth he'd fucking gut me first and ask questions later.

Although, judging by the narrowing of his eyes and curl of his lip, he may not wait for all the information before ripping me a new one.

"You're not fucking helping, Enzo. Is this some kind of two-bit self-help deal you think you need? Do you think Lina needs to see you sporting a new shiner every time your paths cross? Have you even seen the shit she's up to?" With every question, the tone of his voice rises until he growls his grand finale. "Get your shit together or else I'll be the one giving you therapy. With my fist."

On instinct and without even thinking about who I'm talking to, I jump from my seat and find myself nose to nose with my boss. Not just mine, either. He's the boss of all five fucking boroughs. His reach is without measure. My brain, however, has chosen to ignore the fact that he could end me without even lifting his little finger.

Where I'm shaking with palpable energy, my fists at my sides ready to pummel to relieve this pent-up fire burning in my chest, Marco doesn't even flinch. His hands are still in his pockets, his entire demeanor appearing relaxed.

Except I know him better than anyone else. Well, except maybe River and still, I don't think she truly knows this side of him. The cold-hearted killer that wouldn't bat an eye before drawing blood. He's a lot like his father in that way.

"Think before you do something we won't be able to ignore." His voice is like a rubber band just before it's released.

"Everything I do. Everything I say. Every fucking thing I live for revolves around your sister. If I could heal her by bleeding out on your pristine floors, I'd fucking do it in a heartbeat." I speak through gritted teeth, afraid the pressure from my words may cause a fucking tsunami.

Marco leans in impossibly closer, invading my space like he owns it, and whispers. "Then fucking prove it. Bring me Ugo on his fucking knees."

We stand there, staring at each other, frustration like a living beast eating our insides, before I give him a short, tight nod and step away with a grunt.

Marco watches me as I return to my seat like this showdown never happened. He thinks he has some kind of mask on but he can't hide the tension around his eyes, the tightness in the straight line of his mouth. It's stress and it's all about Madelina. I know, I recognize it because I see the same signs in my reflection every fucking morning I wake up and remember Ugo fucking Ambrosio is still living his life somewhere.

"It doesn't help that Aleko killed his own brother. That whole fucking Greek organization disintegrated like fairy dust. So now I have to get friendly with people willing to brag about their bad decisions." Marco turns back to the drops of rain streaming down the large windows.

"We're having a surprise birthday party at that Brit guy's restaurant. River vouched for him and Tino and Galeone secured the perimeter. I need you to make sure she's there at seven tonight. Everyone will be waiting for her." Looking over his shoulder at me, he pauses for added effect before making his point crystal clear. "Make sure Freya is nowhere around us. She's fucking toxic and I promised

River I wouldn't kill her. Yet. However, if she shows up uninvited, all bets are off."

I scoff, shaking my head and closing my eyes as I lean my head back. "You seem to be under the impression that I can control your sister. If that were the case, she wouldn't be club hopping with a fucking psycho and doing more coke than an eighties metal band." It's like my words have dragged the air right out of his lungs, the sound pained and frustrated. "Fuck. Please tell me you already knew."

"Of course I know. River makes Sherlock Holmes look like an amateur, and even though she won't tell me everything because of some preconceived girl code I'm supposed to respect—spoiler alert, I don't—I make sure to eavesdrop at the right times and places." Back at his desk, he opens a drawer and takes out a file, pushing it toward me with three fingers.

Leaning forward, I snatch the manilla folder from the wooden surface and quickly flip through the ten-or-so pages inside. A couple of names jump out at me but no major red flags. "What's this?" I raise a brow at Marco, urging him with my silence to give me information.

"Those are the names of the dealers she may be buying from. Find them and help them find another street corner to sell from." I chuckle at his imagery because, judging from the pictures in this file, they're not exactly two-bit drug runners hustling on the corners of anything. These guys are living the high life and selling to the top crust of New York City.

"You do realize this is bullshit, right? All she needs to do is give them a call and they'll meet her at a club, make the deal, and walk away." I throw the file back on his desk and grunt as I slump back into the chair.

"I don't think I made myself very clear." Marco stands, leans over the desk, and pins me with a look that would make Iron Man piss his armor. "Get them. Off. My. Streets. Do you understand?"

The corners of my lips creep up and my body relaxes just enough for me to feel the welcoming heat of adrenaline burning through my system.

"Loud and fucking clear."

I should already be in Madelina's room, escorting her to the restaurant. River set the whole thing up like they were having a girls' night for her birthday with the condition that I be there with them for safety reasons.

My fingers curl around the edge of the sink as I lift my eyes to the mirror and stare at myself without actually seeing my face. My mind is stuck in the past, lying on the dirty ground—bound and bleeding—as I do my best to anchor the only woman I've ever loved.

It was a ridiculous thought, believing I could help her ignore the fact that some fucking psychopath was taking what she refused to offer.

If I squeeze the sink any tighter, I'm either going to break it or my fingers, but it's impossible to stop my body from reacting to the memory… the sight of her eyes going from wide and scared to dead and resigned. We held each other's gazes as she lost her will to live in those disgusting moments back in Italy.

The home to my ancestors will forever be Hell for us. Just mentioning Naples makes my entire body shake with pent up rage and murderous hunger.

Taking a deep breath, I hang my head and close my eyes as I force my lungs to breathe in and out, slow and steady, until I can look back up and not feel the need to kill the man in the mirror.

I couldn't save her.

I didn't save her.

I had one job and I failed. That failure destroyed the love of my life and now she can't even look at me without needing to snort drugs up her nose to forget that I was there, to forget that I saw what happened, that I was responsible for her pain.

"Fuck. Get your shit together, Beneventi. It's not over until you're six feet under."

It takes me five whole minutes to walk from my suite on the third floor's east wing to Madelina's corner of the house up on the fourth-floor west wing. This place is nearly as big as the convent where my mother abandoned me thirty years ago. Except here, the only suffering I endure is self-inflicted.

By the time I reach her room, my heart is beating against my ribs, threatening to break one or two but before I can knock on her door, I hear the music. Madelina's musical choices have always been directly linked to her moods. When she was a teen, if Eminem blasted through her speakers then she was about to do something that would probably make her parents flip out. Lady Gaga meant she was stressing out about something and needed the girl power vibe to reassure her. Right now, Katy Perry's *California Girls* is practically shaking the walls down, which means she's in party mode.

I used to love this side of her, it meant she was happy and excited about going out and having fun with her well-vetted and protected friends. But tonight, I'm afraid.

Is she high already? Is she feeling reckless?

Fuck.

I knock a few times but the damn music is so fucking loud that there's no way she can hear me.

Taking my phone out, I scroll for her name, a pang of sadness burning my chest when I realize how far down my list it is now. On any given day, Madelina's name would be first or second but she's made it impossible to ignore that the last thing she wants is to hear my voice or see my face.

Pressing the call button, I hear it ringing in my ear but there's no echo on the other side of the door.

I bang harder, three hits against the wood, before a frustrated sigh rips from my throat. I'm out of options and the party is in twenty-five minutes. If we don't leave now, we won't make it to the restaurant on time. New York City traffic this time of night will make sure of it.

There's only one option.

Turning the knob, I crack open the door. The loud music slaps me in the face as I push an arm through the opening and wave it like a white flag.

"Lina, time to go." I wait for her to see me agitating my arm like a fucking idiot but if she's in her bathroom then she's not going to see shit, that room is fucking huge and not at all positioned to see the entrance to her suite.

Before Italy, I would have walked in without a second thought. She would have jumped in my arms and the idea of seeing her naked wouldn't have filled me with anxiety.

But all that has changed.

We've changed.

Italy fucking changed us.

Shaking my head, hoping to dissolve the vile thoughts swimming inside my memory, I take a step inside and head straight to the speaker taking up half the space on the top of her dresser and press pause.

I expect her to yell at me, demanding I turn it back on, maybe even cuss me out for invading her space without permission. What I don't expect is complete and total silence. My ears are ringing with the phantom sounds of Katy Perry, but aside from that, there's nothing. No water running, no annoyed Madelina huffing and puffing, not a single sound greets me.

Looking around, I notice two things.

Her phone is nowhere to be found and the current purse she's been obsessing over is gone. Madelina may be on this side of disorganized but she always leaves her phone on her bedside table with her charger and her purse on the coat rack to the right of the door.

"She's gone." My hand flies to the butt of my gun as I turn on my heel to face the sound of the voice.

Clenching my jaw, I do my best to pretend Stefano didn't scare the fuck out of me, sneaking up here like a fucking sixty-year-old ninja.

"Jesus, Stef, what the fuck? I could have shot your head off." Shaking my arms out, I crack my neck from one side to the other and relax just long enough for his words to register. "Wait, where the fuck is she? We were supposed to leave together."

"Oh, Vincenzo, it took you three seconds longer to reach for your gun than it would have taken me to snap your neck. You're... what's that word you boys like to use?" He snaps his fingers, his eyes to the sky searching out the magic word before he claps his hands together like he's just discovered gravity, his grin wide and proud. "Slacking. You've been slacking off, young padawan."

Christ... River has been watching the Star Wars saga with Stefano on her nights off and now he's talking like a fucking Jedi. Okay, I need to get back to the heart of the matter here.

"Where did she go, Stef? When?" I'm outside her room now and I already miss her signature scent. It's like she bathes in wild flowers while drinking fresh orange juice. It makes me horny and hungry all at the same time.

"I assumed she was heading to the restaurant with you. She left about an hour ago." I narrow my eyes at his words because he knows a lot more than what he's telling me.

"Stef, goddammit, what aren't you telling me?" My fingers pinch the bridge of my nose as I take in a deep breath and hope he's not trying to actively give me a heart attack.

"Freya came to pick her up. I also saw it on the camera feed a few minutes before coming up here to warn you." He hands me a black and white image of my girl stepping into what looks like a new German sports car, Freya at the wheel, as Madelina looks directly at the camera, winking.

Her entire life, Madelina Mancini has been underestimated. We babied her, we protected her, we shielded her from the darkness of our world. All the while, she was forging a cunning suit of armor we never saw coming.

"She's playing with us." I'm not speaking to anyone in particular. Hell, maybe I'm talking directly to her stilled image.

"Clearly, she's playing with you, Vincenzo. She may be pushing you away but she hasn't cut you off. The longer you give her space, the larger the gap will grow."

Annoyed, I raise a brow and pin him with my deadliest glare. "You think you're Yoda, now?"

"Of course not. Yoda would have said it backwards."

I'm still fuming from Stefano's unnecessary humor when I finally get to the restaurant. I'm sure to find one of two things. Either Madelina hasn't shown up and Marco will put a bullet in my skull and call it a night. Or, she's here with Freya, both high off their tits, and he'll put a bullet through my skull and pray to God he's forgiven. Either way, my lifespan has drastically shortened in just two hours' time.

Barely inside the restaurant, it takes only a half a second before Marco is towering over me. It only feels like he's looking at me from above because his sheer presence puts him somewhere up there with the fucking Greek gods, when in reality he's barely has an inch over me.

"Traffic?"

Fuck, he's pissed.

"In my defense, Stefano totally dropped the ball on this one." It's better to beg Stef for forgiveness than to admit to Marco that I fucked up.

"Why the actual fuck is psycho Barbie hanging all over my sweet, innocent sister?" Marco with his hands in his pockets doesn't mean he's relaxed. In fact, that's his pose when he's trying really fucking hard not to unalive someone.

"She left an hour early like a damn jail bird and jumped in Freya's car so she could ride off into the sunset." I hand him the picture Stef gave me, hoping it'll get him off my back.

Pinching the image between his thumb and forefinger like it's made of dog shit, he sighs just as River sidles up to him and snatches the picture away.

"Ah, she ditched ya, didn't she?" River grins like a proud mama before handing the image right back and distracting her husband with what I'm choosing to believe is some kind of witchy potion she sprays on like perfume that snares Marco's attention like lasagna for Garfield.

"Tesoro, your friend needs to get her filthy claws off my sister. She's proven to be a heartless cunt and I don't want her rubbing off on Lina." I grunt my agreement and immediately regret it, having pulled his attention back to me. "She's flying high on God knows what and that Brit chef is eyeing her like she's his next crème brulée."

"Hmm, that sounds so fucking good right now." We both look at River as she scans the room, hoping to find the dessert somewhere.

"I like when you're hungry for dessert before we've even started on the appetizers." When her attention slides right back to his, I know it's my cue to get the fuck away or else be forced to watch them eye fuck each other in front of friends and family.

I mean, who in their right minds is going to tell Marco fucking Mancini to get a room?

Madelina. She definitely would.

Reaching my girl, I decide to take Stef's advice and see if it holds any truth. Where I would usually just sit back and watch from across the room, I decide it's time to take action. My gaze fixed only on Madelina, I plant myself at the bar, my back to Freya and my attention on the only woman I've ever truly seen.

"You're being rude to Freya, Enzo." Her words hold no bite but her gaze won't meet mine.

"Why did you ditch me, Madelina?"

She ignores my question and takes a shot of what I'm guessing is vodka.

"Hey, Lapdog, you're killing our vibe here, man." Slowly, my head turns from Madelina to my other side where

Freya is glaring at me with her lips pursed, her disapproval evident in the pinched lines.

Leaning down, I whisper in her ear, "You're lucky that's the only thing I'm killing right now." I hear her gasp and it feeds my inner monster, that part of me that needs to torment.

"Excuse me?"

"You heard me, Freya. Go home or you'll be leaving in a body bag." She sputters like she thinks I'm kidding or bluffing. To be fair, I am kidding about the body bag. She wouldn't need one of those at the bottom of the East River.

"Be nice, Enzo. She's my friend." I turn back to Madelina and, without thinking, I pinch her chin between my fingers and speak against her mouth.

"If she's your friend then you might want to save her by telling her to get. The fuck. Out. You know me, Madelina. I don't hesitate." Her sweet breath falls on my lips and I almost lose my mind over it. It's been months since I've tasted her, felt her love warming my bed and her laugh brightening the darkest corners of my soul. I'm a starving man and she's the feast that can give me life.

"Well, well, this looks quite appetizing, Treacle. You can use my storage room if you need a quick shag. Just as long as I can join ya."

Chapter Five

Devon

Watching her from across the room, I clench my fists tightly, trying desperately to hold myself back from throwing her over my shoulder and spanking her ass for allowing herself to get into this state again. She may look the part of happy birthday girl in her barely-there sparkling silver dress, but this isn't the Lina I first saw gliding across the stage covered in glittering pink diamonds, the one with a brightness in her eyes and a spark for life. The one who fixed her icey-blues on me and refused me a lap dance in her sister-in-law's club.

This Lina is broken and lost, her fire extinguished, and it boils my blood when I think about the reasons why.

I left England to get away from the kind of shite Lina's had to deal with, only to walk right back into it, following her sweet arse into the flames like a puppy. One of the things I can thank my family for is the connections they've given me across the world, being the biggest crime family in London has afforded them—and myself—some luxuries. And while I want to separate myself from the business side of it all now after the night my dad went too far, I can't deny the benefits of the family connections. Especially when said benefits have handed me all the information I need about the woman I'm obsessed with, including what she went through in Naples because of her fucking mafia don big brother and a dead-man-walking cunt called Ambrosio.

I swear, I couldn't make this shit up.

Finding out about her two boyfriends came as a surprise. The fact that they were okay with sharing her sent a warmth through my stomach, knowing this woman was perfect for me. To be worthy of the love of two men already, she must be something pretty fucking special.

Every time I've seen her since that first night, I have made sure she remembers me, inserting myself into situations and keeping an eye on her, and now that she's separated from the two guys from before, I've been watching her even more closely. The Italian one is a moody fuck and has been completely avoiding her, and the rich one has been moping around like a fucking sap. It's obvious they're still in love with her, and I'm all for it, but for now, I'm not going to complain about the alone time I've experienced with her so far.

I'm so close to the edge of my limits with her, I have a feeling tonight is the night I'm going to snap. I get that she's grieving for a time before what happened to her, but she's a fucking queen in need of a king—or three. It's time she realizes how precious she is and puts that sassy mouth of hers to good use on something other than my cock while dressed as a pink fluffy bunny.

The broody Italian guy's face is full of pain as he approaches her but I can still see the magnetic pull they have together. He's telling her off about something, and maybe it's about time. A grin spreads across my face and I find myself walking over to them, unable to stop, my thread of patience for her finally snapped in two.

"If she's your friend then you might want to save her by telling her to get. The fuck. Out. You know me, Madelina. I don't hesitate."

This statement is something I can agree with. That limpet cunt is bad news. And I haven't had it confirmed yet, but I have my suspicions that she was responsible for her husband's death a few months ago. Grumpy is holding Lina's chin between his thumb and finger, and my dick twitches at the idea of him licking at the seams of her mouth, opening her up for a bruising kiss.

"Well, well, this looks quite appetizing, Treacle. You can use my storage room if you need a quick shag. Just as long as I can join ya."

"Stay out of this, *Chef*."

"Oh, Grumpy, we have cute nicknames for each other already? I thought it'd take a while to get to this stage of our relationship, but here we are. Shall we celebrate with a kiss?"

The veins at his temples seem to pulse and his jaw tightens, his black-brown eyes alight with a fire that makes me smile. Lina's twinkling laugh makes my smile grow even larger, and I glance her way with a wink, enjoying the blush creeping up her cheeks as I do.

"See, the lady agrees." I wag my eyebrows at him, knowing how much he wants to stab me in the eye because psychos know psychos, but he won't do it. Not here, not at Lina's birthday party. The restraint this man has is impressive though. I wonder how long he can hold off on giving Lina the orgasm she so desperately needs?

"Enzo, you're being rude again. Devon is my friend too." Her voice is a little slurred and I know if I don't act soon she'll be too far down the rabbit hole of wasted. She needs sobering up.

Sliding my hand around her waist, I pull her in front of me and begin swaying my hips, encouraging her to move with me. My eyes stay on Enzo, enjoying the way his pupils dilate at watching her move before he growls under his breath and walks away.

"Wanna come back to my batcave, Treacle?" I'm not going to beat about the bush with this woman anymore. I can't continue to sit back and watch her destroy herself and everything she's worked so hard for.

"But it's my birthday party and I'm dancing." Her slurred voice is jovial and I know I can sway her decision.

I slowly move my hand from her hip to her stomach, pushing her against my front so she can feel what she does to me.

"Is that a gun in your pocket or are you just pleased to see me?" She laughs, but it's husky, deep, full of lust.

"I prefer knives, and right now, they're all in the kitchen. Go and thank your brother and sister-in-law for the party and tell them you're coming home with me." I slap her arse and gently guide her in the direction of Marco and River.

"Why do you have to ruin our fun?" The insipid little trollop who goes by the name of Freya is in my space, and if I didn't have a thing against killing women, she'd have been minced meat weeks ago.

"I don't give a shit about your fun. You're walking on thin ice, girl. Take the hint and fuck off."

Turning my back to her, I pull out my phone and text the guy I hired to manage this place, letting him know I'm going home and to organize the clean and close up when the party's over. I slide it into the back pocket of my jeans as I make my way over to Lina, who is being a good girl and talking to her brother.

"...sure you want to go home with him, Lina? If you don't want to stay in your new apartment yet, you'll always have a room at home."

"Marco, baby, loosen the leash. She's your sister, not your daughter." I knew I liked that River chick from the first moment I saw her when she came here for lunch with my girl.

"Ready, Treacle?" I slide my arm across Lina's shoulders, pulling her into my side, and she comes willingly. Although she's leaning quite heavily, letting me know that getting her home and sobered up now is a good idea.

"You know who I am, if anything happens to her while she—"

"Anything? Or just anything bad? Because stopping him from doing anything nice to her or good for her would just be silly." River pulls Marco's face to hers, locking her gaze with his and softly kissing his lips. Then she pulls his face into her neck and quickly glances my way, winking and telling me with her eyes to fuck off with my girl.

The twenty-minute journey home last night was spent with me rubbing Lina's back and holding her beautiful dark hair away from her face. I had to give the Uber driver a few hundred dollars to cover the cleaning bill. She was a mess, but I hoped the sickness helped to get a lot of the shit she'd taken out of her stomach. I don't have coffee here, so I made her a cup of tea and practically forced her to drink a liter of water before gently laying her in my bed.

It's nearing mid-day and I've been awake for hours. I spent the first few staring at the beauty in my bed. Even pale and sick, she's the best thing I've ever had lying next to me. I cleaned her up a little last night, washed her hair over the bath and plaited it back out of her face. Having six sisters and no brothers is to blame for my hair styling abilities, but I won't complain, not when it means I can take care of my new obsession.

Now though, I'm done with waiting, so I'm taking her breakfast in bed—well, brunch. The best morning-after food ever invented.

"What is that smell?" Her throaty voice tells the story of how fucked up she was last night, but the mumbled words from beneath the duvet still put a smile on my face.

"This, Treacle, is your hangover cure." I peel the covers away from her face and she groans, trying to burrow deeper into the pillows.

"Oh, God. It smells gross. I think I'm going to be sick."

"No, you're not. You need to eat. Come on, sit up for me."

"I hate you."

Her vicious words are like a balm to my soul, but I know she doesn't mean them as she moves to sit up. I lean over her to bring the pillows up behind her back, and she glares at me as she tucks the covers underneath her arms. She's still wearing the sparkling silver piece of material she calls a dress from last night. Knowing her past made me wary of removing it without her knowledge, but I can't imagine it was comfortable to sleep in.

"I know, Treacle. Here, a bacon sarnie will settle your stomach. Eat." I place the plate on her lap and make myself comfortable beside her, taking a bite of my own sandwich.

"A bacon what now? It looks like a grilled sandwich to me." She picks it up to inspect it, watching the ketchup spilling from the center with curiosity.

"Tom-ay-to, tom-ah-to. Eat."

"I don't really feel great. I'm not sure if I should risk it if I'm honest." The pain in her eyes is unmistakable as she questions herself. I don't like it.

Turning to her, I pick up one half of her sarnie and break a small piece off. "Open." I push it toward her mouth and brush it against her lips, my tone leaving no room for argument. Like a good girl, she opens up for me, and I slide the food inside her mouth, gliding my thumb across her lip as she closes her mouth and begins chewing slowly.

Without giving her time to think about it, I break off another piece and hold it out, ready for her when she swallows. This time, she opens up for me without encouragement, biting her teeth down on the sandwich before chewing once more. I keep my eyes on hers as I lean across and grab the glass of orange juice I brought in for her, waiting for her to swallow before bringing it to her lips. For a moment, a look of panic and defiance flashes across her gaze, but I raise a brow, demanding she do as I'm asking.

The silence as we eat isn't deafening though... in fact, it's only making the moment more intimate. Never before has a woman made me feel this way, but it's frustrating the fuck out of me that she has these demons.

The tension building as I continue to feed her has my cock standing to attention beneath my boxers, but this isn't about sex. This is about looking after my woman. My girl. My Italian princess.

The last few times I've seen her, she's been high as a kite and practically begged to suck me off, and while I *should* have said no, I didn't want her to go and let out her frustrations on someone else. So I allowed it, and fuck me, she knows how to work my shaft, but that's not how I want her.

I want her sober, clear-headed, and coming all over my face instead of the other way around.

"Is this weird for you? Because I don't think I should be here..." She's swallowed the last bite and a little color is already back in her cheeks.

"Not weird at all. Just a man feeding his woman."

"Erm, I think you're getting a little carried away there, Batman. Just because I've sucked your cock a couple of times doesn't make me yours." There it is, that bite. My bratty girl is showing herself.

"Oh, it doesn't? I guess we'll have to change that then, won't we, Treacle?" I move the empty plates from the bed and place them on the side table before putting all my attention back on Lina.

"I think I need to go. Thanks for the sandwich." She throws off the duvet and slides her legs off the side of the bed, her dress hitched up on her thighs. "Where are my shoes?" She drags her eyes up from the floor and looks at me, uncertainty clear in her gray irises. I'm guessing she's at war with herself over whether she should be here or out there somewhere putting shit into her body to forget her own mind.

One of my sisters had a similar experience to Lina and the signs of self-destruction are all so familiar. I couldn't save my sister, but I refuse to let this woman go.

"By the sofa in the other room."

My home was once an abandoned warehouse. I had it renovated to fit my needs when I moved to New York, so it's pretty open-plan, but I made sure to have my bedroom separated from the rest of it, walls and all.

"Where's my phone?" Her voice is timid again, like she can't decide whether she's up or down, fierce or cowering.

"Come here, Treacle."

Without argument, she turns to me and lays across the bed, resting her head against my waiting chest. I wrap my arms across her front and hold her tightly, giving her every piece of strength I have. The way she responds to my commands is just another thing that makes my dick twitch, and the realization that she is even more perfect for me than I ever imagined fills me with a new obsession for the woman in my arms.

If I do nothing else, I will bring back my bratty Italian princess and that spark I know she's hiding.

Chapter Six

Lina

The way Devon's voice vibrates through my insides when he tells me to do something makes me forget anything else in the world exists. It's better than all the drugs in New York and, in this moment, I'm content. Which is far better than I've been in as long as I can remember.

His fresh ocean scent reminds me of a time when I didn't feel like a shadow of myself and I want to cling onto that memory for now.

"How're you feeling, Treacle?" His tone rumbles through his chest, interrupting the soft rhythm of his thumping heart against my ear.

The question makes me falter, unsure whether I should still be here, and guilt begins to gnaw at my chest. I may have broken up with Tyler and Enzo, but not once did I think it would last forever. I'd like to think I can eventually pull myself out of this downward spiral I've found myself in and make my way back to them as a whole person once more.

I turned Devon down time and time again because, as much as Tyler and Enzo agreed to share me, I don't think I could find it in myself to ask them to share me with someone else as well. No matter how much the annoying Brit called to something inside me.

I miss them.

But there is no way back now. Not since the first time I got on my knees for this man in the back of a nightclub. Freya had gone home with some random dude again, leaving me alone, and Devon had just been there. Like a knight in shining armor ready to escort me home... and I had practically begged to suck his cock. He refused me at first, telling me I was in no state for that, but I could feel how much he wanted me as he held me close.

His weakness for me and the sounds he made were addictive, like a powerful injection of confidence.

I'm not that powerful person though.

I'm a mess.

I'm damaged goods.

I come with too much baggage.

"Hey, where'd you go, Beautiful?"

A tear slowly drops from my eye and trickles down the side of my face into my hairline. I've fucked up so much recently: my relationships, my body, my mind, all of it.

I'm a worthless piece of shit.

"Listen to me now, Treacle." Devon firmly grips my shoulders and encourages me to sit up, then he uses his whole hand underneath my chin to lift my head to face him. "We're going to have a shower, then I'm going to make us both a cup of tea and we're going to stick a film on and watch it. With popcorn." He slaps my ass and urges me to stand at the same time as he gets up from the bed. The small smile on his face doesn't hold a hint of pity or sympathy and he's not asking me if this is okay, this is a command.

There's a part of me that wants to deny him, to see what happens when I don't do as he says, but I'm not sure I'm ready for that yet. What he's offering for now is easy and I kind of like that he isn't giving me choices, because I'm not sure I'd make the right ones anyway.

In silence, I let him lead me to the bathroom, the carpet on my bare feet as soft and grounding as his hand on my lower back. The pale gray-and-black-tiled walls alongside the black porcelain scream masculinity. Considering the room has no windows, I would have expected it to be quite dark in here, but the bright spotlights in the ceiling make the room sparkle in brilliant luxury.

Large glass doors cross over half of the room and I swear at least five people could easily fit inside that shower. There's even a bench seat on one side, like you'd casually have a sit down halfway through showering.

Devon removes his hand from my lower back, causing an immediate chill to run down my spine and goosebumps to erupt over every inch of my skin. Moving to stand in front of me, he does that thing guys do when they're being sexy and lifts an arm to grab the back of his T-shirt, and my God if I wasn't so dehydrated I'd probably drool at the way his muscles tighten, highlighting every curve and line of the tattoos I'd love to take the time to inspect. He pulls his T-shirt up and over his head, not saying a word but keeping his deep-blue eyes locked on mine.

It's really difficult to resist glancing down to see the hard chest I rested my head on earlier, wanting to see if the art from his arms travels further.

The corners of his lips tip up into a smirk, as if he knows exactly what I'm thinking and he's just waiting for me to disobey his silent command. Next, he bends enough to push down his gray sweatpants, and still, my eyes stay on his.

"Your turn." He raises a brow before reaching over to slide open the shower door, leaning in to turn the shower on. Then his attention is back on me.

The fact that he isn't undressing me makes me release a deep breath and I raise my chin a little, wondering why I can't keep this man forever. The things he's making me feel are not at all what I was expecting with him.

I slide the straps of my dress down my shoulders and let it pool around my ankles, leaving me in just my panties. Hooking my thumbs in the sides, I push them down my thighs and let them fall too. Then I step out of them and move forward, all the while keeping my eyes on Devon's. We're inches apart as steam begins to fill the room and suddenly the silence makes me feel self-conscious. I fold my arms across my chest and look down, questioning why I'm even here.

"Eyes on me, Treacle."

He doesn't touch me but his command alone makes me obey and he slowly nods, just the once, before gesturing for me to walk into the shower. Any and all physical contact has been something I've struggled with, unless I'm the one initiating it or in control of the situation, but honestly, it's tiring. Trying to constantly protect myself is wearing me down and maybe Devon is my reprieve.

With him, I don't have to think.

His blond hair gets darker under the hot spray, flattening against his head as he lifts his face and pushes it back. I follow the line of a Celtic tattoo design flowing from his shoulder to his chest, shocked when I see so many scars there—all surrounded by more tattoos, but the raised skin suggests severe trauma.

"What happened here?" I can't help myself, my curiosity getting the better of me as I reach out to stroke my fingertips over a long scar across his collarbone.

He looks down at my hand, water falling into his face before he makes eye contact with me again. I can't tell what he's feeling and I realize I may have just made a mistake. I quickly pull my hand away. It doesn't get far though, because he grips my wrist and brings it back to his chest, using his other hand to uncurl my fisted hand so my palm is flat against him.

"Some wanker tried to slice me open." He doesn't give me any more than that, and I get the feeling he would tell me everything if I asked, but I don't want to talk about my own demons so I'm not going to make him talk about his.

It's then I realize his hand is slowly making its way up and down the scab on my arm, a small frown marring his brow as I slowly move my fingertips back and forth against the thin raised line on his chest.

"The next time I see you, I want this scab healed."

"Excuse me?" Call it embarrassment, call it anger, whatever it is causes me to step back a little in shock. But he doesn't let go, he just pulls me back to him without breaking contact with my arm.

"The next time I see you, Treacle. I want this scab healed. Understood?"

The heat in his eyes is impossible to ignore and the seriousness in his tone seeps through my skin, causing a stir of something I would never imagine. This man makes me feel brave. Strong. I don't quite know how to cope with those emotions right now.

"Yes?" There's an authoritative lilt to his voice that just pulls the word from my throat, and I can tell he's waiting for more, but I'm not there yet.

He waits a few seconds longer, staring deep into my soul, before allowing that grin to creep up his face, flashing that goddamn dimple and making me weak at the knees.

"Okay, Treacle. We'll work on that."

Somehow, he manages to maneuver us so I'm now standing underneath the stream of water. It's warm and soothing against my back and I tilt my head to wet my hair and face, all my self-consciousness evaporating. Devon lowers my hand and moves to stand behind me.

I'm about to question what he's doing when I feel the pressure on my scalp as he begins to massage shampoo into my hair after adjusting the shower head to point further down. I've had my hair washed plenty of times at the salon, but never has it been this sensual. The steam, the silent commands, those magic fingers running across my head… the combination is making me weak in the knees, desperate for him to touch me in other places. To run those fingers over every part of my body.

This man comes across as a sexual deviant, but the way he's so caring and attentive and considerate of my invisible needs are like a complete contrast to my imagination. Although, all those same things have me practically begging him for more.

I haven't felt this way in so long, I want it to last and I'm going to hold on to it for as long as I can.

"How does that feel?" His words are whispered beside my ear and I close my eyes at the extra sensation, moaning an incoherent, "*mmm.*"

"Words, Treacle."

"It feels good."

"Just good? What about if I do this...?" His lips connect with my neck, just below my ear, and I almost jump from the electricity that shoots through me at his touch.

"Mmm. So good."

I tilt my head back further to allow him better access, every inch of my body enjoying his teasing touches, and he chuckles against my neck.

Water begins cascading down my hair from the shower head and Devon uses his fingers to wash out the shampoo before going in with the conditioner. Just when I think he's going to give me more, he surprises me. The simple way he's taking care of me isn't done from pity, but more from a want of his own. I can't explain it because he confuses the Hell out of me, but I'm certainly not complaining. While his attention is on me, I'm going to lap it up.

"We can do better than *so good*."

There's a sharp pain on my neck and I almost pull away, until his soft lips replace the pain, his tongue licking and soothing. He continues this across the skin on my shoulder, his large palms moving to the tops of my arms and slowly gliding up and down. The touch is barely there, like there's a thin barrier between our bodies, and again... I want more.

The sensations rolling through me stop again and the extra heat he was providing at my back is gone.

"What are you...?" I turn around to see what he's doing and find him squeezing a bottle of something onto a black loofah. I don't know why, but it does something to my pussy that I haven't felt in months. My own dampness begins to mingle with the water from the shower and I have to clench my thighs together for some kind of friction.

"Eyes on mine, Treacle." He steps forward, lifting one of my arms by my hand, and begins washing me with the loofah. The scratchy-but-soft texture feels good against my skin and the scent of him becomes intoxicating as it surrounds us.

He moves the loofah up and across my collar bone, around my neck, down my other arm, and to my chest. I wonder if he'll linger, giving me a little of what my body is craving, but he doesn't. He washes me with so much care, dipping his eyes every now and then to watch what he's doing and barely giving my nipples any attention at all before he gets onto his knees. The position is one of the sexiest sights I've ever seen and my breaths become shorter, sharper as he lifts one of my feet to rest on his knee before he begins washing my leg. He begins with my foot, working his way up my calf to my thigh, and just when I think he's about to hit the jackpot, he places my foot down and picks up the other one, repeating the same on that side.

Never has getting clean felt so dirty.

My mind is focused solely on this beautiful man in front of me and everything he's doing to my body; the way his muscles flex with every movement, droplets of water all over his colorful, hard skin.

His eyes are still on mine as he finishes my second leg and moves the loofah around to my ass, moving in slow circles across both of my cheeks. Next, he brings it back around to my lower stomach, and I'm suddenly really thankful that I invested in laser hair removal as he moves even lower. Every touch is so soft, gentle, and full of a care I never thought him capable of.

"Now turn around, face the glass. You can see me in the mirror of the vanity as I wash your back." It's another command, but it's given in such a way that I obey without hesitation.

The scratchy massage continues over my back and shoulders until I feel the hot spray of water cascading over my body. Wordlessly, he taps my chin from behind me, encouraging me to tilt my head back so he can rinse the conditioner from my hair... and my God this man's magical fingers practically work me into a frenzy as he massages my scalp again.

Every non-touch, every unspoken word, the complete concentration he has on his task, all have me practically panting for him.

Once he's finished rinsing me off, he reaches over and slides open the glass door, stepping out and grabbing a large fluffy gray towel from the rail on the wall. Without drying himself off, he holds out a hand for me.

"Come here, Treacle."

Again, I obey, and he wraps the towel around my body, tucking it underneath my arms. Then he grabs another, slightly smaller than the first, and wraps it around his waist before gripping my hand and leading me out of the bathroom.

There's a little chill in the air as we leave the steamy room behind, but Devon grabs another towel from I don't know where and begins rubbing it over my shoulders before gently squeezing the water from my hair.

We work around each other in a comfortable silence as he then dries himself off, and I bite my lip to stop from making embarrassing noises over his solid body.

"Here, put these on."

A black T-shirt and a pair of boxers are thrown onto the bed in front of me, confusing the Hell out of me. I thought this was leading somewhere. This man has me so hot for him that even though I'm now dry from the shower, I'm still totally wet, and he's asking me to put clothes on rather than keep them off.

An enigma. That's what he is. A complete enigma, catching me off guard at every turn. I thought that once he had me in his clutches, he'd want to ravish me, take all he can, but all he's done is give and expect nothing in return.

Okay, so he's had a couple of blow jobs, but I was the one that begged him to let me do that.

Maybe if I beg him to touch me, he will. Maybe that's what he's been waiting for.

Devon pursued me so strongly before now, not caring that I already had two boyfriends, and I had expected him to go in guns blazing when I finally gave myself over to him. My intentions in coming home with him last night had been to let him have his way with me, and leave the next morning... at the same time showing Tyler and Enzo that I'm a big girl and don't need them to treat me like porcelain.

They've both been so placid and accommodating in letting me go and all I want is for them to fight for me.

But now, Devon is a game changer. He's unexpected, and the feelings I have for him run deeper than just a quick fuck.

Great way to make life less complicated, Lina.

Dressed in his clothes and a pair of his socks, which are also way too big for me, I follow him down the stairs where he leads me to the sofa.

"Sit here. I'm going to make us some drinks and grab some snacks. We're going to begin our Avengers marathon with Captain America."

Chapter Seven

Tyler

"Here you go, sir." The waiter places my favorite top shelf-whiskey, neat, on the square, white napkin before he asks if there's anything else he can get me.

"Thank you, that will be all for now." My voice is tight, my tone clipped, but it has nothing to do with this young gentleman and everything to do with Lina and the guy she chose to go home with two nights ago. It's close to six in the evening and the crowd here reeks of old money and high privilege.

Like me.

Choosing to sit in a corner booth with a beeline to the front door, I'm like a hawk watching for my prey to walk through and give me some much needed answers. In the last year, Enzo and I have grown close enough that we could almost use the term friends.

As teenage boys, Enzo was more Marco's friend who wasn't allowed to hang out with us since he started working for Mr. Mancini as soon as he was taken in by the family. He and Marco always had a pretty tight relationship, but that wasn't necessarily between us. It wasn't *hostile*, exactly, but there was definitely a barrier between Enzo and myself that we never really overcame.

Lina changed the dynamics completely these last twelve months when she presented her needs and convinced us that sharing her was in all of our best interests. If there's one thing I've learned in all this time, it's that I have more patience than I ever thought possible.

I'm not used to being told "no". Or "wait" for that matter. Having to schedule my time with Lina was a new kind of torture I didn't know existed. At first, when licking my wounded pride after River's rejection was a necessary evil, it all sounded like the perfect set-up. No hard-core attachments, no need to choose between work and a "girlfriend." It all just made sense.

Until, that is, spending time with Lina was the oxygen I didn't know I needed in my life. She became so intricately woven into the fibers of my lungs that I even accepted sharing her in bed.

So, yeah. Having a sort of joint custody of my woman with another man has created quite the bond, it would seem. Co-fucking or something.

"Didn't think you were going to show." I take a sip of my whiskey as Enzo slides into the booth, his gaze already seeking out the waiter like he's in dire need of a drink.

"Almost didn't." With a back and forth of his index finger between my drink and the empty space in front of him, Enzo is efficient in letting our waiter know what he wants. That's when I notice the fresh bruises and cuts on his knuckles.

"Been busy, I see." I nod to his hands, his only reaction is a curt shrug of his shoulders.

Italy fucked us up. Lina and Enzo more than me, for obvious reasons, but the sheer pain etched over every flawless line on Lina's face is like taking a flogger to our backs every time we see her.

"Tell me about this Devon guy." I decide to just get to the damn point since talking sense into Enzo is about as efficient as driving through Manhattan during rush hour traffic.

"Christ, that guy is hard to figure out." I just stare at him, hoping he's going to continue, but Enzo doesn't do long speeches. We have to work for every syllable he graciously gifts us.

"So, what? You decided to just wait and see?" I can't imagine Enzo sitting on his ass and letting fate do all the work. It's not in his nature, which he confirms when he scoffs and shakes his head at me like I'm a naïve imbecile recently shot out of my mother's womb.

"I've had my contacts on him since the first day I saw Madelina talking to him." We pause our conversation just long enough for the waiter to place our order on the table and walk away.

"And? Jesus, Enzo, do I have to prompt you for every crumb of information?" I raise an expectant brow at him above the rim of my glass just before I take a generous gulp of whiskey. It's Enzo's turn to take his drink and bring it to his lips, probably giving him enough time to think about whether or not he wants to share all his intel. I hope, for all of our sakes, that he's not sitting on something dark and depraved, because Lina went home with the chef and if he's hurting her I may turn into something closer to a version of Enzo and Marco than I ever thought possible.

"Every one of my contacts has said the same thing. The guy is deadly, downright unforgiving, when it comes to his family." I nod at all this as I pull out my own investigative file on him and place it on the table between us. "What's that?" Enzo's question is accompanied by a nod of his chin and his steel gaze is moments away from burning a hole through the manilla folder.

"My own research. Did you know about the South London gang? The..." Opening the file, I thumb through the first couple of pages before finding his family history. "He's a third-generation member." My index finger slides down the page, stopping only when I find the gang name. "The Butcher of Lewisham was his dad, the gang was The Quinns. Christ, they sound like a parody." At Enzo's snort, I raise my gaze, frowning at how he could possibly find any humor in this situation.

"They are the deadliest gang to have ever seen the light of day. Devon's grandfather was a butcher, ran his entire mob-like business from his office in the back of the shop and kept a big ass fucking knife with him at all times." None of this is making me feel better about Lina being within a thousand miles of this guy. "If he even had a suspicion that he was being crossed, he'd whip out his knife and either scar for life or take the life all together. He didn't fuck around."

Raising a brow at him, I lean in and whisper. "Is that respect in your voice? Because that's fucked up."

Enzo only shrugs, reminding me that Marco and his family may be close to me and mine, but our worlds are separated by a mile-high moral wall.

"Look, we don't all have the luxury of being born into a family with money and affection to spare. Some of us had to kill to eat. Take your judgmental bullshit to the corrupt politicians who invest in your companies. Then we'll talk." I lean back into my chair and stare, a little dumbfounded, at Enzo as he finishes off his drink, poised to stand and leave, but I stop him with a hand on his forearm.

"I'm worried about Lina." My words make him freeze mid-movement, just like I knew they would.

Our eyes meet, his pupils shrinking to a pinpoint before he leans in and speaks.

"He won't hurt her."

"How could you possibly know that?" This file on the table says the exact opposite. "Sit down, Enzo, let's forget where we come from, how much money I have and how many lives you've shortened, so we can make sure the woman we love doesn't end up a casualty of some psycho with kitchen knives."

After a few seconds where his gaze takes a faraway trip to some place and time I know nothing about, he gives me his attention and sits back down, ready to talk. It's there, his determination, written along the lines at the corner of his eyes.

"Devon Quinn, thirty-six years old, born in East London to Shelly Quinn and Mike "The Butcher" Quinn. Shelly is the owner of a clothes shop, Mike owned several pubs. Devon was his father's executioner, money collector, he incited people to pay for protection or pay back loans. One day, his father orders him to collect from a single mother with her two boys, about three or four. Her deadbeat ex-husband was gambling his life away, took all her savings along with The Butcher's loan and lost it all at the poker table. The order was to kill her if she didn't pay his debt. Devon refused, shit got heated and he ended up beating the life out of his father. When he was supposed to take control of the gang, he told them all to fuck right off and came here then opened his restaurant. Lesser known fact, he also has an MMA gym where assholes like me get to de-stress."

In all the years I've known Enzo, I could fit every sentence I've ever heard him say into that fucking monologue. I'm speechless, my mouth hanging open in utter shock at the fact that Enzo is capable of speaking for longer than half a second.

"How is that supposed to make me feel better about Lina being with him? You just told me he killed his own father." Pushing my glass closer to the end of the table to let our waiter know I'd like another, I tap my index finger on the manilla folder once, twice, then clasp my hands together. "Plus, my detective didn't get half of that information. How did you find all this out?"

I only hire the best so I'm half annoyed at my employee, not to mention my ego is bruised because I'm not the one holding the greatest amount of information in this meeting.

"I told you. I have contacts in place. People who live there, who know Devon and also knew his father." Enzo taps his thumb on the table, my eyes catching on the open gashes on his knuckles and wondering if he went to Devon's gym before meeting me here.

"Right." I nod to his hand and raise a brow. "So, fighting inside a cage, huh? Not scared of fucking up that pretty face of yours?" With a smirk, he leans back in the booth and quickly runs his thumb over his bottom lip like a boxer wiping off blood.

"I don't need a pretty face. The only woman I'll ever need to impress wants nothing to do with me." He speaks like his fate is written in stone.

"Has she been seeing her therapist?" I ask the question even though I already know the answer.

"No. She's using coke like some people use Xanax." His words make my anger rise exponentially.

"And what the fuck are we doing to stop her?" Through gritted teeth, I spit out my words, my fingers fisting into tight balls of rage.

Except, I almost forget who I have in front of me. Enzo doesn't cower at my sudden ire. He's not a Harvard graduate trying to kiss my two-thousand-dollar Italian shoes in hopes of getting a permanent position in my company.

He's a hard ass. A mobster with blood on his hands, literal blood on his knuckles. Enzo leans in, our faces only inches apart, barely moving his lips as he speaks through his teeth.

"You didn't see her, Tyler. You didn't watch her as her entire fucking world was destroyed in less than five minutes. You didn't watch as the light in her eyes faded to nothingness. As her pain and hopes and all her belief in humanity came crashing down like a house of cards." His jaw ticks as he takes a lungful of air before he gives his final blow. "You may have flown her there, you may have given her what she asked for all those months ago, but in that moment, in that earth-shattering second, the truth is… you were nowhere to be found while she was dying inside."

My self-hate resurfaces as my anger toward him deflates because he's right; I handed her over to that fucking maniac on a silver platter and I was the only one spared from watching her suffer the consequences.

He's right and I fucking hate it.

Leaning back in the booth, we don't break eye contact, as though our staring contest is a conversation in and of itself.

"You're right. I get it. I just can't sit back and watch while she destroys what little she feels she has left."

The tension dies out a little as the waiter comes back.

"Would you like another?" I watch as Enzo slides his attention back to the young man dressed in a white button down and black slacks.

"Nah, I'm leaving. Put it on his tab." Hooking his thumb in my direction, Enzo smirks before rising to his feet and pausing on his way out. "He won't hurt her, but he won't coddle her either."

Then he hands me a piece of paper pinched between his two fingers, waiting for me to take it before he nods and walks away.

Lost in thought, I watch him as he crosses the bar, lifts the collar of his coat over his neck and disappears from view into the night. My thoughts are firmly on Lina, on her suffering and the part I played in her predicament, when I remember the scrap of paper in my hand.

Looking down, I realize there's only one way to ease my mind and Enzo gave me the tool to do exactly that.

Never in my life did I think I'd be taking a page from Marco Mancini's handbook and sitting outside an apartment building stalking my no-longer girlfriend. I refuse to call her my ex because that title comes with a conversation that we have not had.

"Sir, I have your newspaper in the front seat. You haven't asked for it all day."

My driver distracts me from my stalker-mode outside what I'm guessing is Devon Quinn's apartment. Or maybe it's Lina's new place. I'd heard she'd found something but I have no idea where it's located.

"No thank you, Aaron." I never miss a day on the stocks and Aaron has been with me for so long that he must wonder if I'm possibly losing my mind. The Wall Street Journal is my daily dose of market information. I need to stay on top of what's happening in the world and most of all in The City. But right now? I have only one thing on my mind: Lina.

"Is that Miss Mancini up ahead on the sidewalk, sir?"

At the mention of Lina's name, my entire body reacts. My heart rate speeds up, my muscles tighten with the need to bolt from the car and wrap her up in my arms, and my nerve endings come alive like fireworks at an amusement park.

I lean up, looking through the partition and searching the sidewalk on the right side of the street, and sure enough, there she is in all her long, dark-haired beauty.

"Yes, that's her. I'll be back in a bit."

Without taking a second to think my actions through, I open the car door and step out into the crisp fall air. It's almost eight at night and the only light comes from The City—the buildings or the passing cars—but I see her as though she were basking in the sun.

I also see *him*.

I see his arm pressed against her shoulder blade with his hand collaring the back of her neck as he leans in and pulls her mouth up to his but doesn't kiss her. My back pressed against the side of my town car, I watch, pain radiating up my spine with the force of my restraint, as she willingly gives her lips to him. As she eagerly allows his tongue to slip inside her mouth and his free hand to circle her waist. He devours her like she's the only meal he's had in weeks, without a single care that people are forced to walk around them on the sidewalk.

Meanwhile, my dick twitches in my slacks at the scene. A foreign delight at watching the woman I love giving herself to another man, almost tasting her happiness. In mere seconds I'm hard as stone but it doesn't stop me from walking straight up to them and clearing my throat.

"Are you okay, Gumdrop?"

As Lina leaps back and away from Devon, the corners of my mouth lift into a faint smile as my gaze lands on his strangely amused features.

That's right, motherfucker, keep your mouth off my girl. Although I refuse to admit watching them was somehow arousing, the proof to the contrary is difficult to miss.

"Took you long enough to cross the street there, mate. Get a good view?" And now I want to punch his face.

"Tyler! What are you doing here?" Lina squeaks out her words and I get perverse satisfaction at watching the back of her hand wipe away Devon's kiss from her lips.

"A little birdie told me you moved out of the Mancini mansion. Thought I'd stop by and check it out." As the words spill from my mouth, I hope I'm right because eating crow in front of this guy is going to hurt going down.

"Oh, um, okay. You know Devon, right?" She's not feeling comfortable but she won't back away either. It's what I love most about her. My eyes scan her from head to toe, noticing she's practically drowning in an oversized "Oxford" hoodie—subtle much?—and sweatpants that could fit three of her.

When I take a closer look at her face, I realize, however, that she's sober. Her pupils are dilated, yes, but it's dark outside. Her skin looks healthy. Without any makeup to cover up the visible signs of drug overuse, I notice her pallor. Well, as pale as one can be when they're from the south of Italy.

"Yes, we met briefly at your birthday party." Devon grins, showing off all his pearly whites and a single dimple that takes up the entire side of his cheek, as he offers his right hand and I mine.

We shake but it's stiff, like a forced moment of civility.

"You're the billionaire, yeah? The guy with the jet." I have no idea if it's a dig at me but with Enzo's words still fresh in my mind, I squeeze my hold on his hand as we have a bit of a Clint Eastwood moment, where I've placed Devon as the Bad and given myself the title of Good. As we stare at each other, I realize people are still having to walk around us. Though I'd felt it was rude earlier as they were kissing, right now, I feel justified.

I'm here to save her. To take her home and make sure no one takes advantage of her.

I'm here to do everything I couldn't in Italy.

"That's me. And you're the cook?" I deliberately use the wrong title, a childish way of knocking him down a notch.

Devon grins, seemingly unaffected by my jab as he releases my hand and slides it in the pocket of his jeans.

"Feeding one hungry mouth at a time." His smirk is firmly in place and I can't help but hear his words with sexual undertones. When my gaze slides to Lina, even in the dim light, I can see the pink splash across her cheeks and the faint smile at the corners of her mouth.

"Cute." I don't even hide my contempt, even though I'm incapable of putting my finger on what exactly irks me about this guy.

Is it his unwavering confidence? No, I've been around confident men my entire life, I eat them for breakfast around my conference table.

"Um, thank you for walking me home, Devon, but I can take it from here." Lina smiles at him and, without even giving me a second thought, Devon buries his fingers in the long strands of her hair and kisses her with wild abandon. For the second time tonight, I'm transfixed by the sight of my woman kissing another man and, as much as I want to feel jealousy, all I feel is turned on.

What the actual fuck?

Obviously, sharing Lina was not a problem with Enzo, but it was never in my face like this. Never displayed like a blockbuster movie that I had to watch from beginning to end. So why don't I just turn around or lower my eyes to fixate on my leather shoes?

Simple.

Watching them makes me hard as a fucking rock.

In this moment, on this November night, I learn that I, Tyler Fucking Walker, have a kink.

"Enjoy the view, mate?"

Without hesitation, I answer, "I did, yes."

Chapter Eight

Lina

My head feels clearer than it has in days, and for the first time in too long, Tyler isn't looking at me with any pity in his eyes. Instead, they're full of heat—and a little anger if the creases at the corners of his deep brown eyes are anything to go by.

I like it.

It reminds me of a time when I still felt alive.

The last couple of days with Devon have been much of the same, freeing in a way I've missed. But having both of them here, at the new apartment where I've yet to see the finished interior, with Devon basically tongue-fucking my face and making my clit pulse with a need he's refused to fill… yeah, to say it's awkward is an understatement. At the same time, I've never felt so turned on in my life.

Tyler and Enzo may have agreed to share me before, but our relationships were always kept separate. This is something else entirely.

Devon pulls away from my now-bruised lips and turns to Tyler, his hand still gripping the hair at the back of my head. "Enjoy the view, mate?"

Heat flares up my neck but before I can even open my mouth to try and make this a little less whatever it is, Tyler's words send an electric buzz rushing through my body.

"I did, yes."

Devon's low chuckle against my ear doesn't help the panty-melting situation happening, and I don't even question why his hands on me aren't making me flinch. I'm reveling in the attention and all the good feelings flowing through me.

"As much as I'd love to stay and enjoy you both, your man's got some shit that needs dealing with." Devon gently nips my earlobe and Tyler clears his throat.

It's unlike him to be lost for words in any situation. Words are part of his power, but Devon seems to have a similar hold over Tyler as he does on me, and I won't lie, it's hot as fuck.

"I'm good with sharing, Treacle. I know you need them too." Devon's tone is so low and heated that it tickles the hair on my neck as he speaks into my ear before pulling away, flashing that damn dimple at me and winking. "Take good care of our girl, Rich Boy." He pats Tyler on the back as he passes him and heads down the street the way we came without a backward glance.

I should be horrified at his use of the terms 'your man' and 'our girl', yet the corners of my mouth are tipped up into a small smile. Devon is like a whirlwind of confusion, a little tricky to figure out at first, but after spending a couple of days with him I want to know more.

What I *do* know is that he seems to really care about me, and he's not afraid to call me out on my shit, basically forcing a detox of sorts on me for the last forty-eight hours. I know I've still got a long way to go though.

"Do—"

"Wh—"

Tyler and I speak at the same time, then stop at the same time, and I stare up at the handsome face I've missed so much, enjoying the twinkle in his eye and the lift at the corner of his mouth.

"Do you wanna come in?" My voice is timid, afraid he'll say no, that he's just here to check on me, to make sure I'm not about to break into a million pieces again.

"Yeah, I really do." Now this is the Tyler I remember. Firm and in control of what he wants.

Turning my back on him, my heart beating out of my chest, I go about unlocking the door to my new apartment, excitement thrumming through my veins at seeing what the decorators did with the place and having Tyler here with me.

I pause once the door is fully open and we're both inside, closing my eyes and taking a deep breath of the fresh, positive energy the apartment has. River was right yet again. She's been all for me getting my own apartment since before Naples, insisting the new environment would be good for me. Seeing me fly is like a favorite hobby of hers and I thank God every day for sending her back to our family.

The apartment is mostly open plan, with huge windows across one wall, and everything decorated in different shades of gray and creamy pinks. The kitchen, separated only by a high breakfast bar, gleams with new appliances; in one corner of the room, a large deep-gray L-shaped sofa sits in front of a glass coffee table, facing the windows and the short hall with three slightly-ajar doors; on one side the bathroom and a spare bedroom, and the other, my bedroom and ensuite.

Tyler's body heat warms my back as he moves closer and slides a hand around me to rest on my stomach, his chin against my shoulder. Suddenly I feel shy again. It's not like I haven't had sex with Tyler since Naples, he spent a lot of time with me when we got back, but my therapist at the time managed to convince me to push my guys away. River's always talking about the vibes she gets from people, and I never got good ones from that woman.

It's like she enjoys preying on the weak-minded and ostracizing them from society. At least that was *my* experience, which is why I haven't gone back to see her.

How she persuaded me that this man behind me is bad for me is something I'm struggling to comprehend... and I've got to stop thinking about the damn therapist.

Tyler is here, right now, not treating me like breakable glass, filling me with a heat only he can provide.

"Do you want a coffee?" The words just pop from my mouth as I lean my head back against him, simply enjoying how he holds me. I cringe internally at my question, because it's obvious I'm stalling here. My head is saying we need to talk, my pussy is saying take me to bed or lose me forever, and, generally, I'm a mixed bag of emotions.

"No, but I do want you."

I inhale sharply, and I'm pretty sure I just squealed a little as his unshaven cheek glides over the skin of my shoulder.

"And I know you want me too. Your heart is thumping so hard I can feel it against my chest through your back and I bet if I lower this hand, I'll be able to feel how ready for me you are." The hand on my stomach slowly slides down inside the hem of the oversized sweatpants, cupping my bare pussy. We both groan at the contact and I find myself pushing my ass back into his rock-hard length.

He begins peppering gentle kisses across my neck and shoulder before pulling the hoodie up and over my head with one hand while the fingers on his other begin to move back and forth. The pressure on my pussy is electric and I can't help grinding against him.

"Fuck this slow shit." His words are deep, guttural, like he's barely maintaining all the control he usually exudes as he moves to step in front of me. He cups my cheek in his large palm, wiping his thumb over my lips and staring into my eyes with an intensity I crave from this man. "Just fucking beautiful." The way he kisses me is exactly what I've been missing. It's heavy and messy, our mouths and tongues dancing to a beat only we can hear. I taste his need with every stroke across my lips and I smell his longing with every breath that caresses my skin.

Gripping under my ass, Tyler lifts me, encouraging me to wrap my legs around his waist, never breaking the kiss as he walks me toward the door leading into my bedroom.

Devon wasn't wrong, I do need this.

"Let's put you in your real birthday outfit instead of some other man's clothes." He barely breaks his lips from mine as he moves his hands from my pussy and places me on the floor, yanking the sweatpants down my legs. A shiver zaps from my core and up my spine in anticipation. My arms are around his neck as I jump up and wrap my legs back around his waist... and now I'm naked—except for my stilettos because why would Devon have shoes in my size to borrow?—as I cling on for dear life.

"Sweatpants and stilettos, Gumdrop?" He palms my thigh, sliding it down my calf to my shoe digging into his back, amusement lacing his tone.

"I was making a fashion statement. You telling me I didn't look hot?" I stare him in the eye, daring him to disagree with me.

Of course, he doesn't.

"Gumdrop, you'd look hot in a burlap sack."

"Oooh!" I squeak when the cold surface of my wooden waist-high dresser is pressed against my ass cheeks. Tyler places me down and pulls away a little, my arms falling to his wrists where they rest on my upper thighs.

Brown eyes full of heat, lust, and want, scan my body. They trail down from my head to my toes, slowly rising back to my face as he reaches a hand into my hair and strokes some flyaway strands backward.

"Fucking beautiful. Don't you dare leave me again, do you understand?" His palm rests against my cheek and the desperation in his voice has my vision turning blurry. I reach forward, gripping his face in my hands and looking him straight in the eyes.

"I promise." I never imagined he'd want me back, but the last couple of months without him has been its own kind of torture and some miniscule part of me heals with his assurance.

Tyler grasps my head, wrapping a hand in my hair, and kisses me like he doesn't give a single fuck about anything outside this apartment. Outside of me. His tongue, his lips, his taste, he's intoxicating in all the best ways. My already-bruised lips must be swollen at this point, and they practically have their own heartbeat as he pulls away again, bending down and taking one of my nipples into his mouth. He bites down and lets it pop out as he brings his gaze back to mine.

The way his eyes narrow and the corner of his mouth tips up on one side tells me I've been a bad girl and I'm about to get spanked... and my God have I missed Tyler's hands reddening my ass. I put on my best innocent girl look, raising both eyebrows and fluttering my lashes with a sweet smile.

"On a scale of one to spanked-within-an-inch-of-your-life, how bad has my good girl been?" His hands slowly work their way up and down my thighs, and every time he reaches the tops, his thumbs dip toward my center and I'm struggling not to lift myself so he touches me where I'm burning to be touched.

This is his way of asking how I want him to take me, and the memory of the last time I played the bad girl for him flashes through my mind. The thought alone has me getting wetter than before, and even though we still have some talking to do, for this moment, we've come to a truce and he's handing me the power he is always so determined to hold.

"I've been a real bad girl." I run my hands up and down his torso, feeling every athletic ridge underneath his perfectly crisp white shirt, letting out another squeak as he bends a little, wraps his arms around my waist, and lifts me onto his shoulder.

He spanks my bare ass before growling and biting into the side of my cheek.

"You have forgotten your manners."

"Sir! I've been a real bad girl, Sir." The giggle that escapes me is uncontrollable and the vibration of his body beneath my stomach sets my insides on fire.

One, two, three more taps to my right ass cheek, followed by a slow and gentle rubbing massage on the now-heated area of skin.

"On the bed, you know the drill."

Oh don't I!

Tyler allows me to slide down the front of him, pushing my hair from my face. He's still fully clothed, in all his suited glory, and it's honestly just as sexy as naked Tyler.

Before climbing on the bed, I take a moment to lightly kiss him on the mouth, and he breaks character for just a second with a small, encouraging wink. I push up onto my elbows and knees, arching my back and looking over my shoulder at him when I'm ready.

His stance is a powerful one that almost takes my breath away, his feet shoulder-width apart as he stands there removing his cufflinks, then unbuttoning his shirt—I kinda wish he was wearing a tie today. The things he can do to me with a tie...

"Your ass looks incredible up in the air waiting for me." His shirt is now off and the gentle sculpting of his body never fails to blow me away. Slowly unbuttoning his pants, he then hooks his thumbs in the top and pushes them down his legs to pool in a heap on the floor. His cock is standing at full mast beneath his boxers and I lick my lips in anticipation of seeing it in all its throbbing glory again.

I'm not disappointed when the next thing he removes are the boxers... holy Hell, he's gorgeous.

The bed dips a little as he kneels behind me and strokes my heated ass cheek, pushing my head down into the sheets and tickling his fingers down my spine. He dips one inside me and I groan, arching my back further and tilting my hips, encouraging him to continue.

He doesn't.

His soft moan, followed by a pop from his lips, tells me he's sucking my wetness from his finger.

"I love the way you taste." He maneuvers himself behind me, gripping my ass cheeks right before his tongue flicks at my clit. I almost shoot from the bed at the sensation. For a second, thoughts of Naples fly through my mind, but Tyler is not *him*. Tyler cares for me, he loves me, and even though it's been a while since I've used the words, there's no denying I love him too.

He begins sucking at my clit, nibbling, and I mewl with pleasure when he dips his tongue inside me. An orgasm is building quickly, and he laps at me like I'm his favorite meal, adding a finger for just a moment... and oh, God, I think I'm...

"Nooo!" My cry of protest is involuntary when he pulls away and spanks my non-reddened ass cheek twice.

"Bad girls get spanked. You only get to come when I say you can. Can you do that for me, my little Gumdrop?" One more spank to my ass before he gently massages the pink skin while he strokes his cock and I wish I could turn my head all the way around to see him better.

"Yes, Sir."

"Good girl." At his words, the image of Tyler and Devon calling me their good girl at the same time heats my skin. Tyler bites my ass before placing a gentle kiss in the same spot and crawling up the bed, sitting up to rest against the luxurious light-gray headboard. "Come and sit on me. Slide that pretty little pussy over my cock so I can fill you up."

With every dirty word, my body temperature rises and my skin erupts in delicious goosebumps. My desperate heart beats against my rib cage, almost bursting through my chest as every breath becomes harder and harder to control. I immediately comply, placing my knees to either side of his legs and resting my hands on his shoulders for support. He grips my hips and guides me down onto him, and oh my God, yes!

We both groan with pleasure, each letting out what feels like a breath of relief to be together like this once again.

"That's my good girl." He licks up my neck, stopping to nibble at my earlobe. "Now ride me, Baby. Take everything you need."

I don't need to be told twice. Our lips meet in another bruising clash of tongues and teeth, and I slide up and down his shaft, my walls clenching around him, the tingles of my missed orgasm needing little encouragement to come back.

Tyler's hold on my hips becomes firm and he begins to control my movements, slowing my pursuit of that orgasm. He breaks away from the kiss and grips one of my nipples between his teeth, flicking it with his tongue and making my movements quicken again.

The slapping sounds of flesh against flesh paired with our increasing moans are among the sexiest things I've ever heard. Every delicious second pulls at my orgasm until it courses through my body at lightning speed, making it impossible to hold back any longer.

"Oh God, Tyler, Sir... please."

"Fuck it. Come all over me, baby."

"Yes... fuck... yes... Sir!" Each of my words are punctuated by a sharp thrust as Tyler tops from the bottom, taking control of the orgasm now rolling through my body, my clit pulsing and my heart going a million beats per minute.

His response is a deep growl with one final thrust before he stills inside me, lightly kissing my abused nipple and holding each side of my face in his hands to place another kiss on my forehead.

I don't try to move away and he doesn't try to move me. I'm going to have to change my bedsheets but, in this moment, it doesn't matter. I'm content in his arms as he brings my head to rest against his chest, where I can hear his heart beating just as quickly as mine.

My phone rings from the other room, but it's Rex's ringtone, my salon's general manager, and it's far too late to deal with any of that. Whatever he has to say can wait until tomorrow.

"Want me to get that for you, Gumdrop?" Tyler's sleepy voice makes me smile, and I lightly shake my head against his chest, my grin growing with the realization that he's rock hard inside me once more.

"No. I don't want to move from here. Do you?" My cheeky question makes him chuckle and he slowly starts to rotate his hips beneath me.

"Come here."

"What the fuck, Brett? Since when does Cora make your business decisions? You want to go on vacation? Fine. But don't think you're getting a fucking dime out of this deal unless you're here putting in the time and actually showing up at the fucking meetings. We clear?"

I'm not fully awake, my eyes are still closed, but Tyler's raised voice catches my attention. His dumb-ass ex-wife, who is now with his business partner, has caused nothing but trouble for him. I stretch my body out, having slept for yet another night without nightmares, and the bed dips when Tyler climbs on beside me.

"Morning, Gumdrop. How did you sleep?"

"Mmm. Good." I open my eyes and shake my head when I see him pulling back the covers and using the warm, wet cloth he's holding to wipe between my legs. He may like to sleep inside me when we've come, and I really don't mind because of the tender way he cares for me the morning after. He has this way of making me feel like a real princess to him.

Silently, he finishes cleaning me up, placing a light kiss on my abused pussy before standing.

"I'm sorry I have to leave. Brett's a dick and I can't lose this client. Raincheck on breakfast in bed?" As he speaks, he's putting on the clothes he took off last night, and watching him get dressed is as sexy as watching him get naked.

I'd love for him to stay, for us to spend all day together doing more of what we did last night, but as the daughter of a once mafia don, and the sister of the current head of the New York mafia, I understand the importance of business. I would never try to stop Tyler from something clearly important to him. I just wish that Cora bitch would fuck off already. His business partner, Brett, was never as flakey as this pre-Cora, and she couldn't make Tyler bend to her every whim, which is why she cheated on him with Brett.

Money-grubbing whore.

Chapter Nine

Lina

Even though he can't look me in the eyes, and can barely stand to be in my presence, Enzo made sure my apartment has all the best kind of security, meaning Harris can have time off when I'm there like he could when I was staying with Marco and River. But that also means someone is watching my apartment twenty-four-seven and I have a feeling I know who pulls that duty more than anyone else.

I wish things were different between us, that we could get back to what we had. What I ruined.

"Miss Mancini, we're here." Harris's voice from the front passenger seat startles me from my tumbling thoughts, and I'm a little grateful. I'm aware that I've been spiraling a lot lately, and I'm trying to be conscious of when I'm at the beginning of a spin.

River's advice throughout everything has been more beneficial than any therapist I've ever seen. Maybe I should give her a call later. It feels like it's been ages since I've seen her, and I could really use the uplifting sister-vibes she always gives.

"Thanks, Harris." I step out the back of the sleek, black, chauffeur-driven Mercedes, even though I was perfectly okay with getting a normal cab. Harris had insisted and I gave him this one because I was on another amazing high when we left this morning from my previous days with Devon and my night with Tyler.

The light bell that sounds upon entering my salon brings me a hint of familiarity and I vaguely remember coming by one day last week. I feel a little embarrassed for my behavior because I know damn well I wasn't fully sober. That isn't how I have ever wanted to conduct my business. Head held high, regardless, I approach the counter with a wide—albeit fake—grin.

"Hey, Sandy. Ho—" I stop speaking when the phone rings, and Sandy smiles apologetically as she answers.

"Hello, Belle'Vu. How can I help you today?"

I wait patiently as she takes the call, not wanting to be rude by walking away without having a conversation with her before going through to speak to Rex in the office.

"What?! No! Oh, sweetie... I'm so sorry... Okay." Sandy's clear distress has Harris on full alert, and me worrying what on Earth that phone call is about. When she hangs up, she immediately bursts into tears, moving around the counter to hug me. I flinch, her touch triggering dark thoughts that I try desperately to push away.

"Sandy, what's wrong?" Concentrating on my breathing helps to steady me and I tentatively place an arm around her because, in this moment, she isn't just my employee, she's my friend who needs me.

"It's Rex. That was his new girlfriend, he died of a heart attack last night." Every word is said through sobs, and when she's done speaking, her loud cry triggers my own tears to fall silently down my cheeks as I try to comfort her. I recognize this feeling deep in my chest. I'm in shock but I can't afford to be. I'm the boss, I have to step up.

"Stand down, Harris. There's no danger here." My words are quiet to my hovering bodyguard, and I'm struggling to hold it together myself, but I know I have staff here who need me to stay strong. I'm going to have to tell them that Rex is no longer with us, experiencing the heartache from each and every one of my employees over and over again.

Fuck, I'm so not ready for this.

'Pull up your big girl panties.' Thanks, River.

Without Tyler here, my new apartment suddenly feels a lot less awesome than it did when I bought it last week. It's empty. And lonely. I miss Stefano greeting me with his smiling face every time I came home—well, now my not-home, just Marco and River's home. Maybe I'd feel better if I had a Stefano... but that wouldn't be the same. He's been around our family since before my brother was born, loyalty and dedication like that can't be replicated.

Harris saw me to the door of my building and, after he made me call to make sure I got inside my apartment okay, he left to go wherever it is he goes. So I'm alone on my beautiful new sofa that has officially claimed me as one of its own—it's that soft—and the skin on my face is tight from tears.

Rex has always been a great manager for the salon. He was the first person I interviewed for the job a couple of years ago and has been there with me ever since. He was like a part of the furniture... and now he's gone. For a heart attack to take him seems so cruel. The man ate healthily, he exercised, didn't do drugs, he was a model citizen, yet, in the end, none of that mattered.

On the other hand, men like Ugo Ambrosio get to live.

I really want a drink but I don't like the way it's been affecting me. I'm not an alcoholic, but doesn't feeling the need to clarify that make me one by default? Am I in denial? No. I'm not one. But I could very well be close to getting there, and as much as I'm broken inside, I still have a little sense right now.

The last few weeks, months even, have been a bit of a blur. I know I haven't been thinking straight, I haven't been myself. I'm still not, but I want to be.

Tears are falling down my face again, and my head is pounding from dehydration, but I make no effort to move. I can't. It's like I know I should get up and get some water but my body isn't complying. Not that I'm trying all that hard.

Instead of picking at the scab on my arm from fuck knows where, watching the blood pool and seeing how long it takes to start moving, I should be trying to help myself. Getting up, calling someone to keep me company, *anything* else.

Darth Vader music pulls me from my unconscious mind, confusing the Hell out of me. Where is that coming from?

It's my phone. I check the screen and see Freya's name flashing across it and I smile a little because the only person who has touched my phone recently, other than me, was Devon. He's made it clear that he isn't a Freya fan.

Neither are Tyler and Enzo, to be honest.

I miss Enzo. I really fucked up what I had with those guys. Tyler and I may be working things out, and I've hit the jackpot if Devon is still interested, but I don't think I'll ever get my Enzo back.

A sob breaks free and I quickly wipe at my eyes as that damn ringtone begins again.

Why won't she just let me be?

"Hi, Freya."

"Biiiiitch, there's a party in the Hamptons. I've put your name and a plus one on the list. So put your sluttiest dress on, get your driver and that sexy Harris dude ready, and we're going to a partay!"

"Not tonight, Frey. I've had some bad news today, so I think I'm going to sit this one out." Before now, she hasn't seemed all that annoying. She's simply been there for me as a person who doesn't look at me like I'm broken inside, and when her husband, Kai, died, we both let our grief out by partying together. It was fun.

I'm not so sure it's fun anymore. I make my way to the bathroom to grab some tissue to wipe away the blood dripping down my arm from the small now-open wound.

"Fuck off. Don't give me that bad news shit. Come on, come party. You know you'll feel better."

Usually, the way Freya's speaking to me wouldn't grate on my nerves so much, but the small glimpses of happy I've had over the last few days have been everything to me, and something about her voice now feels *off*. I thought that numbing myself to the outside world was helping, but the low I'm feeling today isn't worth it. I'm not a total dumbass, I know how close I am to practically killing myself with stupidity, and I can't allow that man to hold that kind of power over me.

I won't.

"Frey, no. Not tonight." I don't need to explain myself any further than that. She's part of the problem, and even though River warned me about her—in a really subtle way because she's not the kind of woman to just bitch about another woman—I didn't want to listen.

"Come on." Freya's words are basically a whine. "Can you at least call your driver and have him take me? I'll find someone fun to go with."

"Now hang on a minute. There's no need to speak to me like that. It *does* make it obvious, however, that you don't want to spend time with me, you just want my things. So again, Freya... no." I don't know why I'm not just hanging up on her. Maybe it's because I'm not a total bitch and I actually feel a little guilty for being that harsh.

Not that I don't already have enough guilt on my conscience with everything going on. The fact that I didn't answer the phone to Rex last night keeps playing on my mind. What if he was calling for help and he might still be alive if I'd just picked up?

"Are you serious right now? Well fuck you. You're nothing but a mopey cunt anyway. I mean, I know, you were raped. Big deal. Can we move on already? My fucking husband was shot and died, but am I wallowing in my own self-pity? God, you're such a fucking sap. Just come out already."

Something inside me snaps and I'm done.

Angry tears cloud my vision and I don't think I was even this mad when River and I killed Ugo's twin sister, Elizabeth, in my brother's warehouse.

"Fuck you, you vile, twisted, money-grubbing cunt of a whore! Go suck on a bullet!" I throw my phone across the room, not caring if it's still intact or where it's gone, and I scream at the ceiling. My body is shaking with adrenaline, heat, and anger. At Freya, at Ugo, at my goddamn self.

The cut on my arm itches and I scratch at it, leaving long red lines from my sharp nails and removing the newly clotted blood from the scab. I don't know why, but watching the blood pool is satisfying, concentrating and watching how long it takes before there's enough to form a drip. Breathing heavily, anger still thrumming through my veins, I resist pouring myself a shot of something nasty and put my sound system on.

Music begins to play through my speakers around the main living space, and it's my *Mad Max* playlist, full of all the angry and empowering songs that make me want to dance.

Oh, how I miss dancing.

How have I let myself get to this point? I'm stronger than this, and I think it's time I get some real help. The therapist River referred me to actually had some really good write-ups.

Would she judge me for the way I've behaved? For the way I'm thinking? For still wanting to numb everything forever, even though I am fully aware of what a bad idea that is?

Loser by Emily Kinney starts to play and, while not all of the words fit my situation, there are definitely phrases that resonate. It's such a soft and melodic song to dance to, and with tears streaming down my face, blood trickling down my arm, I move. Twirling and stretching, crunching, and flowing in time with the music, feeling every musical note like a soothing balm to my soul as I work up a sweat with each new song, dancing through my pain.

It's heavy, it's tiring, and I haven't moved like this for too long, but I love it. All thoughts leave my mind and I turn the music up until it's the only sound I can hear, covering the noises from the sweeps of my feet or knees as I dance around my new apartment, getting lost with each new song.

I don't know when it happened or how I got here, but I'm on my sofa, my eyes so heavy I can barely keep them open, when I hear a voice I thought I'd never hear again.

"Madelina!"

Chapter Ten

Enzo

Banging on the steel reinforced door that leads to Madelina's brand new apartment, I can't help the rising dread as it begins at the base of my spine and in the depths of my stomach and makes its way straight to my battering heart.

The music is loud enough to raise an army of ghosts, probably pissing them off as well. The insulation in this building is up to par but it's not fucking infallible.

The key in my front pocket burns white hot, calling me to use it.

She can't hear you.
She's ignoring you.
She's in danger.
She's dead.

It's that last thought that has my hand sliding into my pocket and my fingers wrapping around the nickel-brass material, only hesitating a single second before punching it through the hole and hurrying inside.

The music assaults me, the thumping of something aggressive, violent enough to be right at home in a Tarantino movie, slaps me across my ear drums just as I step in and quickly close the door behind me.

The lights are dim, candles scarcely placed around the living room and kitchen as I frantically search for the only woman I've ever loved.

Fucking fire hazard, is my first thought when it's clear she's nowhere to be found, or at the very least, not paying attention to the fucking flames just waiting to burn a hole through the curtains.

The fact that I supervised every aspect of the renovations on this place, gives me the added bonus of knowing exactly where all the rooms are located so I check the guest bathroom first, hoping—no, praying—she's not passed out in a pool of her own vomit.

Praying she hasn't overdosed and I'm too late.

I'm not sure if I'm relieved or terrified that it's empty.

As I round the corner and burst into her bedroom next, everything is just as it was in the living room... dim and empty. The en-suite is littered with her personal things, some still in boxes from her recent move, others neatly clustered on the counter.

Where the fuck are you, Baby Girl?

As it always does when it comes to Madelina, panic rises like bile up my throat, my fist clenching with the need to beat something, or the desire to have something beat the shit out of me.

I can't lose this woman. Not physically. She may not want anything to do with me but that doesn't mean I could survive the idea of her not existing. Nothing could bring me back from that. The world would be a dark, desolate place without her.

It's when I jog out of her room and down the hallway that I see the lump on the couch. I don't know how I missed it before. Although, the back faces the front door so I must have just skimmed over it without actually looking down. I blame the new moon.

The relief is like warm water on an icy day, it soothes my blood and calms my breathing.

"Madelina." I can hear the relief in my voice the moment my eyes meet her blinking eyelashes as she tries to rise from the couch. The comfort only lasts a half a second before my stare lands on her forearm, the blood covering most of her skin and dripping onto her shirt where her arm rests. "Jesus, what the fuck?"

I realize too late that my reaction is violent and most likely having the opposite effect from what I intended. I'm worried, scared to fucking death, she'll do something I can't fix.

Reaching over to the console, I turn the music off, using her password to revive her phone, and sigh as the apartment falls silent once more.

"Enzo? What are you doing here?"

I want to answer her but my mind is reeling, too focused on her wound to remember where she stored the first-aid kit.

"Enzo!" She's more alert now, awake and a little on the pissed off side.

"I was worried." I don't want to admit I've been watching her place like a hawk, fess up to my stalker tendencies when it comes to her. Although, to be honest, she's far from naïve. Growing up in the heart of the New York City mafia, being watched is just another Tuesday.

She scoffs as she spins around and sits upright on the couch. Her gasp as she realizes she's covered in her own blood doesn't reassure me. The fact she's surprised means she's hurting herself unconsciously, proof her mind is still stuck four thousand miles away in a dirty stable, dead eyes staring straight into my teary ones. The protective monster inside me wakes up like a breathing, living thing that hunches over her entire form and acts as a shield against the outside world. At least that's how I imagine this overwhelming burning inside my chest.

I wish I could be by her side every second of every day. I would build an impenetrable bubble around her and kill every motherfucker who gets within a foot of her. If I had her permission, I would do all that and more, no questions asked, all consequences be damned.

"I'm fine. It's just a scab." She's about to get up but my need to take care of her shocks me into immediate action.

"Where do you keep your meds? I'll do it." Madelina blinks up at me and even with swollen, red-rimmed eyes, she's the most addictive woman—no, person—I've ever met. She's still pale, drugs will strip you of your natural tint, but unlike the last few months, there's a pink blush splashed on her cheekbones, a fierce glint in her slight glare. She's alert but, beneath her will to heal, she's still in pain.

I know she's been spending time with the chef and last night Tyler came in and only left this morning. If their presence distracts her from her demons then I won't interfere.

"In the spare bathroom under the sink." I snap my fingers as the memories punch my conscious mind. I can see the red box so clearly now.

I pause for a second, my eyes scanning her features, plump lips I've tasted a million times, golden skin I've licked over and over again, lush black hair I've wrapped around my fists as I fucked her from behind before raining kisses down on her spine and tits.

Focus, Enzo, goddammit.

As I head to the bathroom, my eyes scan the surroundings, making a mental note of every object and checking for anything out of the ordinary. Her phone is lying carelessly on the floor, her signature red-soled shoes thrown haphazardly at the front door, her light-brown coat hanging from the back of the bar chair. The kitchen is pristine, not a spot or a utensil out of place. Normal, I think, since she's barely spent a whole day here since moving in.

Back by her side, I shake my head at her clumsy attempt to wrap her arm and stop the bleeding. It's not gushing and it's not life-threatening but it is an open window to her mental workload and the lingering effects of Naples. She's self-harming... just like me. I may be going to a gym and beating the shit out of a bag or a willing opponent but the result is the same.

Punishment.

It doesn't take a shrink to know I'm punishing myself for not protecting her. My entire existence revolves around her well-being, the Mancinis' safety. But why is Madelina punishing herself? Why the fuck would she feel an ounce of guilt?

Her gaze sears a hole right through my heart, the burning need she awakens in me is always brighter the closer she is to me and sitting mere inches away is sweet, sweet torture.

"What happened?" My eyes dart to her arm then back up to meet her stare.

"Scratching an itch." She shrugs and there's some kind of double-entendre in there. Is she talking about Tyler spending the night? About some kind of medical condition? Should I be worried? Maybe take her to the hospital?

Fuck!

"Relax, Enzo. It's just a damn scab I picked before I fell asleep so it just... I don't know, took time to close back up." We play a short game of chicken as our gazes lock and a million memories pass between us.

The first time I ever saw Madelina, she was an eight-year-old kid whose worries didn't go beyond the next game she wanted to play with her big brother. I used to envy her ability to live her life so carefree, without a single fear of the outside world. She was so innocent that I was uncomfortable even being in the same room. The simplest things used to make her laugh—a bird diving from a roof straight into Central Park, the battering rains against the huge living room windows, or Marco making a face at her while their dad tried to scold them.

I felt like an intruder in their sunshiny lives with my big cloud hanging over my head.

But on her seventeenth birthday, Madelina stepped right up to me, kissed my cheek, then glared at me as she punched her fists into her hips.

I scowled at her, my heart beating with fear behind my ribcage. If her father ever saw me touching her, he'd slit my throat.

"It's my birthday, Enzo. It's kind of insulting that I'd need to kiss your cheek instead of the other way around."

And that was it. That was the exact moment I fell in love with Madelina Mancini. Not that I'd tell *her* that. She was still a child, no matter what she claimed. Screaming at her parents that she was an adult capable of making her own decisions did not make it so, no matter how effective her pouting could be. I was twenty-four, no way in fucking Hell was I touching her. And she made it her life's mission to make sure I knew where she was at all times.

"You'll fall in love with me yet, Vincenzo, I'll make sure of it."

Fast forward ten years and here I am, unable to love any other. She may have been a child but she knew exactly what she wanted and made sure to get it.

Blinking, I lose our game of chicken as memories of our younger selves flash across my mind's eye.

"I hate it when you hurt yourself. You know this." Rifling through the box, I find the bottle of antiseptic and spray her scrape before dabbing it with a cotton pad to get the excess blood cleaned off.

"I know but I didn't do it on purpose." Her lie is louder than her music was earlier. She forgets how well I know her. I've spent the better half of my life learning her every move and laugh and facial expression for every one of her facets.

"Right. Hold the pad there." Scowling, she does as I say but only barely.

"Think you've got enough there, Enzo?" My head snaps up to look her in the eye, making sure she knows her sarcasm is not welcome as I search out the gauze and tape in the kit, grinding my teeth when it's clear the scissors are missing. Damn it.

"Why would I scratch my scabs on purpose, Enzo? That makes no sense." Madelina hates being placated and she knows me just as well as I know her.

"I'm not getting into this, Madelina. We both know what's going on here." I'm suddenly on my feet, grateful that the scissors are across the room from her, all the way in the kitchen.

"What the fuck is *that* supposed to mean?" Her voice follows me, the pain ringing so clearly it wraps around my throat like elongated fingers trying to trap the air in my lungs.

Pulling the utensils drawer with too much force, I'm startled by the loud bang as forks and knives rattle against each other.

"Nothing." I slam the drawer closed and stomp my way back to her like a spoiled brat. That's how I feel. I can't have what I want so I take out my frustrations on the simplest of things.

"Right. Of course. Mr. Mysterious who can't talk about his feelings, what was I thinking?" Her words are clear as day, she doesn't even pretend to mutter. They are meant for me to hear and digest and possibly choke on.

"Lift." I tap the underside of her arm and she obliges while looking out the windows. The night is black as coal and the only thing she could possibly see is… us.

Us sitting side by side while I tend to her wounds.

Us fighting, screaming, though our visible traumas.

Us loving each other until the sun burns out.

It's right there, the mirror of us. This living, palpable thing that keeps bringing us back together again.

Except when I look at the windows, I see my ever-present dark cloud raining down on Madelina's sunshine. Hiding it, snuffing it out, holding it back.

I am and always will be the rain on her parade.

"I miss you." Her words have the exact effect of a sword through the heart.

"You miss the idea of me."

"You're an asshole. Don't tell me how I feel or what I feel. I'm aware of shit, Enzo. I know why I'm fucked up, I understand it but it's fucking hard to just open my eyes and…" Even though every one of her words adds a slash to my flesh, it's her silence that scares me the most.

"And what?" I freeze, my eyes narrowing and fixing on her mouth, waiting breathlessly for her next admission.

Silent, she just stares at the windows. At us. At what we used to be.

"And what, Madelina?" My voice is stronger, more adamant. More desperate.

"See him. When I'm sober and alone, I see him." She turns to me, tears welling in her eyes until twin drops scatter down her cheeks. "When I close my eyes, when I open them, when I'm in a crowd. When I look at you, I see him."

The sound that rips through my throat is closer to animal than human. It's no surprise, really. I already knew this. It wasn't a stretch to guess this. I was there, I witnessed the violence she endured. I held her dying gaze as she lay there suffering inside her mind, unable to speak or scream or fight back.

I was there. I saw it all.

In her mind, I will forever be associated with that moment.

My reaction is about actually hearing her say it. It's one thing to know, it's an entirely different monster to actually hear the confession.

My jaw clenching, I make quick work of the gauze and tape her right up, not too tight, not too loose, and jump to my feet.

"I have to go." I'm nearly sprinting to the front door when her words make me freeze instantly.

"Vincenzo, I love you. Please know that. Please, don't give up on me."

I take in a deep breath before turning back around and facing the love of my life.

"There is no world where we both exist and I don't love you, Madelina. Giving up on you isn't an option." She's crying now, not even trying to hide it, and I have to fight the urge to fall to my knees and sob like a beaten down child.

"Then..." I hang on every breath we take between her words. Giving her the space and the time to speak freely. "...help me."

Jesus fucking Christ. Those two words are my kryptonite and her use of them tells me she wants to heal and she's counting on me to bring her back to where we were.

So I do what I was put on this Earth to do... I help her.

"Go get changed. We're going to the gym."

Chapter Eleven

Devon

The crowd roars as my fist connects with the beast of a man in front of me and he stumbles backwards into the cage surrounding us. This could have been over five minutes ago, but I've been playing, trying to wear myself out, the need to pummel some motherfucker into the ground too strong to ignore completely. At six-foot-five and built like a brick shit house, I'm not exactly a meek man, but this dude looks like he's been growing in manure while taking steroids. Fucking massive.

Not that his size is helping him; his right eye is already swollen, his nose is broken, and I'm pretty sure his left shoulder is dislocated after I flipped him. He's unsteady on his feet, leaning into the steel cage, and I give him a moment to pull himself together because no other fucker here will fight me tonight, so I wanna get what satisfaction I can from this one.

The smells of sweat and blood fill my nose and I breathe it in, the scent of home causing a shiver to roll down my spine. After my eldest sister, Emma, called a couple nights ago, tearing me away from the woman I plan to call mine, I've been antsy. Our sister Lizzy has been sneaking around with one of the hoodrat creeps from the Deptford Boys—a South-East London gang—one of our biggest rivals, and I'm not there to put him in a fucking grave.

It's for the best in the long run, whatever's gonna happen is gonna happen with or without me there. Emma's the only one I've spoken to since I left, abandoning them all after beating my dad to death for being a dick and relinquishing my title as The Butcher to come and live in a different time zone, far far away from all the depravity of the firm my dad built up.

Don't get me wrong, I'm all for teaching people a lesson, making people pay what they owe, causing pain when the time is right, but the shit my dad was getting us all into was something else. Not for me. Being under the thumb of all of those rules, being dictated to by fucking minions... also not for me.

Shouts from the crowd pull me from my thoughts and I smirk at the beast now pushing from the cage and lunging forward, anger etched all over his face as I wag my brows and gesture for him to come closer.

"Come on, big boy. Show me what you've got."

I duck, then swerve, avoiding his giant fists as he yells in frustration while I block his leg aiming for my ribs. Without pulling my arm back, I square my fist up and connect it with his face, all in the blink of an eye—because all this pulling back and giving it a good swing shit only allows your opponent to see what's coming. He stumbles and I punch out again, hitting exactly the same spot on his cheek, his left eye now swelling to match the right one.

Within seconds, he's falling to the mats, and I make a mental note to make sure my cleaners get rid of all the blood and shit properly in the morning. I always block the caged ring area off until it's been thoroughly cleaned after a fight night anyway, but this dude just spat a tooth out and I don't wanna be finding that in my foot anytime soon.

Swaying, the beast lunges for me... only, he doesn't quite make it. Instead, his cheek hits the floor as he passes out, leaving me feeling deflated. I'd hoped to make it last longer than that, thinking this fella could give me a run for my money, but of fucking course not. Blokes like this all think they wanna play with the big boys, think they've got what it takes to get into a cage with the likes of me because they all wanna bring down the English dude who owns the gym to prove themselves.

The only person who's ever come close is Enzo, but he's a different breed of man compared to pretty much every other person that comes to these fights.

They all have something to prove, money to make, people to impress, whereas Enzo acts like he has nothing to live for, like he's trying to punish himself. If he put some actual effort in, I reckon we'd be evenly matched, and I look forward to the day.

If the way she's spoken about him and Tyler—when she's been off her face in a club with the twat supplying her drugs while I've been keeping watch over her—is anything to go by, then these men will be in my life for the foreseeable future. Because she will be mine, even if I have to share her.

That fucking Harris fella who reckons he's her security is a useless prick. I don't trust him as far as I can throw him. Which is why watching over my girl while she's out is my newest hobby. If he was any kind of security or protection for her, he'd have sussed me out already and at least approached me to find out why the fuck I'm following her around. But nothing. Nada. Zilch.

So yeah, useless prick.

The ref opens the cage door and enters to count out the beast, declaring me the winner as the crowd roars out in excitement once more before money begins exchanging hands from bets made. People congratulate me as I exit, clearing a path and not touching me as I pass. The last guy who patted my back at one of my fight nights was lucky he only went home with a broken arm.

I make my way to the back of the room, watching over everyone as the next fight is set in motion. Money is passed around and the two fighters in the cage are introduced, parading around and flexing to the crowd. Whatever's going on, I couldn't give two fucks because my blood begins to heat when I spot my girl on the other side of the room with that fuckwit, Enzo.

Why would he bring her here on a fight night? The people that come to these are mostly low-lives with no morals, and none of them give a shit about my girl's needs and triggers.

Fucking Enzo.

I bet all she did was bat her luscious black lashes at him to take her out with no clue as to where he was going.

However, she's out with Enzo for the first time in months.

That's progress, I suppose.

Plastering on my trademark grin, I make my way over to them, enjoying the way Lina's eyes widen in surprise when she sees me. The black and white dress she's wearing hugs every curve of her body, covering her arms and flaring out a little just above her bare knees.

Even fully covered, this woman's mere presence is enough to have my already-blue balls screaming at me to release inside her pretty pink pussy, or her arse will do. Either way, inside her, on her, any way that doesn't involve me having a wank by myself.

Leaning forward, my nose close enough to her neck to scent the unmistakable scent of oranges and wild flowers she emits, I whisper in her ear, "Alright, Treacle?"

She visibly shudders at my words, and I wink as I pull away, wagging my brows at the brooding Italian by her side. "How's it going, Happy?"

Enzo's only response is to roll his eyes, something I'd spank his arse for under different circumstances. I get the distinct feeling he'd enjoy it if our girl was involved.

"Are you following me or something, Devon?" Lina's tone is flustered, the pink tinge of the skin on her neck also giving her away.

"Nah. Not tonight. Gotta show my face to these things sometimes or they'll forget who owns the place."

The shock on her face at my admission makes me smile. As much as I know about her, she knows very little about me, and I'm slowly peeling away my layers for her. I want her to see me, to understand me... to want me as much as I want her.

"This gym is yours?"

"It sure is. And your boy here has become something of a regular." I turn my attention to Enzo. "Fighting tonight?" I can see it in his eyes, his desire for pain, punishment, the same as every other time he comes here. Only this time, he's a little more wary and I still have no fucking idea why he thought it was okay to bring Lina when he's clearly itching for a fight.

I know she's not weak or unable to take care of herself, but I can't imagine watching someone you care about get punched twenty times before knocking his opponent out with two hits is fun for her.

Now that I'm this close in the dimly lit room, it's obvious that Lina's been crying, her eyes are a little puffy and red. The fact that she's here with Enzo tells me it can't be his fault, which is good for him because my hand has automatically tensed into a fist at the thought of her being upset.

"Oh, look, the Italian stallion has brought a sexy cheerleader with him today."

Oh for fuck sake.

The first time Enzo ever came to one of my fight nights, he beat the shit out of the Road Captain from the Bronx Chapter Sons of Khaos MC, and ever since then, the rest of them have had a thing for challenging him every time they're here. Like, sort this shit out somewhere else and keep me the fuck out of it. But the pussy fucks haven't got the guts to go for him outside of my ring.

I have rules. Well, one rule: everyone leaves my gym still breathing.

And the obvious *we don't talk about fight club*, but that's a given.

My hackles are raised as the President of the club approaches, a couple of others wearing their branded leather cuts on either side of him.

"Rik." I tilt my head a little in greeting, showing as much respect to these douchebags as I'm willing. Which is not a lot.

"D." Rik returns my head tilt but his eyes aren't on me. They're on Lina. "You're a pretty little thing, aren't you?"

Sounds of fighting and jeering behind me aren't enough to drown out the twin growls directed at the Sons. What the pricks don't seem to realize, is that Enzo is the right hand to the man who basically owns them and their territory. They can do fuck all without Marco Mancini knowing about it or approving it.

"Got yourself some protectors there, haven't you—"

"Who says they're my protectors and it's not the other way around?"

My heart leaps into my throat as Lina steps forward and squares up to Rik. My God, this girl is amazing. Enzo and I are both on high alert though, our bodies tensing in anticipation of this going south real quick. Her heels lend her some height, but she still has to bend her neck to look him fully in the eyes.

"Oh, little girl. Look at you being all brave. Do you need a real man to show you how to behave in public? Why don't you come home with me, it won't take long to break a prett—"

His sentence goes unfinished when Lina knees him in the family jewels and his face contorts in pain. Lucky fucker, because I was about two seconds away from flooring him myself, and if the steam coming out of Enzo's ears is anything to go by, then he's feeling the same as me.

"You cun—" Rik lunges toward Lina, who stands her fucking ground like the queen she is, her fist meeting his face at the same time as Enzo grips his neck and I take the prick's legs from under him.

The nameless Prospects—which is what their cuts tell me they are—hesitate for a split second before making the same mistake as Rik, lunging toward the three of us as Enzo puts Rik in a chokehold. Grabbing their collars, I pull both of their heads down, one by one, kneeing them right in their faces and knocking them both out cold.

Enzo's pummeling punches into Rik's face as Lina watches on, a little flush on her cheeks that tells me she's actually enjoying herself, and I make my way back to them, resting a hand on Enzo's shoulder in a gesture to stop. I know actions mean more than words with this dude, and I'm happy to speak his language because, right now, I'm fucking fuming.

I bend down to put my face level with Rik's, where it still sits nestled in the crook of Enzo's arm.

"You ever look at her, speak to her, or even *think* about her again, and you'll regret every moment you've walked this Earth. Because I won't just kill you, I'll happily torture you for fucking centuries. I know you're aware of my fight night rules, so you're a lucky bastard because I don't break my own rules. You three can leave here tonight, breathing, alive, but if I ever see your fucking face again, you'll wish for death. Do you get me?" My words are spoken through gritted teeth as I restrain myself from shoving a dagger into this man's skull for disrespecting Lina and I vibrate with adrenaline coursing through my veins.

"I—" Rik coughs up some blood while trying to answer and I can't help the smirk that crosses my lips at the sight. "Ye..." His eyes are already swelling up, his jaw looks a bit wonky, and blood is pouring from his broken nose. Fucking beautiful sight.

"Enzo, mate, can you let the little prick go now?" He's like a dog with a bone. He doesn't want to let go and I can't blame him, but I also can't have him breaking my fight night code of conduct. It'd send the whole thing down the shitter.

Enzo grunts and lifts his arm, shoving Rik to the floor with the other two, who are both rubbing sore heads as they try to sit up.

"Now fuck off."

Mumbling under their breaths, they help each other up and attempt to push their way out through the small crowd that has formed around us to watch.

A quick glance at Lina tells me she's trying to hold it together, but barely managing. My little Hellcat is still fighting her demons through all that bravery as she holds a strong stance next to Enzo, her breaths heavy.

"Alright, show's over. Everyone out." A chorus of grumbles and groans echo around the room, and the two fighters still standing in the cage throw their arms in the air in frustration. My employees rally the crowd, ushering them all out, and I leave them to it as I turn my attention on the two raging Italians behind me. "Well played, Treacle. What do ya wanna do now?"

What I really want her to say is, "fuck!" But—not for the first time—I'd have to decline her offer until she's ready to beg for me, and it'll be so worth it.

Her perky breasts rise and fall with every breath, and I'm in awe of how strong she is when she rolls her shoulders back, sets those light-gray eyes on mine, and actually pouts.

Fuck, my balls are so blue, I feel like a smurf.

"I was looking forward to watching a fight, but those..." She pauses, as if searching for the right words. "Pricks! Those pricks ruined my fun."

Beside her, the tense mass of muscle that is Enzo visibly relaxes a little, turning his head to raise a brow at our little Hellcat. It's an odd thing to see his face holding any expression that isn't a scowl. It suits him.

"Well, we can't have that, now can we? What M'lady wants, M'lady shall get. Care for a scuffle, big guy?"

"What? Wait, I didn't mean—"

"Don't panic, Treacle Tits, we won't kill each other." Without giving her a chance to object, I grab her ponytail and tilt her head back, holding it in the perfect position to claim her lips with mine, infusing myself into her soul with every stroke of my tongue before pulling away and walking over to the cage in the now-empty room.

"Enzo, you don't have to do this. We can just go home."

The way she's looking up at him is adorable, but he needs a good knock to the head to sort him out because he's just not taking the hint.

"Fuck sake, just kiss her already and get your arse over here."

Enzo hesitates before gently holding the sides of her face, then the fucking sap kisses her forehead before walking over to me. I shake my head at him, disappointed, and he knows why. Man needs to grow his balls back.

"Rules?" Enzo speaks few words, but he's always respectful of my space here.

"Same as always, stay away from my boat race, and no junk."

He nods in acceptance and we both move into a fighting stance, feet shoulder-width apart, knees bent a little for impact.

"Hang on a minute, you have a boat in a race? Wait, why would Enzo go to your boat race anyway?"

My roar of laughter echoes around the room, I can't fucking help it. She's too cute. Even Enzo's cracking a smile and this moment feels lighter than anything has in a long time with Lina's confusion written all over her face. The way her brows are furrowed and her bratty little pout demands answers as she places her hands on her hips.

"Cockney rhyming slang, Treacle. It means face." I wink, enjoying the flush on her beautiful golden skin before turning my attention back to Enzo.

"Come on then, big guy. Let's give the lady a show."

Chapter Twelve

Tyler

"Mr. Walker? I've got Lenny Jenkins on line one."

My hands stop halfway through signing my name for the approval of a pay raise across the board. While the world economy slowly sinks into the depths of Hell, my company has flourished, and a big part of that success must be attributed to those who work their asses off. New York City is its own beast and living here can be the most exciting experience of your life and the most traumatizing. The mere task of searching for an apartment is like walking through an endless maze with no exit.

"Put him through, please." Careful to keep my hopes in check, I slowly place the pen parallel to the document, take a deep breath, and nearly rip the receiver from the unit as I pick up the call.

"Talk to me, Lenny, and it better be good news." Lenny Jenkins has been working for me as a private investigator for years. He and my father went to high school together so when I told my dad I needed a P.I. on hand, he thought of his old buddy right away. It's been seven years now and he's never let me down even once.

Here's hoping his streak continues.

"We found him. Like we discussed, I hired a couple of guys who do freelance work. The perv's currently napping in the trunk of an unplated car at the docks. What do you want us to do with him?"

I'm not a violent man, never have been. I've been told I'm ruthless when it comes to negotiations but violence has never been my knee-jerk reaction.

Except right now. With every word out of Lenny's mouth grows a flame of unhindered rage from my belly to my chest. I clench my teeth hard enough to quell this foreign need to hurt and maim just long enough to answer my employee. My very efficient employee who's about to get a bonus big enough to surprise his wife with a Christmas vacation.

"I'll call you right back." Before I can pause long enough for him to hang up, I add, "And Lenny?"

"Yes, sir?"

"Ask your wife what her dream vacation looks like." I hang up with the sound of his low laughter echoing across the line.

Placing the phone back in its cradle, I grab my cell and immediately dial Marco. Nothing happens in this town without him knowing and I cannot keep this from him or else he'll make sure I can never have kids in the future.

"Mancini."

"What, did you break your caller I.D?" I know for a fact my name pops up on his screen when I call and here he is answering like he has no clue.

"Nah, I've just named too many people 'asshole' on my phone so I have no idea which one is calling." Takes one to know one, I guess.

"Yeah, well, I bet you'll change mine to 'king of New York' in a minute." There's a pause and it's like we're communicating on the same mental wave.

"Doubtful, that's my name, but if this is about what I think it's about, I'll meet you at Brooklyn docks in thirty minutes." I hear his desk chair slam against something and I picture him getting up and grabbing his peacoat. The sound on the other side is muted as he gives his assistant instructions.

"Okay but I need to make a stop first."

"Tyler."

I pause, not sure why he's using his mafia boss voice.

"Yeah?"

"Do not call Lina. She doesn't need to be reliving this."

Is he fucking kidding me, right now?

"That's where you're wrong. This is exactly what she needs." I won't back down on this. Lina needs closure and, although I won't be getting blood on my hands, I'm sure that whatever Ugo Ambrosio's fate will be, it needs to be her decision.

Lina Mancini won't be able to turn the page until she's been given closure. I literally flew her to the worst day of her life, I will allow her to move on in her own way.

The silence on the other end is pregnant with conflict. He knows I'm right but at the same time, his need to protect the women in his life is stronger than anything else running in his bloodstream. Placing his sister face to face with her rapist goes against every protective instinct he has.

"*D'accordo* but, Tyler?"

"Yeah?"

"I want him gagged the whole fucking time. He doesn't get to speak. He doesn't get to beg for his life. The rest is up to her." When it comes to control, Marco is the most predictable prick out there.

"I've got a roll of duct tape I've never had to use before so I guess this is the perfect occasion." He doesn't outright laugh but the tension across the line dissipates just a fraction.

"We'll be ready for you. Don't make us wait." By "us" I'm guessing he means River will be joining him. I wouldn't be surprised to learn that she was also traumatized by the events in Naples. Hell, I'm scarred from it and I wasn't even around for the worst of the action.

We grunt our goodbyes, too preoccupied by the upcoming events to care.

Next, I contact Enzo;

Me: You with our girl?

In under a minute, I have a response.

EB: Why?

Fucking Christ, these mafia fuckers are giving me ulcers.

Me: Yes or no. It's that fucking simple.

I'm typing and walking, my coat over my arm as I close my office door and lock it.

"Cancel my meeting, please. I'll be out the rest of the day." My assistant, Clara, doesn't even pause in her typing.

"Yes, sir. Oh, Mrs. Walker just called—" I stop dead in my tracks and turn around.

"Mrs. Walker, as in my mother?" She never calls the office, she knows to only reach me on my cell.

"No, sir, your ex-wife." I take a deep breath and look down at the floor, forcing myself to stay calm.

"Clara, the only Mrs. Walker I know is the woman who gave me life. If Cora calls, you may call her Devil's Spawn or Satan's Mistress, I don't really care, but I would rather she not share the same name as my mother." There's a pause as Clara's cheeks pink up like two little rosebuds.

"I'm so sorry, it won't happen again."

"Don't worry about it. I'll see you in the morning. Don't stay too long. Go out and have some fun." I know I will.

I'm already walking away when she thanks me, my phone lighting up with a new message from Enzo, causing my teeth to grind.

EB: Why?

Me: I have a present for her.

EB: With the chef

He couldn't just say that in the first place?

Me: Stay there.

I don't bother to check his response, I'm pretty sure he's sent me any number of variations of "go fuck yourself" but he'll be much happier when he hears about my little gift to our girl.

It takes longer to get to the restaurant in the middle of the day than it does to fly to D.C in my jet. This city is insane. There are more reasons to live anywhere else than there are to stay here but we New Yorkers all have a bit of a masochistic side to us. The same shit that pisses us off, like Midtown traffic, is also a familiarity that makes this tiny island our home. When I was at university, I tried taking a cab on a Friday night from Midtown to Brooklyn and the cabbie outright refused. I couldn't give him enough money to drive me out there.

You either love her or you leave her, but you can't feel ambiguous about her, ever.

When I walk into Devon's restaurant, I immediately spot my girl at the bar, Enzo's watchful eye scanning their surroundings, always on constant alert. I'm hoping my news will alleviate some of his worries.

"A billionaire, a chef, and a stone-cold killer walk into a restaurant..." Devon's voice booms from the door that leads to the kitchen as he lets it swing back without a care in the world.

Shaking my head, I make a beeline for Lina, whose ice-blue eyes are fixed solely on me. I don't care that Enzo is following my every move, that Devon is now standing right across from Lina, and that a couple of waiters are prepping for tonight's opening. I don't care about a goddamn thing when I bury my fingers into her cascade of ebony hair and close my fingers around the silky strands before pulling her parted lips to my mouth. I don't care about the barely perceptible growl next to me and the grunt of approval from across the bar. I don't care about anything except the sweet taste of my Gumdrop as she melts into my touch, opens her mouth, and allows my tongue to sweep inside.

Her kisses are life sustaining and being away from her for a couple of days has been nearly torturous.

"That's quite an entrance, mate. Got one of those for the rest of us?" I'd scoff at his remark if I weren't convinced he meant every word.

"I've got better than that." I mutter my words across Lina's lips, but say them loud enough for both men to hear me.

"What's going on?"

I turn to Enzo and grin.

"I got our girl a late birthday present." I've got his attention. I can tell from the furrow of his brow and the narrowing of his eyes that his brain is working quickly to put the puzzle pieces together.

"You didn't have to get me anything else, Tyler. That's ridiculous. You already spoil me so much." She has no idea how I wish I could spoil her the way I dream of doing but she's almost as rich as I am and flashy, fancy gifts are a dime a dozen in her world.

No, Lina is more receptive to the thought behind the gesture.

"Trust me, this gift is going to make you truly happy. But first..." Pulling out a black satin blindfold, I wink at Lina before presenting the fabric to her.

"Oh, kinky. I like it." My gaze darts to Devon and, judging by the smirk proudly smacked on his lips, I'm certain he likes it. The kink, I mean. "Unfortunately, some of us have to work so I'll leave you to it. Take care of our girl."

Placing the blindfold over Lina's eyes, I kiss her once more before nodding to Devon and sweeping my girl into my arms.

"Christ, you're a showoff."

Lina giggles at Enzo's grumpy attitude then leans her head on my shoulder, where it fucking belongs, always.

"Come on, Princess Gumdrop, your chariot awaits."

Chapter Thirteen

Lina

Well, this was an unexpected surprise today. Not that I'm complaining. I've spent the last few days surrounded by at least one of these three men, and while I know I'll never be who I once was—and I absolutely need to speak to River's therapist—they've done something to my insides. Something I didn't think would be possible anymore.

I don't feel so alone, and I'm trying really hard to not get lost in the misery that has been pulling me down. I genuinely thought breaking up with Enzo and Tyler was the best thing for me. For them even. But they're like moths to a flame, unable to stay away from the heat that could burn them whole.

It's still strange to me that the three of them seem so open about the possibility of sharing me, but maybe I'm misreading the situation. This could very well be a friends-with-benefits thing with Devon. Not that the benefits have been anything other than me giving him a couple of blowjobs in a nightclub and him taking care of me like I'm precious to him.

Enzo is still guarded around me, refusing to do much more than grunt or stare into the distance like the world has offended him.

Tyler is acting like we were never apart, but he's still holding back on me. When he used to blindfold me, his hands would be roaming free all over my body.

Ugh, they're so confusing.

I'm so confusing.

The way we are now isn't all on them. I know I pushed Tyler and Enzo away, and the fact that they're so okay with Devon now being in the picture... yeah, I'm just waiting for the last pin to drop.

"We're here, Gumdrop." Tyler's voice breaks through my thoughts, bringing me back to the here and now, sitting in the back of a car with Tyler's thigh pressed up against my left leg and Enzo's pressed against my right.

The silky blindfold is soft against my skin, and I can't help adjusting in my seat for a little friction down below in anticipation of what's to come. The two of them together feels like something from the promised land, and I'm eager to know what the fuck is going on right now.

The cool New York air brushes against the bare skin of my hands and face just as the telltale sound of the car door clicks open.

"Take my hand." Tyler's instruction is firm but soft all at the same time, and while I'm still blindfolded, I can't actually see his hand, so I just hold mine out in the hopes he'll take it.

He does.

"Thank you, Aaron." My Tyler, always polite with his staff.

"Sir."

After managing to get out of the car, with a lot of help from the two men at my side, I feel one hand at the base of my spine—Enzo's—while Tyler keeps a gentle grip on my fingers, and they lead me to wherever we're going.

The hustle and bustle of the usual New York traffic is quieter than usual, and the scent in the air is slightly different, which means we're not central. I literally have no clue where they've brought me, but lucky for them, I trust them both with my heart and soul.

Denying it would be futile.

The screech of a metal door confuses me, because that sounds a hell of a lot like one of my brother's warehouses.

"Where are we, and what is my surprise?" I'm beginning to get anxious as we step inside, the breeze no longer cooling my skin. This doesn't feel like some kind of sexy game anymore.

"Stupid fucking idea." Enzo's words are practically grunted out with annoyance lacing his tone.

"Optimistic as always, I see. If A.A Milne had known you, he would have named Eeyore after you." I can tell from the direction of Tyler's words that he's addressing Enzo and when his breath caresses my skin like priceless silk, I know his attention is right back on me.

"Okay, Gumdrop, I'm going to take the blindfold off in a second. But I want you to hear me out first." Tyler's fingers squeeze together with mine as the hand on my back begins moving in slow circles.

"Ooookay. Is this some kind of punishment for pushing you away? Because I thought we settled that after the other night, and I don't know why you feel the need to gang up on me to get Enzo back. He's the one—" My words are coming thick and fast before Tyler interrupts me.

"Gumdrop, it's not a punishment for you. We just thought you'd enjoy the surprise more if you didn't know where we were going first. This way, there was no chance for you to build an anxious ball in your stomach."

These guys know me so well. Thinking this was sexy time had me in suspense, but now, Tyler's right, that anxious ball is beginning to grow and I'm trying really hard to push it down.

"So wha—"

"Tyler found Ugo, Madelina."

Oh shit.

My knees give out on me, but they don't let me fall. Instead, the blindfold is removed and I'm heavily leaning into Enzo behind me.

"What happened to easing her into it?"

"Taking too long."

"Well look at her now! She's barely standing, Enz—"

"Thank you." I can't listen to them argue. They both thought they were doing the right thing here, and as much as this is the shock of the century and I want to run away, crawl into a hole, and never return, something inside of me is happy.

They both pause as I right myself, standing on my own two feet and taking what feels like a million deep breaths to steady my pounding heart. If I really think about it, what they've done for me here is so romantic, I wonder why I ever let them go.

"Are Marco and River here?" They allowed me to be a part of ending Elizabeth, Ugo's sister, when she had been found, so it's only fair that they're a part of this now. Plus, my brother would have their balls if they did this without him.

"Yeah, they're already in the office, waiting for you." Tyler gestures toward the door to the right of the short hall and, even though we're inside, this place is still so cold. With one more deep breath, I nod and step forward, knowing Enzo and Tyler are right behind me.

"Then let's go and get this over with."

"Hey, Beautiful." River's warm welcome as I walk into the office brings a smile to my face. This woman just radiates positivity and warmth. And some high level of badassery too.

"Hey, Gorgeous." It doesn't matter how much time passes between us, she's always there with open arms. Arms that I readily step into.

River hugs me like my mamma hugs me, with everything that she is, pushing all the love she has for me into the embrace, and it's something special to know she's on my side in all things. Even when I'm intent on pushing everyone away.

I open my eyes and see Marco over River's shoulder, hands in his pockets, power stance and all. There's a softness in his gaze as he watches us hug, and when he realizes I'm looking at him, his expression changes a little. It becomes more intense, reminding me of Papa when he was proud of me. It's a feeling I've missed.

My whole world has practically turned into toxic waste since Papa died, but this here, in this warehouse, is just one more small step to becoming a me I'm proud of again. The barely-there upturn of Marco's lips and the intense stare of his silver-gray eyes tells me he believes in me, and that is everything right now.

Pulling away from River, I move to step into my big brother's arms, allowing a single tear to trickle down my cheek and giving him an extra squeeze, hoping he knows how grateful I am for him.

"We take your lead on this one, *Sorellina. Va bene?*"

Moving back, I look him in the eye, determination flowing through my body, and I nod once. "Does anyone have a—"

I'm silenced with a dagger being held in front of me by Enzo's calloused hand and I turn to look at him. The butterflies I thought were long dead flutter in my stomach at his close proximity and the promise of death in his eyes.

I was born to be strong, I was trained to stand up for myself, and I've allowed Ugo Ambrosio to live in my mind for far too long.

I'm ready.

My hands are shaking, my skin is itchy, and I want to curl up into a ball, forgetting the world exists, but as I step into the small room with my family at my back, I roll my shoulders back and hold my head high.

He's there. In the middle of the empty room, looking surprisingly like his sister did hanging from the ceiling in this very same space months ago. She was found first and, while she wasn't the one to rape me like this motherfucker in front of me, she had played a huge part in allowing it to happen.

There's black duct tape over his mouth and wrapped all around his head, and I can't help smiling at how it appears to be cutting into the skin on his face. His eyes slowly move in our direction and I almost back out of the room when they land on me, bringing an immediate lump to my throat and a burning pain through my veins.

I won't be ruled by how this man made me feel.

Exhaling through my mouth, I approach Ugo with confident strides, a million different ways I can make him hurt flashing through my mind.

This is my focus for right now. I can't—and won't—allow anything else to distract me from what I need to do.

A hint of fear flashes through Ugo's eyes as he watches those behind me, but they're not the ones he should be afraid of in this room. Okay, so yeah, he should be afraid of them too, because none of them would hesitate to end his life, but I'm the one who has the pleasure of doing so.

He stole from me, so I'm repaying the favor.

Words feel impossible, I thought I'd have so much to say to him when we were finally face to face. That was wishful thinking because my throat is closed and the only thing residing inside me is hatred.

Slowly, I raise my dagger-wielding hand, the black hilt firm in my grasp, and the clip point tip glistening under the single dull bulb hanging behind Ugo's head. Images of what happened in Naples begin to penetrate my thoughts, my breaths become shorter, and my heart is almost beating out of my chest as I cut through the tape on his face.

I'm not careful, slicing the skin on his cheeks as I make a hole so he's able to open his mouth. Growls from behind me remind me that my big brother, Enzo, and Tyler are here too. A quiet, "shh," from River brings a small amount of light into the darkness consuming me as Ugo yells out in pain, blood trickling from the wounds on his face.

"You whore!" Ugo spits his words, spittle and blood landing across my chin. I can't control the gag and almost throw up all over him. "Ha, my little treat can't handle some blood. Are you here to give what I deserve? Come on, I like it rough." His laugh echoes around the room, the sound so similar to Naples. He called me his little treat when he...

I'm frozen, staring into dark eyes swirling with hatred, when Enzo appears in front of me, protecting me like he wasn't able to all those months ago. His fist smashes into the side of Ugo's face, quickly followed by Tyler's fist after he appears on my other side. Tyler then turns to me as Enzo continues to use Ugo like a punching bag, grips the side of my face with his clean hand, and forces me to look at him.

"I wasn't there for you when you truly needed me..." I open my mouth to tell him I know that wasn't his fault, he holds no blame in what happened to me, but he pauses and pushes his thumb against my lips. "I wasn't there, Gumdrop. But I'm here now. You are strong, powerful, a fucking force to be reckoned with, and we all know you're not going to allow this douche to consume any more of your fear." The sounds of Ugo being beaten fade into the background as Tyler places his soft lips against mine in a gentle kiss. "You've got this, okay?"

I nod, a hint of a smile playing on my lips, the frozen fear from before dissipating with each second I stare into Tyler's deep brown eyes. He kisses my forehead before stepping away, leaving a battered Ugo swinging in front of me, his face already swelling up from Enzo's beating. He's passed out and his gray slacks are now soaked in piss, the stench burning my nostrils.

Enzo's practically steaming from the nose like a caged bull as he moves his eyes to mine, softening ever so slightly. "Anything for you. Always, Madelina." He steps closer and I have to bend my neck up to keep my gaze on his. He's so close I think he's about to kiss me, but all I feel is his warm breath against mine before he lifts my hand, kisses my knuckles, and walks behind me to the others.

I turn to look at them all. Marco stands proud, nodding his head at me in gentle encouragement, with River tucked neatly under his arm. She has tears in her eyes but the determination on her face gives me strength. Then there are Tyler and Enzo, side by side. Tyler is cleaning the blood from his fist with a wet wipe—probably from River's purse, that woman is prepared for any occasion—and he winks at me while Enzo folds his arms across his chest, bulging muscles and all, nodding his head once like Marco did.

We were all in Naples when we first attempted to finish this thing with Ugo, it's only right that we're all here now to see that through. And for them to allow me the power in this situation is a gift I never thought I'd live to see.

An idea comes to me, and as sick as it may be, it's no sicker than what this man did to me.

"Can someone remove his slacks? I need to get to his penis." The thing that caused me the most pain.

"What the fu—?"

"Tyler, shh." River has been through her fair amount of shit. She might not know exactly where I'm going with this, but she's on board.

"I got it."

"Thank you, Enzo."

Pulling a dagger from behind his back, Enzo steps forward and slices Ugo's pants off, careful to avoid touching the soiled areas. He leaves some shallow slices down the front of Ugo's thighs before moving away.

The pain from the cuts must bring the hanging dead man in front of me back to the land of the living as he begins groaning and trying to open his eyes. His jaw is broken, so his words are nothing but rambled mumbles. I like that better than the words that were spewing from his evil mouth earlier. Maybe Marco had the right idea with the duct tape.

I don't even know why I split it open.

Determination and hatred flow through me as I glance toward the flaccid little dick hanging between Ugo's legs. The disgust almost makes me back out, find another way to kill this man, but I can't. He deserves this.

His garbled moans get louder when he realizes what I'm about to do, and a flash of memory makes me pause, but not in fear this time.

"Hold his legs down." I'm mirroring what he said to his minion when he attacked me, when he stole from me, and I hope the sweet irony of this moment isn't totally lost on him as Enzo does exactly as I've asked. He crouches and holds Ugo's legs still in a death grip.

Ugo struggles to move, to get away, but there's no chance of him escaping this.

Without touching it, I begin sliding the sharp edge of my blade around the top of his shaft, cutting down and underneath his ballsack as far as I can go. I repeat it on the other side, enjoying the way the blood flows over his skin. Then I slice down the center, from root to tip, several times. Rather than one deep cut, I'm creating lots of lighter cuts until the crevice grows. Ugo's screams of pain are music to my ears, and I never considered myself the kind to need this type of violence.

I may have been born into it, lived among men who do it without thought, been trained for it even, but it was never a complete reality until now.

The satisfaction that thrums through my veins at Ugo's screaming pain won't fix me, but I also won't deny that it's helping.

I continue to cut and slash at him until his tiny dick falls to the floor in pieces, closely followed by his ballsack. There's so much blood.

"Christ, maybe she should be Don instead of me."

"We're all going to need therapy after this. Is it wrong that she's still hot as fuck?"

"Tyler, that's my fucking sister."

River's low laugh cuts them off. "A woman's wrath is something to be admired. Watch and learn, boys."

I'm aware this is all kinds of wrong, but it *feels* all kinds of right. I look to Enzo continuing to hold Ugo's legs in place and there's nothing but pride written all over his features. The rare grin on his lips mixed with the splatters of blood covering his skin make him look completely demented, but it gives me the courage to carry on, to keep slicing at Ugo's now-bare chest. The form of torture known as Lingchi is something I saw a documentary about years ago. Death by a thousand cuts. Although, I've lost count now, slashing randomly at all the fresh skin to create lines of blood all over his body.

Ugo isn't screaming anymore and Enzo looks up at me from his crouch, silently asking me if I'm done.

I am.

Tears spring to my eyes as I nod once, dropping the dagger and inhaling deeply, exhausted, as the metal echoes across the stone floor.

Ugo's not the first man I've killed, and he certainly won't be the last. It's the world I was born into.

I'm immediately enclosed in the weirdest group hug I've ever been involved in as River wraps her arms around me, quickly followed by Marco, Tyler, and Enzo. The floodgates open and I can't control the sobs that wrack through my body in relief.

No more looking over my shoulder.

No more wondering if this dead man is going to find me and take from me again.

He's gone.

And I hope he rots in Hell for an eternity with his sister.

Chapter Fourteen

Enzo

I hate group shit. The hugging, the touching, the kumba-fucking-ya of it all. My only saving grace is Madelina, her nose in the crook of my neck and her lips pressing hard against my skin, as she sobs away the pain of the last few months.

I would participate in a group hug every hour, on the fucking dot, if it meant watching the love of my life heal from the inside out. Hell, I would live in a perpetual group hug just to see her holding a bloodied knife and slashing up her demons until there's nothing left.

I'm so fucking turned on right now, it's almost indecent.

I lock eyes with Tyler and he nods. The guy is too observant for his own good. He sees Madelina in a way no one else ever has. Not even me. And right now, he sees *me,* can probably feel the buzzing across my skin from my adrenaline rush. By the time I understand what's going on, Madelina and I are standing alone in the warehouse, her sobs gone but her fists now clenching at my shirt.

"What do you need?" I wait, patient as always when it comes to her, and inhale her soothing scent of wild flowers and fresh oranges.

"I need you to fuck me, Enzo. I need you to do exactly what I just did and let go of that night. Take me to that office and fuck me like you mean it." Lifting her face from my neck, she looks straight at me, eyes swollen, cheeks streaked with tears, and lips the color of lust. "Can you do that for me?"

As if I could ever deny her anything. I can't, it's not in my nature. I was made to serve her, to protect her. I'm supposed to be her shield from the real world, which is why watching her getting raped was my own personal Hell, and that's not even a fraction of what she went through.

Cupping both of her cheeks in my hands, I press my lips to hers and kiss her once, twice, before I pull away.

We just stand there, breathing each other in, appreciating this rare moment of solitude where time is frozen and only the feel of our skin and the sound of our rapidly beating hearts interrupt the silence.

I can't explain the moment my instincts kick in, that inevitable instant when all the pieces of my mind click together and a soothing calm washes over me. It only ever happens when Madelina looks at me or when her eyes turn to molten lava and her breaths hitch up just the tiniest bit. When it does happen, though, my body reacts on instinct.

Bending at the knees, I slam my hands to the backs of her thighs and lift her into my arms, her legs wrapping around my waist, and head straight back to Marco's office. It's only a short distance to go, but it's enough for me to imagine all the ways I'm going to please her. All the ways she's going to tell me how she wants it. All the ways I will be at her command. Just like before and, hopefully, every minute after this.

I'm not sure where everyone else went but, to be honest, I don't give a fuck. As I enter the office and slam the metal door closed, I can only focus on one thing.

Madelina.

Thankfully, Marco's office is just a place to sit and plan. His desk is empty of all pretenses, no computers, no files, no pens and paper. Just a massive oak monstrosity that, for all intents and purposes, will be the perfect size for what I'm hoping will happen next.

Setting Madelina down on the wood surface, I stand between her parted thighs and allow my gaze to travel across her face, along the slender curve of her neck and down to the deep parting sea of her cleavage. Fuck, her tits are perfection with just the right amount of swell peeking out of her vee neck shirt and her nipples like beacons to my lust.

"Get on your knees, Enzo. I want to ride your face like old times." I quirk a brow at her, a smirk fighting to make an appearance at her no-nonsense command. Except, this isn't the time for fucking around. This is the exact time for fucking… full stop.

Dropping to my knees, I shoulder my way between her legs and unbutton her pants, watching as she lifts her ass from the desk and allows me to slide the fabric, along with her panties, off her thighs and down her legs before laying them at my side.

I'm eye level with her dripping wet pussy, her lips slightly parted in this position and her pink nub peeking out at the apex of her slit. She's my oyster and I'm about to get drunk on her taste, but only when given permission.

In my world, I may be a ruthless psychopath with the moral compass of a bloodthirsty killer but when it's just me and Madelina, I'm at her service. She runs the show. Always has and always will.

"Put your mouth on me, Baby. Eat me all up."

There they are, the words that set me free. Hooking my arms around her thighs, I dig my fingers into her flesh and slam my mouth to her wet cunt, licking and sucking and thrusting my tongue so fucking far up there that I pray to lose myself inside her. I'm surrounded by her taste and her smell, the noises she makes every time my teeth nip at her skin make me so fucking hard I'm afraid I might come in my jeans.

To be honest, I don't fucking care if I do. It's been months since I've touched her this way. An eternity since I kneeled at her feet. A lifetime since I've let everything go except my unwavering devotion to the woman who has held my heart since the first time I saw her.

"That's it, Baby. God, yes. Lick me up and swallow me down." Fuck, she knows what her words do to me as she grinds her pussy over my mouth and nose. My chin is dripping with her cum, my lips feel swollen with how hard I'm kissing her, fucking her with my tongue as my hips thrust to the same rhythm. I can't get enough of her, can't pull away, not even for a much needed breath. It's all right though, I don't need oxygen when I have her. Dying with the taste of her cunt on my tongue is more than I ever deserved.

Madelina spreads her legs wider, her hips fucking my face as she digs her fingers into my short hair, her nails nearly breaking the skin on my scalp as she takes everything I have to give her. She takes it because I willingly gave myself to her years ago.

I submitted to Madelina Mancini before I even knew what those words meant and before she could possibly imagine the power she held over me.

"Fuck yes, so good. Suck my clit, Enzo, make me scream." Goddammit, her words make my entire body shake with pent-up need as I flatten my tongue and run it up her drenched slit and over her swollen clit. She's mewling, tearing at my hair, scratching at my scalp as she nearly suffocates me with her need.

I can't get enough. I suck her clit into my mouth and flick it in rhythm with her grinding hips.

"That's it, yes, yes, God yes. Please, Enzo, don't stop!" I couldn't stop if a fucking army tried to pry me away. I won't stop until she gives me permission to do so.

My hands slide over her hips and stop at the small of her back so I can pull her closer, suck her clit even deeper into my mouth.

I suck and lick as she screams out my name. Run my teeth over her sensitive flesh as she nearly lifts off the desk with the power of her orgasm. Still, I don't pull away.

I bury my entire face between her thighs, lap up every fucking drop of her cum as she offers me her wet pussy juices, coating my lips, my tongue, my chin. Still, I don't pull away.

I drink her in, I moan my pleasure between her pussy lips and inhale her wicked scent until I'm so fucking drunk on her that my head is spinning with the potency of her. Still, I don't pull away.

It's only when her fingers give way and her body melts into my touch that I know I have little time to suck in and swallow up every last fucking drop of her climax.

My tongue is so deep inside her that I can barely catch my breath as she cries out my name and tremors rake her body like aftershocks after a magnitude eight earthquake where her cunt is the epicenter of my emotional and physical destruction.

"Stop. Fuck, stop, Enzo, it's too much." I'm consumed by her—her taste and her scent—almost not hearing her command. But my body is so attuned to her voice and her tone that it pulls back, my eyes connecting with her dilated pupils in an instant.

Reaching out a hand to my face, she runs her thumb across my bottom lip.

"I love seeing my cum all over your face. Your lips are so swollen and it's all for me." I don't speak, no words are needed because she knows me. She knows what this moment means to me. "Now, give me your cock, Enzo. I want you to come inside me so I can feel you dripping down my thighs as we walk out of here."

Jesus fucking Christ, this woman is everything I ever wanted and so much more.

Standing, I pop open the buttons of my jeans and push them over my hips and down my thighs as I grab my cock and stroke it once, twice, before she reaches out and squeezes the root.

"You come when I tell you to come. Are we clear?" Clear as fucking crystal. "Say it, Enzo."

"Yes, Mistress."

Madelina smiles, her chest heaving with the power I imagine she feels at my words. She owns me, heart and soul, and I'm sure it's a heavy responsibility to hold my destiny in the palm of her hand.

"Good. Now fuck me to within an inch of my life."

"Yes, Mistress."

Madelina lies on her back down the length of the desk, her arms up over her head and her fingers curling around the edge of the wooden surface so she can hold on to dear life.

I haven't come in months, not even by my own hand, because all of my fucking orgasms belong to her and she knows it.

In one hard and precise drive of my hips, I impale her from tip to root until I can't go any further. My entire body freezes at the feel of her hot pussy squeezing the life out of my cock. She's so fucking tight and warm and it's like coming home after a tour of duty in the depths of Hell.

"Did you miss me, Baby?" I look up at her and the expectancy in her eyes almost kills me. In her dominant position, she's feeling vulnerable. I did this to her confidence every time I walked away from her. I made her doubt herself every time I put distance between us.

There's a stain on her armor from every time I denied myself the pleasure of her but right now, right here, as I stand between her spread open thighs with my dick buried inside her cunt, I promise myself that I will never, not fucking ever, deny her this power again.

I will wipe away the stain of my insecurities with the fabric of my soul.

"Every fucking second of every fucking day." I have never meant anything more than these words.

"Good. Now make me come." Arching her lower back, she wraps her legs around my hips and fucks me from the bottom. Topping me even though I'm the one standing over her.

Palming her ass, I plunge in and out of Madelina like a crazed man. Grunting and growling, I revel in the feel of her velvet walls rubbing against my hungry shaft. With every thrust, I bottom out, grinding my pelvis against her clit and digging the pads of my fingers into the flesh of her ass. Every time the tip of my dick hits her most sensitive spot, the air whooshes from her lungs with a desperate sound of need.

A need for us, for this moment. A need that consumes from the inside as I do exactly what she ordered me to do just minutes ago. I fuck her to within an inch of her life.

When her walls close in on me and her thighs squeeze me with her well-trained leg muscles, I know she's close. Her breathing is erratic, her lips are parted, and her eyes are wild with lust. She's primed for coming all over my cock and I can't fucking wait to feel it again.

"Yes, Enzo, yes... God, don't fucking stop." I couldn't if I wanted to, which I fucking don't. Stopping is impossible, nowhere near my radar.

I'm fighting the overwhelming urge to drown her pussy with my cum but I won't, not until she's ready. Instead, I drill her with my thrusts, fuck her raw until she roars her orgasm into the confined space of this empty office, her eyes on me, her jaw slack as she gives me everything she has.

My movements are erratic and my cock is so slick with her cum that every time I pull back I'm at risk of sliding right out. So I tighten my hold on her, careful not to break skin but unable to control the force I need to keep myself buried inside her. I'm so fucking close to exploding, the months of denial, the time spent apart and missing her. Missing this. It's all so fucking hard to hold back.

"Now, Enzo. Come inside me." Her words are strangled, like she's holding back the last vestiges of her orgasm until we're both giving ourselves completely to each other.

Thrusting one final time with the force of a tsunami wave against the unprotected beach, I ram myself back inside her and shoot my load hard enough to feel the cum filling her cunt like a flood.

"Yes, fuck yes!" I watch her as my entire body shakes and buzzes with uncontrollable energy, watch as her eyes find mine and we hold our gazes through this momentous snapshot in our lives.

We've come back to each other. Slayed our demons together, fucked our doubts away. Without a conscious thought, my gaze falls to her forearm, my fingers grazing the scab that has started to heal. Pride swells in my heart knowing we're on the right path.

"That's my good boy."

And there's that soothing calm washing over me. Her approval, her appreciation. Her unwavering love and devotion.

Chapter Fifteen

Lina

Today has been a lot. I'm positive I've experienced every emotion on the spectrum in the space of the last twenty-four hours. Crippling self-doubt, hopelessness, excitement, fury, lust, relief—in more ways than one—and while I've been all over the place in general over the last few months, today feels like a breakthrough.

Enzo... oh my God, Enzo. I hadn't realized how much I needed him. Letting him and Tyler go was a terrible decision made through some kind of grief for myself, for my power as a woman being taken away from me, but at least now I can recognize that. I'm by no means over what happened to me, but I am done with acting like a victim and I'm going to try my damn hardest to crawl out of this hole I've dug for myself.

I'm not sure of what my future looks like at the moment, but I don't need to figure everything out right now. What I *do* need to do, is take this man who looks at me like I created the moon and show him he is as worthy of love as anyone.

While River would tell me it's not wrong to have been selfish, shutting everyone out, literally drowning my sorrows in drugs and alcohol, I can't help feeling a little guilty for it. We all went through something in Naples and I never for one second considered anyone else.

Both Tyler and Enzo told me they love me and I threw it back in their faces by cutting them loose. Walking away. Fully believing it was the right thing to do. It wasn't.

I need them. And they need me just as much. That feeling is one I thought I'd never get back.

"...Finished. Listen... no noises..."

"I'm not listening to my sister fucking one of my best friends in my office."

"You could listen to her fucking two of your best friends if you let me in."

"Ty, I swear to God, I will gut you if you ever make me listen to that shit."

"Oh, boys. Shh." A gentle tap of knuckles sounds on the door before the knob turns and River pokes her head through the gap. "Did you guys have fun?"

Enzo doesn't move, his eyes boring into mine as if River didn't just walk in on him seated inside me. His beautifully carved face is still covered in blood, but it only accentuates the sharp edges of his cheekbones and makes the blackish-brown of his eyes glow through the shadows in the dimly-lit room.

"Yeah." I'm not ashamed of enjoying myself and River is nothing if not accepting of anyone being sexual.

"Clean-up crew is on the way. Pull your dick out of my sister-in law's pussy, Enzo, and get your pants up. Time to go home." She blows us a kiss and disappears from the gap. Before the door closes all the way, there's a scuffling sound before Tyler opens it fully and casually strolls in.

Enzo and I are covered in blood and sweat, cum now dripping down my thighs, yet Tyler still looks at me like I'm his whole universe. Standing there in all his shiny clean glory, removing his suit jacket and stepping toward me as Enzo follows River's instructions, buttoning up his pants.

"Here, it's cold outside, Gumdrop." He wraps the jacket around my shoulders, unconcerned by the blood staining my skin, gripping the lapels together as he pulls me toward him. "I'm so fucking proud of you." Tyler's deep brown eyes are dark, almost stormy, and full of a need I feel right down to my bones as he kisses the tip of my nose.

I close my eyes and take in the unmistakable scent that is Tyler Walker, with hints of coffee that envelop me like a warm, comforting blanket.

"Come on. Let's get you both home." He wraps his arm across my shoulders and looks over to Enzo and I swear my pussy flutters at the thought of them both. Tyler was the last person I'd ever have expected to be okay with sharing me.

Holding my hand out to Enzo, I give my huge Italian teddy bear a wink and he links his fingers through mine. We manage to do some weird crab walk through the door, heading out to the car we all arrived in.

Marco and River are waiting for us, beside my brother's obnoxious Aston Martin, and River's face is a picture when she sees us walking toward them. If I didn't know her so well, I'd say she's about to cry, but she's happy. She's like a proud mama watching her baby walk for the first time.

"You three look amazing together." She doesn't move to hug me, likely because she doesn't want to break up the little threesome we're in.

"Okay, Tesoro. She's still my little sister." Marco kisses her forehead with a smile and she rolls her eyes dramatically, her own grin playing on her lips. "You two, look after her. Friends or not, it won't be the Reapers that rip your nuts off if you hurt her." To be honest, I think Marco would be cleaner and quicker than the Reapers—led by one of his capos, J.

Enzo nods respectfully, and Tyler just raises a brow while I giggle between them. Oh, man, it feels so good to just be happy. Even if it's only for a short time, I'm clinging onto it for dear life.

"If they're looking after me, does that mean I don't need Harris as a constant tag-along anymore?" I'm being optimistic, but also, why the fuck not? I'm a grown woman, Ugo isn't a threat anymore, and I don't need a constant babysitter.

"Okay. I'll reassign him." Holy shit I did not expect him to give in that easily, but I'm not going to give him time to think about it and change his mind.

"Thank you."

"Ti voglio bene, Sorellina."

"I love you too, big brother. *Grazie per oggi.*" I thank him for today but really, I'm thanking him for every day he's ever taken care of me.

Marco pulls me away from my men, wrapping me in the kind of warm hug only a big brother can provide and kissing the side of my head.

"Okay, Husband. You can let her go now. Polo will be driving Stefano crazy so I think you should take me home. Unless you're willing to let me drive the Aston for a change? Then maybe we could have a little joy ride?"

"No chance, Tesoro."

"Yeah, okay. We'll see." Marco pulls away from me to raise a brow at his wife. She smirks up at him before slowly leaning in for a kiss. At the last second, her hand is in and out of his pants pocket in a flash, whipping out his car keys. She blows me another kiss before turning and rushing toward the driver side of Marco's Aston, climbing in and revving the engine.

Marco shakes his head then winks at me before walking away. He opens the passenger door and climbs inside, strapping himself in before River revs the engine again, covering the sound of Marco's growly demeanor at his wife's antics. The car shoots forward and begins down the street and River's hand is seen waving out of the window before she turns left, toward home.

The drive home to my new apartment is almost as exciting as the drive to the warehouse. I had been blindfolded, and the anticipation for what they both had in store for me sent shivers up my spine. Obviously, it didn't turn out the way I'd expected, but it was still fucking everything to me.

That man is gone from this Earth forever, and that's something to celebrate.

To be honest, I'm hoping that the relationship between the three of us is evolving into every woman's fantasy. If I can get them both upstairs with me, that's at least one step toward it.

Back inside his car, Tyler's palm is warm on my thigh as his thumb strokes delicate circles, the sensations multiplied tenfold by his proximity to my core.

I've always been confident in my own skin but that confidence was brutally ripped away from me. Now, that man has been brutally ripped away from the land of the living, and a sense of peace washes over me as we pull up outside my apartment building.

I'm done with being the shrinking violet. I'll never be a victim again.

I'm a survivor.

Chapter Sixteen

Tyler

By the time we make it to Lina's new apartment, the gravity of the situation hits me full frontal. There was never any doubt of what would go down at the warehouse, I knew the consequences of my decisions, but on the drive back the irony occurred to me.

Just like I handed over my private jet for her to go to Naples, I handed her the proverbial knife in that room. In both cases, I was the catalyst turning her from woman in control to victim, then from victim to murderer.

I wish I were sorry about the latter but I'm not. Ugo Ambrosio's violent and untimely death was, without a doubt, warranted. He deserved every ounce of pain he felt before he died. It was his only gift to our Lina.

"I need a shower." There's a lighter note to her voice but the enormity of this past year will probably sit on her shoulders for months to come and it's our job to make sure she doesn't miss a single appointment with her therapist.

Sliding my hands into the pockets of my slacks, I lean against the door jamb of her bedroom and watch the dynamic between her and Enzo. There's a shift happening to this... whatever this is. A foursome? A poly something or other? I don't actually give a fuck about the label. All I know is that Lina has the sexual appetite of a lioness on ecstasy and I'm fucking here for it.

"You should probably join her. You look like you went ten rounds with a bloodhound and you smell like a slaughterhouse." Although my words are directed at Enzo, my eyes never leave Lina's figure as she peels off her clothes, one torturous piece at a time, and drops them in the nearly-empty hamper. From my vantage point, I can see the specks of blood that stain her naturally tanned skin, the newly erupted goosebumps across her back, and the delicious triangle of space between her legs as she bends over and rummages through the bottom drawer of her dresser.

For all of those reasons, I'm standing here sporting an erection hard enough to break through granite walls.

When Enzo doesn't even pretend to move, I glance his way and see he's riveted, his eyes drinking her in like she's the fountain of youth and he's an old man with unfulfilled dreams.

"I see." Those two little words get his attention.

"You don't see shit." There's zero emotion in his retort and he doesn't even pretend to look at me.

"I see you want to shower with her yet here you are, standing next to me." I lean in like I'm teasing him, wanting to ruffle his feathers. I know exactly why he hasn't stripped down to nothing yet but I want to hear him say it. "Maybe you want to shower with me?"

I expect him to scoff at the idea, maybe even have some kind of homophobic reaction. After all, the world we live in isn't always accepting or even remotely open-minded, but all he does is shrug and I have no clue how to take that.

"Come on, Enzo, let's get cleaned up." Lina's voice is like velvet: smooth and firm. A little bit how I imagine my voice sounds when I give her a command. This time, he's pulling off his blood-stained shirt and soaked through jeans, discarding them in the trash as he makes his way to the shower without completely closing the door.

Hmm, an invitation if I ever saw one.

Or maybe I'm just being hopeful. In any case, it doesn't matter. I'm already stepping across the threshold of the bathroom, a room big enough for an orgy but decorated like it's the most intimate space in the universe, when Lina and Enzo stand under the large pummel spray of the Italian shower.

Just the idea of them putting on a show for me makes my dick hard, the impatient pressure against my zipper becoming more and more painful. I am many things, but a masochist, I am not. As though the bathroom layout was created just for me and my particular tastes in sin, the seat on the suspended toilet faces them at the perfect angle. I don't hesitate, unfastening my pants and pulling out my cock, I watch as Enzo steps up, mere inches behind Lina, lathering her long black hair with her preferred citrus shampoo.

With her head back, she turns in my direction just enough to flash me a coy smile. She's trying to give me her good girl act but I know she's a filthy sexual being who knows exactly what her body needs and wants.

And she wants us. Who am I to deny her?

In no particular hurry, I let my gaze roam their bodies as they run their hands over slick skin and soapy hair. My fist tugs at my cock from root to tip in rhythm with Enzo's hands wringing out Lina's hair. He's taking care of her, soothing her, and my eyes get distracted by the water drops clinging to dear life at the hard peaks of her nipples. I want to lick those drops into my mouth before sucking on her tits, possibly bruising, marring, her perfect complexion.

Running my thumb over the small slit at the tip of my dick, I let my mind drown in the fantasy of tasting every inch of her, of having my mouth travel the expanse of her entire body, when this whole scenario takes a turn.

"Kneel." Lina's voice goes from velvet to steel in a matter of a nanosecond and my attention becomes laser sharp, my eyes glued to her now-dominating stance.

Enzo doesn't hesitate, he drops to his knees, eyes on her, one hand on his cock, the other on her pussy as he flicks her clit with his thumb.

I'd be hard pressed to choose between my Lina, on her knees with a mouthful of my cock pressing against the back of her throat, or this version of my Gumdrop who doles out the orders and spreads her legs wide, expecting an orgasm from the man kneeling at her feet.

Christ, I'm so turned on right now I'm afraid I'll come like a first-timer.

"Are you enjoying the show, Tyler?" Placing a hand on Enzo's head, she guides his mouth to her cunt and pushes her hips close enough for his tongue to reach where his thumb used to be.

"Worthy of an Oscar, Gumdrop." I barely recognize my voice as it comes out scratchy and lacking any control.

"Who's going to come first, do you think?" She watches me then, her eyes molten lava and her mouth slack with pleasure. I can't look away, my hand fisting a little harder and pumping a little faster.

"I'm hoping it's you but the precum on my dick is telling me otherwise." She smiles at my words, a drunken tilting of her lips, as Enzo grabs her ass cheeks and buries his face between her parted thighs. Fucking Hell, I can almost taste her on my tongue, gustatory memory playing tricks on me.

"That's it, Enzo, eat my pussy like it's your last supper." Damn, if she keeps talking like that I'm going to shoot my load in less than two minutes. When she moans into the shower, her pleasure echoing off the walls, I correct my estimations. If she keeps this up, I'll be coming all over my hand in less than ten seconds.

My ears are hyper focused on the sounds of Enzo's mouth as he slurps her juices right up, his own growls reminding me of how fucking good she really does taste. She's like a gourmet meal made especially for me. For Enzo. Hell, for Devon, too, I'm guessing.

Lina takes no prisoners as she steps into Enzo's face and, although she's standing, she's able to ride his mouth, controlling every one of his movements as she holds him down by his hair and fucks him from above. From my sitting position, I can see the pads of his fingers indenting Lina's fleshy ass cheeks, his nails digging deep a testament to his own pending orgasm. He's going to blow, and very fucking soon, without even needing to be jacked off.

I'm actually impressed. My hand is now pulling and squeezing my cock in time with her hips as she takes her pleasure from him. Tilting my coccyx, I reach down and cup my balls, rolling them between my fingers as Lina gives me the first clue that she's about to come.

Throwing her head back, she closes her eyes and speeds up the rhythm of her hips. She's fully fucking his face now, seemingly unable to slow down. Enzo doesn't care though. In fact, he looks like he wants to get in deeper, closer, like he wants to fuck every part of her at once.

I'm briefly distracted as Enzo's dick slaps against his abs before a long strand of pearly cum erupts from his tip and lands unceremoniously on the shower floor, rushed to the center by the waterfall from above. Lina cries out with a long, erotic, "Fuuuuck" that makes my dick give up the fight.

Except I don't want it to end like this.

Quickly and without thinking twice about it, I bolt up to standing and rush to the shower where my hand lands on Lina's wet hair, curling my fingers around the nape of her neck and pulling her face just millimeters from my hungry mouth.

"Your turn, Gumdrop." It's as if a switch went from up to down. Lina drops to her knees, side by side with Enzo and goes from dominating to submissive in the blink of an eye.

"Mouth open, tongue out." My order is for Lina but to my surprise, Enzo follows suit and just the sight of them there at my feet waiting for my cum drives me right to the edge.

"You sure about this?" I'm staring at Enzo, needing his words before I lose what little control I have left.

"Yes." Thank fuck. No sooner does he give me his consent on a silver platter than my dick shoots its first load.

I coat their faces, their necks, their mouths with my orgasm and when everything is ripped out of me, my growls and grunts as the pleasure courses through my bloodstream are that of pure, unadulterated bliss.

I'm high on power, high on euphoria, high on the sight of my seed adorning my woman's features.

Dropping to my own knees, I take Lina's face and bruise her lips with a scorching kiss, my tongue fucking her mouth like my dick wants to fuck her pussy.

"Clean her up and meet me in the bedroom." I can barely walk as I shed my wet clothes on the bathroom floor and grab a towel on my way out.

Now, to plan the next scene.

Chapter Seventeen

Devon

"Lizzy's lost the plot, Dev. She's honestly gone fuckin' crackers over this Ben."

"Ben, as in Ben the *head* of the Deptford Boys gang? Because if it's *that* Ben, Emma, then why the fuck didn't you tell me that before now?"

When I thought my little sister was fucking around with one of the lowly members of the Quinn family's rival gang, I was content to leave it alone. The lower ranked members are usually a little more amenable and less likely to want friction. Kinda like a *Romeo and Juliet* scenario, and who am I to mess with that? But fucking Ben Williams is a whole other situation.

"Uncle Harry said he was dealing with it, but he's done fuck all."

"Oh for fuck's sake."

"I'm sorry, Dev. When I rang the other day, I was worried, but now I'm fucking terrified. Uncle Harry said to leave you out of it, let you live your life, but we need you here. Everything is going to shit. The Deptford Boys keep coming into the pub with Lizzy as if they've got some rights to be there, Mum is going batshit, and cousin Johnny ain't got the balls to take control 'cause he's worried about his dad. Please come home."

Emma is my only elder sister—since Milly died—and she's usually one of the most calm and collected of us all, but her rambled rant about what's going down in London worries me.

I have a new life here in New York. My restaurant has been booming for the last year, my MMA gym and fight nights have grown in popularity, and I'm finally getting somewhere with Lina. Now, I have to go fix shit in a place I swore I'd never return to because, apparently, my family—whom I trusted to be safe in my uncle's hands—can't cope without me.

Washing my hands of the whole thing was a great dream but, in reality, I can't leave my mum and my sisters to the wolves. And by ignoring this, that's exactly what I'd be doing.

Fucking morals kill me.

"Gimme a few days, Sis. Look after Mum, and I'll see you soon."

"Oh, thank fuck. I love you so fucking much, Dev. I'm on top of everything as best I can be for now. Just hurry." Emma hangs up, the beeps to indicate the end of the call the only sound in my office.

Well, it was a great year, I suppose. *New York, you've been fun.*

Not a fucking chance I'm gonna leave without finally claiming my girl though. Fuck that. It may take some work, but I'll need to find a way to get her to London with me. The two tagalongs that come as part of the Lina package, too.

Fuck it, I'll figure it all out after the restaurant closes tonight.

I'm antsy enough as it is. I haven't seen my woman for nearly a week, not since her two fucknuggets whisked her away to that warehouse for the afternoon. According to my sources, what happened there was a fucking massacre, and after a phone call full of grunts with Enzo, I got the gist of what went down. And I'm so fucking proud of my Treacle Tart.

I'm just fucked off that I wasn't able to find that sick son of a bitch for her first.

But I've been giving her the time I think she's needed with her two ex-now-current boyfriends while trying to keep that cunt Freya off her back. She's been hard fucking work. I have a guy that's blocking every call and text the cunt makes to my woman and people making sure she doesn't step foot near her apartment.

"Chef, there's a couple demanding to see you because we haven't got a table for them. They asked for you specifically and said you'd be pleased to see them, but they refused to give me any names." Daisie's been my head hostess for almost as long as the place has been open, and not once have I seen her thick red brows scrunched up with such worry.

"I'm coming, Doll. Where are they now?" I'm up and spinning out of my black leather chair, rounding my desk and grabbing my phone. My favorite dagger is tucked neatly in my sock, as usual. It won't take two seconds to stab a motherfucker in the ribs and lead them out of my restaurant if need be.

"They're at the bar."

"Okay. Thanks, Daisie. I'll deal with it from here."

She nods before turning to leave and I follow her through the short hall to the main restaurant. Her tight little arse is something I can appreciate, but it only makes me yearn to bury my face into Lina's and lick her tight little hole.

Oh you're having a fucking giraffe. Think of the devil and she shall appear.

Freya.

With Rik. The fucking twat president of the Sons. He tried to get into another fight night a couple days ago until I politely reminded the motherfucker with my knife that he wasn't welcome.

They didn't call me The Butcher back home for nothing.

He's sporting some beautiful cuts across his cheeks that I can't help smiling at as he and the cunt he's with spot me heading over to them. Why they're together, in my restaurant of all places, I have no fucking clue, but it's suspicious as fuck. I don't like it.

"Oh, look! You come to finally find us a table, big boss man?" Rik holds out his glass of wine in my direction, his voice far too loud for the environment, and I know the dick's gonna just cause more problems if I try and kick them out.

N.O. ONE

Thursday evenings in New York are much like every other evening, busy as fuck, and stabbing this twat in the ribs might be satisfactory for me, but there are too many people around to avoid someone calling the cops. Weighing my options out leaves me with only one that's gonna get them out of here as quickly as possible; I'll have to find them a fucking table.

I hold my hand out to shake Rik's and, as our palms clasp, I pull him into me so I can whisper into his ear.

"Keep your voice down, Rik. This is a classy place and I don't wanna have to call the razz on ya. I'll find you a table, you'll sit and politely have a one course meal, and then you will both fuck right off. Am I understood?" There's no way I'd ever snitch, but this motherfucker doesn't know that.

"Fine. But you can't ignore me forever, Devon. I want back into the fights." His deep and rumbled tone is full of mirth and I really couldn't give two shits.

Pulling away, I don't even acknowledge the smug cunt by his side. She's clearly high as a fucking kite, but at least she's nowhere near Lina. Thing is, she just keeps popping up in random-as-fuck places, with some dodgy-ass people, and I can't figure her out. To begin with, I figured she was just some druggy in the wrong places at the wrong times, figured she owed some dude money, which is why her hubby was killed, but the more I dig into her... nah. She's fucking dangerous.

The night is running smoothly enough since Daisie managed to find the fuckwits a table. My staff are fucking legends, so I expected nothing less. The head chef I hired—and trained vigorously to cook the way I like in my kitchen—has been banging top notch dishes out all night, the waitresses are smooth as clockwork, and I have no worries that this place will keep going with me back in London. But I'm gonna need to think of something long-term because I'm not letting this go. I worked too damn hard for it.

There's a sense of pride that fills me in knowing what I've accomplished here and, as I watch Cunt One and Cunt Two finally leave my restaurant, I take a deep breath and pull out my phone. I have flights to arrange and a woman to fuck into insanity, but first, I need to let the only other crazy fuck I know in this city—Enzo—in on what's really been going on.

I know he hates Freya as much as I do, and his boss is the head of the fucking New York mafia, so maybe he can do a little more with the information I've learned than I can.

He answers within two rings. Well, I say answers, but it's more like a casual grunt in greeting.

"Enzo, mate. I've got some info on that Freya bird I think you'll find interesting."

Chapter Eighteen

Enzo

Something is shifting. The thought of Devon calling me to inform me of shit going down in my backyard would have made my eyes roll like a five-year-old. But this? This feels normal. It feels natural.

I dart my eyes to Madelina, who's rummaging through her closet, sequins flying left and right as she mumbles shit about losing her favorite body suit. Whatever the fuck that is.

"I'm listening." Why do people announce that they're going to say something? Life is too short for this shit.

"She was just here with the local prez of the Sons of Khaos." I frown at his words, the guy's face flashing in my mind.

"Guy from the gym?" Why the fuck would she be hanging around that idiot?

"Found it!" Madelina's cry of joy and relief has my lips popping at the corners, a strange feeling of happiness warms my chest at her wide eyes and grin big enough to see all her pearly whites. "It was in the box of special dance wear." She shrugs and saunters back to her bathroom without bothering to close the door.

We've been here for a week. Sometimes just Tyler when my job tears me away from her—like taking care of the fuckwit drug dealers Marco wanted gone—sometimes just me when Tyler has to go run the world of billionaires or some shit. Mostly, we're here, all three of us, learning how to navigate this new dynamic. Except something is off, there's an imbalance and I'm guessing it has everything to do with the Brit on the other end of the line who is currently giving me a history lesson on the fucking Sons.

I've known this motorcycle club my entire life, their crimes back in the nineties were epic and because they had a third of the police department on their payroll, they were almost as untouchable as the Mancinis.

The difference is that where the Mancinis stuck to a plan, the Bronx Sons got too damn greedy and had to reimburse their bad accounting with blood.

I know, I was the collector at one point.

Today, they're just a bunch of self-important thugs puffing out their chests to make themselves look bigger than they are.

Marco has spared them—so far—only because they move coke from point A to point B and I'm guessing that's the reason Freya is hanging out with them.

"She's either moving the coke for them, using it, or Hell, my gut says both, mate. The bar for her morals is set lower than my balls." I scoff. Sure, there's a joke there just waiting to fly out of my mouth, but I need to deal with this Freya shit, not play buddy-buddy with the other guy who wants to fuck the love of my life.

"I'll look into it." I'm about to hang up when he calls my name.

"Enzo. She's up to something and it ain't good, mate. She has to be stopped." Now, I know a few things about Devon Quinn. His family back in London? Well, let's just say his nickname isn't The Butcher because he's a genius in a kitchen. Although, his cooking is fucking on point, not that I'd ever admit that to him. No, this guy uses his knife like an artist uses a paintbrush to tell a story. Except Devon's canvas is bad people and their stories are usually sung like a fucking tweety bird once he starts carving. Art is in the eye of the beholder and all that shit.

So, when he says "she has to be stopped," he's not talking about having a conversation. He's already scoping out a patch of land where her bones won't be found. At least not in our lifetime.

"I got it."

"All right then. How's our girl?" His voice softens at the mention of Madelina and it's clear as day that he's fucked just like the rest of us.

"She's in the shower." I grin as he growls over the line.

"You pair have hoarded her enough. Time to share, and soon." With a parting grunt from the both of us, we hang up just as Madelina wraps a towel around her chest and leans against the door jamb, dark, wet hair hanging freely behind her and water drops carving a passage down the goosebumps on her skin.

"Was that business?" I could look at her all damn day, listen to her voice every second of every minute.

"Devon." She nods like she already knew but wanted confirmation.

"Is he coming around, joining us?" There's hope in her voice, a need that I feel deep in my gut when it comes to her.

"Yeah, soon." I stand, walking over to her until I'm close enough to smell her orange-scented shampoo. "I need to know everything about Freya." Her relaxed features immediately morph at the mention of her ex best friend. Those are Madelina's words, but I think they were never friends and Freya was using her for... Hell, I don't fucking know. Everything? Notoriety, money, drugs, a friend to party with? I don't fucking care. She's toxic and Devon is right. She needs to be stopped.

"What about her?"

"Did she mention where she got her drugs or who she was fucking?"

I'm guessing, these days, she's spreading her legs for the Sons, but I don't know how long that's been going on. The problem isn't her fucking who she wants, I'd be a hypocrite to judge, it's the unmistakable danger she put Madelina in every time they hung out together.

"She may have but I wasn't exactly paying attention to the logistics. I was just happy to... I don't know, drown in the darkness of it all, I guess. How I got there didn't matter." I reach her in half a second, my hands on her cheeks, my mouth on her mouth. We're not exactly kissing, just standing there breathing each other in, taking comfort from one another.

"I have my weekly appointment tomorrow, you don't need to worry about me." I pull back and shake my head, a smirk peeking out just for her.

"Name one day since I met you that I don't worry about you." The room lights up with her smile and my heart pauses in my chest just so it can take in her brilliance.

"Fair enough. Still, baby steps, right?"

"Right." I almost choke on my word as she reaches out and cups my cock in the palm of her hand, her eyes dancing with mirth and her smile as mischievous as the devil himself. "Madelina, I have to go. I've got work to do but Tyler should be by soon." Fuck, I wish I could just blow everyone off and hide out here for the rest of... well, forever.

"I hate it when you go. It's always dangerous." Tilting her head up, I kiss her hard enough to almost make me forget my responsibilities. We both know that's not possible. Being Marco's right-hand man comes with promises and non-negotiable terms.

"Gotta go. Rest and I'll see you when I'm done."

Lina brings her hand to my chin and squeezes, her dominating side peeking out and saying hello.

"You be safe, got it? You fucking come home to me, Enzo. Always." Fuck, this girl is everything.

"Planning on it." One last kiss on her nose and I'm forcing myself to walk out of the apartment.

By the time I call J and make my way out to the Bronx, it's already been over an hour. This chapter of the Sons of Khaos used to be a big deal, now they're just a disorganized group of men acting like spoiled brats. Unlike the other few chapters up and down the East coast who seem to have their shit together. And while they're a pain in our asses sometimes, it would be more of a hassle to put them down than to let them think they have a piece of the pie. They barely get a chip from the crust but they don't need to know that.

"Well, well, well, if it ain't the second to the big honcho." God, give me the strength not to skin this douche alive.

J and I both grunt at his words, it's non-committal and it works in our favor. Neither one of us is a big talker so this conversation may become complicated.

"So, what can I do for you? Must be a big deal if it means crossing the bridge to come see us." From the corner of my eye I see J reaching for her blade. She doesn't even try to hide it and when I look up at her face, it's like looking into emptiness. I'd say she's stoic but she's more than that. She's completely shut off from all emotions. It's fucking impressive, if not a little psychotic...

"Boss has questions, I'm here to get him answers." As I speak to Rik, I'm scanning the area and counting the number of bikes parked in front of the club house. Seven with two off to the side and a van that looks like it came out of an afterschool special about "Stranger, Danger." By the time I've scanned the lot, I have to fight the constant urge to roll my eyes when half a dozen bikers step out behind Rik, chests popped out like doped up roosters and chins high like snotty kids from the 'burbs. These guys are jokes. The sound of tires crunching against gravel almost makes me smile.

The cavalry is here because J and I aren't fucking stupid. We don't go into the den of unpredictable assholes with an ax to grind against half the population of New York with just one gun and a knife. J's team steps out of the four Escalades and, without a word, they stand—arms crossed and legs spread—against their vehicles, waiting on our orders.

"Well, what Mr. Mancini wants, Mr. Mancini gets, right?" His smile is about as real as a wrestling match on prime-time television, but I don't give a fuck and neither does J as we both follow Rik inside their biker home.

The cigarette and pot smoke hits me in the face like a two-by-four and I almost chuckle as J mumbles something about loving the single life.

"Could be worse, there could be…" The rest of that phrase dies on my tongue as we walk deeper into the den and a Khaos Khunt—their words, not mine—bobs her head up and down as she attempts to deepthroat one of the members.

"You were saying?"

I just shrug at J's sarcasm. It's not like we haven't seen worse. Not by a long shot.

"Come to my office, it'll be quieter."

The place isn't exactly a mansion but there are a few doors lining the halls. Rik's office is at the back and he's right, the moans and screams don't travel all the way down here.

Settled in, I nod to the chair for J, who snarls at me before raising a brow and daring me to ask again. We don't sit at these meetings. Those extra seconds it takes to jump out of the chair in the event of an ambush could be the difference between seeing Madelina again or sleeping for good.

"Wanna drink?" Rik doesn't even look at us as he pours himself a shot of Jack Daniels.

"We're good." I answer for J, knowing damn well she doesn't drink on the job. "Boss wants to know what you're up to with Freya."

"Why? He want a piece of her?" Fucking Christ, this guy has a death wish. J shakes her head before tilting it back like she's asking the heavens for the strength not to stab this guy in the eyeball.

"I'll be sure to ask his wife that. I'm assuming you're not afraid of losing your balls and swallowing them?" Looking at me over his shoulder, he freezes for a second, like he's weighing his options. Like I said, he's not the brightest bulb in the clubhouse.

"Right, right. Didn't mean nothin' by it. Guess it's just a habit, ya know?" Right. It's a habit to be a fucking idiot. Can we just get this over with and move the fuck on, now?

"So, Freya?"

"Look, all's I know is that bitch can suck cock like a fucking pro. And I mean, an honest-to-God professional whore." He takes his shot glass and downs the amber liquid like it's water before serving himself another.

"How did you meet her?" If he mentions Madelina I'm going to fucking slit his throat.

"Ah, shit. It was a while ago. Back when the Greeks were still here." I frown, glancing at J and finding a matching look on her face. The Greeks were running these parts back when Marco and River were getting hit from all sides. But when the brothers disagreed, it turned bloody. The youngest of the two, Aleko, joined the Sons down south, in some podunk town that loves to hate their presence there. Who knows? Maybe they hate to love them. I'm still trying to figure out the timeline when Rik continues with a total game changer.

"She came by here looking to hire us for a job."

"What kind of job?" I'm gritting my teeth, trying really fucking hard not lose my patience. I hate having to ask questions when it's unnecessary. Why is it so damn hard to just give a monologue with all the fucking answers in it? Do these assholes want me to literally pull their teeth out?

"The kind good guys don't do, if you get my drift."

Yeah, I think I do. Looking at J, I nod to the door, barely acknowledging Rik's presence as we walk out.

We came in separate vehicles, me in my car and J on her motorcycle.

"When River finds out what I think just went down in there? Well, let's just say I hope I'm invited to the bloodshed party." Jesus, I thought I was fucked in the head. This chick makes me look like a fucking boy scout.

"I have a feeling it's going to be a rager."

Chapter Nineteen

Lina

The rooftop of my brother's apartment building is like our own private oasis in the midst of the chaos that is New York City. It's always been a beautiful space, but my sister-in-law's presence is definitely prominent. Flower arrangements full of reds, whites, and greens line the glass barrier; twinkling lights are wrapped around every branch of the small, potted trees; and the small, undercover seating area is like a paradise of soft and fluffy cushions.

At this point, I am one with the cushions. It's so freaking comfortable up here, even in the cold November air—outdoor heaters are a wonderful thing.

River and I have been comatose amid the softness for the last hour. After she picked me up from my therapy session today, she insisted we come up here to decompress. I have to admit, as usual, River knows exactly what I need. Sitting in this comfortable silence has allowed me some time to really think about what I discussed today, and while I'm fully aware that one session isn't going to completely rid me of my demons, I know I'm on the path to recovery.

"Stop scratching, Gorgeous."

I hadn't even realized I was doing it and immediately stop. Luckily, I haven't managed to rip the scab off of the current scratch-mark along the inside of my arm. It's become a habit I know I need to break, and I'm getting better, becoming more conscious of the action, but it's going to take time.

"Sorry."

"Don't you dare apologize." River sits up and holds my arm, her palm covering the deep scratch as she stares into my eyes. "This is a war wound you won't feel ashamed of. But you need to let the scar form, let it heal, let it be a reminder of how fucking strong you are. It's nothing to be ashamed of or be sorry for. Okay?"

I hadn't really thought about it like that, but she's right.

Annoyingly, she always is.

"Okay." Her smile mirrors mine as she nods once before standing, holding out her hand for me to take. Which I do, of course, without question.

She leads me to the edge of the building so we're standing against the glass barrier looking out onto Central Park.

"There's a wooded area in Staten Island where I would usually do this, but this is as good a place as any. Now, I want you to scream at the top of your lungs, for as long as you feel you need to. Like this." With her hands holding onto the barrier, River raises her head to the sky and pushes up to her tiptoes before letting out the loudest yell I've ever heard. Her body is tense as she screams to the heavens. When she's finished, she relaxes and turns to me with a smile. "Your turn."

Questioning this woman is futile, so I shrug my shoulders and take the same stance she did moments ago, raising my head to the sky, gripping the barrier... and I scream.

I scream from the bottom of my soul.

I scream until my toes curl and my vision blurs.

I scream until my throat burns and my lungs beg for oxygen.

I won't lie, it feels fucking fantastic.

I scream, take a breath, then scream again, pushing out all my hatred for what happened to me, all the fear, all the pain, and when I finally stop, my cheeks are wet with cold tears and my body deflates. River is there to catch me before I fall and she holds me so tightly that her warmth and love seeps through my bones. I squeeze her back, hoping she understands how grateful for her I am.

"Thank you."

"No need to thank me, Beautiful. Come on, we should get to the club. I know three men who are eager to see my best dancer back on the stage." River winks at me, and, wow, has she perfected the art of the sexy wink. If I wasn't so into men, my brother would have a competition on his hands for this amazing woman in front of me.

My breaths are heavy, butterflies are flying around my stomach, and I need to pee. All completely normal as I step onto the stage inside Rapture, River's burlesque club.

The room is pitch black, murmurs from the patrons echoing throughout the space, and I close my eyes, blocking everything out. This is my first time back on the stage in too long. I was ashamed of my own dancing, my body, the way I can make it move when the music flows through me, thinking maybe it was my own fault that monster thought it was okay to put his hands on me, maybe I asked for it with my naïvety in how I handled myself.

I know that's all complete bullshit now.

Now I'm stronger, I'm evolving, I'm a fucking gladiator. Which is exactly the reason I chose the song I'm dancing to this evening. *Glory and Gore* by Lorde.

Silence descends as the song begins, the words ringing out around the room with the soft build of music. A dim red spotlight highlights my slow movements as I make my way over to the pole at center stage, and all my anxiety about this performance trickles away into nothingness, all my worries forgotten as I lose myself in the rhythm, extending, spinning, floating to the tune my only focus.

My hands above my head, gripping the pole behind me, I slowly slide down into a crouch with my knees together and head hung low before the chorus kicks in. When the beat begins, and Lorde sings out about something trying to take us, I flip my head up, my long, curled hair part of the routine as it rests at my back, uncovering my face as I part my knees sharply before standing with a *rond de jambe*.

Turning and gripping the pole, I lift myself up, climbing as high as I can, twisting, turning, contorting my body in all the delicious ways I've missed so much, continuing to get lost in the words.

I'm a gladiator.

I'm strong.

As the song comes to an end, I allow my body to quickly slide down the pole, head first, before abruptly stopping, flipping around and extending my legs as I spin away, pirouetting to the big finish. I slide to the front of the stage, the bright lights shining in my eyes making it impossible to see the audience as my body bends backward, my arms stretched out behind my head, knees beneath me.

The applause that comes with the silence of the music almost makes me tear up.

The adrenaline high coursing through my veins after a performance is like nothing else and I'm *so* fucking glad River gave me the opportunity to come back. As the club fills with music once more, the lights flickering with a group of dancers now taking center stage, I make my way down the steps, my vision clearing as I zone in on the booth to my right.

Glittering tassels tickle against the skin of my ass and thighs as I walk toward some of the most important people in my world. People at other tables openly stare as I move past them, and as I near the booth, the matching scowls on all three of the men sitting there warms my heart.

River is sitting among them and she must see the question in my face because she speaks without me even having to ask.

"Your brother is in my office upstairs. Probably watching this booth on the CCTV because, in his words, there's no fucking way I want to see my sister sliding around a pole again."

I knew he wouldn't be far away from his wife, especially when she's surrounded by three men. It makes me smile at how predictable Marco is, how protective he is over River, even though she is more than capable of handling herself.

"Anyway, Beautiful, you were amazing. How did it feel?"

"Like Heaven—"

"If *that* felt like Heaven, Treacle, then just you wait 'til I get my hands on you."

The growls I'm expecting from Enzo and Tyler over Devon's comment don't come. Instead, their gazes heat as they slowly nod in agreement; a development I'm not sad about.

"I can take the hint when it's there. Devon, nice to get to know you a little tonight. Tyler, Enzo, all three of you better look after this woman here and treat her like the queen she is, because if you don't, you'll *wish* Marco was dealing with your punishments. Got it?"

This woman. I love her. I can't help giggling at the looks on all three faces now giving their full attention to River. Respect, awe, and amusement reflects in each of their gazes.

"You got it, Dollface." Devon salutes her before turning his deep blue eyes back to me.

"Understood." Tyler tilts his head respectfully before following suit and fixing his deep brown pools on me.

Enzo just nods once before he too moves his gaze to mine.

This room just became ten times hotter and I swear if I wasn't already dripping with sweat from dancing, I'd be in a pool from their looks alone.

River turns, kissing me on the cheek and softly whispering, "I love you," into my ear as she walks away, probably to go straight up to her office to find my brother.

"You gonna sit down or are you ready to dance some more for us, Treacle?"

"I should go and get changed fir—"

It's Tyler who whips his hand out, gripping me by the waist and pulling me onto his lap, causing a little surprised yelp to escape. Devon and Enzo are sitting on the opposite side of the booth and, as I'm encased in Tyler's arms, his very erect cock digging deliciously into my back, Devon ducks under the table to grab my feet, passing one off to

Enzo before he begins smoothing his palm up and down my calf.

Enzo's fingers move in small circles around my ankle, Tyler's warm breath is against my neck, and I'm in fucking Heaven right now. But it's still so confusing to me how these three strong and powerful men are okay with sharing me like this.

"You were fucking beautiful on that stage, Gumdrop."

"He's not wrong, Treacle. You were fucking glorious to watch. And we're the ones who get to keep you."

Enzo silently agrees with Tyler and Devon, a small smile tipping the corners of his plump lips.

"Okay, I'm just going to say it. How are you all okay with this?" It probably isn't the time nor place for this question, but it's on my mind and just kind of popped out.

Surprisingly, Enzo is the first to speak.

"You deserve the world, Madelina. They make you happy, they can stay."

"What he said." Tyler's words vibrate through his chest at my back and I look to Devon, interested in his take on this.

His face, as usual, is full of amusement and warmth, his blue eyes practically twinkling with mischief.

"Well, my little Treacle Tart, my brother-husbands are right. You deserve the world. One man was never gonna be enough for a woman like you. So you get three." His wink sends a tingle straight to my clit, making me push my thighs together to ease the building ache.

"But we haven't even—"

"I was giving you the time you needed." Devon's face turns more serious than ever before as he leans forward, still gripping my foot in his palms. "And you've had more than enough time. Lads, I need a chat with our girl, so I'm stealing her away for as long as it takes to give her at least three orgasms." He doesn't take his eyes off of mine while he speaks and I feel Tyler's grip around my waist loosen as Devon stands.

Enzo squeezes my foot before lowering it to the floor, raising his brows knowingly at me with a sexy as fuck glint in his eyes.

"Have fun, Gumdrop. We'll be waiting."

Devon grabs my hands and pulls me to standing. Before I can say a word, his lips are on mine in a searing kiss. A sharp slap on my ass makes me jump. When I realize it was Tyler and not Devon, a thrill flows through me at the thought of all three of them working together. Heated growls of lust come from the two sitting men as Devon groans into my mouth, his tongue battling mine for dominance and winning.

"You're so fucking sexy." Devon speaks over my kiss-swollen lips before giving me that devilish grin and flashing his knee-weakening dimple.

The world is suddenly upside down and I squeal as I'm thrown over his shoulder, him holding onto my ass as he makes his way to the backstage door. Enzo is giving me one of those smiles he reserves just for me and Tyler turns to wink. All I can do is finger-wave at them as I'm hauled away by the caveman.

Mimi, the head of security for Rapture, casually makes her way over to halt Devon in his tracks, her concern for my safety prominent. I wouldn't want to get on her bad side because I've seen her throw men five-times her size out of this place.

"It's okay, Mimi. He's my... er..." Devon's body shakes a little as he clearly tries not to laugh at my uncomfortable explanation. I know what I'd like us to be, and I'm well aware of the position I'm in right now, but it feels too soon to call him my boyfriend. Although, he did refer to him and the others as brother-husbands. Just thinking about his ridiculous remark makes me smile.

"I'm her boyfriend, Doll."

Ignoring him, Mimi addresses me directly. "Lina, is this what you want?" I love that she's double checking for my safety, taking her job seriously as always.

Before I am able to answer, she holds a finger to her earpiece, listening to someone on the other end.

"Let me down, caveman."

"Since when did I get demoted from Batman? Batman is much cooler than caveman."

"Okay, you can be Batman again if you let me down. I've got legs, I can walk."

"But this is so much more fun. I just have to turn my head and I get a face full of arse. Why would I give that up?"

Heat warms my cheeks with the way he speaks to me, like he's in awe of every part of me and can never get enough.

"Like I said... caveman."

"This caveman wants a taste of this juicy rump. You better get Ms. Trunchbull's pretty sister out of the way or I'm gonna have to take you right here."

"You can't do that. This is a respectable club and it belongs to my sister-in-law."

"Well I wanna do very *un*-respectable things to you and I don't wanna wait."

Mimi clearing her throat brings our attention back to the world outside of us, and she's smirking. "River has given the all-clear. You can go through to your dressing room. She said to tell big D to make sure he keeps it in his pants until you get there."

"Big D, ey? Have you been talking about me with your friends, Treacle?"

"Incorrigible!"

"Have fun, Lina. Good to see you back." Mimi turns and walks away, that knowing smirk still on her face.

"To the dressing room." I laugh at Devon as he whisks me away through the backstage door then pauses. "Shit, where's your dressing room?"

"I'm surprised you don't already know."

"Stop being a brat or you'll have to wait even longer for those orgasms I promised you." He nips at the top of my thigh, where my sequin panties stop over my diamante fishnets. "Dressing room."

Part of me wants to not tell him, to let him punish me for being a brat, but the other part needs us to be in a room where that's possible first. Clearly, that side wins out.

"Third door on the left."

"Good girl." His hand on my ass moves around so his fingers slide between my clenched thighs, and he gently rubs, putting pressure on my clit and making me jump at the sensation. Just as quickly, his fingers are gone and he's clutching my ass cheek once more as he heads toward my dressing room.

The door clicks behind him and suddenly I'm nervous. It's not a small space, but it's also not very large. Big enough for a dressing table, a small closet, an ensuite, and a deep-red three-seater sofa for me to chill on between sets. Every dancer is assigned their own room for comfort, definitely not for what I'm sure is about to go down in here.

Devon slowly slides me down his front, never taking his hands from me, making eye contact as soon as my feet touch the floor.

"You, my little Treacle Tart, have invaded my mind since the moment I laid eyes on you." He takes a step forward and walks me around so my back is now to the door instead of his. "There was never a moment that I doubted you'd be mine."

I go to protest, to remind him that isn't how this can work. Worry begins to spread now at the thought he wants me all for himself. Maybe I jumped the gun by assuming this could work with the four of us, too optimistic that a girl's dreams really could come true...

"I can see your beautiful little mind working. You don't need to worry, Treacle, I know you come as a package deal. One I'm all too willing to accept, but this first time..." He pauses and breathes me in, the wooden door at my back easing the flush no doubt covering my skin. "This first time, you're all mine."

His mouth descends on me and he bites my bottom lip before sliding his tongue into my mouth and groaning, pushing his hands to the sides of my face, his fingers in my hair adding to the punishing kiss.

Devon consumes me, taking away my ability to overthink, to worry, to experience anything other than all that is him. It feels like only a few short seconds have passed when he pulls away again, resting his forehead against mine and breathing just as heavily as I am.

It's like he's a man starved and the only thing that can fulfill him is me. We've been together before, but it was only a couple of hazy blowjobs and that amazing few days we spent mostly sleeping and eating. Like my own personal kind of rehab.

If he really wanted me, he could have easily taken me then. As we try to control our breaths, my eyes remain closed and doubt begins to creep in.

"Devon?" My voice is timid, barely a whisper. I don't want to ask but I'm trying to get back to me, to speaking what's on my mind rather than burying my head in the sand.

"What's up, Treacle?"

"Why haven't you tried to have sex with me before now?" I may be being presumptuous, but that's exactly what I'm expecting this to turn into.

"Oh, my beautiful princess. Open your eyes and look at me." I do as he asks, his tone brokering no argument. "Don't you ever doubt yourself. You're fucking amazing and my balls have turned blue waiting for this day. You weren't ready for me yet. I'm a different breed."

"Ever the romantic." I'm unable to contain my grin, every fiber of my being telling me to give myself to this man, knowing he is the final piece to my fucked up puzzle of happiness.

"If you want romance, Rich Boy is your man."

He claims my lips again, a hand sliding over my chest to rest against my throat, and I can't help running my fingers over his tight, muscled arms. The black T-shirt he's wearing hugs his body in all the right places and I'd be doing a disservice to women all over the world if I didn't appreciate that by touching every part of him.

The kiss is over too soon and he rubs his nose against mine before gently nipping my lips.

"I'm going to tie you up, have you at my mercy. Do you think you're ready for that, my princess?"

His tone is deep, low, and I almost melt at his demand and question all at once. For someone who always has something to say, at the moment, there's nothing. I have no words, afraid they'll come out a panting mess and I'll drool at his feet. So I just nod, eagerly, ready for anything this man wants to do with me, because I have zero doubts it's going to be good... and he did promise three orgasms.

"Words, Treacle."

Damnit.

"Yes, I'm ready."

I yelp as he spanks my ass, the sharp pain making my clit throb and my pulse race. I know what he wants, but that bratty side of myself wants to see what he'll do if I don't comply.

"What was that for?" Pouting at him and batting my lashes does the trick, his lust-filled eyes widening just a fraction as he slowly grins.

"Oh, so you wanna play brat, do ya?"

"I would never..." Another spank in the same place as last time.

"Strip me down." Now *that's* surprising, but I'm all too happy to comply, gripping the bottom of his T-shirt and slowly pulling it up to reveal his tattooed chest covered in delicious ridges I want to lick.

Devon's eyes stay on me as I pull the T-shirt over his head and begin to unbuckle his jeans. Rather than making two trips, I push his boxers down with his jeans and slide his boots off at the same time. Then he pushes his fingers into the back of my head and grips my hair, encouraging me to straighten up again instead of sucking his large, studded dick into my mouth.

"Ah ah ah. No treats for you, yet. Your turn." Reaching down, he cups my pussy, pushing his fingers into the material covering me before sliding his hand away and grunting in satisfaction. "Already so wet for me." Devon moves to sit in the center of the sofa, his legs spread and arms behind his head, completely confident in his naked form.

"Fine." If he's not going to strip me down himself, he can wait a little longer.

Slowly, I unbuckle my shoes and step out of them before reaching around to unclip my jeweled necklace.

"The longer you make me wait, the longer you wait for your first orgasm. Up to you, Babydoll."

The smug fucker, I believe him too.

Narrowing my eyes at him, I move faster, removing my bra-top, quickly followed by my panties and fishnets, leaving me bare before him. I hold my arms out to show him I'm done, waiting for my next instruction.

"Good girl. Now get me some rope."

"Wha—?"

"No questions." He raises a brow at me, daring me to go against him, and I swear my ovaries are having a party down there.

I don't actually have any rope in here but I *do* have plenty of ribbon, that will have to do. Pulling a long, thick length of black ribbon from my dressing table drawer, I saunter over to him, dangling it over him as I stand between his thick thighs.

The tattoos across his body are mesmerizing and I'm looking forward to the day I can explore them properly. His cock is standing to attention, the tiny silver balls something I can't wait to experience inside me.

"Palms together."

"Wh—?"

"Are you questioning me, my little brat?"

"Never."

He's yet to touch my naked body—except for spanking my ass—and the anticipation is driving me fucking insane.

"Palms together." His firm tone makes me want to melt into a puddle at his feet, so I comply, biting my tongue and smirking.

Devon shakes his head, grabbing the ribbon and folding it in half before wrapping it once around my wrists. The material is soft against my skin as he loops it into a knot and I watch in fascination as he concentrates on wrapping it around my thumbs and fingers in an elaborate tie I've never seen before.

"It's called a Prayer Tie. Thought I'd start you out with something simple, but I promise we'll play with ropes when I have the proper equipment."

"Okay." I'm quick to answer, excited at what else he can do with ropes because this simple hand tie already has me a panting mess for him.

"Okay, what?" There's mischief in his eyes, the light from the lamp in the corner of the room reflecting in his blue irises.

"Okay, Daddy D." Fuck knows where that came from, but calling him sir feels disrespectful to Tyler.

We both freeze at my words, his hungry eyes searching my features, assessing me, trying to hold himself back. I can see it in the tightening of his jaw and the fire burning in his dark-blue irises. He's turned on but he also has questions.

I'm sure there's a conversation that needs to be had about this newly born kink but that time is definitely not now.

"Well, it's better than 'old man', right?"

"Ooh, you cheeky little brat."

"*Daddy's* cheeky little brat."

"Oh fucking Hell, you're gonna make me bust a nut before I'm buried deep inside your wet cunt, aren't ya?" Quickly, his hands move to grip my hips and he pulls me down on top of him, lifting my tied palms over his head and leaving my breasts in his face as I stumble forward a little. "Your tits are fucking glorious." He punctuates his statement by sucking a nipple into his mouth, flicking at it with his tongue and biting down hard enough to make me flinch.

Palming my ass, he squeezes both cheeks tightly, pulling them apart and moving his fingers between my crack. One hand moves between my legs, finding my wet pussy ready and waiting for anything he has to give. The buildup has been so intense that I'm afraid I might burst as soon as he touches my clit.

"So fucking wet." He moves to the other nipple, sliding a finger inside my pussy and making every nerve ending in my body prickle with desire. "I was gonna make you wait for the first one, but I think I'm gonna come like a pre-teen if I do that, so you better sit on my cock before that happens."

"Oh shit, yes!" The studs lining his cock scrape against my walls as I slowly lower myself onto him and, dear God, he's so fucking big.

Before he's fully seated, he thrusts up into me, letting out a growl of satisfaction. One hand reaches up, nestling in my hair as he pulls my head toward his and claims my swollen lips again. His other hand remains on my ass, the tip of a finger pushing gently against my hole, and he continues to thrust up into me.

It's fast, it's rushed, the tingling orgasm already building in the depths of my stomach as we fuck like starved beasts. With my hands fastened behind his head, he has me exactly where he wants me, unable to move away—not that I would.

His finger breaches my hole and he pushes it inside at the same time as he sucks my tongue into his mouth, then he moves his lips across my jaw, nipping at my neck and driving me crazy with desire. I want to move my hands, to touch him, to discover him, to grasp at him...

"You're fucking beautiful." His words are like a whispered prayer into my ear as he continues to nip and lick at my sensitive flesh. They're like the detonator to my orgasm, because it's now impossible to hold back.

"Fuck, yes!" It's coming and I'm not in control. My whole body tenses as an orgasm tears through me and I yell, loudly, attempting to squeeze my thighs together—which is obviously impossible with this god-like creature between my legs.

As I cry out, Devon's thrusts get sharper until he grunts a, "Fuck!" Stilling inside me, he kisses me again, but this time it's slow and sensual as he strokes his fingers down my face. "Fucking perfection."

"Mmm." It's all my voice will allow me to do, the only noise I'm capable of making right now.

Devon chuckles as I practically fall against him, our sweat-covered bodies still joined, and I can feel him hardening inside me again as he begins to slowly rotate his hips.

"One down, two to go, Treacle."

Chapter Twenty

Tyler

The Chef: We're ready for you.

"Bout fucking time." Raising a brow at Enzo's grumbled words, I slide my phone into the inside pocket of my jacket and down the last drops of my top shelf bourbon before turning to fully face the man.

"You know, you're like an addict when it comes to Lina." I watch as his eyes become slits, the creases multiplying at the corners, and wait for him to snark something back to me.

"Right, because you're immune to her?" He has a point but I can't say it's exactly the same thing. Our addictions are equally potent but for different reasons and in different ways.

"I'm more of an alcoholic for her, if you will." It's his turn to raise a brow as he reaches into the back pocket of his jeans and takes out his wallet.

"You're a pretentious little fuck, aren't you? Is this your way of pulling rank on me?" I'm taken aback by his off-the-cuff remark and, for a moment, it distracts me from the original conversation.

"What the hell does that mean? What rank am I pulling?" We're in two different worlds, two distinctly different areas of expertise. I buy companies and turn them over for profit while Enzo is the reason the Mancinis are safe. He's been Marco's detail and right-hand man for decades.

"Forget it, Lina's waiting." Fuck this, I'm not going into this thing if there's even the tiniest resentment happening between the men in her life.

Placing my hand on his shoulder, I squeeze to get his attention, the muscles beneath my fingers flexing and stiffening like he's two seconds away from knocking me out cold. Which he could, by the way. His right hook is legendary, or so Marco tells me.

"Answer me." Without conscious thought, I realize I've used my dominant voice, which is usually reserved for Lina, but this feels important. It feels right. In fact, his muscles relent under my touch. Not completely but enough for me to notice it.

"Rich educated guy versus the charity case. Madelina is my crack while she's your, what? Chardonnay?" He rolls his eyes at me and my inner Dom wants to slam his face against the bar and hold him there until he apologizes. I realize this is not the ideal place to be having a conversation that—clearly—has years-long baggage to it, but I'm not stepping a foot into Lina's dressing room until we've got our shit together.

So I do what I do best. Stepping up to him, our chests inches apart, my lips close enough to his ear that he can hear my words as clear as fucking crystal.

"I was thinking more like a deep, ruby, Bordeaux aged to perfection. So potent that when you bring the cork to your nose, you can taste the red velvet on your tongue. When you swallow the first drops you can feel that tiny burn in your chest like a beacon of pleasure." When I pull back, Enzo's eyes are dilated, his breathing heavy and his mind clearly on a long-legged beauty whose pussy should be choking our cocks right about now.

Instead, I'm putting out fires before they burn down our futures.

We are eye to eye now, my words coming out clear. "She's your drug because she makes you high, forcing you out of your deep, dark cave and getting you out into the sunlight. Me? She's my wine because she's like a soothing balm to my overly-active mind. It never stops, it's always going, going, going. But with her? I can breathe. I can think." Enzo doesn't speak but I can see understanding in the way his entire body relaxes. He'll probably never admit it but I'm sure he agrees with me.

"So what does that make the chef?" His question makes me grin because, just like for everything else, I've thought about this for hours.

"He's an adrenaline junkie and she's his most extreme sport. That guy would jump off a cliff if only to touch her once." Enzo's smirk may as well be a full-out grin. He gets it.

"Tyler Fucking Walker." He shakes his head like all of this is ridiculous, yet he can't deny how much sense it makes.

"We good?"

It's Enzo's turn to lean into me, crowding me as the bartender slides his change on the pristine counter. "Yeah, we're good, but if you ever touch me like that again, I'll break your fucking wrist."

I grin, a pretentious, cocky one that is sure to get a rise from him, before saying what needs to be said. "No, you won't. And we both know it."

My phone vibrates in my inner pocket and when I look at the message I snort.

The chef: If you two are done fuckin' about, I've got a very horny little pussy here waiting. Keep it up and you won't be tasting her tonight.

"Our little Gumdrop is getting impatient, let's go." I throw down a fifty and nod at the bartender before heading for Lina's changing room. I know exactly where it is, been there before with the hope that she'd returned to dancing back when she was shutting me out.

It doesn't take long to reach our destination. I turn the knob then push the door open enough for Enzo to walk in. I follow him, then close the door and lock it. The four of us in this small space almost feels like a claustrophobic's nightmare scenario, but just being in her presence quiets the constant buzzing of my mind.

"'Bout fuckin' time."

I chuckle at Devon's words, the exact same ones Enzo mumbled earlier when I received the text message. In many ways they are so different, but they're so similar in everything that matters.

"We were having a meaningful conversation." Lina's eyes widen at my admission, like she's half scared of what we said to each other but curious as fuck at the same time. She's curled up in Devon's arms, her legs pulled up to his ribs with her feet tucked into the back cushions of the couch. Gloriously naked except for the robe he's draped over the visible parts of her, she doesn't try to lift her head, as though she were too exhausted to bother moving.

"Right, well, as you can see, our Treacle has been fully satisfied." The thrusting of his hips gets our attention and I realize he's probably still buried inside her. Fuck, I wish I could see it. My dick has an immediate reaction to the idea, pressing painfully against my zipper. "Which is good because I've got shit to say."

Enzo leans back against her dressing table while I slide my hands inside the pockets of my slacks, leaning casually against the door. He's got our attention and I hope it's not bad news.

"I've got business in London so I'll be leaving in the next few days. While I'm go—" Lina interrupts him, her head snapping up and her smile like crystal in sunlight.

"I haven't been to London in forever!" Before anyone can process what the fuck is happening, Lina is pulling herself up, Devon's eyes almost crossing, confirming my earlier thoughts of him still being tucked away inside her pussy. "Oh my God! I need to tell River so she doesn't freak out. Also, she can tell Marco so he doesn't freak out. Oh!" Sliding her silky robe back on, she whirls around and points to Enzo. "He won't be too happy about you not being there for a while. Oh, Tyler!" Now she's looking at me with stars in her eyes like she's five and Mickey Mouse just kissed her cheek. "We're gonna need your jet and do you think we could stay in that little hotel you told me about? The one where the London Eye is right there at the tip of your finger?"

It's like, half a mile away but who am I to kill her dreams?

"Uh, Treacle—"

"I know, I know, last time Tyler lent me his jet..."

"Madelina, I can't—"

"Don't worry about Marco, I'll take care of him. He'll listen to River."

"Gumdrop." I use my voice, the one that always gets her attention.

"Yes, Sir?"

Fuck, my dick is now rock hard and anything I was going to say to her that could potentially ruin this high for her dies on the tip of my tongue.

"When do we fly out?"

Going into work on a Sunday is the last thing I wanted to do but with Lina's excitement last night, I had to make sure everything was in place at the office. In fact, I could take advantage of this trip to land a deal I've been working on for a few months now. It's not ideal and there are a million other things I need to be doing here instead of planning to cross the Atlantic on a whim, but it's physically impossible for me to refuse Lina anything. After it was clear that we were taking a weird family vacation to London, Enzo and I went our separate ways and left Lina and Devon to their own devices. I had a feeling that the next time we'd see each other, she'd finally taste us all at once.

Leaning back in my chair, I feel a smile tick up the corners of my mouth just thinking about her reaction last night. Her excitement was palpable and for the first time in months, I saw my Gumdrop again. I saw her bright eyes wanting to live again and, despite the fact Devon and Enzo were most likely plotting my death behind their murderous stares, I couldn't think of anything worse than extinguishing that shimmer of hope on her face.

"Okay, Tyler, get your ass back to work. Call the pilots for the flight plan and get these contracts in order."

Talking to myself out loud helps me to organize my thoughts, it's a mechanism I've had since I was a kid.

As though thoughts of my childhood physically summon my mother, my eyes dart to my buzzing cell phone shaking around my desk, the name "Mom" flashing across the screen.

"Mother, I was just thinking about you." Well, it was more about her techniques to help me concentrate but, as Devon would say, tamayto, tomahto. Suzannah Walker is nothing if not a fixer. When she saw that my mind was like a computer with fifteen tabs opened at once, she researched for months, wanting to find the perfect strategies to keep me focused.

"Tyler, darling, I haven't heard from you in ages. Your father and I were getting worried. How are you?" Her tenderness and concern always bring a smile to my face. There are a million horror stories out there about rich parents treating their children like nuisances instead of loving them unconditionally, but I can firmly say, I'm the exception. If anything, my sister Angelica and I were cherished like gold during a market crash. When she died, our grief was overwhelming. It was a living, breathing entity wrapped around our souls and as I would imagine any parent would, their entire focus landed on only me. Still today, I am their priority in all things.

That singular focus is exactly how I feel about Lina.

"I've been busy, distracted, running around trying to rule the world. You know, normal stuff." It's our running joke.

"Yes, I saw the article about Satan's Spawn, a few weeks back. She's playing golf with the bigwigs now? I didn't think she could be out in the sunlight. Isn't that supposed to kill creatures like her?" My mother was never a fan of Cora's. When I proposed, she tried really hard to stay out of it, to let me make my own choices. Except one night, about two weeks before the wedding, she'd had a bit to drink and cornered me in the upstairs hall of their Hampton's home, telling me I was making the biggest mistake of my life.

Obviously, I ignored her. Never made that mistake again.

"Not my circus, Mom."

"Well, it is if she's speaking on your company's behalf, isn't it?"

I sigh, softly, hoping she doesn't hear me.

"You're right. I'll talk to Brett about it."

"Oh, please. That boy lost his balls somewhere between building an empire and tripping into bed with the devil. Just... be careful. I don't trust her." We've had this conversation a million times and just like every other time, I reassure her that everything is fine and that if all else fails, I still have one hundred percent control of the company she signed over to me. Which reminds me...

"How are you feeling?" My question always holds a certain heaviness to it. Painful-yet-sweet- memories.

"I'm good, darling boy. I'm good. Had a doctor's appointment yesterday for my yearly check-up and I'm still in remission so you don't need to worry about me. It's why I'm calling, to be honest." My relief is palpable, as always.

"Thank God. Dad must be relieved." Their love? It's for the ages. It's the thing that makes me want to settle down, create a family. Hell, I'd go for a white picket fence, but New York City isn't the best place for that.

"How long are you going to deflect, Tyler? Last time we spoke, you said you and Lina Mancini were back to seeing each other. Is everything okay?" Well, I suppose I should tell her about our trip, then.

"It's all good, Mother. In fact, we're taking a little vacation to London on Tuesday for about a week." My family and the Mancinis have always been close. Marco's family has donated large sums—I won't pretend it doesn't help their money laundering, but I choose to ignore it—to my mother's breast cancer charity.

"Oh, that's wonderful news! You'll be cold, it's dreadful there this time of year, what with the rain and everything." She hates rain yet won't leave the north east.

"Oh, you mean it'll be the same as here?"

"Yes. But if I'm honest, your father and I do love England. I wish you had time to stop by, I've knitted a beanie for you. It's all the craze among the Millennials." Oh, for fuck's sake. "Have you knitted anything lately, my boy? It does help settle your mind, doesn't it?" It does, knitting was our down time when mother was in chemotherapy. I made a shit ton of scarfs that year.

Our conversation slowly drifts to her new friends, her charity work, and all the other subjects we love to talk about.

Fifteen minutes later, we hang up, and I may be a grown ass man but I already miss her voice.

Placing the folder with the signed documents in the outgoing box for Clara, my secretary, I slide over the profiles of our new employees. I like to know who works here, greet them by name when I can and, because I don't always see everyone every day, I make sure to keep up with the new hires. Thankfully, they are few. I pride myself in treating my teams fairly, which means our turnover is slight. My father gave me the most valuable advice I could ask for when I first started hiring. Keeping staff happy is about respect and teamwork without taking your eye off the ball. It's important to make sure they know where the company is headed, how they can help to achieve our goals and, of course, showing my appreciation for their hard work.

So, knowing their names from day one is just a small gesture on my part. No one knows I do this, I've kept it my little secret all this time because nobody likes a boss patting himself on the back.

This file has six new employees, which is more than usual. I wonder what happened, did I miss retirements or did anyone quit? Reaching for my Post-it notes, I ask my secretary about this and stick it on the outgoing box as well. Flipping through the new files, I frown.

Ventura McBeth is now working in IT. What happened to Jordan and Kelly?

My phone buzzes on the table, again, and I grin when I see Lina's name pop up.

"Missing me already?" My voice is two octaves below normal. That's what her presence does to me.

"So much so that Devon's fingers are in my cunt." Fucking hell, she's trying to actively kill me.

"Is that so?"

"Yes, Sir." She drags out the last syllable and I can see the scene in my mind's eye. Lina lying on her back while the chef pumps his fingers in and out of her hot pussy.

"Put the phone down so I can hear how wet you are." I know she's obeyed when I hear the sounds of her juices with every push and pull from Devon.

"Spread 'em wider, Treacle. Show Daddy D how badly you want to be fucked." Looking around my office, I wonder how important all of this truly is when, instead, I could be burying my face in her cunt and drinking from the fountain of pleasure. "That's right, suck in my fingers, take what is yours."

Fuck this shit. Unzipping my pants, I pull out my cock and wrap my fingers around my shaft, keeping my attention solely on the sounds Lina is gifting me with from the other end of the line.

"Oh, God, yes!"

I pull a little harder, jack myself off a little faster. Eyes closed, mouth open, I imagine Lina's spread-open legs, her hips fucking Devon's hand as she tries to top from the bottom.

The sound of flesh against flesh, with a clear yelp that follows, tells me Devon isn't allowing such bratty behavior.

"Who's in charge here, Lina?" He growls his words and the whimper she offers him makes the head of my cock weep with lust.

"You are." I barely hear her, her words are soft and airy like she's just whispered them.

"And who am I?"

"Daddy D." I shake my head at the idea that he's her Daddy, but who the fuck am I to judge anyone's kinks? In fact, I like that we all have our own preferences, it means that when we do end up in the same bed, Lina's orgasms will be that much more potent. And, fuck me, watching Lina come is my second favorite thing in the whole world. The first being my tongue scooping up all her cum from said orgasms.

As he continues to fuck her, his fingers making sexy music to my ears, I brace myself for climax, checking to see that I have a box of tissues nearby.

I do.

My hips thrust off my chair as I tighten my hold on my dick, pumping up and down and running my thumb over the leaky slit at the head of my cock. I'm almost there, all I need is that final push.

On the other end of the call, I hear Lina's cry to the heavens, begging for more, for harder, for God to save her, and my control flies out of the window.

Covering my cock with the palm of my hand, I shake and grunt as my dick releases stream after stream of cum.

My breaths are heavy, my eyes still closed as I picture Devon bringing his juice-covered fingers to his mouth and licking up his reward. Fuck, I need to be inside her. And soon.

"Don't say I never did anything for ya, mate." Devon's chuckle has me smiling as I hear the click of the phone call ending.

Well, I guess I need to clean up and get ready for what will most likely be the greatest flight to Britain ever.

The mile high club is about to witness a whole new level of kink.

Chapter Twenty-One

Devon

Fucking sisters.

Thinking I could walk away from my family forever was clearly a deluded wish, because here I am, on a private jet owned by my girlfriend's boyfriend, on my way back to London. The last time I saw my mum, she was in tears, begging me to stay, grateful that I'd finally taken her husband's life—my dad's life—but I broke her heart and left anyway. It was too much; the responsibility of the family, the businesses, the fucking drama. I needed to go, to live for myself for once, to know who I am without the expectations, the pressure. Everyone wanted a piece of me, be it money, attention, more this, more that... always more.

"Hey, D, you okay?" My body immediately relaxes at the sound of Lina's soft velvet tone by my ear, the feel of her delicate fingers wrapped around my bicep, the rich, sweet scent that invades my nose, and I turn to look at the vision in white beside me.

"I'm good, Treacle."

She raises a perfect dark brow at me and purses those fuckable lips, telling me she doesn't believe a word, but I won't ruin this trip for her. It's just a few days, a week max. She has Thing 1 and Thing 2 to keep her occupied while I deal with business, she doesn't need to worry herself with my shit.

"Hmm, why don't I believe you?"

"Because you're a sensitive little sausage with a huge heart." Her brows furrow in confusion, making me smile as I pull her closer to kiss her forehead.

"What was that about a little sausage?" Tyler's hand is on her thigh as he leans forward to look at me with a smirk from where he's sitting on the sofa-style seat to the left of Lina.

"Talkin' *about* ya, not *to* ya, mate."

Lina doesn't hide her chuckle at my comment very well, which causes the giant Italian sitting opposite her and massaging her feet to smile, just a little. That smile I've seen on his face when he looks at our girl, and I know he's feeling the same as me.

We're lucky bastards.

"Are you laughing, Gumdrop?" Tyler's mock-horror turns into him tickling her ribs, and it's a side to him I actually enjoy. I haven't seen it often yet, but the more time we all spend together, the more comfortable we're becoming. We each have the same goal, to treat this woman giggling between us like a fucking goddess.

"Never, I wou—" She cuts herself off, giggling again and trying to crawl into my lap away from Tyler's twitchy fingers.

"Hey, Treacle." I nip at her ear as she sits on my lap, side-on, her feet now curled up onto the plush cream leather seating. Everything that is Lina consumes me, she soothes my soul and I've just remembered the bag full of goodies I brought for the flight to keep my mind from the destination.

"Hey." She looks up at me and smiles before gently placing her lips on mine, as if she's completely unable to help herself. I'm not going to complain, but as my tongue connects with hers, she ends the kiss just as quickly as it began, jumping out of my lap to go and sit in Enzo's.

Smug fucker wraps his arms around her, looking like the cat that got the cream.

"Right, we've got about six and a half hours of flight time left, and I've got a little surprise for everyone." I stand, grabbing my black duffel from the overhead locker, wagging my brows at the three people staring back at me with a mixture of expressions.

Tyler is trying to hide his confusion, Lina's eyes are wide with excitement, and Enzo's as stoic as always, unbothered by my declaration.

"Ooh, what is it?" Surprising Lina just became one of my new favorite things, and I'm vowing, here and now, I'm gonna do it as much as possible. Her simple reaction to something so small is addictive.

"Well, my little Treacle Tart, you and I are about to head into that handy bedroom back there to get prepared before we call the boys in."

"And what if I'm comfortable where I am?" A completely sober and aware Lina is my favorite kind. My dick is hard from her pure sass alone. She snuggles further into Enzo's lap, like he's going to protect her from me.

He won't. I can see the intrigue in his eyes. He wants to know what's in my bag as much as Lina does.

"Enzo, mate, hand her over." I haul the handle of my duffle over my shoulder and open my arms out, Tyler's dark chuckle spurring me on.

We're all still getting to know each other, but with our main focus being this sexy-as-fuck woman, we seem to have come to some kind of mutual agreement and understanding.

"Don't you dare!" The last word is said on a squeal as Enzo silently stands with Lina wrapped tightly in his arms, easily passing her to me. Without putting up a fight, she removes her hands from around Enzo's neck and clings onto me instead. "Caveman."

"We discussed this. It's Batman, Treacle." I wink down at her before turning and heading toward the bedroom. "I'll call you in when she's ready, fellas."

The bedroom is small, barely enough space for the large king-size bed in the center and large leather chair in one corner. Seems our billionaire has a thing for watching if the set-up in here is anything to go by. The room is decorated in luxurious creams with gold accents, showing just how fucking rich one quarter of our little pack is.

I mean, I'm not exactly poor, but Tyler takes the fucking biscuit. At least he's not a complete prick about it like some of the rich twats I met in New York when first trying to build my restaurant.

Placing Lina down onto the bed, I pull my duffle from my shoulder and put it next to her, silently sliding the zip open.

"What's in there?"

"Patience, young Padawan."

"Oh no, don't tell me you're a Star Wars nerd, old man..."

"Old man *and* nerd? Treacle, you wound me!" I hold a hand to my chest and dramatically fall to the bed, crushing her beneath me. "I'm too old to stand, I need resuscitating, get the blood flowing through these old bones again..." I plant a long kiss on her perfect red-stained lips before rolling away, one hand on my head and the other on my heart, giving her my best pout.

"Dramatic much?" Her addictive laugh as she straddles me makes me grab her throat and pull her back to my eager mouth, wanting to catch every sound for myself.

"There, that's better." Spinning us over again, so she's now underneath me, I grin down at my woman. Her dark hair is spread out, like veins of ink running over the cream bed sheets, her silvery eyes sparkle like diamonds in the light, and her perfect tits are begging to be set free and put on display.

I have the perfect Shibari tie in mind for just this occasion.

"I'm not gonna hog you all to myself for too long, Treacle. Just enough time to prepare you for us." With a chaste kiss, I sit up, grabbing my bag and pulling out the first length of jute rope. Lina's eyes widen as I pull out a few more lengths, placing them neatly side by side on the bed.

"That's a lot of rope." She moves to rest on her elbows, curiously analyzing my actions.

"I want you to strip for me, then stand at the end of the bed when you're ready."

"Yes, Daddy D." Her playful tone makes me smile and the name is almost as unexpected as the last time she said it, but fuck is it hot when she calls me that. Excitedly, she practically jumps from the bed and starts taking off her clothes, starting with the low-cut tight white top she's wearing, then unbuttoning her light-blue jeans and rolling them down her legs.

With the pre-prepared ropes I need on the bed, I place the duffel on the floor in the corner of the room, just in time to watch my eager beaver rid herself of her lacey knickers.

"Done. Now what?" Hands on her hips, completely naked, she's every man's wet dream.

"Cheeky." Picking up the first length of rope, I begin by folding it in half and wrapping it under her tits, looping the length through the bight at the center of her spine. Immediately my mind is calm as I work the rope, concentrating on making sure it's snug, but not so tight that she can't breathe. Leaning down from behind her, I whisper in her ear, "Do you trust me, Treacle?" After experimenting with the simple hand tie in the club and seeing her reaction to it, I know she's okay with this, but I need to make sure.

Shibari isn't always about sexual pleasure, in fact it's often not about that at all for some people. For me, it's like meditation, a way to clear my thoughts, concentrating on the beauty I'm able to create with a few knots.

Lina takes a deep breath, and for a really brief moment I'm unsure of what she's going to say.

"I really do, yeah."

Thank fuck for that.

Balls firmly back in place, I spank her pert little arse, enjoying the high-pitched sound she lets out as she jumps.

"What was that for?"

"Yes, what, Lina?"

She shivers and I watch her body as her thighs close together. "Yes, Daddy D. I trust you."

"Good girl."

She really is down for this, the bratty attitude she loves to flaunt put aside in anticipation for what I'm doing to her.

Wrapping the rope around her one more time, I tuck it before winding it twice around her front again, this time above her luscious tits with a little loop at the top of her spine. Lina watches in fascination as I work, gently stroking my fingers against her beautiful tanned skin, and her nipples could cut glass, they're so hard.

I really want to suck those pert little things into my mouth and feast on them but I refrain, the wait and suspense for touch an extra addition to the sensations for my woman.

Taking a second piece of rope, I fold it in half like before and loop it together with the first piece, extending the length I'm working with. With a nice little handle now at her back, I bring the rope over her left shoulder and tuck it into the piece beneath her tits, bringing it back up in a V over her right shoulder and tying it into a half hitch at the top of the stem. I finish it off by using the last of the rope in a figure of eight weave on the stem, creating a wider handle to be used when needed.

"Turn around, Treacle." She follows my instruction like a pro, and I admire the beauty in front of me. The simple chest harness looks fucking stunning on her, encasing those perfect tits, every inch of her still accessible and easy to move. "Fucking perfection. We'll try something a little more restraining next time, but we've only got a few hours to play."

"I like it, makes my tits look gre—Oh, fuck, yes!"

I push two fingers into her soaking wet pussy at the same time as biting one of her nipples into my mouth, sucking hard and loving how her body tenses up in pleasure. She scratches her manicured nails across my back, hopefully leaving her mark for all to see, and I suck harder, using my thumb to rub at her swollen clit.

Gripping the stem of the harness, I hold her in place as I thrust my fingers in and out of her pussy, hooking them for that sweet spot. Lina's screams get louder and I know the fuckers in the main cabin can hear. Just a little more teasing...

"Who does this pussy belong to?" I switch to the other nipple, holding it between my teeth until she speaks.

"My kings!"

That answer was unexpected, but fuck me was it perfect.

I bring her closer to orgasm, her knees buckling as I keep holding her in the position I want her. Thumb rubbing, fingers thrusting, tongue flicking, and lips tasting, I could nut in my boxers from this alone. She's fucking perfect and the sounds she's making are the world's best high.

"On the bed, on your knees." My voice is raspy, lust consuming every nerve ending, and I'm trying real hard not to keep her all to myself, worshiping the naked goddess at my mercy.

Her pout as she complies is cute, but she knows that complaining about me stopping right before her orgasm hits will only make it take longer. And it seems we've got our good girl to play with today so she's being compliant... for now.

"Lads, we're ready for ya." I slowly strip, standing at the edge of the bed and gripping the stem of Lina's rope harness so she's on display for them. They've got a nice full-frontal view of me too, but I know they're not paying attention to that when their eyes land on our girl.

"You should probably catch up and get ya kegs off, she's wetter than the Atlantic."

Without waiting for them to undress, I push my fingers inside Lina's pussy and suck her nipple into my mouth again. I fucking love these nipples.

"Move backwards, Baby, let Enzo lie underneath you and sit on his face."

He doesn't question my instruction, lying down and sliding his head between her legs as I move my fingers.

"Oh fuck!" Lina begins grinding against him and I smile, looking to Tyler. He raises a brow at me, as if allowing me to take charge this time, and I nod gently, appreciating the silent agreement we have. I know he likes to be in control as much as I do but, also like me, he's happy to relent when it comes to our princess's orgasms.

"Mouth open, tongue out, Treacle." She complies immediately, already a beautiful, panting mess as Enzo goes to town on her pussy. "You're going to suck Tyler's cock like it's your favorite snack, and don't you dare come until I say so. Understood?"

She nods her head, unable to reply with her tongue eagerly waiting for Tyler's dick. Watching him slide it into her mouth as he stands by the side of the bed has my own cock hardening further.

She sucks dick like a fucking pro. Just imagining the sucking and swirling of her tongue against my own skin has me palming myself, kneeling beside her and sucking that perfect tit into my mouth, grasping and squeezing the other one so it doesn't feel left out.

Her moans and screams are my high, my ever after, my Eden, and I grab the stem of her harness, pulling her up off Enzo's face before she orgasms. Her body had begun shaking, the vibrations a tell-tale sign she's close.

"Nah-ah. Not yet."

Enzo actually growls, gripping her thighs and pulling her back down, and I chuckle. He's such a soft touch when it comes to her orgasms, not as into denial as Tyler and me. That's okay. We're working as a team here, and I'm loving every fucking second.

I go back to playing with her tits, her nipples, perfectly placed within the harness and now covered in my marks. Her movements become more erratic as she grinds against Enzo's face, her screams mixed with Tyler's low grunts tell me they're both about to come.

I'll allow it. She's been a good girl.

"Come now, Babydoll."

"Oh, God! Fuck, yes!" She just about screams out, her body tensing up and her body movements slowing, but she doesn't let up with her mouth. It's still wrapped around Tyler's dick as he stills and pulls out, shooting his load to the back of her throat as she opens up and takes it all, swallowing and sucking the end of his cock to clean it off when he's finished.

I have to stop jacking myself because we're not finished here yet, and if I carry on I'm gonna come all over my hand.

Enzo is still beneath her and she's leisurely moving against his face again. I think the man would die down there given the choice. Tyler grips the back of her head and kneels on the bed beside her, claiming her mouth in a searing kiss that has me slowly rubbing myself again.

"On all fours." I'm too worked up to use all my words. This woman is driving me nuts. "Wanna watch or join in, Rich Boy?"

I know he enjoys both so giving him the option only seems fair. I hope he'll extend the same courtesy to me when he's in charge of play time.

"I'll watch, Chef Boy." He smirks and seats himself in the plush chair in the corner of the room, giving him a perfect view of the bed.

"Enzo, get on your knees in front of her, let her wrap those blood-red lips around your cock and milk you dry."

Wordlessly, he moves into position in front of her and I line myself up with her pussy from behind, slowly easing myself in. More to extend the moment than anything else, because watching the silver balls on my dick disappearing into that pretty little pink pussy is a thing of art.

Fully seated inside her, I spank her arse just to see the pink color taint her perfect skin before gripping the harness stem and making her arch her back. She sucks Enzo into her mouth, squeezing his large thighs and no doubt bruising him with her fingertips. Lucky fucker.

I use my grip on her harness to control her movements, thrusting in and out of her, making my own fingerprint bruises on her thigh. The sounds of her slurping, our bodies slapping, and her juices from her release combined are a thing of beauty, and I push inside my woman fast and hard. Wanting to imprint myself on her soul.

Her pussy pulses around my cock as Enzo stills, spilling himself into her mouth before she screams out with another orgasm of her own. My body isn't my own as I thrust harder, deeper, losing myself in her as my movements become jerky. I yell out in ecstasy as I come inside her, the pleasure rolling through my body in waves and I slow my thrusts, enjoying the silky feel of her walls.

"You're fucking perfect."

The whole fucking Scooby gang insisted on coming with me to the Anchor Pub near the center of Lewisham—one of my family's first establishments bought by my grandfather—to meet my sister, Emma, for a chat about what's going down. I won't say I'm happy about it though because it could be dangerous if any of the Deptford Boys realize I'm back in town.

In aid of leaving in a blaze of glory, I burned down one of their local haunts with two of the fuckers inside. The pricks aren't picky when it comes to dealing to kids and I've never been okay with that.

It smells like stale lager as we step inside and, for a Tuesday night, it's pretty busy. Not a good sign for me.

"Stay by my side, Treacle. You know what to do if it starts to get hairy in here."

My cousin, Johnny, met us with a car at the airport and made sure I'm well prepared for being home. Which means being armed to the teeth because this city is as dangerous for me as New York is for Marco.

Enzo was all too happy to accept a couple of guns, easily sliding them into his chest holster, which he'd worn as if he knew he'd need it. Tyler reluctantly took one and stuffed it into the back of his trousers, mumbling something about offering money to solve the problem, and

Lina... that woman! She made my fucking dick stand to attention with the glint in her eyes as I handed her a gun too, with strict instructions to only use it if shit goes down.

I head straight for the bar, Enzo leading the way as he walks slightly ahead of us, in front of Lina, who is holding my hand. Tyler is just behind her, and I realize we've instinctively formed a protective barrier around her as best we can.

"Three pints of lager and a lemonade and lime for the lady, please, Dave."

"Holy shit, Butcher! When the fuck did you get back?" Dave's smile is contagious, and never did I think I'd have missed his fucking mug. He's been loyal to the family since he was a kid and he's never wanted anything more than to work behind the bar. He's been offered other positions but he says he enjoys the variety and responsibility of being a barman. Can't fault the lad. He does a banging job.

"About an hour ago, mate. Have you seen Emma?"

Dave gets to work pulling our pints after placing a tall glass in front of Lina. She looks at it curiously before taking a sip, raising her eyebrows in surprise and delight at the taste. "Ooh, I like this."

"Knew ya would, Treacle."

"Emma's over in the corner by the pool table." He finishes our drinks and I nod my thanks, handing one each off to Enzo and Tyler before downing half of mine and heading in the direction of my sister.

"I was expecting you half an hour ago, Little Brother." Emma's blonde hair is a few shades lighter than mine and it hangs in waves to her shoulders, looking as though she's run her fingers through it one too many times.

As the only one who inherited our dad's height, I literally look down on all of my sisters, my big sis being no different.

I take in her loose cargo trousers and thick hoodie, noting the dirt marks on her shoulder and sleeves. It's unusual because she's usually so well put together and it puts me on high alert, ensuring Lina is back within our protective unit.

"Well, you know London traffic, Sis. Fucking taxi drivers are menaces. Do I get a hug, or what?"

Emma's smile is so much like Mum's, and now I'm home, I feel guilty for not going to her straight away. She wraps her arms around my waist and squeezes tightly.

"The kids have missed their uncle Devvy almost as much as I have. You need to call more."

"Yeah yeah, Sis. I get it. Guilt trip me with the kiddos, why don't ya? I promise I'll call more, okay? I'll even come and have a visit while we're here."

"They'd love that. Bethany's getting so big now, she's reading all by herself, and Charlie started walking last week. Won't be long before he's running around and causing mischief."

"Good lad, just like his uncle." I laugh as Emma shakes her head and rolls her eyes.

"So, are you going to introduce me to your new friends, or what?"

"Yeah, *Devvy*, where are our introductions?" Lina smiles up at me before turning her attention to my sister. "Hi, I'm Lina. The broody Italian is Enzo, and this is Tyler." She gestures to each of them in turn, stroking a hand down each of their chests before resting her head against my shoulder, and my sister's eyes widen a fraction in amused surprise.

"Okay then. Lucky girl! I'm Emma. Lovely to meet you all."

"Anyway, come on. What's up? Talk to me, Sis."

Picking at the label on her bottle of cider, Emma fidgets and takes a deep breath before looking me in the eyes.

Something isn't right in here but I need to hear what she has to say about Lizzy and Ben.

"Lizzy's besotted with him, Dev. I think she's got that Stockholm Syndrome thing because he took her to get to you. And now... now she won't leave him. She says she loves him." Emma's whispered words are getting louder, more intense, and I can practically feel her pain as she speaks.

When our younger sister, Amelia, left to go and be a bigshot lawyer, followed by the youngest two, Olivia and Sophie leaving to follow their dreams and travel the world, Emma was hit the hardest with missing them. She's cared for all of us in her own way, as the big sister taking on an almost-motherly role, and each time one leaves the nest, she gets a little emptier inside. So whatever Lizzy is going through, I know Emma's feeling all the guilt a person could possibly feel in this situation.

"I tried to reason with her, tried to get her to come round Mum's for a roast, for a cuppa tea even, but nothing. He won't let her leave his side, Dev. It's fucking psychotic. And then... oh, God. I'm so fucking sorry. If I only kept a closer eye on h—"

"Stop that shit right now, Em. It's not your fault."

"But if I'd just stopped it before it all started, then you'd still be off living your best life, and I wouldn't be standing here making a prat out of myself in front of your new friends. And yes, I know I'm being totally rude and haven't even said hello, but this is so bad, Dev. It's all gone proper fucked and Uncle Harry might as well piss in the wind for all the good he's doing to help."

"Who's this posh twat and this big fucker then, Butcher? Got yaself some muscle, have ya?"

Fucking fantastic.

Travis Peters. Cock sucking cunt and one of Ben's errand boys.

Turning away from my sister, I look over to the bar to have it confirmed. Travis is standing there with five other pricks surrounding him, and they all clearly have a death wish. The police around here are paid well, so I have no problems if these twats want a proper fucking shoot out. We might have to cover Tyler a bit, with this not really being his thing, but I trust that the people I walked in here with today will be walking right back out with me.

"I don't need extra muscle, ya puny cunt. What the fuck are you doing in this pub? This ain't your turf." My voice is deep, demanding, and I'm barely containing my anger at this entitled motherfucker.

"It ain't exactly yours no more either, is it, Butcher? Or are ya back now? Oh look, boys, he's brought a pretty little whore back home. You can't tell me she ain't ridden all three of your little dicks. She looks the type."

The six of them laugh and the growls surrounding me get louder. Even my little tigress is primed and ready to pounce on these pricks.

"Shut your cunt mouth and have some fucking respect, Travis. See, that's the difference between me and you. You'd never bag a woman like this one right here because you have no fucking idea how to treat a lady. So why don't you go and crawl back between your mother's legs until you've grown a pair and have figured out what a clitoris is."

Travis's eyes widen at my growled response, and a warmth spreads through my chest at the violence etched on Lina's face. I squeeze her hand before reaching to my belt, ready to grab my dagger or a gun because the fuckers at the bar look like they've got twitchy fingers and I'd bet everything in Rich Boy's accounts that they'd take me to Ben dead or alive.

Chapter Twenty-Two

Enzo

I have been called a psychopath more times than I can count; starting at fifteen when I took my first life. It was life or death, kill or be killed, and I don't regret a second of it. By the time that word had been used on me for the tenth time, I actually looked it up in the Mancini library, one of the six different dictionaries placed by date of publication.

According to Merriam-Webster, a psychopath is "a person having an egocentric and antisocial personality marked by a lack of remorse for one's actions, an absence of empathy for others, and often criminal tendencies."

I remember sitting there, in that dim library where the only light came from the fireplace, and thinking about the words on the page. Yes, I had criminal tendencies but not because I was born violent. I just wanted to survive in a world that wanted me dead. Antisocial? Sure, but only because getting to know people meant talking about my past and that shit is locked up tight and far away. At the end of the day though, I knew it wasn't true. I carry around too much fucking guilt to be a psychopath.

That being said, I've been around them my entire fucking life so, as I stand in the middle of this London pub, my palm on the butt of my gun, I know two things:

One, I'm going to kill that motherfucker who disrespected Madelina and I will have zero remorse for doing it. Two, these cunts—when in Rome and all that shit—are Merriam-Webster descriptions of psychos and getting rid of them is a kindness to the Brits.

"Devon!" As I'm watching the Travis guy, I hear Dev's sister screaming at him a half a second before sound explodes in the pub, the air changing inches from my cheek as though something were whizzing by, most likely, a bullet.

My first instinct is to push Madelina down to the floor but she's already got her gun out, aiming at the now-shattered window.

"Get the fuck down, Madelina." She may be the one calling the shots in the bedroom but when it comes to her safety, she's mine to protect. If only she'd fucking let me.

"I'm fine! Get Tyler to safety!" I don't have time to argue with her, bullets are flying all around this place and I cover my tribe by shooting at the fuckers outside. Devon is going crazed-commando on the guys at the bar, his knife in one hand, his gun shooting out bullets like he has mind control over them.

"Tyler! Get under that table and don't fucking move!" I scream at the guy and, thank fuck, he hears me. Taking cover behind the knocked over table, he pulls out his gun and shoots. Pretty sure he missed all vital organs or even people, but it's helping to cover us. At least Madelina is with him, taking cover from both sides.

Kind of.

In a crouch, one gun aiming at Travis and his merry band of fuckers, but only as a precaution since Devon is going all *Peaky Blinders* on their asses, my other hand is aiming at the last half-dozen fuckers outside.

I have no idea how long we've been at it, my attention too focused on surviving and protecting what's mine, but it sure as fuck feels like an eternity. Glancing back at Devon to see if he's done playing with his food, I can't help the grin on my face.

He's standing behind Travis, who is on his knees, his buddies lying dead at his feet, a big fucking knife at his throat. Two twin streaks of blood are running down his front but the guy is still very much alive and probably pissing his pants.

"We ain't gettin' any younger, mate. Mind pulling a little weight there?" I don't bother to remind him that I've put down a dozen guys while he was playing Brit Rambo in the back, and just fake salute him before running to the entrance to get my sights on the last two assholes still shooting at us without really seeing us.

Fucking amateurs.

One of them is hiding behind his passenger door, which is on the wrong side of the fucking car, and just when he peeks his head out to cover his buddy, I take aim and decorate his forehead with a perfectly round hole.

"Bloody fucking Hell, Butcher. Why d'ya have to kill us all?"

And who the fuck is this whiner?

"Is this guy serious? They come shooting at us and now he's complaining because we shot back?" Devon just shrugs at my words like he doesn't understand either. That, or he just doesn't give two fucks.

"We had orders to take you to Ben, that's it." Again with the douche outside.

"What do you want me to do?" I mean, I'll gladly kill the fucker for putting us in this situation, but hell if I know the code of conduct in the London mafia. If that's even what it's called.

"He put Lina in danger. He dies." I grin at Devon's words. He sounds so much like Marco that I can't help but respect him.

"Um, hello! I'm here and I'm fine. Maybe we should hear him out?" Devon and I both roll our eyes at her naïve words, but I still look at Devon for instructions.

He's staring out the window, grunting at the fucker before he fixes his attention on the guy kneeling at his feet.

"Change of plans." Grabbing the guy by the hair, he drags him to the door and, without even wondering if he's about to get shot, walks outside and presents Travis to the whiner.

"You tell Ben that if he wants to see me, he can text me. I don't take well to disrespectful cunts." Then, as though he were prepping his next recipe, he brings his knife to Travis's mouth and cuts off his tongue like it's butter.

"Next time you see me with my girl, you kneel at her feet and bow your worthless fucking head or else the next thing to go is your tiny dick."

I take it back. This is much better than killing the fucker.

Just as Travis starts screaming in pain, blood gushing from his mouth like he's the source of Dracula's next dinner, two cars pull up, tires screeching on the asphalt.

Devon seems to still be in the killing zone, that mental state where everything that moves is a possible threat, when Emma comes out from behind the table yelling, "I called them, Dev, they're with us!"

I'm pretty sure she's the only reason those two guys don't die today.

As Devon wipes his hands with a handkerchief like he's not covered in blood, I wrap my arm around Madelina's waist and pull her behind me. These guys do not need to look at her or speak to her or even breathe in the same space as her.

"You tell Benny boy that The Butcher's back and he wants his sister to come home."

With my gun in a firm grip, I notice the slight tremble in the whiner's hand as Devon makes his announcement.

I have a feeling the name The Butcher means a lot more than what I initially thought.

"Get this piece of shit away from me before I change my mind and dice up his insides."

The guy jumps into action and grabs his friend who is lying on the ground practically passed out. I'm guessing the blood loss and the pain are doing quite a number on him.

Without another word, he drags his guy to his car and drives away on screeching tires.

"How come the cops aren't here? Marco runs a tight ship but gunfire always has the PD running when the calls come in." Tucking the gun back in my holster, I run a quick assessment of Madelina, right down to her fingernails, making sure she's not hurt. "Also, what the actual fuck just happened? Do we need to be on high alert here?" I told Marco I would be here watching over his sister and that it was just a vacation. It's the only reason he accepted that I take a week off to travel. Hell, convincing J to play "babysitter"—her words not mine—was actually harder. She made me swear on my favorite gun that I'd return to take my job back.

"Don't ya fret, mate. They'll be here as soon as I'm gone." I frown because what the actual fuck?

"Ha! You sound like they're waiting in the shadows for you to leave. Is the police station like, really far away?" Madelina is laughing, convinced he's joking.

He's not.

"The station is about two hundred meters that way." He points to a road perpendicular to ours then turns back to us. "They're waiting for me to leave so they can come here and say it was a drug deal gone bad or some shit. Who the fuck knows anymore?" Shrugging, he takes two steps to Madelina and grabs the back of her head to plant a kiss so fucking hot it makes the asphalt melt.

"Interesting. That's got to cost you a pretty penny." I pin Tyler with a frown. There are more than a dozen bodies lying around the street and nobody, not a single fucking person, is around except the drivers still waiting for us, and Tyler is worried about how much it costs him to pay off the cops?

Billionaire world problems, I guess.

"What we pay the cops we gain in legal fees. I like it better without the hassle, mate." Grabbing his sister around the waist, he hugs her tight and grins. "Ya know, a cake and balloons would have been just as great, Big Sis. You didn't need to throw me a welcome home shootout too." The siblings laugh while Madelina, Tyler, and I watch, in awe.

"I could go for cake." Shaking my head, I grin at my girl. Because of course she'd say that.

"Me too, Gumdrop. Let's get some London cake with no bullets."

Chapter Twenty-Three

Lina

Growing up in the world of the New York mafia wasn't exactly difficult for me. As the Don's daughter—now sister—I'm protected, treated with respect, regarded as a prized possession to be kept safe at all times, never wanting for anything. I was given a full ride to college, funds to help set up my salon, vacations, whatever my spoiled little heart desired.

A gun was handed to me for my thirteenth birthday and I was taught to use it to defend myself, but I was also told I'd never have the need for it. The men would take care of any threats against me.

The weapons, the training, all things meant to give me power and control should I need it because being a mafia princess was 'dangerous', only for that control to be ripped away in an instant by a cruel man, because I wasn't as prepared as I should have been. I walked into that situation in Naples with River, severely underestimating the world I lived in.

I took that control back the day I sliced Ugo Ambrosio's dick off, vowing to never underestimate a situation like that again.

Well... Devon's world has just shot that vow right out of the park because there is no way in Hell I was expecting what happened in the pub earlier this evening. The thing that really makes my heart soar though, is the fact Devon gave me a weapon before we stepped inside. He armed me without even asking and gave me exactly the same instructions as he gave Tyler and Enzo.

It might seem a little fucked up that a man handing me a gun could make me swoon, but I really don't care what anyone thinks other than this family unit we're creating between the four of us.

It took about half an hour to get back to our hotel at Westminster Bridge after a quick goodbye and promises to speak with Devon's sister tomorrow. Who, by the way, is a whirlwind of chaotic energy. The shootout—as Devon's been referring to it—didn't even phase her. She just walked out of that pub like there weren't dead bodies lying around. I mean, I've seen my fair share of dead people at this point, but she just stepped over them as if they were mere obstacles on her way to hug her little brother, who just so happens to be three-times her size.

Our hotel is beautiful, something my big brother would be proud of. In fact, it'd be great if he opened one of his hotels in London, spread the Mancini Luxury Hotels chain across the pond. We're in the penthouse suite with a perfect view of the London Eye. Everyone has showered the blood and grime away and Devon insisted on making us all the best bacon sarnies we've ever tasted—his words.

It might be just past midnight here, but our body clocks are still on New York time, which means it's really only about seven in the evening.

One of the guys who dropped us off at the hotel had been sent out to get the supplies needed, and he was only too happy to do what the infamous Butcher asked. To be honest, I thought the whole Butcher name had something to do with Devon being a chef. Turns out, I couldn't have been more wrong. After watching him slice into people in the pub, a wide grin on his face as blood splattered everywhere, the reason behind the name became clear. The respect and fear he instilled in everyone around him echoed through to Enzo, Tyler, and me too, and it was an adrenaline rush like no other.

The four of us, we just work. I don't know why, I don't know how, but I'm never letting these men go.

Sitting around a large table made of some fancy-looking dark wood with Tyler and Enzo on either side of me, I watch Devon move fluidly around the kitchen space in his boxers. His usual carefree smile isn't there all the way, it doesn't quite reach his eyes, and his beautifully sculpted body is tense.

"So are we going to have a discussion about what the fuck happened this evening?" Tyler leisurely sips his whiskey, not addressing anyone in particular, as his hand gently strokes up and down my bare thigh. I grabbed one of Enzo's large plain black T-shirts after my shower, so I'm about as half dressed as Devon.

"We absolutely are. But grub first, chat later. I need to cook and fuck, maybe both, before I'm gonna be calm enough to talk properly."

With the adrenaline from this evening still running through my veins, I'm totally down for both of those things. Devon doesn't help my libido when he looks up at me, frying pan in hand, and winks, panty-melting dimple and all. That, combined with the men on either side of me, each with their hands on me, and I'm surprised I'm still functioning.

"Do you want any help?" We're all just kind of watching him make us food and I don't think I'll be able to eat a thing if the hands on my thighs get any higher.

"You could butter the bread if you want, Treacle."

"Do what now?" I've never buttered bread to make a sandwich in my life.

Enzo stands to help me up, like the gentleman he's always been, and I admire his version of casual. It's unusual to see Enzo or Tyler in anything other than a suit of some kind. I only ever see them dressed to the nines or naked. We haven't really done this whole thing very often—sat around and talked, spent evenings all together, as a unit, a family. Enzo's black sweatpants are old, clearly well-used, and I wonder if they're part of his gym-wear. The black tank top he's wearing with them accentuates every muscle on his tanned skin and I think I have a new obsession with wanting to lick these men. They're all so deliciously handsome.

Tyler has gone for gray sweatpants, which are very obviously brand new because I've never seen him wear sweatpants in my life, and a white T-shirt. The T-shirt hugging his thick arms like it wants to hold him inside forever, and I can't believe I'm jealous of clothing.

Practically fanning myself from overheating, I curiously head to the kitchen space.

"Come on, Treacle. If you want the best bacon sarnie ever, you've gotta do it right. That means buttering the bread. Here, like this." Putting the sizzling frying pan to one side, he moves behind me to stand us at the black marble countertop and pulls out the sliced bread.

Our hands are linked, one on the surface, the other holding a knife as he scoops up some butter and begins spreading it over the bread. It's surprisingly sexual, but everything with these men turns me on, so I take that back. It's not surprising at all.

Warm breaths tickle my hair against my neck, and there's no doubting whether Devon is as turned on as I am. The hardness at my back tells me all I need to know.

"Why not just put mayonnaise on the bread? It's not toasted or anything so butter feels pointless."

Devon pauses to look up at Tyler.

"Mayonnaise in a bacon sarnie? Mate, come on. Ketchup. Always ketchup, maybe brown sauce if you're feeling fruity, Worcestershire sauce if you wanna spice it up, but never mayonnaise." Mock-tutting, Devon shakes his head and continues to use my hand as his own while spreading butter on all the slices. "I thought he was the classy one."

Somehow, we all made it through what was actually a nice sandwich filled with crispy bacon cooked to perfection and ketchup without getting naked. The sexual tension in the room felt like electricity zapping through my veins with every small touch they found excuses to make and the silent promises of pleasure written all over their faces.

As Enzo and Tyler clear the empty plates, Devon shows me that dimple again, a little of his usual spark visible once more. He wags his brows and blows me a kiss before following them to the kitchen area that is clearly visible in this open plan space.

"What are you three doing?" They're huddled together and whispering, each of them grinning like the Cheshire cat. "Don't make me come over there!"

"Oh, Gumdrop. We wouldn't make you come over here. *Yet.* You're going to come *on* the dining table first." Tyler turns and stalks toward me with something I can't quite make out in his hand. "You got the ropes, D?"

Oh my. These men are going to kill me and I'm going to die the luckiest woman on Earth.

"T-shirt off, then lie down on the table, Treacle."

"But it's going to be so cold!"

"There's our little brat. Don't worry, we'll have you warmed up soon enough, Babydoll."

I huff, pouting my lips for good measure, but we all know I'm not going to say no. We had a discussion after our session on the plane about hard limits and what we'd be willing to try in the future, and me being completely at their mercy like this is something we're all up for.

There's a definite chill as the skin on my back touches the cold surface of the table, my nipples pebbling to points and causing each man to do that sexy growl thing under their breaths. Having this kind of power over three strong men is something I won't take lightly, treasuring every moment we all have together.

Devon begins wrapping one wrist in an elaborate tie, no doubt he'll tell me its name later, before attaching it to one corner of the table. At the same time, a very naked Enzo looks down on me, that special smile he reserves just for me shining on his face.

"Kiss me." They may be in charge here, but I can always count on Enzo. When he's around, the other two don't deny me orgasms for as long.

Leaning down, Enzo kisses the shit out of me, owning my lips, my tongue, as he palms one breast and uses his other hand to pin my arm down for Devon to tie back. I yelp at the wet, sticky feeling between my legs, sending an electric shock all over my body in the most delicious way.

"It's a good job you're not allergic to nuts, Treacle."

Confusion brings me out of my lusty haze for a moment, does he mean their nuts? Why wo—

"Rich Boy's got a hell of a job cleaning up all that peanut butter down there, and woop, there it is." My back involuntarily arches as Enzo spoons some blackcurrant jam over my breasts, going straight back to putting every inch of them he possibly can into his mouth. "You're the P.B. and J. and we're the bread."

My confusion is quickly forgotten when Tyler pushes two fingers inside me as he punishes my clit with his mouth, sucking and biting, and fuck me, I'm not going to last long. One of my legs is pulled down and Devon begins tying my ankle to another corner of the table, the restraints only adding to the haze of desire I'm drowning in.

Oh no, I think I need to pee. "Oh fuck! Wha—Oh!"

Tyler laps me up as I convulse with pleasure on the table, every nerve ending alight with fire burning through my veins, my skin ten times more sensitive than before.

"And we have a squirter! I get to make her squirt next time, Rich Boy. That's so fucking sexy."

"One orgasm down, five to go."

"Five!" Not that I'm complaining, but Tyler's declaration for five more orgasms, after just one nearly made me pass out, has me a little worried for my sanity.

"We get two each, Madelina. Only fair." Well, when Enzo puts it like that, who am I to stop them?

Chapter Twenty-Four

Tyler

I'm fascinated by Devon's Shibari techniques, the intricate ways the ropes create an entire story on Lina's body is like nothing I've ever seen before. When we discussed Lina's limits, it wasn't any different than a dom to sub conversation. She talked about her willing fantasies, like getting fucked in all of her holes at once, and her hard limits. Most notably: humiliation and degradation. We weren't disappointed since those two kinks don't concern us.

"Shibari isn't just about tying up our girl and fucking her until she passes out, although I wouldn't complain." Devon's words are aimed squarely at Lina and even though she's mostly boneless, all tied up and looking regal, she still manages to swoon at his over-the-top flirting. "It's about the emotional connection it provides. Our girl is a tight ball of conflicting feelings swimming inside her and these techniques can liberate her." Reaching out, Devon traps her nipple between his fingers and presses hard enough to make it ruby red and engorged. That's when he looks to me and nods his head. "Taste her, mate, she's like a strawberry waiting to be sucked."

I mimic his position and pinch her other nipple between my own fingers, bringing it to my mouth and sucking it with the vigor of a starved man, my tongue flicking it twice and making her moan to the ceiling.

"It's all about communication and open conversations with our little Treacle. She probably has triggers we need to avoid like…" Devon looks to us and Enzo is the first to respond.

"Certain words are a no-go." He's right. Ambrosio used the word "treat" over and over again and she gets a faraway look in her eyes every time she hears someone say it. It's impossible to catch without the context of her past, but we see it because we expect it.

Maybe one day, it'll just be a word again. It's what she's trying to do with her use of Daddy with Devon, taking back her power, and we're here to help guide her through the process.

"Let's move this to the bedroom, shall we, boys?" Before he steps away, Devon bends forward, his mouth leveled to her pussy, and takes a slow, long lick at our girl. "Hmm... delicious, indeed." He then unties her wrists from the corners of the table, freeing her for a short time.

Enzo scoops up Lina and walks her to the bedroom in the back of the suite, me at his heels with Devon right behind me, whistling as he grabs his bag of treats and hauls the sack over his shoulder.

Over Enzo's shoulder, Lina's delicate features peep out. Her eyes bright with excitement, she winks before falling back into her bodyguard's arms.

"Have you ever seen her cry from too many orgasms?" Cocking a brow at Devon, I shake my head.

"I haven't, but I have a feeling you're going to show us."

"That I am, mate. That I am. You wanna watch or participate, Rich Boy?" He always asks me this and, usually, I get off on watching them bringing her to the edge before taking her back down but tonight, I want to play. Tonight, I want to see her cry.

After Enzo lays her on her back, Devon frets around and places her in a kneeling position like a pious woman begging for forgiveness. She looks like a nun who's just taken off her habit with her long black hair draped over her back and her wrists roped up, loose ends hanging down her thighs.

"Fuck." Enzo's words are choked, his usually impassive face tight with pain or shock or... something.

"You alright, mate?"

"Yeah, fine." Neither one of us believes him but it's not the time to have a sit down. Right now, it's all about Lina and her pleasure. It's about giving her some freedom by tying her up and watching her submit to us.

"Look at me," I place a finger under her chin and lift her face up to mine. As her eyes open, I almost lose my footing at the trust written within her irises, the overwhelming way she's giving us the reins without a shadow of fear or doubt. "Hard limits."

With a smile, she repeats her words from the other night, "Humiliation and degradation." I smile and, because I can't fucking help myself, I bring my mouth to hers and lick a path across her bottom lip, demanding entrance. We kiss for a while, our tongues dancing together like we've been practicing for years and this is our big performance.

Except no one here is acting. This is real for us. This is the manifestation of our deepest, darkest fantasies and Lina is the reason they're coming true.

Devon takes her wrists and while Enzo guides her backward across the bed, I climb on top of her and straddle her hips to avoid breaking our kiss. With her flat on her back, Devon places her arms wide along the line of the bed with a length of rope dangling to the floor. Rummaging through his bag of goodies, Devon takes out two twenty-pound kettlebells and places them just below her hands, tying the loose rope with practiced efficiency. Just like that, Lina is helpless once again. There isn't a single ounce of fear or regret in her eyes, which turns me on more than I could have ever imagined. That's not true. As soon as Devon mentioned Shibari, I knew I'd be one hundred percent on board.

"Here, we're going to do two half-hitches so she's secured to the kettlebells." I watch him as he basically does what looks like a double knot but at the end of the second one, he goes back through the loop and tightens only one end of the rope. "See that?" Pulling on the rope attached to our girl, he shows me how efficient it is. "But if you pull here," he pulls on the other end and everything comes loose. "She's free in half a second."

"Impressive." Almost as impressive as him carrying a bag with that much weight like it was nothing.

As Devon continues to secure Lina, her hands, then her ankles, so she's open wide and spread eagle, he nods to her naked form and grins. "Keep our girl busy while I decorate her body."

Enzo kneels beside her, his hands on her face as he bends down to kiss her while I kneel between her legs and play with her clit. Devon is alternating between harnessing her flesh in intricate ropes and kissing and biting every inch of her skin.

Lina's panting, her breaths heavy and quick. Curious, I press my forefinger to her pussy and push in just enough to know how wet she is for us.

"Fucking Christ, you're soaked, Gumdrop. You like being at our mercy?" Her mouth is too busy sucking on Enzo's tongue to answer me but she bucks her hips and begs for more of my touch.

And who am I to deny her?

With two fingers, I push inside her and hook them just enough to make her cry out into Enzo's mouth. "I need actual words, Lina."

Enzo pulls back an inch, freeing her mouth, as she aims a breathy, lusty "Yes," my way.

I'm not surprised by her answer, I know her hips thrusting toward me means she wanted more but it's important that she talk to us. It's vital for her to express her feelings when it comes to sex.

"Good girl." I swear to fuck, her body visibly melts into the bed at my words and I wonder if being praised is part of her own fantasies. If that's the case, I'll tell her how good she is fifty fucking times a day.

With Enzo thoroughly ravishing her mouth as he tweaks her nipples and Devon kissing and biting her chest and stomach as he riddles her with silky rope, I push her to the brink of orgasm and let her crash.

Screaming into Enzo's mouth, she moves her hips in a circular motion, as best she can with the ropes biting into her skin, while I continue to fuck her with my fingers. Just as she's about to explode, her body shaking and her toes curling into the rope, I bring my mouth to her pussy and suck on her juices, lapping up everything she gives me and fucking her with my tongue.

"That's two, Treacle."

When Lina opens her eyes, we're all three staring at the erotic masterpiece laid out in front of us, naked as the day is long, with hard dicks pointing to the heavens. Devon slaps her pussy, once, then twice—hard muscles rippling beneath his tattooed skin—with a stupid grin on his face while Enzo follows up with a soothing caress and two fingers inside her wet cunt. It's pain followed by pleasure and it's her preference.

We were all tested and cleared weeks ago, knowing damn well we would one day end up like this. Fucking together, loving her together.

"Enzo, got hard limits, mate?" With a tight jaw, he looks up at Devon and hesitates before shocking me with his words.

"No. Whatever Lina wants, she gets." I smirk, I can't imagine he'd ever—Devon's voice cuts off my internal rambling.

"Have you ever bottomed?"

"Yes."

"Consensual?"

Whoa. What?

Enzo pauses again then looks to Lina for guidance. Nodding, she silently urges him to be honest.

"Not always."

At Enzo's admission, I feel complete and utter rage. Not aimed at him, of course, but at whoever took advantage of him.

"And here, would it be consensual?" Enzo looks to me then to Devon before his gaze softens as he stares at Lina.

"For her pleasure, yes." Devon leans forward and palms the side of Enzo's face, their foreheads pressed together.

"We're a family now. Honesty and openness is the only way this works." Enzo nods and they both close their eyes. A warm feeling of... something builds in my chest at the intimacy I just witnessed. It's like seeing Enzo for the very first time, his armor vanishing, his impassive mask melting to give way to vulnerability and transparency.

"Rich Boy, hard limits?" Devon's attention is on me now and I feel as though I'm on the spot because I've always been the Dom in any relationship, so I'm usually asking the questions, not the other way around.

"Today, I'd say I don't bottom, but like you said, we're a family now. Who the fuck knows what can happen in the future?" Lina's face is one of complete awe and unbidden happiness.

"Thank you for this. I love you all so fucking much for what you're giving me."

We all freeze at her words. Sure, she's professed her love for me and I for her and I'm sure she's done the same for Enzo but it's been months since things have been normal. The difference here is that we're all together, all naked in more ways than one, and I don't think we could get any more vulnerable than we are right now. Physically and emotionally, we are stripped of all coverings and I've never felt freer.

Devon's eyes land on Lina's, grinning from ear to ear and popping out those ridiculous dimples, as he crawls over to her and straddles her chest, his dick rubbing over the silk rope. I've never been attracted to men but the two of them together, where she's at his mercy and he's getting off on the very thing holding her hostage, is making my dick weep with lust.

"We love you too, Treacle, and soon we're going to show you just how much." Lina's body bucks again, my attention moving from Devon to Lina's wide-open cunt begging for my cock.

"Hey, Brit Boy, are we going to talk her into an orgasm or are we going to fuck her until she cries? I was promised tears." My words earn me a grin from Enzo as he shakes his head, his fingers rubbing circles at the top of her pussy, dipping to her clit then coming back up, teasing our girl to the extent of madness.

"Did you hear that, Treacle? Rich Boy upgraded me from Chef to Brit. I think we're getting somewhere." Lina giggles then gasps as I slam my cock inside her and hold the position long enough to remind myself that this is for her, which means I need to hold my eager dick back from coming the moment I'm inside her tight little cunt.

With my hands planted on her thighs, just below the rope, I press my groin as close as I can get. And that's when I get it. The rope isn't just for her pleasure, for the hundreds of sensations she probably feels, it's also for us. The fabric is soft and silky and it's making it really fucking hard to keep my cool.

"Ah, you get it now, don't ya?" I have no doubt the expression on my face is one of complete awe and surprise.

"Fuck. It feels fucking fantastic. Like her robe but harder and with her pussy so goddamn wet, I can't separate the two sensations, they're just... one." I look at Enzo and nod to my cock. "Want to try it?"

I don't wait for his response, I pull out and exchange places with him at her side. Devon finishes up whatever he was doing to the ropes and stands behind Lina's head like a conductor about to lead us into the performance of a lifetime.

We watch Enzo as he places his hand on one of the rope loops and pushes inside her to the hilt before dropping his head back and breathing out a slow, pleasantly tortured breath.

"Christ." Exactly that. "She's soaked... and the ropes..." He doesn't finish his phrase. He doesn't need to, we both know exactly how he feels.

Devon claps his hands as his attention pins Lina down with a sultry look of chaos. We're on and we all know it as he walks back to his bag and takes out the lube. I recognize the brand, it's the same one I like to use and I feel a sense of camaraderie in this moment because safety is my main priority and, clearly, he's done his research too.

"Bodyguard, heads up." Devon tosses the lube to Enzo, who catches it with ease, and just like that, we all know which pleasure we're giving her. Teasing her nipples with my mouth, flicking and biting at the twin peaks, I roll the pads of my fingers around her clit while Enzo begins to prep her for more.

Devon kisses her mouth, upside down, Spiderman-style, crazed and needy for her lips, as he positions her neck and mouth just right so she can take his erect cock—piercings and all. She licks him, her tongue playing with the head as she laps up every inch of him. Between Enzo lubing up her ass and Devon getting his cock sucked into next week, my dick is begging for friction.

Holding out my hand to Enzo, I silently ask for the lube, which he gives without a second's thought. Lina can't see me, her head hanging off the side of the bed while she's busy choking on Devon. I rub her tits nice and slick so I can get some relief. Straddling her ribcage, I press her exposed tits together and slide my shaft between the smooth, warm globes, fucking them slowly as the head of my dick taps out against the base of her neck. The underside of my cock rubs against the Shibari ropes and I'm not confident about how long I can hold out like this.

"Watch it, Rich Boy, I don't need her biting off my dick." I shrug like it's his problem but we both know we're all being careful, working together to give her maximum pleasure. Behind me, Enzo uses the thick lube to more easily access her pretty little hole.

"Let's try something different." Devon pulls out of her mouth and gives her a quick kiss before freeing her wrists and walking around the bed, giving me the universal sign for moving away. I don't do well with orders, much less with the waving of fingers in the guise of words, but I'm too curious to argue.

Unhooking her ankles, the slip knot indeed convenient, he pulls her back up to kneeling. "Rich Boy, lie down." It's my turn to lie down as Lina is guided on top of me, the rope dangling from her hands pulled back for Enzo to take and use as his reins.

In this new position, her pussy is mine and her ass is for Enzo.

"That's more like it."

Lina is writhing, pushing her ass back and sliding her pussy on my all-too eager cock. I slap her ass cheek, followed by another to make sure she knows who's in charge. Hell, I'm not even sure who's in charge, to be honest, but I know it isn't our little Gumdrop.

Although, to be fair, she does have all the control.

Devon is right back on the other side, standing in front of her face as he presents his cock to her again. "Whose cock is this, Treacle?"

"Daddy D's."

"Who's going to choke on it?"

"I am."

"Mouth open, tongue out."

Then he pins me with one of his no-nonsense glares right before he slides his dick into her mouth, slow and deliberate, until she gags on him. I've got prime tickets to the show.

Fuck, I love that sound. It says, your dick is so big it doesn't fit in my mouth. It says, give me more. It says everything I love to hear.

With both of his large hands on her face, he pumps in and out of her mouth as Enzo positions himself right behind her and, with my hands on her hips, I guide her cunt over my cock. Slow and torturous.

It's when she whimpers and I feel her pussy grow tighter that I realize Enzo is breaching her hole. It's not his cock, yet, just his fingers, but it's enough to get a reaction out of us all, and it's fucking glorious.

"That's it, Lina, suck on my cock and take Tyler's dick so deep we could head bump." I roll my eyes at his words, but Lina's imagination must create a pretty little picture because her pussy is instantly gushing, her juices coating her walls so much that I have to make a conscious effort not to slide out of her.

All of that is forgotten the moment her walls squeeze my cock enough to make me grunt. Enzo's face is pure, unhindered lust and pleasure as he slides his dick into her ass, her pussy walls constricting with every inch he feeds her.

I have to grit my teeth to not lose all fucking control.

"Goddamn, she's so fucking tight. Not sure how long I'm going to last." We've all fucked Lina. I know I've taken her ass before and I'm guessing Enzo has too. Not sure about Devon, but one thing I know is that we've never fucked her all at the same time. I've never shared a woman like this before, period, and I'm fucking ecstatic that the only time I have is right here and now.

We get into a rhythm, my hand latching onto the ropes at her back, pulling her down as I push up into her. As we learn to work together, pushing and pulling and thrusting and waiting, I realize that Enzo is caring and careful, I'm rough yet attentive but Devon? He's ruthless with her mouth and she's loving every fucking second of it. With saliva dripping past her lips and down her chin, the sight is almost too much for me. It doesn't help that Devon is giving us a play by play of every thrust inside her tight little throat.

"That's right, coat my dick with your saliva. Drool, baby, you're so beautiful when you choke on me." The bed is sturdy, barely making a sound as we all fuck her to within an inch of her life. She's groaning and gurgling, her back arched in an awkward position and her roped up legs straddling my chest, rubbing against my flesh every time I plunge into her cunt.

She's at our mercy, giving us the gift of herself, and as I watch the three of us losing our fucking minds over her, I realize she's never been more beautiful than she is right now.

"That's right, Babydoll, cry for your Daddy D. Give me your fucking tears." Devon turns her head just enough so we can see the black streaks from her mascara running down her face but instead of sad eyes and scared features, Lina looks lust-laden and bright-eyed, almost begging for more.

Reaching up, I pinch her clit—the hard nub peeking out from between her lips—because I'm about to come like a fucking volcano and there's nothing that can stop me.

She's so sensitive that it only takes one pinch for her to explode all over my dick, her screams pushed back by Devon's cock and Enzo cursing behind her as her entire body tenses, making her ass and pussy tighter than we ever thought possible.

And I lose it.

With both hands on her hips, I slam inside her to the fucking hilt and let loose strand after strand of my cum with a crazy thought running through my mind for the very first time in my life.

I hope she gets pregnant.

I hope *I* get her pregnant.

I hope we're literally creating a family right now.

Enzo grunts, his dick buried deep inside her ass as she comes for the third time when he squeezes her ass cheeks, rubbing them against the root of his cock. With his head thrown back and his mouth dropped open, I admire his come face and realize it's the first time he looks relaxed and not ready to kill someone.

Slowly, I pull out, my cum trickling down her thighs and coating my dick. Fuck that. No fucking way. I slide myself back in, my cock half hard still, enough at least that I can push my cum back inside her.

When Enzo pulls out, I get a peek at the head of his cock connected to her ass by a strand of his cum and, for some reason, it makes my dick twitch. She's full of us. Of our very essence.

"Ready, Treacle? Swallow me whole, Baby. Swallow every fucking drop I give you." Enzo and I watch, transfixed, as Devon fucks Lina's face like he owns her. He's got her head between his hands, his dick thrusting in once, twice, and on the third time, he slams back inside her mouth and grabs her throat, squeezing his fingers.

"Fuck yeah, I can feel you swallowing me down, Baby. It's so fucking hot."

Just then, I realize her body is seeking us out so, naturally, I give her what she wants.

My thumb reaches up to her clit and rubs quick circles around it, her own juices coating it enough to bring another orgasm. This time, when she squeezes my cock, it pops out so I slam two of my fingers inside and Enzo does the same as she swallows the last of Devon's cum and we finger her to her fourth orgasm.

I suppose that one was a joint effort. It counts as one for us all.

When Devon is done, his demeanor changes at once. Gone is the beast and in its place is the caring man he's always been around her.

His nimble fingers make quick work of all the slip knots off and he releases her from the intricacies of the Shibari, caressing her skin and running his fingers around the grooves from the ropes. Enzo runs to the bathroom, I'm guessing for her after care, while I massage her tits and stomach, twisting us so she's on her back and I'm half lying on her, kissing her lips and her come-and-saliva-covered chin. Her neck and collarbone.

Soon, Enzo comes back with three small towels, all wet with hot water as we take care of the part of Lina that we took. She moans, talking nonsense like she's drunk on us. Drunk on our cum.

Devon begins kissing her mouth, licking and nipping at the corners, as I run my lips over her swollen pussy, my tongue flicking her clit with tender tongue lashes. Enzo wipes her down, kissing the inside of her thighs, soothing what I'm guessing is a sore ass.

Today, in this London penthouse suite, we became one. One unit for Lina, but also for each other.

We became a family.

Hours later, I wake up from our sleep-fest where Lina was lying across the bed with a body part on top of each of us. Her head on Devon's chest, her stomach on my groin and legs tangled in a weird scissoring thing that touched both Enzo and me. It wasn't easy but I managed to slip out of the bed and head for the bathroom to take a much needed piss.

Grabbing my phone on the way, I slow my steps when I see more than a dozen messages from my secretary, Clara. Not to mention the missed calls.

Well, fuck.

The time says just past five in the morning here, so that means it's midnight in New York. Nothing I can do about it now except listen to the messages and maybe jump on my laptop to minimize whatever fire I need to put out.

But first things first.

After relieving myself, I wash my hands and make sure the door is closed before listening to the messages.

My mind goes back to a few hours ago and the thought of starting all over again makes my dick twitch, albeit not as enthusiastically as earlier. I need some rest, then we will see what other positions we can make her try.

"Mr. Walker, we have a situation here. it's... Mrs. Wal—I mean, Cora. You need to come back." Her first message is calm but by the time she sends her fifth, she sounds like she's a panicked mess.

I know exactly what's going on and I don't plan on being there anytime soon. In fact, I'm the reason the situation is happening. Using my secretary's cell phone number so I can reach her this time of night, I send her a quick text.

Me: "Don't worry, everything is going to be fine."
Clara: "But Sir, something's not right over here."
Me: "I know."

Chapter Twenty-Five

Devon

Fuck me, waking up in practically a dog-pile with my woman at the center is like waking up in Heaven. The beds in this place aren't made for four fully-grown adults, but we made it work.

"Need to pee." Enzo is the first to move, efficiently untangling himself from Lina's legs and heading to the en-suite to use the loo.

Tyler is next to get out of bed—even though he's already been awake for hours, he even showered and spent a while on his phone before coming back to our group nest. He's already fully dressed in dark gray trousers, a matching dark gray waistcoat, and a white collared shirt with the top few buttons undone, and I can appreciate what our woman sees in him. He rolls Lina over so she's fully rested on my bare chest, her delicate fingers against my scarred and inked skin. Men have never really appealed to me as life partners, their tits just aren't as fun to play with as a woman's, but this little family unit we're creating is everything I never knew I wanted.

My girl chose well.

"What's going down, T?" I keep my voice low, not wanting to wake our princess, knowing Tyler must have been awake for a while, considering he's already dressed. I bet the clean-freak showered more than once after the amount of juices and sweat we all ended up covered in last night.

The heavy sigh before he speaks tells me there's something on his mind. "Just putting out some fires at the office, keeping the ex-wife off my back... the usual." He's tapping away at his phone as he speaks, and I remember reading about the ex-wife in his file. Platinum blonde, plastic tits, personality of a water pump, and now engaged to Tyler's business partner.

"If she's an issue, mate, I know a girl who'd be happy to get rid of it for the right price." His problems are Lina's problems, which makes them mine now too, and I know his ex-wife is shady as fuck. To what extent, I haven't been able to figure out properly yet, but it's easy to see that she's trouble.

"Thanks for the offer, but I've got it all under control."

"I don't doubt it, Rich Boy. Let me know if you change your mind." He looks up from his phone and tips his head in acknowledgement before furiously typing away once more.

"What are we changing our minds about?" Lina's sleepy voice is like a purr against my chest, and I stroke my fingers through her silky ebony strands.

"He won't let me have his ex-wife killed, Treacle."

She chuckles, her body vibrating against mine. "She's a cunt, but harmless enough." I fucking love when Lina uses words like that, it sends a shot of lust straight to my dick every time.

"For now." The words are mumbled under Tyler's breath so Lina can't hear, but I see it, the tensed jaw, the narrowed eyes... this ex-wife may need to be looked into more than I already have.

Vibrating on the bedside table draws my attention to my phone and I roll my eyes when I look at the name flashing on the screen. Most people send a text and wait for me to get back to them. My mother, bless her soul, isn't most people.

She hasn't spoken to me since I left for New York, or *I* haven't spoken to *her* since I left for New York... either way, it's been a while and I can't find it in myself to ignore her call. Picking up my phone, I tap to answer and bring it to my ear. Lina tries to wriggle away, but I hold her firmly against me. Just a few more minutes.

"Hi, Mum."

"Devon Quinn. Why is it that I hear you're back in the country from your sister and not directly from the horse's mouth?" Her tone is scalding, yet loving all at the same time, relief evident in every word.

"Sorry, Mum. We arrived yesterday and had some shit to deal with first."

"Hmm. Emma did tell me about what happened when she called this morning. I suppose I can let you off if you're planning to come over for a cuppa tea any time today." There's the hint of a question there, like she's unsure if I'll say yes, but it's also a demand. This is her way of letting me know that we're good, she understands.

All the world's problems can be solved over a cup of tea.

"Of course." That's total bullshit. I had planned on spending the day buried inside my woman before going back to real world crap, but she's extending the olive branch. I can't deny her. "We'll be round in a couple of hours." After last night's fiasco, there's no way my Italians or my American will let me go anywhere in this city alone now.

"We? Ooh, who's we? Have you brought some friends home with you? I'll get Emma to bring me some shopping in and make you some lunch, or I can just get your Uncle Harry to stop off at the chippy on his way home from his meeting." She's on one now, completely in her element. She always has loved playing the hostess, wanting hers to be the house my sisters and our friends chose to hang out in after school.

"I have, yes, there are four of us. And I won't say no to a proper chippy." I know Tyler especially would prefer lunch in some swanky restaurant, but there's no way in Hell I'm coming to London and not having chips from the chippy—much better than those skinny things the Americans call fries. I may even go the whole hog and introduce them to pie, mash, and liquor; fucking delicacy.

"Chippy it is. I'll see you soon, my darling boy. Stay safe, okay? Love you." I swear her voice cracks, but I'm not sure and I don't want to upset her any more by asking.

"Okay, Mum. Love ya too. See you soon." Sighing, I put my phone back on the bedside table and wrap my arm around Lina, who's tracing her fingertips across my chest.

"Everything okay?" Her big bright eyes stare deep into my soul and I smile down at the woman who holds my heart in the palm of her hands.

"Of course it is, Treacle. Today's the day I introduce you to my mum."

After a morning of lounging around and a couple more orgasms, I park the Range Rover I hired on my mum's small driveway. The house isn't the same one we all grew up in, my dad figured they needed to downsize once we all moved out, but it's still huge for just two people. Although, Mum has always said the spare rooms are there ready for when any of us want a sleepover. It's a detached three-bedroom house with bay windows, the wear and tear of the brickwork showing the age of the property.

The front door opens before I've even turned the engine off and my mum stands in the doorway, apron on, tea towel in one hand, and her trademark fluffy slippers on her tiny feet. Her hair is whiter than the last time I saw her, the lines on her face deeper, and guilt immediately hits me for leaving her like I did.

"Oh my God, she's so cute!" I thought Lina might've been nervous to meet the parents, or parent, singular, in this case, but she surprises me at every turn, because she's really excited, almost bouncing in the backseat.

"I wouldn't call her cute to her face, Treacle. Where do you think I got my knife skills?" I wink at her before stepping out of the car, and the others follow me as I approach the front door.

My mum's smile warms my heart just a little, the tear in her eye she'd have my balls for mentioning a clear sign that she's missed me, and I wrap my arms around her. The hug is quick as she pulls away to get a clear look at my face.

"Welcome home, my sweet boy." She kisses my cheek and looks past me, raising a curious brow at Lina standing there holding both Tyler's and Enzo's hands. "And hello to you three. Do they only breed good looking people over there, Devon?"

Pushing me aside, Mum holds her arms out to Lina first, giving her a brief hug and a kiss on the cheek. Lina is all too happy to oblige, winking at me over my mum's shoulder. Tyler is next, and he politely greets her, allowing her to give him the same treatment as the rest of us. Finally, she stands in front of our giant Italian, Enzo. She looks up at him with a huge grin as he remains unmoving, unwilling to initiate contact.

"They must've left you in the manure for longer than the rest of them. Come here, you're not too big for a hug either." Enzo's eyes widen in surprise as Mum reaches up and grabs hold of his face, pulling his head down so she can kiss his cheek too.

With the pleasantries all over, we follow Mum inside, straight into the kitchen, the hub of this home.

"The kettle's just boiled. Tea or coffee?" Mum begins placing mugs on the side next to the kettle, preparing the one she uses for me exactly how I like it.

"I'd love a tea, please, Mrs. Quinn, coffee for this pair of mutes."

"Ha, I like you. None of this Mrs. Quinn business either, young lady. You can call me Shelly." Turning to look at me, Mum raises a brow. "Or is she calling me Mum? Hmm?" As if she's forgotten the most important thing in the world, her eyes widen and she covers her mouth. "Oh no, you must think I'm so rude. I didn't even ask your names."

"It's fine, Mum." I sigh and sit down at the breakfast bar in the center of the room next to Lina. Enzo stands by the door, kind of hovering and a little unsure what his place here is, and Tyler sits on Lina's other side. "This is Lina Mancini, the love of my life." The stilted intake of breath from the beauty next to me makes me smile, and I rest a hand on her thigh, wishing to fuck that she wasn't wearing jeans. My mum's eyes twinkle with a joy I've missed, like she can suddenly see the big white wedding none of my sisters have given her the chance to attend yet. "This is Tyler Walker, CEO, and the big one is Enzo Beneventi, New York mafia, and they're also Lina's boyfriends."

Hiding what we all are is never something I've even considered, and I love that we're all on the same page with this, because to hide it would just tell people we're ashamed. And I'm really not. The look on my mum's face, though, is priceless. It's like she's not quite sure how she's supposed to react to that information, and I don't blame her, to be fair. It isn't exactly something you hear every day.

"Well, okay then. Lucky girl!" Mum smiles and winks at Lina before turning around to make the hot drinks.

I squeeze Lina's thigh, and she looks at me with a huge grin on her face. "I really am."

"Your sister finally got the balls to call ya then? I've been telling her for months to let you know what's going on with Lizzy and those bloody Deptford Boys." The metal spoon pings against the mugs as Mum stirs and finishes off our drinks before bringing them over in twos to place on the counter in front of us.

"*You* could have called me, Mum." This is where she puts me through the guilt trip.

"I didn't know if you'd answer after you left the way you did. You could have called me too, you know." She pulls out a small plate, arranging some Rich Tea biscuits, some chocolate digestives, and a couple of others, in a decorative pattern, then brings it over to us. "Biscuits?"

"That one looks like a sugar cookie—"

"Let's not get started on the differences between cookies and biscuits, Treacle. Here, dip this one in your tea. It'll melt in your mouth. They're my fave." I hand her a Rich Tea biscuit and grab one for myself, dipping it into my hot tea and making sure to remove it before it gets too floppy and breaks off. "So what's Uncle Harry done about all this crap going on then?"

I'm choosing to skirt over the whole me leaving for over a year thing, wanting to get to the point so we can get done and go back to New York. Obviously, I'll make more of an effort to keep in touch.

"You know Harry. He's never really been one for the details. He thinks Lizzy's just going through a phase, that she'll come around in her own time. He's refusing to acknowledge them encroaching on Quinn family turf, in our pubs, our betting shops, it's really getting out of hand." Mum cradles her mug of tea between her palms, gently blowing and sipping on it because she can never wait for it to cool down.

"Do we know what their end game is? What it is they want out of all this?" There's always something, it's the way it is with the gangs of London. No one is ever satisfied with the power they already hold.

"Yeah, we do, darling. They want you."

Chapter Twenty-Six

Enzo

I'm not a college educated guy. Everything I know I learned from the Mancinis and the streets. Luckily for me, my birth parents didn't leave me with nothing, at least one of them gave me strong enough DNA to be able to survive in this fucked-up world. A world they threw me into without a fucking care for my safety but still, at least I was equipped to make it out alive.

Just barely, though.

When Alberto Mancini found me, I was running cons to pay off my room rental after running away from the convent in Upstate New York a few years earlier. I was already big for twelve and it's no secret that anyone kid-shopping at an orphanage isn't looking for a preteen, much less one with an attitude as big as Lake Ontario. Tired of the beatings and the "alone time" with the fucking rats in the basement, I packed my shit—two pairs of jeans and a few ripped T-shirts—and got the fuck out of there.

I walked for hours before a truck driver picked me up, saving me about a hundred and fifty miles on my trek to The City. We started with a little small talk—his name was Mills and he had a wife with two kids—but then my body gave up on being awake even though I knew it was probably a bad idea to be so damn vulnerable. I woke up with a start when I felt the truck wasn't moving anymore and a hand was now firmly on my leg, shaking me. Before my eyes even opened, I had a knife at the guy's throat, my lips snarling like a beast until he slowly took his hand off me and grinned like he was proud of me.

"Hey, now, I was just trying to shake you awake, little man." Blinking, I looked around at the rest area, New York City like a distant post card in the background. Slowly, I pulled my knife down and mumbled an apology. "Someone must've done quite a number on you, huh? Look, I'm gonna give you some unsolicited advice, kid." I fought the urge to roll my eyes and nodded for him to continue. After all, I was too young to know much about anything at this point. "The only thing you can trust in this world is your gut. It's the reason you got into this truck and the reason you gave your body permission to fall asleep. Your gut is your ally. Everyone else? They're an enemy until proven otherwise." Staring at Mills, I studied his face for a while before nodding and thanking him for the ride.

Funny how this guy I only met once has been a constant voice in my head for the last twenty years. His advice is the only reason I'm alive and it's that same advice that has my mind going a million miles a minute right now. There are too many pieces on the table and the puzzle has too many holes in it for me to see the whole picture, but one thing my gut tells me is that the uncle is a shitty leader.

As we drove up to the house, I only saw one security guy walking the perimeter with his face in his phone, probably playing some stupid game, and he didn't even blink when our car drove up and we all got out. At home, nobody walks inside without being frisked and searched to the point of awkward. Those are the orders and they either follow them or they die.

Another red fucking flag is him letting the Pet Shop Boys or the Lost Boys, or whatever the fuck they're called, encroach on their properties. That means that he's either a weak piece of shit or he's a sell-out. It doesn't matter which one he is, both options piss me off.

"Dev, we need to head out." I'm in full protective mode as I look out the window and see telephone-guy lift his head and stare straight at the house. His phone is now at his ear and he's talking, eyes darting from window to window as I lean back enough that he can't see me. I'm guessing he wasn't playing after all, he was giving someone the heads up. "Right fucking now."

Tyler has Madelina in his arms as he quickly leads her to me. Shelly pats Devon on the shoulder, mouthing him to "go, go" like she's done this one too many times in her life. I don't miss the movement from the cupboard to Devon as she hands him a gun and a knife—as if he wasn't already carrying—and kisses his cheek.

"Be careful now, son. It's not like it used to be." Devon pauses, staring at his mother, assessing her words, analyzing every intonation and every breath.

"Love ya, Mum. Don't leave this house. I'll have someone secure it within the hour." She nods, no doubt knowing the drill.

"That guy," I whisper to Devon. "Is shady as fuck."

With a grunt, Devon walks out of the house like he hasn't just been told the devil is out to get him and makes a beeline straight to the security guy obviously working for the wrong team.

"You know who I am, mate?"

"Yeah, you're the Butcher, sir."

"Right, right. Know who the lady in the house is you're supposed to be protectin'?" Oh shit. Devon's voice takes on an eerie calm that, in my world, means shit's about to go down. I push Tyler and Madelina into the car and they both turn around in their seats, watching the exchange go down.

"Yes, sir, she's your mum." I wish I could find sympathy for the kid, but wrong decisions get you killed.

"She is that, mate. And I protect what's mine." In a move that I know to be experience talking, Devon wraps one hand around the guy's neck and turns him quickly around so Devon's chest is to his back. Then, quicker than a gun's kickback, Devon slides out his knife and opens the idiot's neck right up before throwing him to the ground. He crouches down, wipes his knife off and closes the guy's eyes before standing and putting his weapon away.

When he walks back to us, he waves at the house and that's when I see the silhouette in the window. Yeah, Mrs. Mancini and Shelly would get along just fine. In fact, maybe they will if this relationship lasts long enough.

By the time we make it back to the hotel suite, Devon put in place a security detail worth its name and had a clean-up crew get rid of the snitch. Same shit different continent.

I make sure to keep in touch with Marco by calling him once or five times a day. J is doing her job like a pro but Marco wants me to come home. Apparently, J has told him that she understands the appeal to working with the boss, but she prefers working the streets and being in the nitty gritty of things. I get it, but there was no way I'd work entire days without seeing Madelina. I promised them both that we'd be back before the end of the week.

Now it's time to get down to business.

"Okay," Tyler breaks out his boardroom voice and everyone, except Devon, falls in line as we all sit at the dining table where I feasted on Madelina's Michelin Star worthy pussy. "I may not be of the criminal world... well, that's not entirely true when I see the way some of the CEOs manage their companies but that's not the point. With Marco, it was just a thing he was involved in, I was just on the outskirts of it all, my hands completely clean of it." We all nod.

"My brother made sure of that." Madelina's whispered words are filled with pride and, when she looks over at me, we grin at each other because what Marco wants, Marco gets. *I* make sure of that.

"Right, right. So, here's what I need." Devon scoffs at Tyler's demand and I realize that with two dominant personalities in one hotel room, shit's gonna get interesting fast. "How long are we here for? What are the risks? What do we do to make sure Lina is safe?"

Fucking Hell, our Rich Boy even has a pad of paper on the table with his rich boy's fountain pen ready to take notes. Shaking my head, I look across the table to see Devon grinning from ear to ear like he's enjoying the show. Tyler may be a shark in the conference room but he's a minnow swimming among piranhas in our world. The whole reason shit is deadly is because the fuckers we deal with are too unpredictable and hot-headed. Take the Greek brothers back in New York. Nothing they ever did made sense on paper but for them, their decisions were obvious.

"Mate, if I could lay out a plan for every stupid move these twats make, I'd be living the high life." It's Madelina's turn to scoff, throwing her arms out like a game show host showing off the grand prizes. "Good point, Treacle. I *am* living the high life." Reaching out, he plants his two hands on her waist and hauls her up on his lap, burying his face in her neck. We watch as she squeals and pretends to want to get away but from the way she's fisting his shirt, I call bullshit.

With a quick slap to her ass, Devon shushes her. "Be a good girl now and listen to what your Sir wants to say." The room falls quiet and the roles are clearly assigned.

"Yes, Daddy D." And now, I'm willing to bet my entire savings that we're all hard as fucking rocks with that little answer.

Tyler clears his throat, readjusting himself as he narrows his eyes at Devon. "Moving on. What do you need to do to get Lizzy back home safe? Are we talking another shootout? Are the police getting involved?"

"No one's calling the bobbies, especially not me. If I have a problem, I take care of that problem. End of." With his mouth planted on Madelina's neck, he barely looks at Tyler as he answers.

"Wait, who's Bobby? We haven't met him, have we?" Tyler jots down the name then looks to me. "Did you catch a Bobby at the pub?"

"Ah, Christ. It's like lettin' loose two toddlers in the sea without a lifejacket." Devon gives Madelina a playful bite before raising his eyes to Tyler. "Bobbies are the cops. The police. That's what we call them." Now we both frown because that's just fucking weird. Taking pity on us, he continues, "Named after the bloke who established the London police, Sir Robert Peel. Could've called them the Peelers but that would've confused you even more."

Brits are weird, but then I think about it... "No weirder than 'cops', I guess. I don't fucking know where that word comes from so I'm not judging." I stand because sitting for too long makes me nervous.

"It's from the verb 'to cop' which is slang for 'to catch'. Mid nineteenth century if memory serves right." The room goes completely quiet except for Tyler's pen scratching against the paper. No doubt feeling all eyes on him, he raises his head and frowns. "What?"

"Do I need to change your nickname to Harvard?" Devon laughs, his eyes bright with mirth.

"He went to NYU. It's closer to home and has less douchebags." Madelina blows a kiss to Tyler and I have to shake my head at their antics. This all feels so fucking normal and fun, but there's always a yin with the yang and I need to be prepared for that shoe to drop.

"You know what we need?" Devon's voice booms across the room as he stands abruptly, taking Madelina right with him. Meanwhile, my gut is convinced that the next words out of his mouth are going to be a hard no for me. "Fun! We should go sightseeing. The big wheel, the big clock, the big palace..." He kisses our girl squarely on the mouth and whispers, "My big cock is for later, though, I promise."

"No, Dev. Absolutely fucking no." I'm adamant about this. He's got people coming out of the woodwork for his ass and he wants to, what? See the sights?

Lina squeals, jumping up and down, clapping her hands like we've just offered her the world on a platter.

"I don't think that's a very good idea, Chef. Not with all the threats around the city, not to mention every-fucking-body knows who you are. It's careless and dangerous. I veto this idea." No sooner his words are out of his mouth that our girl throws herself at Tyler, arms around his neck and pout firmly in place. We all know she's manipulating him and he may be her Sir, but she's his Achilles heel.

"Please, Tyler? Just for an hour. I haven't been to London in so long and I really, really want to see how pretty Big Ben is now that it's been renovated. Last time I went I couldn't even get a picture."

Damn, she's good.

"Lina... I..." Fucking Hell, good thing I'm here.

"Fuck no. We are not going out on the town to be all fucking touristy and shit when people, actual criminals, want to kill us. No. Not happening and that's it."

When Madelina turns her doe eyes toward me, I realize just how fucked I truly am.

Almost three hours later, we've seen the fucking wheel turn and turn and Madelina got a picture of Big Ben. Spoiler alert, it's the same as before the renovations. We're walking back from Buckingham Palace by way of Westminster—something about Queen Elizabeth and her final journey, who the fuck knows—and about to cross the Thames so we can get back to our hotel when my stomach tightens and my eyes dart around the space.

"Oh! We need a selfie with the London Eye in the background and the river, it's just so pretty!" She's pulling a grinning Devon with her as she gestures for us to hurry up, but I can't focus. There are too many variables and I can't be both a bodyguard and a participant in this game. I can only be one if I want to be efficient.

"Come on, Enzo! Tyler, your arm is the longest, you can take the picture."

"I beg to differ, Treacle."

"Just take the fucking picture and let's get the fuck out of here." Yeah, that's me. I'm the fucking Grinch. But, to be fair, we're just sitting ducks here.

"Oh, Enzo, you're actually growling in this picture, I can practically hear you. We need to—" Her words die with the sound of screeching tires and the slamming of a sliding door on a van.

By the time I turn around to grab Madelina and let the other two idiots shoot their way out of this shit, I've got a bag over my head and we're being thrown into the fucking van. It all happens in less than ten seconds before we're rolling with the tight turns the driver takes.

Goddamn it, I knew this was a bad idea.

Chapter Twenty-Seven

Lina

For the second time in my life, I'm fucking helpless. Being thrown around in the back of a van with a bag over my head might just be the most cliché way to be kidnapped, but fuck me, it's effective.

What these guys haven't done though, is check me for weapons. Rookie move. Because there is no chance I'm going to allow myself to be in the same position as last time.

Grunts and grumbles of protest from my three protective men let me know they're still with me, alive, and likely in the same position I am. Arms tied down with something around my waist, bag over my head, and a little bruised from slamming against the floor of the van. To be fair, the thick jacket I'm wearing has cushioned some of it, but the driver is handling the van like a lunatic. It's as if he's purposefully trying to throw us around.

I won't lie and say I'm totally calm right now, but I'm doing my best, channeling all the powerful people in my life and combining their strength with my own. These people will not get to see my fear.

"What's that on ya face, mate?" The voice is raspy, coming from somewhere near the front of the van.

"Bitch cut me with her shoe. Reckon Ben'll let me keep her like he's kept the Quinn pussy?"

A trio of growls echoes through the small space, followed by an almighty roar from Devon. "I'm gonna slice out your fucking tongues and feed them to the pigs as soon as I get out of here. And trust me, I *will* get out of this."

I have to be honest with myself, as disgusting as that is, the way he threatens anyone who so much as questions my honor is hot as fuck. This whole situation somehow feels different from last time. The dread isn't like lead in my stomach. I'm invincible with these men by my side.

"Ooh, the big bad Butcher gonna get us, Steve. I'm shiverin' in ma boots." They laugh, joined by maybe one or two more voices—I can't quite tell—but what I *can* hear is the tremble in his voice as he speaks.

The van stops suddenly after what feels like half an hour and we all go sliding forward. I land against a body that sounds a lot like Enzo when he grunts as I slam into him.

"I've got you, Madelina." His words are whispered into my back, meant for me and me alone, and the power behind them only adds to my hope that this is all going to work out.

The door to the van is opened, sunlight brightening my vision through the clothy material over my face, and I can hear scrapes and footsteps as people get out.

"Be fucking careful, cunts. I'm noting every fucking scratch and mark on our bodies, because I'm gonna pay them back tenfold." Devon's voice is getting further away as someone grabs my arm, pulling me up and out of the van. I tumble, falling to my knees on the floor before my arm is yanked hard, pulling me to standing and dragging me in the direction they want me.

I'm being amenable, for now, waiting until I know all of my men are safe and in sight before I try anything that could be considered stupid. My breathing is controlled, even, because if I allow myself to begin spiraling about this for one second, I know I won't come out of it any time soon.

The person gripping me roughly pushes me down into a chair and rips the bag from my head. It takes a minute for my eyes to adjust to the light again, but when they do, I take in the room.

A fucking pub.

Enzo, Tyler, and Devon are also now seated on separate chairs beside me, bags off, and their arms tied to their sides like mine. We're all in a row, facing the bar with a small blonde woman sitting on the top surrounded by ten, maybe more, men... no, boys in hoodies. One of them has a tattoo covering half his face, another is cracking his knuckles as he tries to stare Devon down, but mostly, they're all holding guns by their sides.

"Big brother! I got impatient. Didn't wanna wait for you to come see me, so the boys said they'd fetch you." I'm guessing the woman is Lizzy then.

"Lizzy, what the actual fuck? Tell them to untie us if all you wanted was a visit." Devon is seething, his voice an angry growl.

The sister hesitates before jumping from the bar, landing on her feet and stepping closer to Devon. Her eyes hold a hint of respect, of love, and I thought she was about to do as he asked when the sound of wood banging against wood makes her jump. Still trying to control my nerves, I look around, noticing a tall athletic-looking man in a navy-blue hoodie stalking toward us from what I'm assuming is some back room.

"Get away from him, Lizzy." There's no kindness in his tone. Just pure hatred, and this couldn't possibly be the Ben they've all been talking about.

"But, Benny, he's my brother. I can trust him, it's fine. I'm gonna untie him."

"You fucking won't."

Lizzy jumps back, head bowed, obeying who is clearly her master, and not in a fun sexy way. Because this guy is a douchebag.

"Sorry, Benny."

"It's okay, babe. Come here. Have you told your brother the good news yet?" The smile is back on her face and she bounces over to him, sitting in his lap with her arms around his neck. His eyes never leave Devon, watching his reaction, no doubt trying to get a rise out of him. "Or should I say, *our* brother?" Ben's fake laugh grates against my nerves and I want to punch him square in the face for the way he's handling Lizzy. Pawing at her breasts and groping at her pussy in front of us.

Luckily, it's winter and she's fully clothed, but she still writhes around on him as if there's nobody else in the room, forgetting we're mid-conversation here.

"Go and get me a beer." As abruptly as he began, he pushes Lizzy off his lap. She stumbles a little but manages to stay upright, straightening out her tight black sweater before running off behind the bar.

Come to think of it, I recognize this place. I think it's the same pub we came to on our first night in London.

"Oh, Butcher Butcher Butcher. Did you really think you'd be able to blow up my betting shop without repercussions?" Ben leans forward in his wooden chair, resting his elbows on his knees. "Did you really think that running away to another country would protect you?" His eyes are full of glee, like he's just won the best game of chess he's ever played.

It doesn't last long. Confusion and anger are all I see when Devon starts laughing maniacally.

"What's so fucking funny?" Spit flies from Ben's mouth as he stands, waving his arms out to the sides in question, like he's posturing.

Devon continues to laugh, but it's not that real, joyous, carefree laugh that I love to hear, it's dark. It's evil. It promises bad things.

And fuck me, I'm here for it.

Wriggling a little because this shit is uncomfortable, it hits me, and I can't believe I didn't figure it out before now. With the way the rope is tied, if I can shimmy it upward, I can pull it straight over my head. Fucking idiots should've had lessons in rope tying from my sexy Brit.

"Here's your drink, Babe." Lizzy interrupts Ben as he stalks toward a still-laughing Devon, and the furious look he gives her sends a chill through my bones.

"The head on this pint is worse than the head you fucking give, Lizzy. Do it again." Quicker than a flash, his arm swipes out and he cracks her across the cheek, knocking her to the floor. "Get your bitch arse up. You're making the place look dirty."

Silence descends. Everyone's eyes on the situation playing out in front of them.

Heavy breaths, followed by a growl and the smashing of glass draws my attention to the right, where Devon has escaped from his ropes and is now standing toe-to-toe with Ben, a broken bottle held against Ben's neck.

"We only had the carpets in here replaced yesterday, thanks to your boys treating me to a welcome home shootout. I think I'll go for laminate next time, easier to clean." Devon's tone as he threatens Ben is as sexy now as it was earlier. Deep, guttural, demanding… shivers race up my spine and I take a deep breath to calm my out-of-control libido.

I guess now's as good a time as any to shimmy myself out of these ropes.

Chapter Twenty-Eight

Tyler

Dealing with gangs is a lot like dealing with power-hungry businessmen. Some are quietly amassing billions in the shadows and others are like this posturing wannabe. I should probably be afraid for my life, and I suppose on some level I am, but I'm fascinated by the theatrics of this whole fucking shitshow. It's like theater but deadlier.

Movement in front of me catches my attention and I see my Gumdrop shimmying out of her rope get-up. Rule number one in any given situation, "Never underestimate your opponent". These idiots didn't even bother to tighten the ropes on her, probably thinking she'd be some powerless wallflower. Where they thoroughly checked us for weapons, it's obvious from the bulge under her jacket that it didn't even occur to them to check her.

My attention is now on Devon, who's not only out of his seat but he's got a broken bottle at Benny's throat, prompting the guns to rise up from every other hooded idiot in this place, threatening him with talk of laminate flooring. I do agree. At this rate, carpeting would be a huge financial loss for this place but it would take away from the warmth. Okay, now is probably not the time to analyze the pros and cons of pub designs.

Just as Lina throws her ropes over her head, she grabs her own gun and points it at no one in particular with one hand as she unties the ropes on Enzo with the other. I'm last to be free, thanks to Enzo's quick work, but I feel weird just standing here with my billions that seems to be as worthless as a knife at a gun party. Dipping my hand inside my jacket, I take out my unharmed phone and, thank fuck, I got Emma's number that first night at the pub. I knew it might come in handy.

Me: Need a little assistance at the pub. Benny's boys are gun happy.

Emma: On our way.

"Devvy, let him go, please, Big Brother. I love him!" Lizzy sounds half feral, half out of her mind with worry.

"This piece of shit just backhanded you like you're his personal punching bag." Devon is speaking to Lizzy but his eyes are on Ben, his voice as lethal as a nuclear bomb.

"No, no. It's okay. I like it a little rough, ya know?" Her words are like a slap to the face. Confusing rough play with physical abuse is all too common in our society and just as I'm about to explain the difference to her, Lina steps up like a fucking goddess.

"Sweetheart, I love a little bit of rough play but make no mistake, if any of my men"—she points to the three of us with pride in her eyes—"were to slap me around like a worthless bitch, I would cut his balls off." Her gun still pointing at the boys behind Ben, she leans in and faux-whispers. "The difference between Devon, Enzo, and Tyler is that they are kings of my pleasure while this asshole isn't worth the toilet paper he wipes his sorry ass on." Damn, I love this woman.

"No, he's just been stressed out and I didn't do his lager right. Ya know what I mean, Devvy, right? He's... he... too much head is gross, right?" Devon doesn't answer her but instead brings the bottle closer to Ben's neck, letting the sharp edge cut into the skin of his throat.

"Devvy, if you hurt him they'll shoot you. They will! They've been given orders, ya know?" Enzo takes a protective step in front of me while Devon steps even closer to Ben, the scratch on his throat becoming a small gash.

"Tell me, Benny Boy, you think too much head is gross?"

"You hurt me and she dies, those are the fucking orders to my boys."

Devon leans in to speak directly into Ben's ear and whispers something I can't hear, but it makes Lizzy gasp, her face frozen in shock. Not a moment later, the beer bottle dives into Ben's carotid artery and his body falls to the floor, but not before Devon grabs his gun from his waist and shoots three of the boys taken off guard.

Lizzy drops to the floor, kneeling at Ben's side, wailing in pain and despair at the loss of her... captor? Because no man worthy of the title fiancé would treat his woman the way he did.

Enzo pushes me behind one table while Lina takes cover behind another, shooting at the rest of the guys.

I can't see everything from here, but I don't like Lina being so fucking far away and in danger of catching a bullet.

From the corner of my eye, I see movement at the door, my relief palpable when I realize reinforcements have arrived. Five or six men come barreling in, guns drawn, as they dispatch to different corners of the pub. That's when I see Emma, Devon's sister, on her haunches, making her way to me since I'm the closest to the door.

"What the hell happened here?" Emma's talking to me but her eyes are darting left and right as bullets spray from every which way.

"One minute we're taking pictures of Big Ben, the next we're being kidnapped by Shitty Ben." I swear, this continent does not like us.

Emma pops her head up to shoot but misses whoever she was aiming at, dropping back down behind our cover.

"You wouldn't happen to have an extra one of those, would you?" I'm no gun expert but surely I can point and shoot, right? I mean, not to brag but I'm pretty certain I'm smarter than half the guys in here combined. How hard can it be?

"Sorry, mate. Like my brother, I'm more of a knife girl. Got this because you mentioned guns in your text and I'm not stupid enough to show up at a literal gun fight with only a knife." Right, makes sense.

A bullet hits the top of the overturned table, making me flinch and crouch a little lower, my eyes locking immediately on Lina to make sure she's okay. Again, the warmth of relief settles in my veins when I see her reloading her gun with a clip she was hiding in her boots. Damn, why is that so fucking hot?

"I need to get to that guy, I can't see him from this spot." I turn to Emma, who's popping her head up over the table every once in the while, shooting then taking cover once more. I can't comprehend how anybody survives these types of situations. "All right, I'll be right back. Stay covered!" Her words prompt me to grab her by the waist and pull her back toward me, to safety.

"Are you fucking crazy? You're going to get yourself shot if you go anywhere right now." As I peek out from around the table, I see the guy she's talking about and realize that she's right, being just two tables down would give her a clean shot. Still, I can't let her go.

When I turn to lay it on her again, she's lunging for the next table over, too quick for me to grab a hold of her again. "Fuck!"

It only took one second.

One pop.

Peeking out to make sure Emma made it across safely, I'm met with wide open eyes and no life behind them, a perfect round circle just beneath her hairline.

"Shit. Fuck." I'm stunned into silence, frozen in place, my eyes fixed on that little red circle that seems so insignificant, yet the enormity of its consequences is too great to understand. I don't know why my first instinct is to pull her body to safety, it's not like she can get any more hurt, but it feels disrespectful to leave her there on the glass and debris. To be honest, I'm afraid that if Devon sees her, the beast inside him will annihilate us all.

Hell, seeing her like this, knowing she's Devon's older sister, brings unwanted images of my sister flashing across my mind's eye. I know what he's going to feel, how he's going to try and push that hurt and confusion down, because grieving a sister is unlike anything else. The pain is profound, it's deep, and it's going to destroy a little piece of his heart.

Before I'm shaken back into the moment—the brutal, deadly moment—I vow to be there for him when the time comes. He's going to need someone who knows and that someone is me.

My gaze darts over to Lina as she looks to me, her eyes falling to Emma then rising up to mine. It's like she can read my mind, her head shaking vehemently, her mouth giving me the order to stay put, but I can't.

I won't just sit here and watch the woman I love fight her own battle. Picking up Emma's gun, I peek out from the side of the table, again, making sure it's as safe as can be before leaping over to where Lina is handling a gun like a fucking master. I don't have time to admire her ease, her poise, the fierce look on her face as she protects the men she loves, but it's impossible to miss.

Launching myself across a few feet to get to Lina, I feel a burning sensation in my stomach, like someone took a laser and sliced my side open. If I had to guess I'd say I've either been shot or I got glass caught in me as I tried to slide across the debris-laden pub. Either way, it hurts like a motherfucker, but I'll deal with that later.

"Goddammit, Tyler, you were safe over there, why the fuck did you—" She cuts her rant off with a sinister grin. "Gotcha, you piece of shit." Jesus, why is Lina killing people making me fucking horny?

I don't want to get in her way, so I twist and turn before leaning against the table and wincing at the biting pain in my side, my hand coming away with wetness seeping between my fingers. The sight exacerbates the pain for a second, forcing me to drop my head back against the table in hopes of regulating my breathing.

Fuck.

"All yous put your fucking guns down or I will shoot this cunt."

It was a second too long. What was chaos a minute ago is now complete and utter silence as Lizzy presses the barrel of her gun against the back of Lina's head. I have a gun but no plan. I have billions of dollars in my fucking bank account that mean absolutely jack all right now. In this moment of utter clarity, it occurs to me that everything I've ever worked for means nothing if I can't have Lina by my side.

"Lizzy, look around. Ben's boys are down for the count. You're free, Baby Girl. Let's go home and—" Devon doesn't get the chance to finish his phrase and I have no idea what his face looks like behind me, but I can clearly see the struggle and confusion on Lizzy's pretty features.

"That's what you don't get, Devvy. He *was* my home."

In the haze that is my mental state right now, all I hear is the deafening sound of a gun being fired before Devon roars loud enough to make the fucking walls shake.

"Noooooo!"

I blink twice and now Devon is towering over his younger sister just as he sees Emma's body lying on the floor across the way from us. Guilt drops on my shoulders like an endless weight, knowing I should have stopped her sooner.

"Dev, it's my fault. She was too quick and I—" Devon's murderous eyes land on me, assessing my wound before darting over to Lina, who reaches up and takes his tightly closed fist.

"You okay?" His tone is deadly but his concern is written in the dilation of his pupils. When he looks back at me, he's no longer a bloodthirsty animal but the man we've all come to love. "You're hurt." Lina's head snaps to me and we lock eyes, a drunk smile popping up on my lips.

"Flesh wound." I'm slurring, like we came here to put away beers instead of getting pushed into a van and forced to participate in a fucking shootout. Again.

I must have passed out because the next thing I know, we're in a car, speeding away, my vision blurry and my side burning.

"It's just a graze, he'll be fine with some pain killers and a thorough disinfection." My head turns to Enzo, his features tight, his voice low and submissive, almost.

Nothing is quite clear right now but my mind brings me back to the pub, something I need to know. Something I need to find out.

"We need to teach him how to use a gun. This shouldn't have happened."

There it is. That's what I needed to know.

"Gumdrop?"

"Yes, Sir."

Chapter Twenty-Nine

Devon

Not once in my thirty-six years of life did I imagine I'd have to shoot my damn sister.

What the fuck was she thinking?

Lizzy is my family, my blood, and I love her so fucking much, but she screwed up big time the second she aimed that gun at my woman. Lina is the very air I breathe, the reason my heart beats heavily in my chest, my priority in all things. I would rather slaughter every living thing and bathe in their blood than live in a world without her.

My little sister will be spending a lot of time in a rehab facility once she's healed from the hole I shot in her shoulder, maybe even the local nuthouse. Either way, there's no way I'm letting her near Lina again.

There's no way I'm letting her near anyone I care about again.

Emma is dead because Lizzy fucked up, and she may be my little sister—which is the only reason I let her live—but I never want to see or hear from her again. My fucking heart is broken and there's shit all I can do about it. Charlie and Bethany have lost their mum, their everything. They don't even have a dad to take care of them since that sniveling little prick picked up and left when Emma was pregnant with Charlie. I was on my way to find him and skin him alive for hurting my sister but she made me promise to wait. Somehow, she believed he would come back one day. Well, he's gonna have to now, because I'm going to find that fucker and give him a choice. Either he takes good care of his kids or he'll wish to die by the time I get done with him. It guts me to think of their little faces when they find out their whole world has been tossed upside down.

I know Mum will take care of it, she always does. Between us, we'll make sure my sister's babies know they're loved and have the best start in life, but Mum's going to be fucking devastated when I tell her everything that happened tonight. No parent should ever have to experience the loss of a child, let alone two of them.

Fuck, I don't know how I'm going to tell her without breaking down myself. Staying strong, keeping my head held high, these are the things I need to do to keep our family standing. Showing any kind of weakness just isn't gonna cut it, but I'm fucking hurting inside. The pain of losing another sister is indescribable, it cuts so deep that I'm almost numb to the whole thing.

While I want to scream and shout and tear apart the Deptford boys again for their part in this, I'm also very aware that won't help. Nothing will. Time is literally the only thing that can make any of this more bearable.

Seeing Tyler down, blood seeping from a wound in his side, was almost as gut-wrenching as the image of my sister's bleeding skull, which tells me how much I've come to care for the fucker. Luckily, he's going to be okay or my woman would be inconsolable, and I'd probably be taking revenge on the entire fucking city right now.

Falling apart isn't in the cards though, I can't.

The shady shit that's going down around here is doing my head in. I need to find out what the fuck's actually happening and my uncle Harry should have some answers. There's no way the Deptford Boys should have been anywhere near The Anchor Pub, again, but for them to be using it the way they did this afternoon tells me they've been allowed some privileges not meant for them.

And right now, that's Uncle Harry's problem.

Enzo and I are sitting in Mum's kitchen waiting for my Uncle Harry to arrive, with Lina, Mum, and the doc in the bedroom upstairs with Tyler. The babysitter for Charlie and Bethany is booked overnight as the kids are already in bed sleeping. I don't want to break their little hearts just yet. I want to let them have one more night of peaceful sleep before destroying their entire world.

Fuck, it hurts. I take a deep breath, needing to concentrate on the here and now. What I can actually do to make things better somehow. A lot of people rely on me to be strong, to be their relief, to be everything I don't feel right now, but I'm not the kind to fall into a pit of depression. I'm well aware that loss is a part of life, and living the way we do means danger is around every corner. It's the price we pay for trying to protect the bigger picture.

Regret for staying away this last year eats away at me. If I had been here, I'd have had more time with my big sister...

No, I need to dig myself out of this hole and get the job done. At least Tyler will only need stitches and maybe some antibiotics. Thank fuck. I might've allowed the darkness to take me if I had to see my woman's pain from that.

I'm fucking furious at what's happened, devastated even, but watching Lina shooting the shit out of those cunts was some of the best foreplay I've ever had. It may have been dampened by seeing my dead sister, but that doesn't mean our girl isn't gonna get fucked into next Tuesday when we get out of here.

"How's ya coffee, big guy?" The way Enzo raises a brow at me makes me smile. For all the brawn and bravery of this man, he's too polite to tell me he thinks my mum's coffee is shit. Compared to the stuff they have across the pond, I can't deny he's right. "You could have said no when she offered."

He shakes his head, the corners of his mouth tipping up, which is happening more often the longer we all spend together. I like it. A smile looks good on him.

"You know you don't have to pretend everything's okay with me." The smile turns into a concerned frown. "I don't have siblings so I can't imagine what you're feeling, but I like to think we're family now. The four of us. Your pain is our pain and we shoulder it together. Okay?"

"I hear ya, I do. And I think that's one of your longest speeches ever." I laugh, but it's a little forced. I know it, he knows it. "Thanks. I appreciate it, but I can't let all that into my head with everything going on, ya know?"

The way he looks at me tells me he understands exactly what I'm saying, and it's like something switches inside of him too. That switch that turns off the emotional shit and brings it right back to business.

"What are we involved in here, D?"

"Whatever it is, is bollocks." I breathe a heavy sigh, not entirely sure myself what's going on. Aside from my dad going rogue and having to be put down like the dog he was, things usually run relatively smoothly around here. Most of our business is done behind closed doors, not in the middle of my fuckin' pub.

"Gangs are rife in London, but they usually stick to their own turf and the collateral damage is minimal. The Quinn family, my family, run this area, we supply the drugs and offer protection to the businesses and people around here. We keep the kids out of trouble and offer the adults a better life. Sometimes, rival gangs try and encroach on our turf, or think they can get in on the action somehow, which always turns out badly for them. We have a tentative relationship with other gangs, some are on our side, others aren't. The Deptford Boys never have been. Before I left for New York, I found out they'd been dealing to some kids at a couple of the secondary schools—like high school for your lot—so as a leaving present to my family, I dealt with the matter and fried the fuckers responsible. That should have been the end of it." I pause to down the rest of my cuppa tea, needing to take a moment to try and figure out how to deal with all of this.

Bringing my woman into the middle of a gang war was not my intention, but it's done now. Fuck all I can do about it. I won't regret my decision though, because having these three here with me has literally saved my life.

"So what does all that mean for us?" Marco is a lucky fucker to have Enzo by his side. This man is straight to the point. No messing, no fuss.

"It means, old mucker, that The Butcher is back in town to sort shit out."

He nods once, telling me what I already knew. He's here for whatever I need.

"Knock knock. Shelly? You home, love?"

Uncle Harry.

Enzo's body tenses at the newcomer, and I don't blame him, my uncle doesn't exactly give off good vibes. Why I ever thought he'd be responsible enough to head our family, I'll never know.

"She's upstairs, Harry. We're in the kitchen." Relaxing back in my chair, I wait for him to make his way through to us.

"Holy shit. Who's the giant, Dev?" The shock is evident on Harry's face and the cocky swagger he entered the kitchen with, dissipates immediately.

"It doesn't matter who he is, Harry, but I wouldn't piss him off if I were you. Now, what the fuck's been going down around here?"

The spotlights in the ceiling reflect off the top of Harry's shaved head as he turns his back on me to put the kettle on. He hasn't even mentioned Emma yet and I'm fucking fuming. It's like he doesn't give a shit.

He clears his throat before speaking, avoiding eye contact completely. "You weren't supposed to come back, kid."

"I ain't been a kid for a very long time, Harry." I remain seated but my muscles are tense, anger rippling beneath the surface. "Now tell me. What. The. Fuck. Is going on?"

With a heavy sigh, he turns to face me, head bowed, and still, the motherfucker won't look me in the eye. "The Deptford Boys had a good offer. They wanted to partner up, ya know? Make us stronger."

"The Deptford Boys are fucking maggots, Harry. Always have been. Do you have any idea how Lizzy, your fucking niece, was being treated by their wanker of a leader? I would hope fucking not, because your balls will be on my wall as a display if you did. Their leader is dead. They're fucking done for, Harry, but so is your fucking niece, Emma. Not only did they fuck Lizzy up, Emma is dead. Or do you just not give a monkey's? Because you sure as shit don't look like you do."

Shifting from foot to foot, Harry shakes his head. "Of course I care. I loved the girl, but she shouldn't have been th—"

"Oh fuck off with that shit. *You* should've been there, Harry. As the head of the family, it was *your* responsibility to sort the problem out, not make shady fucking deals on the side. Charlie and Bethany have no mum because of you, and only you. Those two little babies are going to wake up in the morning and be given the worst news of their lives. I'm not even sure Charlie will understand it, to be honest. He's not old enough to speak, let alone remember his mum. And you did that, Harry. Fucking *you*." I'm seething, shaking with rage. I want to shoot this cunt in the skull.

"Listen, Kid. It ain't your problem anymore—"

"I told you, Harry. I ain't no fucking kid. You will address me properly."

Harry's eyes widen as he grips the kitchen counter behind him. Stoic as ever beside me, Enzo glares daggers at my uncle, ready to strike at any given moment and I wouldn't even need to ask. This man reads a situation better than I can read a book.

"Devon. It—"

"No, Harry. Try again." My tone is quiet, barely above a whisper, because I'm about to lose my shit at my uncle. He's being a disrespectful cunt, he's responsible for the losses, the pain, and I killed my dad for less shit than this fucker's putting us through.

"B-Butcher." He doesn't move from where he's standing, but I see the fight or flight decision flashing through his eyes.

"Exactly. Now try and tell me again that my sister being dead isn't my problem."

Before he can get a word out, his mouth flapping open and close like a damned fish, I interrupt again. "You can't do it, can ya, Harry? Because you're a fucking weed that needs to be ripped from the Earth. Now, I think me and you should step outside because if you get blood in my mum's kitchen, it'll hurt more."

Enzo stands, towering over my uncle, and I smile, a menacing and satisfied thing.

"Can't we talk about this, Ki—Butcher? Come on, I'm the head of the family. We're blood. There's nothin—"

"Get the fuck outside. Now."

The scowl on Harry's face is a thing of beauty, and I've found my outlet for the rage boiling inside me. He moves quickly through the French doors of the kitchen and into the garden, standing firm with his hands behind his back like he thinks I didn't just see him grab a knife from the side.

Two can play that game. I grab a bigger one and follow him out. I can feel the heat of Enzo close behind me and he positions himself a few feet away as I face my uncle.

"Why don't you just go home? We don't need you here."

"I can't do that, Harry. My woman had a gun to her head today and my big sister is dead." The growl beside me coming from Enzo fuels my own anger and my smile doesn't reach my eyes as I take in my uncle. "You fucked up, Harry. You let the fucking rats in, put my people in danger, and I've already had three local families beg me to stay because they don't feel fucking safe anymore!" I'm shouting now, unable to help myself, but I try real hard to keep my relaxed posture.

"They're not your people anymore, Dev. You gave it all up when you jumped ship and moved to New York." Cunt's getting brave but I can sense the hesitation in his tone.

"They've always been my people, Harry."

"You're an ungrateful little prick. After everything I've done for you and this family, you think this stand-off is going to actually solve anything?" The shakiness in his tone gives away his nerves. He knows he's about to die. There's no way out of it at this point.

"All you did for this family is bring it down and get people killed. You're a fucking stain on human existence, Harry. The pigs will enjoy the feast they're getting from your worthless fucking meat."

"You wouldn't."

"I fucking would. And I will." With a step forward and a quick slash, Harry's cheek is now bleeding as he screams out in pain.

"Wait! You don't wanna do this with your mum watching, do ya?" He looks behind me, waving at someone in the house, and I deflate a little, because no, I don't need Mum to watch this. Turning so I can ask Mum to make herself busy was a mistake.

Harry is and always has been a fucking liar.

Nobody is standing there.

In a split second, Enzo is roaring, moving at lightning speed, then there's a loud crack and a thud. Uncle Harry is on the ground, his neck broken, and Enzo is breathing heavily, like he used to do in the ring at the end of a fight. Like he's eager for more.

Fucker just saved my life. I don't even care that he took the pleasure of killing Harry away from me.

"Didn't know ya cared that much, mate." It's actually a beautiful moment. I fucking love these guys.

"Fuck off. You know I do. Is there anywhere we can get a real coffee?"

"Here ya go, lads. You get to open two today." I throw two chocolate advent calendars on the coffee table in front of the dark-gray sofa. The sofa Tyler is currently lying on because our girl is worried he'll pop a stitch if he moves around too much. He won't, it wasn't even that deep, but her worry for him—for all of us, really—is cute as fuck.

Every now and then I'll catch her staring at me, ready to pounce and be my rock if I need her. The woman is everything and just being in her presence is enough for me. Death is shit, but it happens. Moping about it won't bring my sister back. My three younger sisters, Amelia, Sophie, and Olivia, came to Mum's as soon as they heard the news. They're rallying around Mum and each other to hold themselves up for now as funeral arrangements are made. It'll take a little time, considering the circumstances, all the red tape we need to jump through, but it'll get sorted.

Tyler's legs are resting on Lina's lap and Enzo is on the floor between her legs, leaning against the sofa and giving her a foot massage. Coming up behind her, I grip her shoulders and knead her tense muscles between my fingers. She leans her head back to look up at me and her smile and the gleam in her eyes are fucking perfection.

"What about me? Don't I get one?" Scrunching her eyebrows, she gives me that pout, the one that makes me wanna do dirty things to my bratty girl.

"Of course ya do, Treacle. But yours is extra special." I lean down to kiss her forehead, giving her shoulders a final squeeze before bending to grab the chunky advent calendar at my feet.

"Wow, that's huge!"

"Not the only huge thing in this room, Treacle." I go back to massaging her shoulders as she inspects the box.

"Oh my God, this is an erotic advent calendar! I love it. Thank you, Daddy D." Oh, there it is. My cock twitches at her words, but I'll let her open the first two doors before playtime. I'm as eager as she is to see what's inside because, whatever it is, we're using it. Twenty-four days of new toys to play with.

The huge purple box opens up like a really thick book, two halves with twelve doors on each one. It takes seconds for Lina to open the first two doors, and her squeal as she pulls out the first one has my cock twitch turning into an ache to be inside her sweet cunt.

"It's a clit stimulator thingy. This might mean I don't need you guys anymore." Her twinkling laugh makes me shake my head.

"Woah, hang on a minute. No, Gumdrop. D might have given you the toys, but you won't be using them without one of us."

"Agreed." Enzo reaches for his advent calendar on the table, opening the first two doors and happily munching his chocolate. Our Italian Stallion has a secret sweet tooth.

"Reckon this place will let me rent it out permanently? I'm gonna need to start spending more time here in London to sort all this shit out and I wanna remember your sweet little cunt on that dining table every time I eat."

"It would be more efficient if we bought a house here instead of wasting money on long hotel stays." Tyler's voice is a little deeper than usual, but that probably has a lot to do with the meds, and his comment surprises me.

"Yes! I've always loved those cute cottages this country has. You know, the ones in the movies where they're surrounded by fields of flowers, wooded areas to get lost in, wrecked and abandoned castles nearby..." Lina trails off, lost in her head as she daydreams about cottages.

Enzo leans his head back to look across to Tyler and they both tip their heads as if they've just had a silent conversation. The comment about spending more time in London seems to have taken a turn and it's not one I'm mad about. With the easy way they're accepting what I need to do, I can now picture a life here, with them.

"Ooh, what's this? Oh, it's a baby buttplug! That's so cute. Look, it has a little red gem on the end shaped like a heart." She holds it up for me to see and I smile at her enthusiasm, ideas running rampant through my mind. It's just the right size for a beginner...

The shrill tone of my phone ringing interrupts our moment and I roll my eyes, pulling it from my back pocket to see who's calling.

It's Liam, the guy managing my gym back in New York.

"What's up, bud?"

"Oh thank fuck, Boss. The gym's gone!"

"What d'ya mean *gone*? Did you lose your GPS?" This guy's cracking me up, except his tone is all too serious.

"No, Boss. I mean, it's been burned to the ground."

Chapter Thirty

Enzo

We barely had the chance to get used to the time zone change in London before we were flying right back to The City to put out new fires. Literal ones.

When Devon gave us the details, it was a no-brainer. We all packed our shit and were ready to head out within the following couple of hours. Even Tyler popped two pain meds and walked out like it was nothing.

To be honest, it's basically a flesh wound and if he wants to be a part of this family, he's going to have to get used to it. The blood, that is. Hopefully, we won't be getting shot again anytime soon and definitely no dying. Emma's death was enough to nearly break Devon's spirit.

We all tried to convince him to stay for the funeral but he just ignored the attempts, sometimes even growling at us, before going back to whatever he's doing. I get it. Devon and I are different types of beasts compared to the rest of humankind. We don't grieve with love and memories. Our grief comes in blood. If I had to guess, I'd say whoever decided to fuck with Devon in The City is going to be paying for Emma's death. At least, that's how I'd deal with it.

The other thing that sucks about getting shot and losing a loved one is having a doting girlfriend who refuses to see you in pain. Translation... the flight back wasn't nearly as much fun as the flight over. In fact, the only fun we had was inside the bottles of Tyler's in-flight bar.

"Looks like I've got some pyro lovers on the loose." Crossing my arms over my chest, I nod at Devon as we stand in front of what used to be the best fucking gym in all five boroughs. I can feel his rage buzzing around him and I have to be honest, it's fucking contagious. I'm pissed on his behalf and when we find these fuckers, we'll have some fun of our own with them.

"When we catch these cunts, we'll see if they like fire up close." I start at the sound of Devon's laughter, like the sonic boom from a jet crossing the sound barrier. It's so out of place with the scene in front of us that it makes me laugh too. Pretty sure we look certifiable standing in front of a burned down building laughing our asses off.

"Hmm, I do like using fire to make my enemies repent." And now, he's back. The tone of his voice leaving absolutely no doubt that he's going to charcoal some baddies and he's going to enjoy the fuck out of it.

"Less blood to clean up. Win win."

"You're not wrong, mate. It's a great fucking point."

Walking around the perimeter, I look for any signs of anything that could help us figure out who would do this and why. It's not like Devon's out here making enemies across The City. He's got a good business, fair rules, and a successful restaurant. The only thing I can think of is jealousy and, in this world, it comes in spades.

"Have you called the cops?"

"Yeah, they're looking into it. I made a healthy donation to their union rep as soon as I arrived, hoping to get my case at the top of the pile. Back home, it'd be easy to throw cash, here I gotta be a model citizen or else lose my work permit."

I keep forgetting he hasn't been here for very long.

"What about the cause?" I bend down to look at the tire burn next to the sidewalk. I'm no expert in motorcycles, but I've seen my fair share of bikers celebrating the smallest of victories by burning out a back tire.

"Fire department's on it. Donated to them too, but they made it clear that, with or without the money, the investigation would take as long as it needs to take." Devon shrugs before he grins at me. "So I doubled their donation because I respect honesty."

Raising my head, I look around the neighboring buildings, hoping some fucker around here is paranoid enough to have a personal security camera, but no luck with that.

"Come on, Marco's got a guy."

By the time we make it to the Upper East Side, I'm wondering why so many fucking people drive in The City. What the fuck do you need a car for here? And yeah, the irony of me driving doesn't escape me.

"One thing about New York that makes me feel at home is this bloody traffic."

I grunt, not sure what more there is to say as we push through the heavy doors of Marco's mansion and get attacked by a vicious white ball of fluff barking like it wants to eat my balls.

Sucks for him, he can only reach my ankles.

"Devon, Polo. Polo, Devon." Once the introductions are made, I hear the click-clacking of expensive shoes across the marble floors and know without seeing, that's Marco coming to greet us.

It's only been a few days but seeing him reminds me so much of his father. The regal, bigger-than-life persona that is the Mancini don demands respect and when River joins him, I realize what it means to be standing in front of royalty.

"Boss. *Regina*." I'm never so formal, but for some reason I feel a step further from them than I ever have before.

Marco walks up to me and gives me the one armed hug with the handshake thing we like to do.

"Enzo, *come va*? I thought J was going to spontaneously shoot people just to kill the boredom." I chuckle because that woman is something else. She called me, threatening to cut off my dick if I didn't come back.

"Oh! Maybe she's the one who burned down your gym? You know, to get you back here faster." We all look at River with frowns on our faces because that makes no sense. "Oh, come on! Like nobody thought of that?" She picks up Polo, who's still yapping with his high-pitched bark. "Here, he wants to sniff you because you're new and a possible threat."

"No, Tesoro, I don't think anyone thought J would burn down an entire gym just so she could leave the Upper East Side." River cocks a brow at the most powerful man in the five boroughs and, without an ounce of God-given fear, she rolls her eyes at him and ignores his sarcasm.

"So, Polo, huh?"

Here we go.

"Yes, that way I can call both of my boys in one simple breath."

"Marco Polo, I can respect that." Devon pats Polo on the top of his head and grins; they're now new best friends.

By the bright smile on River's face, it's clear she's proud of herself and the name she chose for the pup. "I'll leave you boys to it then." Just as she turns on her heel, she sticks her tongue out at my boss, but doesn't get two feet away before he's got his hand around her neck and his mouth on hers, kissing her like there aren't people here waiting for him.

"I'll find better uses for that sassy tongue of yours, Tesoro. You can even start without me. I'll be right there." In any other house, no one would have heard him, but with the echo in this mammoth of a place, we get an earful of his pseudo threat.

"Maybe I'll finish without you too." River's words aren't as quiet as she throws them at her husband, a quiet Polo staring at us over her shoulder with his little black eyes.

"Consequences, Dolcezza."

When River first burst into our lives, I wasn't a fan. In fact, I was wary and suspicious of her and her motives. Now, I can't imagine our lives without her. Sure, it would be a more peaceful, quieter place, no doubt, but not nearly as fun.

"Fuck me, I reckon Marco and I were separated at birth."

I smirk at Devon and nod slowly because he's not wrong.

"*Bene*, let's see if Stefano has found anything. Drinks?"

I look at my watch and frown.

"It's only eleven in the morning."

"Tea time in London, mate."

"Motherfuckers." My mumbled words are drowned out by the whirlwind that is Madelina coming into Stefano's office. She kisses him on the cheek and hugs him from behind. He's been like an uncle to her and Marco their entire lives. As Alberto's second in command, he was asked to stay on because no one knows more about the business than he does.

"Those pricks decided they wanna play? Well, we'll fuckin' play."

"I thought you smoothed things over with the Sons?" Marco aims the question at me since I thought I *had* worked shit out with them.

"Clearly not." I mumble the words but the rage inside me is real.

"Wait! Rewind that last part." I'm looking at Marco when Madelina speaks, a silent conversation happening between us where he tells me to take care of the problem. I get it. They may have burned down Devon's place, but going behind my back after we agreed to a truce is a big old middle finger to Marco Mancini. And that shit does not fly on this side of the world.

I nod when he jerks his chin up. We have an understanding.

"Yes! Right there." Madelina leans in close, her index finger pointing at the blurry figure next to a very clear Rik practically looking into the camera. "Who's that?" Her voice is low, like she's talking to herself, trying to magically unblur the image with only the power of her will.

We all shrug. "There's no way to keep up with the Khaos Khunts." Madelina's head jerks up, her narrowed eyes throwing flaming daggers at me. "What?"

"Khaos Khunts? Rude."

Devon's booming laughter startles everyone but I'm trapped by Madelina's penetrating stare.

"Madelina, the club named them, not me." She relaxes a bit and takes my hand, squeezing her fingers. She knows I can't stand it when she's upset with me. For any reason.

"To be fair, I'm an equal opportunity cunt namer." Fucking Devon always adding his two cents.

"Gentlemen, I think you have business to deal with. Do you need my assistance in any way?" Marco is being polite but we all know what he really wants to do is go back to his bedroom to finish what he started with his wife.

"All good, mate. Time to fuck shit up. But first... we plan."

We go our separate ways—Devon heading to the restaurant to check on things while I escort Madelina back to her apartment. We even take the subway, at her request, like regular New Yorkers taking advantage of the greatest underground system in the world. Her words, not mine. They all smell like piss and fried food to me.

"Need a shower." Between the clinging smell, burned down remains, and the subway tunnels, I need to scrub the day off before taking Madelina into my arms. We have shit we need to talk about, plans that need to be made.

"That sounds perfect." I don't have time to take off my shoes by the front door before Madelina is already kicking off her heels and pulling her sweater over her head, throwing it at her feet. "Saving the planet one joint shower at a time."

I have no idea where my clothes fall, all I know is that by the time I reach her en-suite bathroom, we're both naked.

"Where's Tyler?" I'm getting the water heated to her preferred temperature while she takes her makeup off and brushes her hair.

"At his office. Something about…" She pauses for added effect and deepens her voice to, I'm assuming, imitate Tyler. "Take care of business." Her little scoff at the end is proof she's not happy about it.

"He is a hot shot CEO, Madelina. You can't blame the guy." There, the water is now hot but not scalding.

"He was shot, Enzo! He needs to rest."

I don't roll my eyes but damn, I want to.

"It was superficial."

"He had stitches."

"I got more stitches on my chin when I was three. He'll be fine."

"You're impossible."

Hooking my arm around her waist, I pull her to my front and pepper open-mouthed kisses up and down her neck as my free hand whisper-touches her ribs, the underside of her breast, and the flat surface of her stomach.

"I was, Madelina, but you made me possible. You made a good-for-nothing kid want to be a better man. For you. For us. You made this life possible." Turning in my arms, she brings her hands to the longest strands of hair at my nape and curls her fingers enough for me to feel the sting.

"You did that. *You* made you possible. All the horrors you lived through, the abuse and the concessions. The things you did to survive? Your scars narrate your story." Sliding her hands to either side of my face, she gently presses a kiss to my lips and whispers. "You're the reason I survived that night in Naples, Enzo. Your strength, the way you forced me to focus on you?" I'm gifted another tender kiss, and this time I can taste the saltiness of her tears on my lips. "It's what we do, Baby. We save each other, we always have. When one of us is down, the other steps up. That's what love is. It's imperfect and it's bigger than reason, but it's always there when you need it."

I pick her up by the back of the thighs and guide her legs around my waist as I step into the large Italian shower. The hot drops falling like a waterfall create this haze around us, like a cocoon where nothing can touch us. Pressing her against the tiled wall, I kiss her neck and collar bone, running my tongue down her cleavage before pushing her perfect tit to my mouth and sucking on her tight little nipple.

"God yes, that feels so good." I can feel her getting slick against my lower stomach as she begins to writhe in my arms, my dick all too eager to find its home.

"Madelina?"

"Yeah, Baby?"

"*Ti do il mio cuore.*"

She gasps, pulling away to look me in the eye.

"You never speak Italian! I didn't know you could." I don't, really. Everything I've learned was in the Mancini home or on the streets working for one guy or another. But the day I realized that Madelina was and always would be the love of my life, I memorized that phrase. I practiced it all day and night for weeks until the pronunciation was perfect.

Then I waited.

I waited for the perfect day, the perfect moment, to tell her that I was willingly giving her my heart forever, praying she would give me hers in return.

I just didn't think it would be in the shower about thirty seconds before rearing back my hips and pushing my cock inside her perfect, hot, and wet pussy.

"No, I don't. I may look Italian and my name is Italian, but my parents gave me up before I could truly know that part of me. But, Madelina, you're my family. And now, Tyler and Devon. *We're* a family."

"We're a family."

"We need to tell your brother."

"He already knows, silly. It's not like we've been hiding." She's giggling like I'm being ridiculous, but we're having two different conversations right now.

"No, we have to tell him that I need to get out. I need to be one hundred percent in our unit. I can't protect him if my mind is only with you and the guys." I know we haven't spoken outright about it, but I have a gut feeling and it's telling me that I'm going to be forced to choose.

"No one gets out, Enzo. You're in or you're dead." She's worried and I get it, but I'm sure we can find a way.

"No one is dying, Baby Girl. We've all just learned how to live."

Tears are freely falling down her cheeks as she squeezes the muscles of her pussy hard enough for me to gasp from the pressure. I freeze my movements to avoid coming too quickly, instead, filling my hands with the flesh of her ass while I alternate kissing and nipping at her skin. I leave my mark on the swell of her tit and grin at it.

"Why do you look like you just won a prize?" I point to her skin with my chin.

"Think he'll punish us for this?" My girl laughs. She throws her head back and laughs like she used to. Like she doesn't have a scar on her soul. Like she didn't almost lose herself. She laughs because she chose to survive and I've never been more in love with her.

"Daddy D is going to double up, is what he's going to do. For every mark you leave, he makes two. And, Enzo? I am not the canvas for your big dick energy contest."

It's my turn to laugh and it almost feels foreign.

"What the fuck, Madelina? I don't need a contest, I *am* big dick energy. You heard them in London, I'm 'The Big Guy'."

Madelina is suddenly serious, her mouth on mine and her pussy squeezing the life out of my dick before relaxing and pressing her hips closer to my groin.

"Less talking, more fucking."

Turning us to the opposite wall, I slam her against the tile and plunge my cock back inside without another word out of my mouth. We kiss, a sloppy, hungry, no fucks given kind of kiss that says everything. It says this is us. We're far from perfect but when we're together, we're flawless.

With every thrust into her, I grind my groin, rubbing the root of my cock against her clit, and wait for her to release her breath. Then I pull out slowly and dive right back all over again. My mouth never leaves her skin as I kiss her, or run my lips against her, or whisper that I'm going to make her come so fucking hard.

My good girl with a dirty mind likes it when we say filthy things to her. But she also likes it when we are free with her.

"Oh, God. I'm going to come."

As soon as her words are out of her mouth, I pull out my cock and drop to my knees, holding her thighs open so she can sit on my face. I lick her and suck on her labia until I feel her warm cum spilling over my mouth and tongue and chin. I drink it all up, I lap up every drop as she rides my face and gives me the gift of her orgasm.

I've got one hand on the base of my cock, squeezing so that I don't come. Not yet.

Boneless, Madelina kneels over my cock and sinks right back onto me. I pump once, then another and finally... fucking *finally*, I spill my climax deep inside the woman I love.

"Enzo?"

"Yeah?"

"My shot expired a few weeks ago, I just realized it on the plane ride back."

"Your flu shot? You'll be fine. We can go get it tomorrow or the next day."

"No, not my flu shot."

I'm confused and it must show on my face. To be fair, my brain has lost most of its blood flow, so thinking is a bit difficult.

"I'm not on birth control, is what I'm trying to say."

I blink. Once, then twice. She's not on birth control. I just came inside her like a fucking race horse.

A thought comes to me and I swear to fuck it's the best mental image I've ever had.

"So, you could be getting pregnant right now, as we speak?"

"Well, the chances that it would be happening *right now* are slim to none, but sure." Her eyes are searching my face, wanting to know how I feel about this little revelation.

"I guess we'll find out whose sperm is the fittest when the baby comes out."

"Jesus, you three are going to be a handful."

Chapter Thirty-One

Lina

Today's the day the sisters do it for themselves. I totally listened to that song this morning and it's stuck in my head, but River and I are—according to the men—having a girls' day out. No need for all the security details anymore with Ugo being out of the picture, life is almost back to how it once was.

What we are actually doing is exactly what the men think, with a little added twist.

The CCTV footage I saw the other day played on my mind for a while until I finally figured it out. I know the Khaos Khunt on the back of that bike, and cunt is too polite a word for her.

Freya.

When I told River, I saw the dark and angry side of my sister-in-law come out to play. Turns out, she's been sitting on some information of her own and was already in the midst of her own plan. Like me, she wants Freya to suffer a long and miserable life. Death is too good for her.

Not only did Freya encourage my downward spiral by using me for everything she could get and help the Sons burn down Devon's gym, she hired someone to kill her husband, Kai, before he could divorce her. We all thought that had something to do with the Ambrosios', but we were wrong.

Fucking Freya was responsible. All because she didn't want to lose her easy income. She figured his insurance and savings would set her up for life, but the greedy bitch blew it all on drugs. Which is where I came in, keeping up her lavish lifestyle because I was too broken to care.

The minute I began to find my way back to myself, she turned to the Sons, her current drug dealers. It's highly likely she's fully taken on the Khaos Khunt role and has banged every one of them to get her fix.

The thing is though, Kai was River's best friend, as close to her as her brother, Everest, and she blamed herself for his death because of her choice in husband. That blame was entirely misplaced. For months and months, River has mourned him, and as much as anyone tried to tell her that it wasn't her fault, I know she never believed a word. Until now.

It would be easy to torture Freya, bleed the bitch dry in one of Marco's warehouses, but that would only be satisfying for the time it took her to draw her last breath. This way, she's going to suffer for a lot longer.

Our main reason for not telling the men is because River wanted to do this herself. Without Marco's influence. If he had any idea, he'd shoot first and ask questions later.

Nobody hurts his queen.

I know Devon won't mind that I kept this information to myself, they're off dealing with the Sons anyway. *Freya is ours.*

Wind whips around our faces in the cold December air, and I'm just glad it's not raining or snowing as River and I walk through Central Park.

"How was London?"

I can't help the snort that escapes before I answer. "Apart from all the shootouts, being kidnapped, and Tyler getting shot, it was actually great. Their accents are so cute and the main city is amazing. It could really do with a Mancini Luxury Hotel though." This is the beginning of me planting the seed. If River thinks it's a good idea, she'll tell Marco and it'll happen.

I have a feeling my men and I will be spending a lot more time in London. Tyler was more relaxed—when we weren't being kidnapped or shot at—Enzo seemed to blossom and come out of his shell a little more, and Devon is needed over there. I saw the way his mom—or mum as he would say—hugged him goodbye when he told her we were coming back to New York.

"Subtle much? Is this your way of telling me you're moving to London?" Nothing ever gets past this woman.

"Well, no, but also... maybe? I don't know the logistics yet, but I think it might be a good idea. For a while at least." Not only did my men come alive in London, but I did too.

It's not like I've thought a lot about it or anything. I'm lying to myself, I totally have. Enzo would be able to help oversee the renovations and management of a London hotel, meaning he wouldn't have to die because that's the only other way he's able to leave his mafia life. Devon would be able to deal with his family and businesses over there. Tyler has already told me about his business plans, which I won't deny makes me a very happy girl, especially considering what I discovered this morning. And me, well after the last year, I could do with a change of scenery.

"I think it's a great idea, Gorgeous. We can come and visit and do all the things people visiting London are supposed to do! Be a nice excuse for a vacation."

Her reaction warms my heart, and I don't know why I expected anything less. Being supportive is just who she is, willing to be the cheerleader for anyone she loves and their new adventures.

"I'm going to keep the salon. I've got several applications to look through for someone to run the place for me, and I can still dance in a guest spot at your club when we come to New York. I'm not much more than that at the moment anyway." River squeezes my arm with hers where they're linked as we near the Central Park Med West Spa.

"I thought you were only thinking about it. Sounds to me like you've already decided. I'm going to miss you."

"Oh God. Don't do that. Not now. I'll cry, and I really don't want to cry just before we put this bitch in her place." We both laugh, pausing in front of the large wooden door filled with glass panels to hug. The way River hugs is like she's encapsulating you with everything she is, impressing her positive outlook and love into your very being. I'm going to miss her too.

Pulling apart, we grip each other's arms and take a deep breath.

"Okay. Ready for this?"

She nods, still getting used to the world of ruthless monsters she now lives in, which makes doing things like this difficult for the kind-natured soul she is. That's why I'm here. I'm her support, her anchor, her extra strength if she needs it.

Freya is already sitting in the waiting room as we walk in. Her skinny ass looks lost in the wide cream leather chairs. Not that there's anything wrong with a skinny ass, but Freya's a cunt, therefore everything about her is an insult. Brown hair... looks like shit. The shiny black Louboutin's on her feet that I lent her... never want them back because they're tacky as fuck.

River easily slides on her mask of happy and friendly when greeting Freya, wrapping her arms around her in a hug the cunt definitely does not deserve. "Hey, you."

There it is, the very finely veiled insult. River always greets people she loves with, 'hey, beautiful,' or gorgeous, or some endearment. Never 'you'.

"Hey, girls. Thanks for inviting me. I'm so excited to try Botox."

The vain bitch happily accepted our invitation to a spa day that, of course, she wouldn't have to pay for. But what she doesn't know is that nobody in this building today works for the spa. J was all too happy to help us out with filling the place with people willing to pretend to work here, on the promise that we'd tell Marco as soon as we were done.

"Oh my God, yes. It's going to be so much fun!" And it really fucking is. This whole elaborate plan to fuck Freya up almost has me giddy, so I'm not faking my excitement.

A stern-looking woman rounds the corner with a tray of champagne, a glass for each of us, and River and I exchange a knowing look.

"Champagne! We really are having a girls' day." Freya grabs her glass and takes a huge gulp before rubbing at her nose. Girl's got zero class.

"Please, follow me through the back for your first treatment. We have you each booked in for a pure gold radiance facial first." The woman gestures with her head before turning and leading the way.

There's only one treatment chair in the small room that we all pile into and I know this isn't the way places like this usually work, bringing everyone into one room, but today's special.

The woman looks over a list on her clipboard then peers up over her round glasses. "I have Freya first?"

Freya claps her hands together like a child and bounds over to the chair, downing the rest of her champagne before lying back without even being asked. "Of course I'm first. I'm the guest of honor." Her laugh, like she expects us to laugh with her, grates against my ears.

If only she knew. She's the *only* guest today.

"Please close your eyes and put your arms down by your sides."

Without question, Freya complies. And I smile.

Game on.

The woman looks over to us and nods, waiting for one of us to come over to help with this first part. I glance at River, letting her have the choice in this, considering she's been hurt the most by the cunt in the chair. The moment she makes the decision, I see it. It only takes seconds for the whole exchange, but I know she's ready. The hard glare in her eyes tells me that mask of hers is firmly in place.

Walking over to the chair, River gets into position opposite the woman, so I make my way to Freya's feet, shaking my head at the poor shoes I now hate forever because she's tainted them. The three of us standing make eye contact, saying everything we need to without words. When the woman nods again, giving us the first cue, I bend down a little and spot the ties dangling beneath the chair, ready to be wrapped around Freya's ankles. With practiced ease, the three of us quickly and effectively strap her down, immobilizing her limbs.

"What the fuck?" Eyes now open, Freya starts struggling against her bindings, frantically trying to get free. "Let me go. What are you doing?"

I laugh, it's impossible not to.

"Psycho bitch. I always knew you were fucked up."

"Didn't stop you wanting to party with me or spend all your time with me while I was funding your little habit. Didn't want to know me when I cut you off, did you?" I know this is River's show, but that doesn't mean I'm going to stay quiet.

"Cut me off? *Me?* Ha! I cut *you* off." She spits her words, not even trying to play nice anymore.

"Okay, whatever you want to tell yourself." I look to River, silently handing her the reins.

"I know what you did, Freya. How could you?" Her tone is soft, full of the pain I know she's been holding on to after losing Kai.

"Do what? I didn't do anything. You're just as crazy as she is."

"You really are delusional, aren't you? Stop playing dumb and admit it. Admit what a dirty little snake you really are." Venom coats my words at the way she's treating River. It's not okay to speak to her that way. I won't allow it.

"I wanted you to realize how much you need me, okay? I thought if someone else important to you died then you'd break again and come crawling back. There. I admitted it. Can you let me go now? I'm sorry, okay? It was a silly mistake an—"

"Wait, what?" I'm wracking my brain for what she's talking about, because even though Kai's death was sad for me, it happened while I was already on my downward spiral.

"Rex. That's what you're talking about, right?"

No.

I'm actually speechless, trying to form words that are impossible to let out.

"You know I was dating him. Are you telling me I just admitted to that for no reason?"

It's like my instinct completely takes over and I clench my fist, punching the cunt in the face. Satisfaction thrums through me at the immediate swell forming on her cheek and her scream of pain.

"You fucking bitch. Rex had kids! You killed him so that I'd need you? Are you actually kidding me?"

Not only did the sick bitch have her husband killed for money, but she killed or had her boyfriend killed for fucking attention. Like some freak-ass Black Widow. The way she's speaking is as if she's completely detached from the situation, like she doesn't know how fucked up her actions have been.

"What the fuck, Lina?"

Anger surges forward, rumbling through my entire being, and I'm struggling to not stab the cunt between the eyes.

"River, please do what you need to do because I can't look at this bitch for much longer."

My patience is worn, fraying at the seams, and Freya's stupid face isn't helping.

"So what is it you think you know if it's not that? I haven't done anything else." Her eyes widen in faux-innocence, flitting from me to River to the woman standing next to her with a giant injection needle.

Realization dawns in her eyes that she's never getting out of this. It doesn't matter what she says at this point, she's fucked.

River shakes her head. "I really thought you were just a little lost. All this time, I treated you like family, included you in my life, and you've thrown it back in all our faces like the ignorant and spoiled little cunt that you are. Well, Freya, you know how much I believe in karma? Today, and for every day for the rest of your worthless little life, *we* are your karma."

The woman wastes no time stabbing the needle into Freya's arm, injecting LSD directly into her bloodstream. It starts working almost instantly, her eyes almost clouding over as she fights against her restraints.

After a few minutes of watching Freya struggle so hard she might as well be frothing at the mouth, giggling in between bursts of energy to escape, two more women enter the room with a stretcher. Freya's on her way to a psych ward where she will get treated like shit every day, fed debilitating drugs that she won't find fun, and given the occasional beating... all while keeping her alive.

We have a special facility privately funded by the Mancini family, and they're all too happy to oblige the New York City don.

Kicking and screaming, Freya is half-dragged, half-carried from the room and out into the waiting van. River and I watch, smiles on our faces and arms around each other's shoulders.

"Well, that was fun."

We both burst out laughing and River turns to really look at me as though she's staring into my soul the way her brother's wife, Petal, does all the time.

"I fucking love you, woman. Don't ever change."

"I love you too."

"You're going to be an amazing London queen."

Chapter Thirty-Two

Tyler

"Ladies, Gentlemen, please, please... stay seated. There's a lot for us to cover today so I'm hoping you read the memo and had your mornings cleared?"

Those seated around this table are some of the smartest, most talented business people I know. Except for two of them, of course.

Brett, my partner and former best friend and Cora, my ex-wife and former decent human being.

"You could have given more notice, you know." I barely give Cora a glance as she speaks, wondering, still today, what I ever saw in this woman.

Around the table that seats the exact number of board members, I check that everyone nods their understanding. I called this meeting last week, made sure that all my paperwork was verified, twice, photocopies made for every person at this table and a digital version scheduled to be sent to their secretaries as soon as this meeting is over.

Truth is, for the first time in my career, I'm nervous about my next move. I've never been a spontaneous man, never liked spur of moment decisions because if I can't see three steps ahead from the present moment, I don't feel like I'm in control. Although half of this plan has been in motion for the last six months, the other half is only two weeks old. Herein lies that nervous ball in my stomach.

"Tyler!" From the gasp at the far end of the table, I'm guessing some have already skipped to the end of the proposal. "Is this an April Fool's?"

"We're in December, James."

"No shit."

"Hmm, early Christmas gift, maybe?" I ignore my ex-wife, pretending she didn't just piss in her two-hundred-dollar panties from glee.

"Gentlemen, please. Let's all finish reading the documents and we can discuss together."

"Oh, Tyler. Are you ill?"

Of course they'd think this. Why else would I give everything up and step away from my life's work?

"Again, we'll discuss once everyone is finished." Sitting back in my chair as I head the meeting, I think back to when Brett and I first created this company straight out of business school at NYU. We were hungry, of course, but we had morals... or so we thought. Cora and I had started dating shortly after my senior year of college and all through my Master's. She was different back then but I suppose we all were. Being young, in good health, and with the means to make your dreams come true, everything seems so cut and dry.

Brett was our friend, my best friend.

Cora was my girlfriend.

That's it. Those roles never should have crossed into different dimensions. As I sit here today, about to negotiate the terms of my retirement, I realize that the dreams we had never did come true. Our morals were incinerated, our personal happiness put on hold, our company growing so fast that my ritual of getting to know all of my employees is becoming more and more difficult to uphold.

Then Lina happened and all the pieces found their places without a single effort on my part. Not to mention the added benefit of having Enzo and Devon to complete our circle. We all bring something different to the table, giving her the best of all worlds at any given time because she's our focus.

But that's not all, is it? Enzo and I have grown close, we confide in one another and give each other different perspectives on life. Marco and I grew up together, Enzo was always a little on the outskirts of that friendship, but it's easy to love the guy when you know him. When you know how far he's willing to go for his family.

Devon? Well, he's the reason we're all working. He's the conductor that makes our music possible. He may be a legit sociopath but when it comes to us, he's balls in. Quite literally.

To be fair, Enzo has the same viewpoint on the whole organized crime shit but Devon actually jokes about it. Who does that?

What did he call us? Brother-husbands. Fucking Hell, I never thought I'd be sharing the love of my life with two other men and feel completely at ease about it.

Now, my new plan is to expand our family. Make it grow and grow and grow, and I want to be there for every second of it.

Which is why I called this meeting.

"Tyler, you can't be serious." Brett's words are laced with sadness and regret. The opposite of Cora.

With my hands steepled at my chin and my narrowed eyes on my former best friend, I have a brief moment of regret, myself. Brett was a good guy, he was smart and conscientious, came from a middle-class family who had to take out a huge loan for him to get a great education in The City. He knew he had the brains for this career but he wanted to make a difference too. *We...* wanted to make a difference. Buy out struggling companies that were a detriment to the environment, relocate the staff or help with their retirement, then resell the company in parts to businesses interested in clean energy. It was a pipe dream back then and today, we are the leaders in this market.

I take a deep breath and grin.

"I am. Ladies and gentlemen, I am officially retiring as your CEO and would like to commence negotiations for my retirement plan." Angling my wrist, I check the time. "We have three hours before I have to leave and you can enjoy your lunches."

Thirty minutes later, Cora is the only one arguing every single point in my proposal. I'm taking too much money, she says, as though it was her money in the first place.

"Cora, this is quite standard. Between the annual salary, the bonuses and stock options, ten percent for the owner and CEO is legitimate." Mark turns his attention to me, his glasses pinching the end of his nose so he can see me over the top and read the document when he looks down. "Are you sure you don't want to keep a few stocks? Except for Thunder God Holdings, your mother's original umbrella company, you wouldn't have any say in what happens here anymore. After all, you built this company—" He's cut off by Cora's gasp.

"Excuse me! He did not build this company by himself. Brett, my husband, built it with him. And three point six billion dollars is highway robbery." The room goes quiet as we all look at my ex-wife and I can't help but feel sorry for Brett and the poor decisions he's made because of her. "Besides, he's probably retiring because he's too busy fucking an escort. High end, of course." Gasps and chuckles echo throughout the room, a grin spreading on my face at the fact that she, as always, is short on her intel.

"I would hardly call Madelina Mancini an escort, Cora, and even if she was, I don't see how it's relevant to... well, anything, really." This comes from Margot, our oldest and most trusted board member who has made sure our equity policy in this company has been on point. "Personally, I think it's great, Tyler. It's high time to take care of yourself with a woman worth her salt." I nod my thanks to her, for her support, now and always. Margot knows the Hell

I went through with Cora, and the fact I had to work in the same space as the woman who betrayed me so openly caused quite a few doors to slam these past years.

A heavy-handed knock gets our attention and a frantic Clara opens the door then shuts it behind her, whisper-yelling with tears brimming in her eyes.

"Sir, the FBI is here. What should I tell them?"

I blink at her, open then close my mouth before turning to Brett and frowning. "Do you know anything about this?" I can see the panic in his eyes as he turns to a very uncomfortable Cora.

"No, of course not." The tremble in his voice gives too much away.

"Clara, do you know if they have a warrant?" I stand, straightening my suit jacket and pulling at my cuffs.

"Yes, they have a warrant for two arrests." My secretary's eyes dart from one end of the conference room to the other before landing back on mine.

I'll have to make sure she gets a huge bonus for her acting skills.

"Well, then. By all means, we don't have the choice but to let them in to do their jobs."

Cora gasps and all eyes are on her. Gotcha, you little snake.

"You can't do that, Tyler. We need to see IDs, to read the warrant. Brett, call our lawyers, make sure they're here and, for the love of God, nobody speaks to them. We have rights, you know?"

Jesus, look at her go. Of all the people in this room, Cora is the only one panicking.

Because she's been skimming off my company for as long as she and Brett have been together. What they don't know is that the money we'll save from what they'll have to pay back will be redistributed to our employees as bonuses for a job well done.

As a screaming Cora is hauled off by the FBI, Brett stops right in front of me and whispers, "For what it's worth, I'm sorry. I was in too deep." I nod, a smidgeon of understanding that, when it comes to Cora, her manipulation skills are honed to perfection.

"And deep is where the sharks swim." He nods at my words, a solemn look in his eyes. I would feel sorry for him but sticking your dick in a snare will always cut the fucker off.

"Oh, my God! I wish I could have seen her face when the agents came in! And did she seriously call me an escort? I bet she thought she was insulting me. Being compared to River is like winning the lottery." I cup Lina's chin with my palm and bring her mouth to mine, silencing her long enough to get a word in edgewise.

"You are an icon in your own right. A mafia princess who has stolen the hearts of three unworthy bastards—" I'm interrupted by the owner of the restaurant who always seems to show up during a great speech.

"Speak for yourself, mate. I knew my dad and killed him for being a proper cunt. World's better off without him, you know what I mean?" Jesus, I wish I could say he was speaking only to us, but he isn't. Half the fucking patrons just heard Devon Quinn admitting to murder. Not just murder but patricide.

"Christ, Dev, a little louder for the old couple in the back, maybe?" Enzo's words are tight, his jaw a little tense as he scootches his chair back like he's preparing to jump and save us all from good Samaritans wanting to take down the bad Brit.

My money's on everyone here thinking he's joking since half the shit he tells them is exaggerated. I think it's his plan. The bigger you make it, the easier it is to tell the truth when needed.

"When do you close, Daddy D?" Oh fuck, I know that look in her eyes.

"Last meal just went out, so we're waiting for the newly engaged couple to enjoy their dinner while I enjoy mine. But first, duty calls." Devon steps up to Lina and kisses her squarely on the mouth before doing his rounds and charming the pants and the money off his clients. He's all smooth and hard-edged at the same time, it's fascinating.

Most of the women in this place want him while their men want to be him. Hell, I'm guessing the opposite is true too. Men who want him and women who want to be him. He's that fucking good. No wonder everything went to shit back in London when he left.

My thoughts are interrupted as Lina leans in and giggles, taking Enzo's hand under the table and bringing it to her lips. "That woman just 'accidentally' grazed her fingers over Devon's ass and the look he just gave her added ten years to her face." I love how confident she is that we would never betray her. Jealousy isn't in Lina's handbook but revenge most definitely is.

Her little stunt last week with Freya, case in point. She got a good spanking for that, too. We all took turns making sure honesty was branded in her memory.

"Come on, trouble maker, eat your dinner." I take the fork from the table and bring the last asparagus to Lina's mouth as Enzo pours her a glass of red wine from the Veneto region. We know this because Devon can't stop bragging about how thoughtful he is by having her favorite wine added to the menu when he first met her.

It takes the last couple an hour and twenty-three minutes between their plates being served and them walking out the door of the restaurant. At one point, Enzo asked if they planned on sleeping here but I'm guessing the subtle hints from Devon—and by subtle I mean like an elephant at the water park—toward the end, there, prompted them to leave sooner than they'd wanted.

"You haven't touched your wine, Treacle, is it corked?" I bring the glass to my nose and take a deep inhale but it smells fruity and deep. We drank from the same bottle so I can't imagine it would taste differently.

"I'm sure it's perfect but I just don't feel like wine tonight." Taking my hand, she brings my index finger to her mouth and sucks on like she's sucking my cock. "I want to keep my wits about me."

"Everyone out!" Suddenly, his staff are scurrying, making sure they leave with the last table's dirty dishes and hurrying into the kitchen where we hear the sounds of glasses and plates and silverware dropping in the sinks. "What my lady wants, she gets. No questions asked."

Show off.

"I want..." Lina bites her bottom lip as she stands and slowly walks to the door that separates the dining room from the kitchen and before she even walks through, she looks over her shoulder and drops her skirt to the floor. "A tour of your kitchen, Daddy Chef."

It takes us a second to react, our mouths dropped and our imaginations running wild with the different scenarios we could work out.

"I'm not getting any younger, lads."

Snapping into action, Devon locks the front door, turns off the lights, and pulls all the shades down for maximum privacy.

Enzo and I are in the kitchen, mere moments ahead of him, hoping to get a little striptease from Lina, but she's already naked and sitting on the stainless-steel prep counter, legs crossed, hands on the edge with her fingers curled around it.

"Took you long enough. I thought I'd have to keep myself busy." Enzo growls at her words, stalking her as he reaches back and pulls his shirt up and over his head. Fucking hell, he is a big guy, all hard and sturdy in all the right places.

Unbuttoning my shirt slowly, I keep my eyes on her while I wait for Devon to give us instructions. After all, he's the chef so it's fitting he gives the orders.

"Enzo, mate, you look like you're still hungry." Devon takes out a couple of knives and I wonder what the fuck he thinks he's going to do with them.

"Well, you do serve portions for toddlers out there. Men like me need sustenance." At his words, Lina uncrosses her legs, a smile making her face look like a ray of sunlight, and spreads her thighs enough for Enzo to get his large shoulders between them.

"Let us see you eat that cunt, Bodyguard." Lina leans back, one hand on his head while the other hangs on for dear life. Enzo's face is buried in her pussy, the sounds of tongue against flesh and their moans mixing together only make my dick harder by the second.

"That's right, mate. Fuck her with your tongue, make our girl come in your mouth." Enzo doesn't hesitate and

Lina isn't gentle as she pulls his head close enough to choke him between her thighs.

"Fuck, that's hot." It takes me a minute to realize I've said those words out loud and if Devon's grunt is any indication, not only did he hear me loud and clear but he also agrees.

"Treacle... if you could have any dish in the world right now, what would be your fantasy come true?" And by dish, I'm guessing we're not talking about food.

Lina's eyes pop open, her mouth a pretty little *O* as she pulls Enzo's head away from her pussy and stares him straight in the eyes. They're having a conversation we're not privy to but, when he nods at her, I'm taken aback by the scintillating beauty in her eyes.

"Are you sure?" The question is for Enzo but the answer is for us all.

"Anything for you, Mistress. I want to." Enzo using Mistress during sex means he's taking on the sub position, he's letting her have complete control and, since we've already touched on hard limits and role play rules, Devon and I know exactly what's about to happen tonight and none of it will be FDA approved.

With his eyes on Lina, Devon speaks to me, "You wanna do the honors or do you want to watch?" As always, I'm given the choice but tonight, I want to watch, feast on our family as we break another barrier. After that, I'll make our girl come one last time, on my cock.

"You okay with that, Bodyguard?" All eyes are on Enzo, as he stands, takes Lina's hand, and kisses her palm before answering Devon's direct question.

We pride ourselves on consent and it has to be verbal.

"Yeah, I'm good with that." Just as Enzo finishes his phrase, Devon sits beside Lina, his chef's whites discarded at his feet.

"Good. Now suck my cock and make sure Lina comes before I do." I jump up on the work table across from them and reach inside my slacks for my rock-hard shaft. They look beautiful together, regal in some ways. Enzo moves to Devon with his eyes on Lina, he darts out his tongue and circles the head of Devon's dick before sucking on it. One hand is at the base while the other is at Lina's pussy, playing with her clit before pushing two fingers inside.

We all moan in unison, me from the sight and them, and the rest from well... obviously from the feeling.

"I'm so proud of you, Baby. You look so good with your mouth on Daddy D." Where he was tentative before, Enzo gets more aggressive, more daring as he opens wide and gets more cock inside his mouth. Lina moans, her eyes on them and mine on her pussy as Enzo buries his fingers deep, not moving an inch.

Meanwhile, my hand is sliding up and down my dick but something is missing...

Looking around, I wonder if I can get something to lubricate myself up a little. "Whatcha need, Rich Boy?"

"Lube."

Devon points to the end of the counter where a bell dish lies. Butter. Works for me.

Reaching over, I pull the dish closer to me and grab a handful of homemade butter, making my hand nice and slick before resuming my strokes.

"Oh, fuck yeah." It feels *that* good.

"I concur, mate. You sure you don't want to try *this*?" He points to Enzo and I realize I do want to join in. I want us to be a unit in all things.

"As soon as Lina comes." My words surprise her, head popping up and eyes full of love for my acceptance.

Lina grabs Enzo's hand and starts to fuck it in earnest, riding his fingers until she cries out with delight. As Enzo pulls out his fingers, Devon takes them and brings them to his mouth, sucking one then holding the rest out to me.

"Fine dining, right here, mate." Bringing the butter with me, I jump down and suck Enzo's cum-covered finger in my mouth.

"Better than anything I've ever tasted before. But, it's not enough." Spreading Lina's thighs apart, I bring my face to her cunt and drink up every drop of her orgasm. "Now, that's much better."

Standing, I cover my cock with a little more butter as Enzo steps up to me, eyes clear and face open like a fucking book.

I reach out, my hand on his jaw, my forehead pressed to his. "I didn't know you were bi, Enzo."

"I'm not anything in particular. Sex, for me, is linked to love. Always has been. I've only been with Madelina since I've known her and now with you two." Fuck me, I'm choked up from his declaration.

"I love you, too, man. Thank you for your trust." With those words, Enzo drops to his knees and slides my cock deep into his mouth, making my eyes roll to the back of my head. I've heard, here and there, that men give better blowjobs and right now, at this very moment, I can't deny that.

"He's got skills, yeah?" I force my eyes to open, my hand resting possessively on top of Enzo's head while I watch

Devon kiss Lina, his tongue demanding entrance into her mouth at the exact moment he pushes his cock inside her pussy.

This whole kitchen smells like sex, raw and passionate, the sounds bouncing off the stainless-steel surfaces adding to the erotic feel of this whole moment.

I don't think I've ever been more turned on in my entire life.

As Devon slams into our Lina, I get rougher with Enzo. With every thrust of Devon's hips, his ass on full display for me, I push my cock deeper into my little sub's mouth.

"You choking on my cock, Enzo?" He doesn't answer but I can feel the back of his throat with the head of my dick. Fuck me, I'm so horny right now but I don't want to come. Not yet.

Devon roars out a fuck that makes the hanging pots tremble. Lina is about to scream but he takes her mouth and swallows her every sound as he continues to pump his orgasm into her.

"Fuck, I need to be inside her." Enzo releases my cock, standing aside so I can slap Devon's ass. "Move away, Old Man." Devon pulls out, his teeth latching onto Lina's bottom lip and pulling it just enough to make her moan.

"I got it nice and wet there, Rich Boy." My smirk tells him everything he needs to know. She was already wet before he spilled his seed inside her.

"Want some help with that monster hard-on?" Lina and I both turn at Devon's words, surprise etched all over our faces. I don't know why I assumed he'd only take a blowjob and not give one.

"What? Don't look so surprised, I give a helluva blowie." The sight of Devon dropping to his knees in front of Enzo does something strange to me. My body heats, my blood buzzing in my veins and my libido going in overdrive.

"Yes, yes! Oh, God, Tyler, harder, please." Taking Lina's nipple in my mouth, I suck until her screams consume the slurping sounds from Devon and the fucking sounds from me. We're all hyped up like animals, needing a release to survive. It's all too much, my climax hitting me like a fucking hurricane in peak season. I plunge inside Lina one last time, spurt after spurt of my cum filling her up until I can feel it leaking out between her lips and the base of my cock.

Devon's mouth pops off from Enzo's cock and, with a grin to rival Cheshire Cat, he stands and pats Enzo's cheek. "Your turn, Bodyguard."

Devon and I watch as Enzo fucks our girl with everything he's got. Her legs are tightly wrapped around his waist, his ass pistoning in and out of her cunt like he's on a mission.

I suppose he is, and his destination is Orgasmville.

"Reckon we have a little dessert? You up for that, Rich Boy?" Devon's question is followed by Enzo's grunts, moans and a final groan as he, too, gives her his very essence. She has got to be filled to the rim with us.

That's when I get it.

Turning to Devon, my brow slanted in a frown, I ask, "Lina?"

"Hell yeah, mate. Three kings of kink drinking from our queen."

Enzo pulls out and because, fuck it, this is my family and I'm guessing we won't end our experiments with his, I immerse myself in my new reality.

Lina spreads her thighs wide, one hand on my head, the other on Enzo's as we each take turns lapping our cum from her perfect little cunt.

Bonding has never been so erotic.

Chapter Thirty-Three

Devon

Five days before Christmas and it's all hands on deck in the restaurant business. Luckily for me, I've found a Michelin star chef who cooks almost as well as I do and a couple of people recommended by Marco to co-manage the place for me while I'm in London. It could be for a few months, it could be a few years, it could even be longer. However it works out, I'm not letting this place go.

Having the mafia don of New York City as practically my new brother-in-law has its perks, and he's agreed to keep my restaurant under his protection at no extra cost to myself. Fucking bonus.

Before meeting him, my opinion of Marco was low. Allowing his sister to get into the kind of situation she did was fucked up, but I really can't talk. One of my sisters topped herself, one was shot in the head, and another is basically incarcerated because of her own choices. I should've given Marco the benefit of the doubt. I didn't, but now I understand him. We're made from the same cloth and I understand every decision he has to make, realizing that sometimes shit goes bad no matter what you do.

With the restaurant under control, almost everything is in place for our move to London. The fact that they're all coming with me still has my insides alight. Tyler is on a jet to London to put the payment down for our new cottage, although it's more of an estate than a cottage, but it has everything our woman could dream of. The three of us all pulled together to buy it for her, knowing this is just one step that solidifies our family unit bond. She doesn't know about it yet, it's one of her Christmas presents, but she did swoon over the property when we were all searching a couple of days ago.

After some lengthy discussions, we've all decided to spend half our time here, and half our time in London for now. Lina wants us to all be together, and it's difficult with mine and Enzo's responsibilities being on different sides of the pond. Tyler made it easy for everyone by taking an early retirement. None of us were sure if it was the best idea, knowing how much he has put into his companies, but he convinced us it's what he wants. His decision was based on the fact he's got enough money to last a hundred lavish lifetimes over, what's the point in bustin' a nut when you can spend time with your family.

The next thing on my to-do list is to teach those cunting Sons of Khaos a lesson. Well, I say teach them a lesson, but really, I'm going to slaughter the motherfuckers. Firstly, I've provided the President of the lead charter with details of what's about to go down, and secondly, Enzo is on his way here with some fireworks, ready to go and play.

Speak of the handsome devil, his black Escalade is pulling up outside the restaurant. He doesn't move to get out and let me know he's arrived, instead he continues to sit and wait until I come to him. For someone so submissive in the bedroom, he's a cocky fuck outside of it.

"Right, I'm off, Daisie. Enjoy your Christmas bonus, and I'll be back to visit in a month or two."

"Okay, Chef. Merry Christmas!" She doesn't move from behind her station, preparing for the dinner service beginning in about thirty minutes, but she does wave before getting her head back into her work.

I smile, happy in knowing I have good people here. My restaurant is in good hands.

Enzo looks every bit the bad boy Italian with his shades on, one hand on the steering wheel, as he waits for me to jump in the passenger side. My woman has great taste.

"S'up, big guy. Got the bangers?" Sliding into the seat, I pull my seatbelt on just as Enzo puts his foot on the accelerator.

"In the trunk." Eyes on the road, Enzo expertly maneuvers the car through the busy New York streets, glittering with Christmas lights and decorations, toward our destination.

The Sons of Khaos' main hangout in South Bronx.

It's taken nearly an hour with the traffic, but we're finally here, in front of what the Sons call their clubhouse. J and a team of her people joined us on the road about ten minutes before we arrived. We may be big bastards capable of handling ourselves, but we're not stupid fucks that think we can take on twenty members of a motorcycle gang by ourselves.

There are a variety of beautiful looking machines parked out front of the building, which is on its own gated compound. The area is run down, like a forgotten piece of land that nobody cares about, which is fucking perfect for what we're about to do.

Checking my knives and my gun are in place, I step out of the car and look to Enzo before checking J and her crew are ready. A grin creases the edges of my face at the sight.

"Let's get this shit show on the road then."

Walking and looking like something out of a bad action movie, we enter the one-story building with blacked out windows. Stupid fucks think they're fucking untouchable because they've done some shit for the Mancinis. Ha, wrong.

There's no wasting time with the whole fucking speech thing, explaining why we're here, why they have to die, blah blah...

With a knife in each hand, I let one fly straight into the skull of the first motherfucker who looks up from sniffing a line from a table by the door. The second knife lodges in the throat of the guy standing behind the makeshift bar in the far corner, at the same time I grab another knife and my gun.

Shots are going off all around from our guys and it takes the pricks we're here to kill a whole minute to realize what the fuck's happening before they pull their own weapons and start fighting back. Not that it does them any good. Rik is in the far corner, throwing a Khaos Khunt to the floor—one who was attached to his now-flaccid dick—and he reaches for his gun on the table in front of him.

Too late, motherfucker. My first bullet flies through his open palm, the second one through his shoulder and he flies backward. I love to play with my food.

I stalk toward a now-cowering Rik, knowing the rest of our crew are taking care of everything around me.

"What the fuck, man? It was just a gym!"

This man doesn't deserve any of my words, my responses, my reasoning. All he deserves is death. I laugh, unable to contain the joy I feel when I get to fuck shit up like this, and the fear in his eyes as they widen at my approach.

The gunshots around me stop, followed by a few thuds, some groans, then silence.

"All down, Dev."

"Thanks, Enzo. Does anyone have one of those fireworks we brought with us?"

With all of his men down, Rik doesn't make a move as I turn to look around. Every one we brought with us is still standing. There are a couple with some nice new bruises and cuts on their faces but, for the most part, they're unscathed.

"Here." J pulls the bag from her back and unzips it, grabbing a rocket-shaped firework from inside.

Perfect.

She hands it over, along with a lighter from her pocket, rolling her eyes at what she knows I'm about to do. "You're a sick fuck, but I like it."

"Yeah, but it's gonna be so pretty." I laugh again as I turn back to Rik. "Can someone hold him face down?"

Enzo is by my side within seconds, manhandling a struggling Rik and pinning him down. J helps by holding his legs in place to stop him from kicking out.

Rik's trousers are already halfway down, so I don't need to even touch the prick to shove the firework up his arse as far as it will go. His scream is music to my ears.

"Make sure the exit is clear. Everyone else wanna find somewhere to put some of them fireworks. Then we'll all light up and run the fuck outta here. Got it?"

Mumbles of agreement pass through the room and I wait a few seconds for the crew to get set up.

"Ready? Light 'em up!"

Chapter Thirty-Four

Enzo

"You look weird, what's wrong with you?" J's words are breathless since we hauled our asses out of that clubhouse just in time to avoid being part of the fireworks. The sky is alight with reds and blues and greens, the thunderous sound like a beacon to the chaos. Won't be long until we hear sirens. Unlike in London, the cops will be here within minutes.

"It's called a smile, J. I seem to bring out the best in this fucker." Devon answers for me and he's right... this was the most fun I've had in years. So what if my guard is down for a minute, my grin wide and my eyes bright? Being the right hand man to the most important criminal family in The City is not always giggles and laughs. In fact, it never is, not for me. My job is to make sure no one fucks with us. I retaliate, I make sure no one gets close.

So yeah, having a partner in crime and fucking shit up like it's the Fourth of July has my adrenaline coursing through my body.

"I think our Italian Stallion's got a bit of a hard on." My grin dies and my narrowed eyes fix him. "Sorry, mate, was I not supposed to say that out loud?"

"You're an asshole. And before we ran out of that dump, I got your knives back but I think I'll keep them until you deserve them." A smirk plays on my lips as Dev's eyes light up like a fucking Christmas tree.

"Christ, and he jokes now too. What the fuck did you all do to him?" J's readjusting her leather clothes just as she straddles her Sportster and pulls on her helmet. Her entire get up is black and chrome, right down to her riding boots, without a single distinguishing sign to talk about.

"I made him see the light, J." Dev holds out his hand to her, his tone changing from playful to serious at the drop of a hat. "Thanks for your help, let me know if I can ever repay the favor."

"I'm sure there will be. Now let's get the fuck out of here before we get made." Slamming her visor down, she speeds off, leaving us in her literal dust.

Not a minute later, we're out of that shithole and casually passing the line of black and white police cars—lights and sirens blaring—as they speed in the opposite direction to figure out what the fuck is going on. I'm guessing half the force won't give a fuck about that place and hopefully they'll make innocent victims elsewhere their priority.

We basically took out the trash for them.

Devon takes out his phone and links it to my center console, rap music blaring as he grins at me like a fucking toddler who's just eaten his favorite cake.

"I'm pumped up and, when that's the case, I like to listen to some gangsta music from home." With his knives in hand, he's twirling them like batons while rapping along to the song. The screen says Russ Millions *Talk to me Nice* but I've never heard of them. Then again, I'm more of a Metallica fan—old school shit—than I am of rap.

Sparing a look at Devon, I can see the tightness at the corners of his eyes, at the square line of his jaw, and no matter how pumped up he claims to be, I know for a fact it's all adrenaline. The pain of losing his sister is there, written all over his features. Who the fuck am I to blame him for pushing it all down? I'm the king of suppressing feelings, it's just who we are.

As I make my way through The City's traffic, I try to anticipate the conversation I'm about to have with Marco tomorrow. It's risky, me asking to leave my position, but hopefully he'll accept my terms and no one will have to die for it.

"Tyler just sent me a text. He's got the keys to the cottage." He then laughs, a booming sound that drowns out the rapper. When he shows me the screen, I can't help but laugh with him. "Looks like Rich Boy is learning all about emojis." There are three eggplants and a cat with the words "Lots of space to christen our new home."

"When's he coming home?" I swerve to the right, my hand on the horn as an idiot from some midwestern state opens his car door without checking for oncoming traffic. Fucking idiots. They should take the damn subway and leave their cars in the hundreds of garages across Manhattan.

"Some time tomorrow." I nod, a feeling of warmth burning inside my chest. I feel better when we're all in the same place. I don't like us being dispatched. Like a shepherd dog, I like my sheep to be close by, where I can protect them.

"Good."

"Same, mate. Same."

It's like we understand each other without having to speak. And goddamn it, I love that feeling.

"Have a seat." Marco points to the chair opposite his as he walks to the other side of his desk, one hand unbuttoning his suit jacket before he sits. "You wanted to speak with me?"

I've known Marco Mancini my entire adult life. Hell, I've known him since my teen years when his father picked me up from the streets and saved my ass from imminent death. We're about the same age, give or take a year, but he's always seemed larger than life. He was groomed from birth to take over the family business, taught to look impassive and urged to push down his emotions when it comes to doing what needs to be done. And sitting here in the luxurious office of his hotel headquarters, he looks every bit the don he was born to be.

That mask? It's rightfully in place now, which does not bode well for me.

Nobody leaves the mafia. At least not alive. No exceptions are made, none. Not even Marco would be exempt from walking away if he chose to do so. You don't leave the life, the life leaves you.

So me sitting here, asking Marco to let me leave is the same as putting a gun to my temple, my finger on the trigger. My next words are the bullet that's going to blow my head off.

"Yeah. I wanted to discuss... no, negotiate... a transfer." My knee is bouncing up and down like it's got a life of its own. I've never been nervous like this in my entire life. Not before a job, not when I'm face to face with death. Not ever before.

Sitting here, face to face with my boss, I realize how much I have to lose if Marco abides by the strict rules of the family. Hell, of the mafia.

Marco sits back, elbows on the armrests as his fingers press together in an upside down vee pressed to his lips. His gray eyes—so much like his sister's that I almost get lost in them—boring holes through me don't tell me a thing. He's completely shut off, in don mode through and through.

"You don't like working for me, Enzo?"

Christ.

"I do, you know that." He's not going to make this easy for me. Maybe it'll be easier to just run away and hope he never finds us. Who the fuck am I kidding? His resources are far and beyond what anyone can imagine.

"So what's the problem?" Cocking a brow, he waits, like a lion ready to attack.

"I love your sister, Boss. That's it."

"I know you do or else you'd be dead. Still doesn't tell me why you want to transfer. And where, exactly, would you like me to place you." Here goes nothing. I can't even defend myself because I don't have any weapons on me today. It's our way to show respect. When we want something, we walk in naked—not literally.

"Devon has to go back to London to take care of his business over there. Tyler retired, he's going too and, of course, Madelina." Marco nods like he already knows all of this but doesn't add to the conversation. He wants me to give him all the details.

Straight-up power move because that's how he rolls.

"We thought it'd be a great opportunity to implant the Mancini name in London. Devon has all the contacts you need and tourism is off the charts there. I thought, maybe, I could run one of your hotels there or maybe the underbelly side of it." Fuck it, I'd be a fucking messenger if it meant living with my family.

"Hmm," Marco nods slowly, his mind whirring as he searches my face for... I don't fucking know what the hell he's looking for since I've never been more transparent than I am right now. "You know what this means, right?" He leans forward, his elbows on the desk and his eyes two deadly lasers.

"Yeah, I do. But Boss, I've been loyal my entire life. I just want to be with Madelina. And the guys..." I mumble that last part because I'm still not used to saying it out loud. He ignores my words and just continues.

"It means that J is going to have your balls for making her take your place."

I open my mouth to tell him that I'm not asking to leave the life, ready to beg him to not break the rules but just rearrange them when I cut myself off, brows slanting in confusion.

"What?"

Marco's mask falls completely, his eyes bright and inviting like he didn't just scare the fuck out of me.

"Come on, Enzo. Lina spoke to River and, of course, she came to me with the proposal. It's a great idea, the London thing. I've been researching the city for a couple of years now, but so much has been happening around here that I've tabled the project a few times." He walks around the desk and places a hand on my shoulder. "I was just fucking with you, man. Come on, it's all set up but I want to take you for a tour, talk about your new responsibilities as my Mancini London Properties Manager."

I stand, a little bit in a haze with the bomb he just dropped, and shake his hand. "So, all that posturing?" There's a bit of a harsh edge to my tone but I tamp that shit down. I can't forget who he is, not now, not ever.

"I negotiated with River. I would accept your terms but only if I got to have a little fun with you. Consider it my going away present. Marco Mancini, the prankster."

Who the fuck is this guy and where is my don?

"Anyone else and you'd be dead for making me sweat it." Marco laughs at my words—they're harmless and he knows it—one hand coming to my cheek and cupping it as his face turns serious. This time there's no joking.

"I have nothing but respect for you, Enzo. You're like a brother to me. But hear me out. Anything happens to my sister over there and I will come for you with everything I have and I will make you suffer a hundred times over. *Hai capito?*"

"Si." Yeah, I understand him loud and clear.

"Bene." Tapping my cheek again, he leads the way out of the office and, for the next two fucking hours, I get an ear full on the topic of running the hotel business.

I'm going to miss killing people for a living.

Chapter Thirty-Five

Lina

Tingles race up and down my spine, my back arching from pure pleasure as I writhe around. There's a soft pressure against my lips, a tickling across my chest, and my clit is throbbing with need as something nudges against my entrance.

"I think she's finally waking up." Hot breath warms my mouth as Enzo speaks and I slowly open my eyes, the bright morning light shining through the windows of my bedroom.

"There's our little Treacle Tart. Good morning, Beautiful. Merry Christmas." Devon is to my left, his fingers tweaking my nipple as he begins to massage my breast before taking it into his mouth and sucking.

"I was hoping to be inside you before you woke up, Gumdrop. But this will do." Tyler's face is hovering just behind Enzo's kissing lips, and he slams inside me easily, letting out a groan once he's fully seated. "Good morning, Princess."

"Mmm." It's all I'm capable of with the three of them playing me like their favorite toy, electricity quickly building inside me.

Enzo kisses me like his life depends on it, exploring my mouth with his tongue, his lips, his teeth, and I kiss him back with just as much need. Vibrations against my nipple from Devon's groans shoot straight to my clit, and the way Tyler's thrusting in and out of my pussy has me practically seeing stars.

"Oh fuck, yes!" Breaking away from Enzo's lips, I yell out, my breaths coming faster as my release reaches new heights. It's coursing through my veins, my insides, from the tips of my toes to the top of my head and I don't know why I'm waiting for permission to come, but I am, letting the pleasure reach an almost painful point.

"Come all over his cock, Treacle."

There it is. I scream out as my orgasm spreads through every inch of me, fireworks exploding behind my eyes as

Tyler pushes once, twice, before he joins me, warm spurts of cum filling my channel.

"Good girl." The kiss he places over my nipple jolts me, the flesh sensitive to every touch now. "Now come on, let's get dirty while we get clean before we head downstairs."

Two hours and the longest shower in the world later, Enzo leads the way downstairs, Tyler is walking beside me, clasping my fingers between his, and Devon's hand is resting against my ass on my other side. We're in my brother's house because River insisted we all needed to spend this Christmas together. It's not her usual holiday, but she's embraced some of our traditions, along with her own hippy ones, and she's going for it hard this Christmas.

The lounge has a huge decorated tree in one corner—one made from natural fibers of course because there's no way River would allow a real tree in here, she's the kind to go planting more trees rather than chopping them down for decoration—mulled wine scents the air, and the warmth radiating through the room is just one reason I love Christmas.

"Buon Natale, figlia."

"Buon Natale, Mamma." Releasing Tyler's hand, I rush toward my mom, who is sitting in her favorite chair by the window, from which she can survey the whole room.

We embrace for what feels like a small eternity before she squeezes me and pulls away, kissing my cheek as she does. This is our first Christmas without Papà, so today is going to be difficult for all of us, especially my mom. Now that I have them, I can't imagine my life without the loves of my life.

That's a lie. I can, actually... it's shit and fueled by drugs and alcohol. My mom is a formidable woman, her strength like no other in the world, and I want to be just like her when I grow up.

"Where's Mar—?"

The yapping Pomeranian enters the room first, trotting along like he rules the world on his tiny paws, followed by a giggling River and a growling Marco. Stefano isn't far behind them, carrying a tray of coffee and pastries.

"There they are." They no doubt have been spending the morning the same way me and my men have. "Buon Natale!"

"Merry Christmas, everyone!" River is the first to hug me, wrapping me in her arms the same way my mom did, before she bounds around the room with Polo on her heels to hug everyone else.

"Buon Natale, Sorellina." Marco is next, enveloping me in his embrace like only a big brother can.

"Okay, enough hugging. Is it present time yet?" Devon's impatience is playful and I love how eager he is. The gleam in his eyes tells me he's really looking forward to this.

If only he knew.

Marco chuckles, deep and low against my ear as he pats my back and we move over to the new family we've created between us. Life wasn't shit before River first came along, but it was dull. Same old same old, day in and day out. Now, Marco and I are more alive than we've ever been.

Butterflies flutter around my stomach in anticipation, and I have to take a deep breath before I burst into tears from just looking at the happy in this room.

"Marco already gave me a gift this morning." River sits on Marco's lap, Polo on hers, and curls her legs up onto him with a smile.

"Wahey. Top man." Devon holds his fist out to Marco and my brows rise in surprise when Marco does the same and they do a bump thing.

"No! Not that, although, yes, there was that." River blushes a little as Marco pokes her ribs before continuing. "There's a large wooded area in Staten Island that was going to be chopped down to make room for some new shopping mall, but now it's mine!" As if she can't help herself, she turns to kiss Marco, and he grabs her throat possessively, changing the soft kiss into a demanding one.

The large three-seater sofa is left for us to sit on. Tyler sits on one end, pulling me down next to him, Devon sits next to me, and Enzo adjusts my legs so he can sit on the floor in between them. They're all touching me in some way, and if we weren't in the same room as my mom, Stefano, my brother, and sister-in-law, I'd jump their bones in an instant.

"Okay, our turn then." Devon squeezes my thigh before standing, grabbing a large red envelope from under the tree. "There you go, Treacle."

"It's from all of us, Gumdrop."

"Thank you." Eagerly, I rip it open and slide out the card from inside. There's a picture of one of the properties we looked at a few weeks ago, the pipe dream house surrounded by fields of flowers. Flipping the card over, I read the notes on the back. There's one from each of my men.

A woman as amazing as you, deserves the home of her dreams. I love you. Always and forever your man, Tyler.

I can't wait to fill this home with mini versions of us, and I'm gonna have a great time trying. I love you to the moon and back. Daddy D. ;)

You are my shining light, my beacon in the darkness, my world, my everything. I'm looking forward to our next adventures. Ti amo. Enzo.

"Oh my God, you guys! This is the best. I love you all so much." My words are spoken through the tears streaming down my cheeks. I can't help it, they just started falling from my eyes as I read their little notes. "Argh! Look, this is my new house!" Excitedly, I show the picture to River and Marco, then mamma and Stefano, and the pride in my mom's face has my tears falling heavier.

I've never been this happy in my entire life, and this isn't even all the surprises happening today.

With a deep breath, I decide now is the time to let my men know what their gifts are. I'm a little nervous with how they'll take it, but they've just bought a fucking house for us all to live in.

"Okay, my turn? Enzo, can you take my seat?" I stand from between the two giants caging me in, making room for Enzo. I want to see them all as I hand over their presents. "Now, you all need to open these at the same time." Picking up the bag full of gifts from under the tree, I hand one to mamma, one to Stefano, one each to River and Marco, and finally, one for each of my men.

They all begin unwrapping them at the same time, as instructed, and I watch from by the tree, excitement thrumming through my veins. River is first to get into hers and see what's written on her new T-shirt. She keeps her mouth shut and tears spring to her eyes as she looks from me to my men. Marco sees it, just as he's opening his, and River covers his mouth with her hand before he says anything.

Mamma's face is as tearful as River's, and pride is written all over Stefano's features. Next up, my men. I watch them as they unwrap their gifts, Devon tearing his apart, Tyler meticulously peeling away the tape, and Enzo already has his open, his eyes on mine, seeing straight through to my soul. Enzo raises a brow, and I nod gently, letting him know that yes... it is what he thinks it is.

"I'm not sure your brother wants to see this." Devon laughs and holds his T-shirt up. 'I'm the Daddy' written across the front.

"Holy shit, is this what I think, Gumdrop?"

I nod again, unable to speak for fear I'll blub all over everyone in happiness.

"What does yours sa— Oh shit. We're gonna need to come up with a new name for you to call me, Treacle. Get your fine arse over here!"

Quicker than I can move, Enzo is up off his feet, kissing the ever-loving fuck out of me, his palm gripping the back of my head possessively before he lifts me to the air, spinning us around. Devon and Tyler join in, encircling me within the three of them, and my tears now fall freely again.

"I'm going to be an auntie again!" River's squeal makes me laugh, and her enthusiasm is contagious.

"Congratulations, Lina." Marco's small smile belies the pride he has, and I would hug him, but I'm still surrounded by testosterone.

"Out of the way, boys. Nonna coming though." Mamma shoves my men out of the way and they all obey, letting her through for a gigantic hug. "I'm so proud of you, Madelina. And Papà would be over the moon. I know he's up there and smiling down on this moment." That's it, my tears fall heavier than before, my mom's joining them as we embrace.

Devon, Enzo, and Tyler surround us, Marco, River, and Stefano too, and Polo is yapping around our legs, and this moment right here, is what dreams were made of.

Epilogue

Lina

Three months later

Ours isn't the typical story of boy meets girl, falls in love and marriage and kids soon follow. We had some twists and turns on our road to happiness but as I stand here in my home on the outskirts of London, I can't think of a better place to be.

It's springtime, the flowers outside in the back yard have popped up all over the place with pinks and yellows and reds creating organized chaos all around our home. Devon says we need to mow the lawn to make sure I don't develop any allergies. Tyler has baby-proofed the entire—and I mean every fucking inch—house to the point where I couldn't open the damn fridge yesterday.

My baby bump is visible enough that I can rub the underside of my belly and the thought of having a baby in my arms in less than five months is both exciting and terrifying. For now, I'm basically throwing up every few hours which means Enzo is following me around with crackers and ginger ale, just in case I need them.

As I look out the window, I smile at the guys play fighting while they clean the pool, getting it ready for the summer. Devon is shirtless and wearing shorts like we're in the middle of July, but apparently the Brits lose their clothes at the tiniest peek of the sunrays. Enzo and Tyler aren't that brave, they've got sweats and T-shirts on because it may be sunny but the light breeze still carries a chill to it.

Our monthly visit with the midwife is happening shortly and we're confident everything is going fine. As Devon likes to remind me, it's probably his sperm donation that's growing in here since everyone knows he's the strongest motherfucker of them all so, obviously, our baby will be perfect.

Tyler and Enzo just shake their heads because there's no rationalizing with him about this.

As expected, the firm has reeled in the shitshow from our last visit here. The Butcher being back has eased the minds of a lot of his people, his enemies staying on their side of the city and leaving the rest alone. Obviously, Enzo and

Devon are staying on top of that situation so I'm not too worried about it.

Marco and River will be visiting soon. Enzo has all the paperwork and permissions for his new hotel "Mancini London" to plant their first proverbial shovel in the ground. There will be a cutting of the ribbon or whatever. Devon believes a press picture with Marco Mancini standing by his side would forever hyphenate the names Mancini and Quinn making the hotel untouchable by the standards of the firms. We may not be married but our names are practically hyphenated at this point. Although, Lina Mancini Quinn Beneventi Walker is a fucking mouthful. We'll figure it out along the way.

Tyler has declared he's going to be a stay-at-home dad, taking his new role very seriously already. We've got a shed full of brand new tools for whatever work the house may need and an attic full of whatever the baby may need from now until he's thirty. Or her. We don't want to know the sex... actually, let me rephrase that. Tyler doesn't want to know and I don't care either way. Enzo is confident it's a boy because apparently, in the Italian old wives tales, the more weight at the bottom of my belly, the higher the chances it's a boy. Devon though? I think he might threaten our midwife with her life if she doesn't tell him the sex. Patience, no matter what he likes to say, is not one of his virtues.

"Hey, Gumdrop, you look like you're miles away."

"Just thinking."

"Shauni is here, you ready?" Turning my gaze away from the window, I smile at Tyler as he wraps his arms around me, his hands cradling mine over my belly. "Those two are going to be over the top dads, aren't they?"

Shifting, I turn just enough to look at him over my shoulder. "Oh, because you won't be?" He reels back like he's offended until I cock my brow and he just shrugs.

"What can I say, I had good role models." I do love his parents. And I can't wait to see them next week as they fly in for a visit, no doubt doting on their son.

"Ready for our four-month checkup?"

"Let's do this."

"Who's going to tell the boys down there?" I giggle at Tyler's choice of words. I don't think Devon would agree with the description.

"I will." Opening the window, I call out. "Hey, daddies, midwife is here so get your asses in gear!" Two sets of eyes flash up at me and suddenly, I'm wet. To be fair, I'm in a constant state of arousal these days and I'm pretty sure it'll be the story of my life until my last breath.

"Watch the tone, Treacle. I'm not afraid to silence you with a mouthful of cock."

"Oh my." Tyler and I both turn at the sight of Shauni, who has a blush running from her cheeks right down to her chest.

"Oh, God. I'm sorry, Shauni, he's just... well, he's... um..." I'm fumbling because what the fuck do you say in these cases?

"It's why we don't take him out very often." Okay, we could say that. Although, I wouldn't in front of Devon.

"What's that noise?"

"Is that echo normal? I feel like the machine is not working properly."

"Is that his wiener?"

I'm going to murder one or two of these men here. I mean, I'd still have one left, it's doable.

"You three need to let Shauni speak and not interrupt her because she has other patients." She's had to explain every single move she makes. From the gel on my belly to the cold paddle to the noises and visions on her portable ultrasound machine.

We need rules STAT.

"Okay, okay… just let me take a look here and I'll answer all your questions. First, that noise is the baby's heartbeat. But…"

There's a collective intake of breath as we all wait for whatever is going to follow that "but".

"For the love of God, woman, there better be something good after that 'but'." Devon looks feral, Tyler is about to break one of my fingers, and Enzo is growling… actual growls are coming from his throat.

"So, the reason the heart beat sounds like it's an echo is because… do you see that?" We all lean in at Shauni's words, my eyes narrowed into slits as though it'll help me to see better.

"All I see is grains of sand." Enzo's face is right next to mine as we try to decipher the image.

"I definitely see a wiener."

Oh for fuck's sake, Devon.

"Is that…?" Shauni looks at me and her smile tells me I'm right.

"You're having twins."

Silence.

"Like... two babies?" Enzo chokes on his words.

"At once?" Tyler whispers.

"Can someone please fucking tell me if there's a wiener in there?"

"Shauni, can you see the sex of the baby? Erm... babies? Or else he's going to drive me crazy."

"Yes. You have two fertilized eggs. See that? That's possibly a penis although it's early and it could just be a clitoris at this point. But there? Nothing is protruding so we can't say it's male sex as of yet so possibly female."

"I knew it."

"Um, guys? Did you all just hear that we're going to have *two* babies in five months?" Why is no one freaking out?

"Babydoll, two is just the beginning because we plan on filling every fucking room in this house."

I frown.

Not if I have a say in it.

The Blonde One

KOK... Did you know this book was nearly called something else? But Brunette and I were chatting one day and thought it'd be really funny to have KOK as the shortened version of the title... And thus, Kings of Kink was born! Lina's story is one that we felt needed telling. With what she went through at the end of The Escort series, there was no way we could hold off from letting you in on what happened next for her. The relationship between Lina and her men may not be 'the standard', but it worked for them.

We wanted to show this kind of relationship in a way that had zero shame, because we know the world can be a judgey AF place. And judgey is not what we're about! There is of course a super sensitive subject we cover during Lina's story, and it's something we tried to do with care, but also in a very real way. Everyone who has experienced and survived any kind of SA will have reacted in their own way, followed their own journey of healing. Sometimes it's rocky as hell, while others are able to easily block it out. There is no right or wrong reaction. You do what you've got to do to survive.

Thank you to everyone who has followed us from The Escort series, and to all the newbs trying us out for the first time! You're all awesome, and we're so so grateful to each person that reads our books <3

Zoe, Lydia, Sam, Hilary... thank you for being our first BETA beeches ;) We LOVE your enthusiasm for our words. Lil, you're still awesome for getting Brunette and I together! David, thank you for helping to make our words shine. Kirsty-Anne, our KOK cover is banging! You're a genius, thank you. Gabriella, thank you for being our awesome Italian checker! All the readers, authors, fb groups and everyone who has ever shown us kindness and love for our books... we friggin' love the shiz outta you all! <3

We have a duet planned next... featuring a certain Capo who's really good at dispatching people... Any guesses as to who...?

Until next time ;)

The Brunette One

Y'all... is it wrong to say you love a book you wrote? I seriously adore these characters. Don't get me wrong, Marco and River will forever be my BFFs but Lina... man, she is so fucking strong it makes my heart soar. Especially with Tyler, Enzo, and Devon who have fueled her strength in different ways. I think it's why I love them so much. They lift each other up and in our community, it means everything.

It means everything because that's what you all have done for us.

Blondie pretty much said it above but I feel it's necessary to reiterate.

Our Alpha/Beta/Editor teams are freaking stars! I can't imagine publishing without your input and guiding thoughts. How lucky are we to have readers ready and

willing to drop everything just to read our words? So, Zoe, Sam, Lydia, Hilary, and the almighty, David Michael...
thank you for being our pillars.

I also want to thank our three special ARC readers who didn't know us from Adam and still took time out from their busy schedules to help us girls out. So, Melanie, Miranda and Tara, we are so grateful for your quick reading and thorough input. Bless you.

I hope our KOK was very satisfying and left boneless by the end of the last page.

A girl can dream, right?

If you have been a victim of Sexual Assault please find comfort and assistance in any of the safe spaces near you.

UK Website for help: https://www.sarsas.org.uk/
USA Website for help: https://www.rainn.org/

BOOKS BY N.O. ONE

Dark Romance

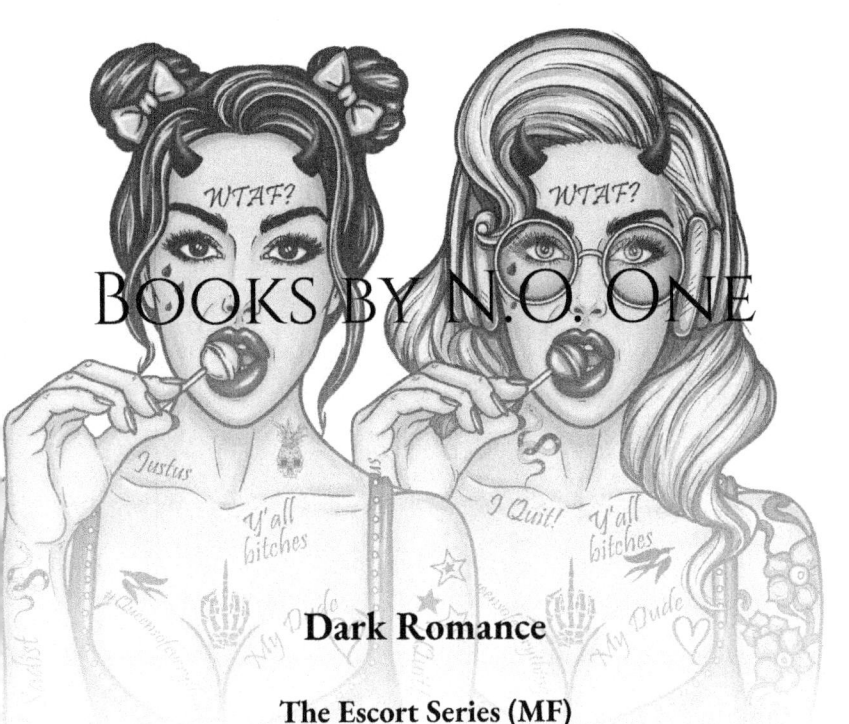

The Escort Series (MF)

The Rich One ~ https://geni.us/TheRichOne

The Kinky One ~ https://geni.us/TheKinkyOne

The Filthy One ~ https://geni.us/TheFithyOne

The Broken One ~ https://geni.us/TheBrokenOne

The Almost One ~ https://geni.us/TheAlmostOne

The Forever One ~ https://geni.us/TheForeverOne

KOK (RH)

Kings of Kink ~ https://geni.us/KingsOfKink

Books we think you should read:

by Molly Shelby

Dark Romance

Date with the Devil (MF) ~ https://geni.us/DWTD

BY EVA LENOIR

Eva LeNoir
Fun Flirty Romance

Contemporary

The UCC SAGA

Disheveled ~ http://amzn.to/2arpbXp
Disarmed ~ http://amzn.to/2myvxNn
Discarded ~ https://amzn.to/2vWTRPf
UCC Boxset ~ https://amzn.to/3ljvepE

Contemporary Standalone

The Wish ~ https://amzn.to/2FTiKQB

Rom/Com

The Woolf Family Series

Screwed ~ https://geni.us/Screwed
Screwed Up ~ https://bit.ly/3IbfWKb
Screwed Over (coming soon)

Supernatural

Soul Guardians Series

Reprise ~ https://bit.ly/3cT9nPe

BY LILY WILDHART

Dark Romance

The Saints of Serenity Falls series (RH)
(You will find crossovers from The Escort series by N.O. One in the Serenity Falls series by Lily Wildhart, and vice versa!)
A Burn So Deep ~ https://geni.us/burnaltcover
A Revenge So Sweet ~ https://geni.us/revengealtcover
A Taste Of Forever ~ https://geni.us/tastealtcover

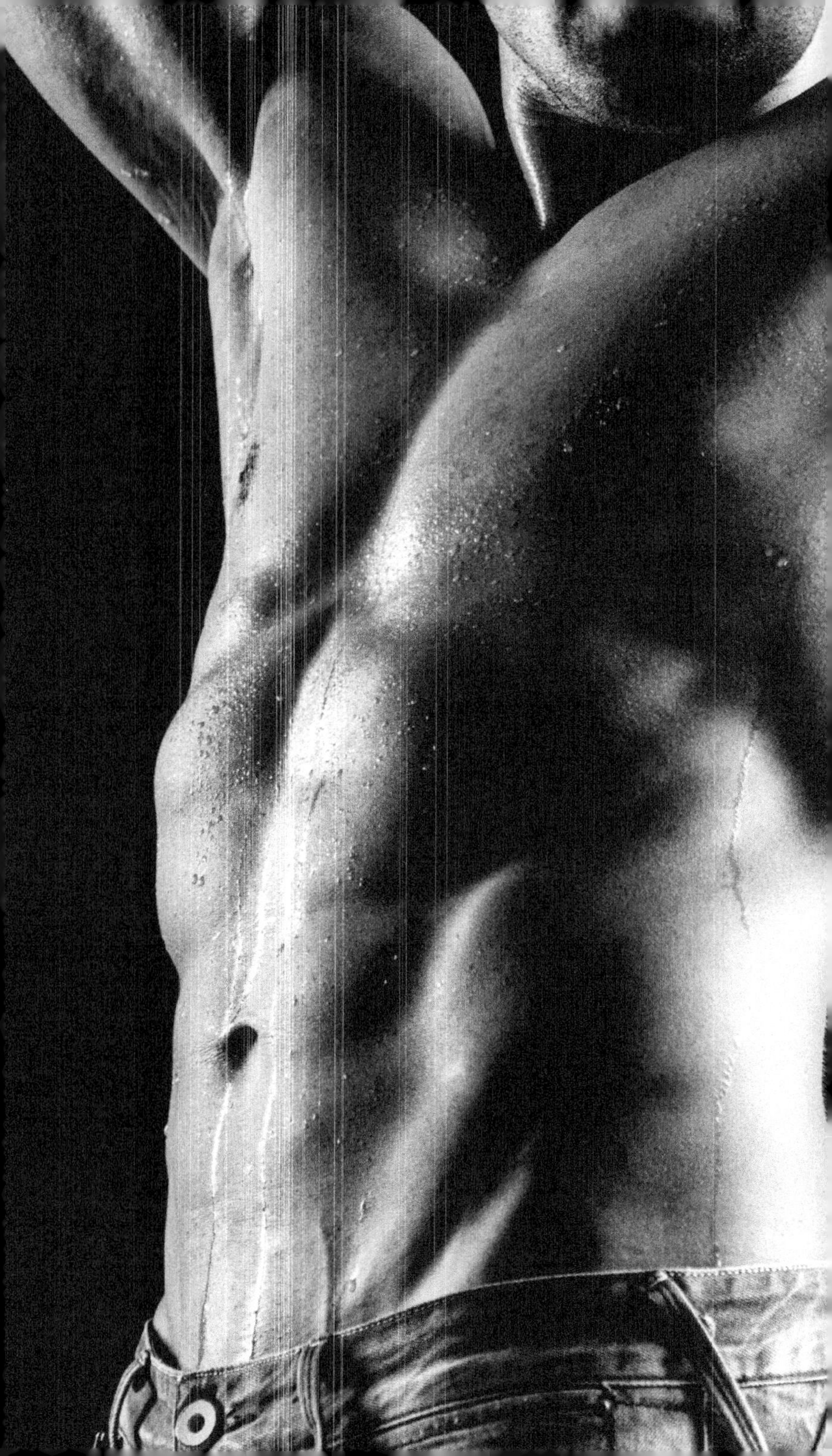

Printed in Great Britain
by Amazon